Romancing

Miss Brontë

Romancing Miss Brontë

A NOVEL

Juliet Gael

BALLANTINE BOOKS   NEW YORK

Copyright © 2010 by Juliet Gael

Published in the United States by Ballantine Books,
an imprint of The Random House Publishing Group,
a division of Random House, Inc., New York.

BALLANTINE and colophon are registered trademarks of Random House, Inc.

Library of Congress Cataloging-in-Publication Data
Gael, Juliet.
    Romancing Miss Brontë : a novel / Juliet Gael.—1st ed.
        p. cm.
    ISBN 978-0-345-52004-3 (acid-free paper)
    1. Brontë, Charlotte, 1816–1855—Fiction. 2. Women novelists—Fiction. 3. Brontë
family—Fiction. I. Title.
    PS3607.A3535R66 2010
    813'.6—dc22   2010000560

Printed in the United States of America on acid-free paper

www.ballantinebooks.com

987654321

First Edition

Book design by Elizabeth A. D. Eno

A mia cara, Ursula Terrasi

Certainly, at some hour, though perhaps not *your* hour, the waiting waters will stir; in *some* shape, though perhaps not the shape you dreamed, which your heart loved, and for which it bled, the healing herald will descend.

Charlotte Brontë, *Villette*

Romancing
Miss Brontë

Chapter One

He rode in on the back of a wagon loaded with crates of chickens and bales of hay, driven by a brutish farmer who had not uttered a word throughout the journey except to curse his horse. Arthur would have enjoyed a bit of conversation as the wagon lurched along the muddy ruts, but the natural world was a thing of splendor and inspiration to him, and he was content to gaze upon the vistas opening up before his eyes. It was September and the wind was balmy and thick-scented with heather. Each climb to the brow of a hill revealed rise after rise carpeted in swirls of purple, green, and gold, each growing paler until the moors faded into a violet haze, and thereafter only shelves of mist the color of blush that might be land or might be clouds. The upper reaches of the River Worth flowed from these hills and fed the becks that fed the mills that fed the people, when times were good.

Arthur and the Church of England had been an arranged marriage of sorts, but he had been one of those fortunate few who had fallen deeply in love with his bride despite her many foibles and warts. He had no tolerance for those who sought to strip her of her liturgy and beauty, and undermine her authority. He was a proud young man, conscious of the dignity vested in him as the newly appointed curate to Haworth, so it was understandable that he was a little vexed to be arriving in the village atop a bale of hay in a lowly wagon full of chickens. There was something unsavory about it, a hint of degradation. He meditated on Christ's entry into Jerusalem on the back of a donkey but could not reconcile this image with the squawking birds all around him. He wished he had a horse, but a horse was not within his means.

By the time they arrived at the bottom of Main Street the sky had darkened and lead-gray clouds were moving up swiftly from the south. The wind rose. Workers from the outlying mills were returning home across the fields, hurrying down to the village and disappearing into the dense, hidden warrens of the poor.

At the tollgate the farmer ordered him down. "I'll deliver yer box but ye walk from 'ere," he muttered as he swiftly pocketed the coin Arthur dropped into his hand.

"Where might I find the parsonage?" Arthur asked stiffly. "I am Reverend Brontë's new curate."

For this bit of introduction all he got was a scowl and a sharp jerk of the head indicating the top of the steep hill.

A cold drizzle had blown in, sharp as needles.

The street was a long, brutal climb, and several times he threw an anxious glance over his shoulder at the old mare laboring slowly up the steep cobbled way. To the right the hillside fell off sharply, with ramshackle sheds and small garden plots scattered along the slope below. On the left rose a straggling row of small stone cottages built from millstone grit quarried in those treeless moors. A sense of oppression and harshness hung over the village.

Halfway up, Arthur paused to rest. Glancing back down the hill he saw that the horse had stalled and the farmer had resorted to a whip. Arthur was accustomed to dealing with recalcitrant draft horses, and he had a winning way with stubborn beasts, a talent that did not always translate to his own species. So when he turned back down the hill, it was more out of sympathy for the horse than for the brutish farmer. Drawing close, he could see the panic in the horse's eyes and the strain that rippled along her muscled flanks. Arthur had once witnessed the carnage when a horse hitched to an overloaded wagon had been dragged backward down an icy slope, and he knew the animal had reason to fear. Arthur stepped up beside the horse and spoke soothingly to her, but when he reached for the bridle he was startled by the crack of the whip just over his head.

"Away with ye," the farmer shouted. "Git away. Git yer hands off my horse." Without warning he lashed out again with the whip, barely missing Arthur's cheek.

Arthur's eyes flashed with anger. He was a powerful man, with a good height and an oxlike build. He had it in him to drag the farmer from his seat and give him a thrashing, but his only concern was for the safety of the horse. He steeled his mind to the task and ignored the cursing, the whip, and the rain. With a firm, coaxing voice, he spoke to the beast, and after a moment she began to move.

Arthur stubbornly led the animal to the top, never relinquishing the reins until they reached a junction at the heart of the village where the road widened and leveled.

The farmer pulled his cap down around his head and waited in sullen silence while Arthur unloaded his trunk from between the bale of hay and crates of chickens. Without so much as a nod of gratitude, the man took up the reins and drove away.

Arthur looked around and found himself in front of the Black Bull Inn. Just a few feet away, up wide steps and through a gate stood the parish church: an ugly, dreary edifice, hardly more inspiring than the gloomy village that lay at its feet.

It was a disappointing revelation, but he was not the kind to ponder disappointments.

At the Black Bull he got a civil reply to his inquiry and learned that his lodgings were just up the lane. He arranged to have his trunk delivered and then set off up the cobbled street.

Past the church, the graveyard came into view. It spread up the treeless slope, climbing to the very walls of the parsonage and spilling into the fields beyond, an insidious thing that swelled its stomach with every harsh winter, famine, and plague. The parsonage stood alone at the top of the steep hill, anchored firmly in this sea of dead. Beyond lay the vast stormy sky and the wild moors.

The house was a two-storied Georgian thing, brick with a pair of whitewashed columns flanking the door. Respectable and unexceptional in any way.

Daylight was waning and Arthur was rain-soaked and out of temper, but he was curious about the aging reverend who had written him such elaborately courteous letters in an old-fashioned, grandiloquent sort of language. Patrick Brontë was an Irishman, like himself, and Arthur had hoped to come to the end of his journey and find a little bit of home. A bit of Irish humor, and perhaps a glass of whiskey or port to revive his flagging spirits.

He hesitated at the bottom of the graveyard, nearly blown back by a stinging gust of wind. At that moment a woman appeared at the lower window of the parsonage. She held a candle that cast a warm light across her face, and she paused to peer out at the evening sky. After a moment, the shutters were drawn. One by one, upstairs and down, she appeared at the windows until the house was closed to the world.

At that moment a sudden, agonizing wail poured from the house. It sounded only briefly before being carried off by the wind as it swept, lamenting, past the sharp corners of the parsonage and out to the open moors, where there was nothing to impede its passage.

But Arthur was convinced it was not the wind he had heard.

He was not the superstitious sort; nonetheless, he turned his back on the parsonage and strode across the lane to the stone cottage where he had taken lodgings with the family of the local sexton, John Brown.

A stonemason by trade, John Brown tended the church and the grave-yard; he inscribed the names of the dead on the tombstones, as his father had done before him. It was a large family, and all they could offer him was a small room looking out on a dirt yard where chickens scratched around slabs of granite. But Arthur was a practical man, and the situa-tion was both affordable and convenient. The church school, which would fall under his supervision, stood adjacent to Sexton House, and the parsonage was a stone's throw away.

John Brown and his wife gave him a warm welcome. His room was ready; there was hot water to bathe his face and a light supper of boiled ham. As he knelt by his bed for prayers that night, Arthur consoled himself with the thought that he need not stay in Haworth longer than a year. Once he was ordained, he would seek his own incumbency elsewhere, in a more congenial place.

If it be God's will.

Chapter Two

Charlotte came into the kitchen with a letter in her hand. She knew at a glance that Martha was in a sour mood by the way she was handling the meat cleaver. Tabby, who was too old and infirm to do much work, sat in her corner slowly peeling potatoes with her arthritic hands. Tabby was growing deaf, and whenever they had some private bit of news to tell her, they had to take her out on the moors, where they could shout without being overheard.

"Where's Emily?"

"Has better things to do," Martha muttered. She pushed up her sleeve, grabbed another hunk of meat, and brought down the cleaver with a thud. Martha Brown was the sexton's seventeen-year-old daughter. She had grown up with the parson's family and had been in service to them for two years; the Brontës were as close as kin.

"What?" Tabby asked.

"I asked where Emily was," Charlotte shouted.

"Roamin' about on the tops, I reckon," Tabby said. "Heather's in bloom. The girl's gone mornin' t' night when she can get away with it."

Martha replied curtly, "Well, this is not when she can get away with it. I was needin' a bit o' help in the kitchen. This is washin' day an' I have sheets sittin' in a tub of water. An' Miss Anne's gone into the village."

Charlotte merely tucked the letter in her pocket and reached for an apron hanging beside the door.

"Here, let me finish that, Martha. You keep up like that and we'll have a finger in the stew for sure."

Martha gave one of her put-upon sighs, put down the cleaver, and wiped her bloodied hands on her apron.

"If you're going out to do laundry, you change that apron," Charlotte said to her.

"Yes, miss," she replied. Quietly, she added, "We're glad ye're stayin' home, Miss Brontë. Oh, fer sure, Miss Emily's a fine cook, but when ye was in Brussels, why, we like to never had a meal on time, an' ye know how the reverend likes everything done on time."

"Oh, indeed I do know, Martha."

Tabby, who had followed the general flow of the conversation, chimed in loudly, "Breakfast at nine sharp. Dinner at two. Tea an' light supper at six. Master hasn't changed his habits in all these years an' likely never will."

The house had run like clockwork when their Aunt Branwell had been in charge, but she had died the year Charlotte and Emily were away at school in Brussels. Both sisters had come home; Emily had stayed to keep house for their father but Charlotte had returned to Brussels for a second year. It was a decision that would define her life in ways she was yet to discover.

"Now, should we set a place for Mr. Branwell?" Martha asked.

"Is he still in bed?"

"Hasn't been down for breakfast."

Charlotte shook her head and began chopping the meat into small pieces. "Well, if he sleeps through meals he'll just have to go hungry," she said sourly.

Martha fed another log of wood to the stove, and when she had disappeared into the washroom behind the kitchen, Tabby spoke up.

"What was ailin' the boy last night? 'e was makin' out like the devil'd got into 'im."

"Just never you mind, Tabby," Charlotte answered, but of course Tabby knew very well what was ailing him.

"Well, best to let the boy sleep." Tabby rose, holding her apron full of potato peelings, and emptied it into the compost bucket. "He needs to get over it. Men take t' drink when their hearts are broken."

"That sort of indulgence is exactly what's wrong with him," Charlotte answered sharply. "He's been given far too much freedom."

"Aye, she's a Jezebel, that Mrs. Robinson. It's a wicked woman that seduces a young man under her husband's nose . . . wicked indeed . . . an' her husband sick an' dyin', too."

"Branwell's twenty-five. He's not some innocent child. He should have removed himself from temptation. He should have offered his resignation and left the house. That would have been the moral thing to do."

"Aye, it would've been the right thing t' do, but we're all of us made of the same stuff, miss, sinners before God, an' none o' us do the right thing all the time."

Charlotte scooped a handful of flour out of the bin and sprinkled it over the meat.

"He's lost his position now, and he makes no effort to find another one. I'm quite fed up with his moaning around the house."

Tabby, who often missed vital parts of a conversation, gave a nod and frowned as she gathered up her potatoes. "Aye, miss, it's sad for us all."

"It's so upsetting for Papa," Charlotte muttered. She fell silent and scooped up the meat and dropped it into a pot on the stove.

They heard the back door open and the dog's nails clicking on the stone floor, followed by Emily's light footsteps.

"Emily," Charlotte called out, "take off your boots before you come in the kitchen. And wipe Keeper's paws. The floor's clean."

They heard her voice, speaking affectionately to the dog, and after a moment the big lumbering mastiff trotted in with Emily behind. She carried an armload of heather in bloom, and her face was fresh and rosy from the wind. She greeted them all with a breezy hello and one of her rare smiles, and then dragged out a bucket for the heather. Her skirt was splattered with mud and wet at the hem from jumping ditches and bogs.

"Where's yer bonnet, miss?" Tabby scolded.

"On the hook, where it always is."

Tabby gave an admonishing shake of the head. "You'll ruin yer complexion like that."

"It's after one. Dinner's going to be late now," Charlotte said with a hint of accusation.

Emily ignored them while she pumped water into the bucket. She looked over Charlotte's shoulder at the stew meat browning in lard and said airily, "That's not enough flour." She reached into the bin for a handful and sprinkled it into the pot. "Did you save any scraps for Keeper?"

"There," Charlotte said, indicating a pile at the side of the table.

"Ooooh," she crooned to the dog. "Look what you're getting for dinner." She picked up a wooden spoon and stirred the browning mutton. She was in an ebullient mood. In the summer she came home like this, sweet-natured and impossible to perturb.

"Is Anne back yet?" she asked.

"No."

"We must all go out this afternoon. It's divine. A perfect day. We can take our sketchbooks."

Charlotte cleaned her hands and then reached for the letter in her pocket.

"This came this morning. From Mrs. Busfeild. The vicar's wife."

Emily looked up with interest. "What did she say?"

At that moment they heard Branwell's heavy-footed tread on the stairs, accompanied by a low groan. It was all quite dramatic and intended to draw their attention to his entrance, but his sisters kept their eyes stubbornly fixed on the simmering mutton, their backs to him.

Branwell paused in the doorway, looking ridiculous with his shock of bright red hair flattened against one side of his head, his eyes barely open. He had slept in his clothes, which smelled strongly of smoke. He steadied himself, shook his head violently to throw off the sleep, then rubbed his face briskly.

"Tea. I need some tea. Very strong and very black, thank you."

"You may get it for yourself, thank you," Charlotte said. She took Emily in hand and headed for the doorway. "Excuse us, please."

"Don't be so cruel," he whimpered in their faces. "I'm a sad man. A lost man. And if you had ever loved like I love, you'd know how it feels."

His breath reeked of sour beer, and the girls winced as he stumbled past them. He dropped into a chair and collapsed with his head on the table where the meat and flour had been worked.

"Oh, my head," he muttered. "Oh, my heart."

Emily and Charlotte stared at him in sheer disgust. Only Tabby came to his aid, waving them out of the kitchen.

"I'll get the lad's tea," she said, and with slow, painful steps she hobbled to the stove to put on the kettle.

Branwell lifted his head a little. His cheek was white with flour. "You're an angel, Tabby." He smiled. It was a grotesque smile, with his eyes half-closed.

"Aye," she said, "but it'll take more than a crippled old angel to beat the devil out o' ye."

In the dining room, they found Flossy, Anne's fat little black-and-white spaniel, nested on the sofa. Emily shooed him off and plopped down, stretching her legs before her. Her stockings were stained with mud and a toe peeked through a hole. She wiggled the toe triumphantly. Keeper followed her in, still panting heavily. He circled briefly and dropped with a thud onto the cool wood floor.

"Here," Charlotte said, handing over the letter. "It's the same thing we heard from the Whites. She believes our situation is too retired for a boarding school, that we're too isolated, et cetera, et cetera."

They heard the door handle turn; Flossy's ears pricked up. Anne entered quietly.

"Tabby said I should find you." She spoke softly, her large violet eyes swelling with curiosity as she untied her bonnet and laid it on the table.

Emily patted the sofa. "It's a reply from Mrs. Busfeild. Come sit down."

The two sisters read the letter together, their lean bare arms intertwined and their heads inclined in a way that hinted of an exclusive bond. In appearance they were strikingly similar, with their long faces and sensual, pouting lips that in another time would have been thought alluring. Anne came off the better of the two, having retained something sweet and as close to prettiness as any of them would ever have. On Emily, the same features left an impression of haughtiness, as if her very nature had stamped itself on the contours of her face.

Charlotte paced the room nervously with tiny steps.

"We are remote, yes, but she wouldn't get those same terms in a boarding school in a larger town. And the fact that we have only enough room to take in a few girls is an advantage."

Emily finished the letter and glanced up. "Moderate or not, if there are no pupils, then there are no pupils."

"Are you saying we should give up?"

Emily shrugged. "Even if someone should show an interest, do you think any mother in her right mind would entrust her daughter to our keeping, with a drunken brother and blind father stumbling around the house?"

Anne added, "She's right, Charlotte. We must rethink our scheme in the light of our present predicament."

Charlotte stopped pacing and turned to face her sisters. Her taut little body seemed to lose its fire.

"I'm deluding myself. I know I am."

Emily and Anne stared at her solemnly.

"I've heard Branwell talk about finding a job on the railway," Anne said. "Then he'd be gone. And things would be back to normal."

"But it's all talk," Charlotte replied. "I'm afraid that's all he's ever been good for. He's done nothing with his life. After all the sacrifices we made so that he could go to London and follow his dreams . . . and then he never made it out of Bradford . . ."

"That wasn't entirely his fault," Emily said.

"Papa would have found the money if he had shown the resolve. All of his boasting, it's all come to nothing."

"We mustn't give up on him yet," Anne said.

They were all disappointed in him—the prodigy, the wildly talented brother who entertained everyone who met him with his stunning flashes of wit and raw brainpower.

As children they had forged a unique bond, creating imaginary worlds of astonishing complexity and spinning them into tales that had brought excitement and enchantment to their lonely lives in this dull little village. Just as Emily and Anne had belonged to each other, Charlotte had belonged to Branwell. She alone was his true intellectual equal. But intellect was a useless quality in a girl, and so Charlotte kept her hopes bound up tightly in her imagination. She locked them into her little boxes, her writing desks and secret drawers, and she watched her brother walk out into the world to live his dreams in her stead. He would be a great artist or poet. She would fly up to Olympia on his wings.

When he failed—recklessly, wantonly—no one was as disappointed as she.

Emily said, "Even if Branwell found a position, we have Papa to deal with now. He needs more and more of our time."

"But what else is left to us? If not this school?" Charlotte asked.

There was a hint of desperation in her voice. They knew what this scheme of opening a school meant to her. It represented more than a means of income and independence. It was a way to keep alive what she had brought back from Brussels.

As Charlotte stewed, Anne watched her with sympathetic eyes. Not so Emily. Emily slid from the sofa and crept over to the great mastiff that lay in twitching slumber on the floor. As she crawled up to him, he raised his big head. She lay down beside him and draped an arm over his barrel chest; he fell back with a deep sigh, blissfully content.

Emily had never concerned herself with their finances. Her material needs were few; she still wore the old-fashioned gigot-sleeved dresses she'd been wearing since she was fifteen. Charlotte did her best to keep them mended, but they were worn and faded, and Emily had no interest in making new ones for herself.

After their aunt had died, Emily had laid claim to the task of caretaker to their father. She ran the house and left the unpleasant business of wage earning to everyone else.

"It would be nice if we could all stay home together," Emily sighed.

Anne replied, "That was the great advantage of our school. There would be inconveniences, to be sure, but we would be home and together."

Charlotte frowned. "I cannot brace myself to go back into a home as a governess. I don't have the temperament for it."

"Nor do I," Emily said.

"Well, that certainly goes without saying."

They had all three tried their hand at service. Only Anne had endured.

Charlotte turned to Anne. "How you survived five years at Thorp Green, I'll never know."

"Oh, but the Robinson girls weren't so difficult once they got older."

Anne had been reticent, had said next to nothing about Branwell's dismissal. It was Anne who had found him the position at Thorp Green as tutor to the little boy. He had stayed for two years and fallen madly in love with the mother.

Charlotte tried again, prodding gently, "My poor Anne, was it too dreadful? You must have heard things."

"There were rumors, but I thought they were nothing more than that. I could see that Mrs. Robinson was very fond of him. But so was everyone else. He was very well liked." She paused to take a deep breath, then pronounced firmly, "And you mustn't suppose that I left because of his conduct—I am not so weakhearted. I quit my post because the girls had grown up and didn't need me anymore. And I, for one, have no intention of being a burden on this family. I shall find myself another position."

Charlotte said, "Oh, Annie, how willing you are to deny yourself for others."

Anne's face flushed with pleasure at this rare bit of recognition from her older sister. "I deny myself as you have done, Charlotte. Out of duty."

Charlotte gave a lighthearted shrug. "Well, I suppose the last resort is to marry."

"Oh, she's in a witty mood now," Emily said.

"Charlotte, dear, you're the only one who's had an offer of marriage," Anne said.

"Yes, from Ellen's brother." Charlotte said wryly. "I fancy that was more like a business proposal. And I imagine it will be the only one I shall ever get."

"Annie's the pretty one." Emily smiled. "I vote her most likely to snare a husband."

Anne blushed again and smiled in return.

"Well, we all know Emily's not going to find a man—neglectful creature that she is. Look at that hole in her stocking."

Emily stretched her leg into the air for all to admire her toe.

"Take it off and leave it for me to mend. If you keep wearing it, the hole will only grow bigger."

"I shall find myself a gypsy husband," Emily said dreamily. "Tall, violently passionate, and very much like a Walter Scott hero."

"Oh yes," Charlotte tittered. "I think we would all like one like that."

"Not I," Anne frowned.

"In truth, I cannot imagine living anywhere but here," Emily said wistfully.

Charlotte grew somber again. "Well, the reality is that Papa will not live forever. And when he's gone we'll be chased out of here. How shall we survive? Where shall we go?"

"Oh, Tally, that's too many questions to answer all at once."

The door was thrown open and Branwell entered. He wore his spectacles on the end of his nose and had donned a dressing gown over his shirt and trousers—a faded old woolen thing with the pockets coming unstitched. Breakfast had revived him and he shuffled in energetically humming a tune, clutching a fistful of dog-eared pages.

"Ah! Here you are!" he cried.

The girls stared at him with closed faces.

"Oh, such sourpusses," he said good-naturedly. "But I have an announcement that will put a smile on your faces."

"You've taken an offer of employment," Charlotte said dryly.

"God forbid, no. I'm speaking of literary exertion. I have the materials for a respectably sized volume of poetry, and if I were in London personally I might perhaps try Henry Moxon. He's a well-known patron of the sons of rhyme, though I dare say the poor man often smarts for his liberality in publishing hideous trash." He gave a sigh of tedium. "It all seems so hopeless. A book of verse like this that requires the utmost stretch of the intellect—why, I'd be lucky to get ten pounds for it. But a novel—I could get two hundred pounds for a novel. That's what's really salable in today's reading world. And I could dash off a piece of commercial fiction in the time it takes to smoke a cigar and hum a tune."

He announced this in the manner of a man accustomed to constant adulation, but the faces before him remained frozen.

"I must attempt something. . . . ," he grumbled as he stuffed the pages into his pocket. "Sitting around here with nothing to do. Roasting night and day over a slow fire. I am tormented. Tormented."

He caught sight of the letter on the sofa.

"What's that?"

"It's not for you," Charlotte replied.

"The post has come?"

"Yes."

"And there's nothing for me?"

"No."

His spirits drooped as quickly as they had risen, and he sank onto the sofa beside Anne.

"How can I live without her? My life will be hell. What can the so-called love of her wretched husband be to her compared with mine? If he loved her with all the powers of his puny being, he couldn't love as much in eighty years as I could in a day."

They listened in uncomfortable silence to his ravings. Charlotte would have loved to throttle him but managed restraint.

He raised his sad eyes to them in a glance and muttered, "God help her. I know she's as miserable as I am. She'll die of a broken heart. We'll both die of a broken heart."

"One doesn't die of a broken heart," Charlotte snapped.

"Oh, hear the mighty oracle, Tally, speaking of love!"

Emily rolled over and stared up at him from the floor. "I don't like your hair like that. It's too long."

" 'Tis my laureate, sister dear."

"It's a wonder it doesn't give you a headache," she replied.

He glanced around the room at them, then, in deliberate provocation, pulled a flask of gin from his dressing gown pocket.

"Branwell!" Charlotte cried sharply.

"Only way I can survive all of you is to drink," he smirked. Anne watched him in frozen horror as he unscrewed the cap. Emily rose to her knees and crawled toward him.

"No you don't," he cried, snatching it from her grasp.

Anne said softly, "God have mercy on your soul."

"Mercy? Why, on the contrary, I shall have great pleasure in sending my soul to perdition, just to punish its maker. Here's to hearty damnation!" He took a long swig and screwed the cap back on the flask.

"Now, *that* will kill you," Charlotte said emphatically.

"You mustn't talk like that, Branwell," Anne pleaded. "Have you no shame?"

"None, sweet Annie. Kill me? I think not. Unfortunately, my constitution defies me. I wager I'll outlive every man this side of Lancashire and go to the grave a stooped and white-haired old sinner."

Branwell had been sitting on the letter, and now he tugged it out and opened it.

"Ah," he muttered with sincere remorse after he had scanned it. "So sorry, Tally. Two years studying in Brussels gone to waste. All that fluent French and German. All that Chateaubriand and Hugo. And not a soul to share it with. As for Emily, I can't see what good Brussels did her. She came back as savage as she went."

"That's not true," Anne interrupted. "Emily worked like a horse in Brussels, didn't she, Charlotte?"

"That's nothing new. She's always loved her studies—haven't you, Em? Never so content as when she's got her nose in a book."

"I'd like to see you play that Beethoven sonata as well as I do," Emily said smugly.

"But you have no audience, dear sister, apart from us."

"I wish for none, apart from you."

"There. Proved my point. But honestly, can you blame folks? Who on God's green earth would pay to come here? Most of us would pay to get out."

It was a sad truth, and the recognition of their shared plight momentarily erased the tensions. In an instant they became the close-knit family of their childhood—traumatized at a very young age by the loss of their mother and the deaths of their older sisters, taking refuge from sorrow in one another's company. And thus they had grown up and turned inward. The four siblings, the dogs, cats, and pet geese, the servants banging around in the kitchen, the father aloof and secluded in the parlor two walls removed—and the outside world nothing more than a memory or a dream.

There was a moment of sweet unruffled silence, and then Charlotte rose. "We should set the table."

At that moment, Keeper began to growl and they heard the crunch of gravel on the walk. Charlotte stepped to the window.

"Now, who is that?"

Anne rose and came to stand beside her.

"He's wearing a clerical collar."

"I've never seen him before."

"It's probably Papa's new curate," Branwell said with a yawn. "John said he arrived last night."

"Good gracious, why didn't you tell me? I didn't expect him until next week!" Charlotte flew into action, straightening the chairs and clearing the sewing off the table.

Emily made a dash for the door.

"Emily Jane Brontë! Don't you dare! Your books are scattered all over the floor!"

Emily snatched up the books and vanished in a flash, with Anne close behind. Branwell immediately appropriated the entire sofa for himself and stretched out on his back, hands crossed over his stomach, toes twitching to the music in his head.

"Branwell, do please stay out of sight. You look appalling and smell even worse."

"John said he's a stiff sort. Invited him down to the Black Bull with us this evening but he declined."

"Well, you can't expect a clergyman to keep company with the likes of you."

"I beg your pardon. Sutcliffe Sowden and I are on very friendly terms. He's the only curate I can stomach."

The doorbell rang.

"Branwell, go! Get out! Upstairs with you!"

She hurried out, nearly tripping over Keeper, who was making his way to the front door in good defensive form. She crossed the entry hall and knocked on her father's study, then entered.

He was at his desk with his glasses perched on the tip of his nose and a magnifying glass in hand, struggling to read a letter that he could see only dimly. Charlotte had been back from Brussels since January, and still she could not come to terms with how he had aged. His snowy-white hair bristled around his face, and he kept his neck swaddled in yards of white linen to ward off colds. At sixty-eight, he was still a handsome man, with an upright air of dignity that age would never diminish, but the forcefulness of his will had drawn unflattering lines on his face, and the mouth let you know that this was a man who would not be contradicted.

He had been irritable at breakfast, and she could tell at a glance that his humor had not improved.

"You must give me some of your time this afternoon, Charlotte," he said sternly. "I need you to read this for me. I have to respond today."

"Papa, it's your new curate," she announced.

"Ah, at last. God willing, they've sent me a good one," he said, straightening in his chair and laying down the glass.

"Can you see him now or should I show him into the dining room?"

"No, no, show him in."

"Good, because I can't dislodge Branwell from the sofa."

"My son is up?" The eyes took on a baffled look. "That poor boy. That evil woman has quite devoured his soul."

The doorbell rang again, sending Keeper into a barking frenzy. Charlotte raced back to the kitchen, calling for Martha. Martha appeared in the doorway to the back kitchen, her face wet and red, her sleeves rolled up, and her hair dangling in her eyes.

"Why haven't you got the door?" Charlotte exclaimed.

"I'm up to my ears in laundry, miss."

"Oh goodness, you do look a fright. I suppose I'll have to go myself." Charlotte took off her apron and patted back her hair.

"Do ye think he'll be stayin' for dinner?" Tabby asked.

"I should hope not. We've not planned for him."

"Those curates're pushy," she scowled. "They hang around like dogs an' won't let up till ye toss 'em a few scraps."

Charlotte was already on her way to the door, smoothing down her skirts. It was her thoughts that needed smoothing, however. Home was no longer a place of retreat. Home was an overindulged brother wallowing in self-pity, an irascible father with failing eyes, and fading dreams.

As for the clergymen who traipsed through their doors, she thought them more trouble than they were worth—the underpaid, newly ordained who came to Haworth to assist her father on their way to greater futures. She thought them vain young men who thought too highly of themselves and too lowly of the lower orders, men of petty jealousies and narrow minds.

The tall, broad-shouldered man who stepped into the parsonage that morning struck her as unusually reserved; he had a proud, statuelike face that might have been handsome had it revealed the slightest hint of feeling. He offered no smile and yet showed every sign of courtesy. He removed his hat, bowed to her, and introduced himself as Mr. Arthur Bell Nicholls. Keeper, who had once driven a terrified curate up the stairs and into a bedroom, smelled no fear on this stranger and treated him accordingly. Arthur let his hand linger before the dog's inquisitive nose, allowing himself to be thoroughly inspected, and if Charlotte had not been so eager to deliver the curate to her father, if she had taken just a moment to inquire about his journey or the suitability of his lodgings, she would have seen a softer side to the man. She would have noticed how he slid his hand underneath the dog's chin and gave it a good scratch; she would have seen the stiff reserve melt and a smile break from ear to ear and a twinkle light up his blue eyes. Instead, she ushered him into her father's study, closed the door behind him, and shut him out of her thoughts.

There was in Arthur Nicholls much to recommend him to Charlotte Brontë, not least of which was the disparity between surface and soul, and it might be argued that Mr. Nicholls was the hidden gem of the two. Behind a veneer of a quiet, ladylike demeanor, Charlotte concealed an acerbic mind and ruthlessly harsh opinions on the weaknesses of the human species. Arthur, on the other hand, was the blustery, bigoted sort who could barely open his mouth without offending someone. Yet when the gloves came off, he had a great and tender heart, and was capable of love that would bear all wrongs, endure all tempests—in short, the very stuff that Charlotte took great pains to fabricate in her stories and that she was convinced she would never find.

Chapter Three

For several days Arthur slipped in and out of the parsonage with no more than his usual deep-voiced greeting and a dip of the head, but already things were beginning to run more smoothly. Apart from the one Sunday service that Mr. Brontë preached, all the other services and responsibilities, the never-ending rituals of burying the dead and blessing the living, were immediately assumed by the new curate, leaving the reverend to focus his energies on the reform issues so dear to his heart. There were opinions to formulate, editorial letters to write, opponents to answer, influential men to persuade; there were issues to address: the appalling sanitary conditions, the scarcity of safe water, church tax reform, and the perpetual nasty spats between the dissenters and the established church.

The warm weather held through the week, and on Monday after dinner Charlotte walked to Keighley to exchange her library books, returning late in the afternoon. She came in through the back kitchen, exhausted and muddied after her eight-mile jaunt across the hills, and found all the women in a tizzy. It seemed that Mr. Nicholls had dropped by. He had been followed in short time by Mr. Sowden, who had walked from Hebden Bridge to introduce himself to the newcomer and, upon learning that Arthur was at the parsonage, had followed him there. No sooner had the women settled back to their baking than the doorbell rang yet again; it was young Mr. Grant, the incumbent of nearby Oxenhope, with the odious Mr. Smith in tow, come on the same welcome mission. Tea had been requested and now tea was being prepared, but they had not made provisions for such an assault on their reserves, and Emily, who habitually worked to a relaxed tempo, was rushing to get scones into the oven and was in a foul temper because of it. Anne had interrupted her dressmaking to run to the village and bring back meat pies, which she was now arranging on a tray, and Tabby was slicing ham into slivers so fine that you could see light through them.

"Not quite so thin," Charlotte said to Tabby, stepping up to speak loudly in the servant's ear as she untied her bonnet.

Tabby wiped a broad callused hand across her dirty apron. "It's bakin' day. If they had any care at all for folk, they'd know better than to come on bakin' day."

"They are men," Charlotte replied. "They only care if the bread is baked or not. Anne, I picked up the silk you left to be dyed."

She set her parcels on a stool and quickly took charge. With Charlotte there, Tabby's anxiety eased, and the tired old servant lowered herself onto a stool.

"Papa will want the good tea service, Martha."

"Yes, ma'am, I was just on my way to fetch it. An' the urn?"

"How many are there?"

"Four of 'em."

"Good grief."

At that moment the sound of loud laughter drifted in from the parlor.

"Is that awful Mr. Smith here too?"

"I'm afraid so," Emily grumbled as she removed the tray of scones from the oven. "Pompous little toad of a man."

"Poor father. That man really tries his nerves. Has the post arrived?"

"Aye!" Tabby replied.

Charlotte's eyes snapped to life. "Where is it?"

"If they'd only be civil, I wouldn't mind so much. But these young parsons is so high an' scornful," Tabby waffled on.

"There was nothing for you, Charlotte," Emily said gently, flashing a look of sympathy. "Only something for Papa."

Emily and Anne exchanged a knowing look. Charlotte had been wait-ing for months for a letter from her professor in Brussels. Early on there had been a flurry of correspondence between them, but he wrote rarely now, and Charlotte never spoke of him anymore.

Charlotte's return reinstated a bit of composure to the preparations, and soon the trays were ready and Charlotte and Martha set sail for the dining room. As the women entered, there was an immediate halt in the conversation, not so much out of respect as anticipation of filling their stomachs.

Reverend Brontë looked up and saw only a shadow at the door.

"Martha? Is that you?"

"It is I, Papa," Charlotte replied as she set down her tray on the din-ing table.

"Ah! You're back. Good," he said with obvious relief, gazing in her di-rection with clouded eyes. He relied heavily on her when there was en-tertaining to be done. "Mr. Nicholls, I believe you've met my eldest daughter, Charlotte."

"Not formally, sir," Arthur said, rising to his feet and greeting her with a deep bow. He dwarfed her tiny figure, and Mr. Smith exchanged an amused smile with the others. She was too nearsighted to read their mocking glances, but Charlotte could feel their eyes on her, and she knew quite well what they were thinking. They considered her an unat-tractive old maid, and any encounter with an eligible bachelor made her the subject of gossip and ridicule.

She held her composure and extended her hand to Arthur, who clasped it firmly.

"I'm honored, Miss Brontë," he said. "In the short time that I have known your father, I can say I have a very high opinion of his worth and character, which can only give me a very high opinion of yourself."

At this Mr. Smith ejaculated an awful sound that came out like a cross between laughter and an effort to clear the throat of phlegm. It was intended to tease Arthur for his overblown courtesy but instead came off as offensive to Charlotte and had the effect of startling them all. Martha, who was busy laying out the plates of ham and scones, looked up in horror at his outburst.

Mr. Brontë turned his head toward the sound. "Are you quite all right, sir?"

"Ah, yes, he's fine, just a little tickle in the throat." The reply came from Mr. Sowden, who turned to his colleague and slapped him a little too heartily on the back.

Charlotte had quickly turned away but Arthur saw the heat rise to her face. He would have liked to say something to put her at ease, but he feared he would only exacerbate her discomfort, and so he sat back down and assumed a stony silence.

When Charlotte had entered, he had just begun to tell them about his arrival in town and the unfortunate incident with the farmer and his horse, but after Mr. Smith's rudeness to Charlotte, Arthur took a sudden disliking for the man. He recognized a mean spirit and thought it best to avoid giving him any more fodder for ridicule. So when Mr. Brontë prompted him to continue, Arthur shrugged it off.

"It's nothing. I merely meant to comment on the lack of civility I encountered, nothing more," he said.

Unfortunately, the news had already come to Mr. Smith's ears.

"Oh, but you must tell it, Nicholls."

"It's not worthy of telling, I assure you."

"Oh, but it is! It is!" Mr. Smith said with glee.

The tea was laid out, and the men eagerly brought their chairs to the dining table. Faced with Arthur's stubborn refusal to entertain them, Mr. Smith gladly took up the tale and told what he had heard, that the new curate had arrived in town in a most unceremonious fashion— leading a tired old workhorse up the hill with an old farmer cracking a whip over his head. Mr. Smith could be amusing when he wished, and he elaborated the incident in a manner that made them all laugh. Martha suppressed a giggle and even Charlotte was tempted to smile, but one glance at Arthur's solemn and petrified face stifled the urge. She felt his humiliation just as he had felt hers. She did her best to distract them by passing around the cups of tea, and they took the bait and grew quiet. All but Mr. Nicholls, who set down his cup and seemed to be quietly gathering his thoughts.

After a pause, he said, "I believe in upholding the dignity of the cloth. I am ever mindful of my position, and I seek to conduct myself at all times as a representative of the holy church. The treatment I suffered was not only a disgrace to myself personally, it was a disgrace to all men of the priesthood and, by implication, an insult to the church."

"Ah, but farmer Clapham's a tough old Methodist," Sutcliffe Sowden said kindly, attempting to lighten the mood. "I heard he once went after a curate with a pitchfork. By Jove, you're fortunate you made it here alive."

Patrick Brontë spoke up. There was a momentary hush as they set down their cups and listened respectfully. "These men are a product of generations of isolation," he said, "and their natures reflect as much. They have learned to rely only on themselves, which is quite necessary to their survival. The outcome is that they have no faith in strangers. If they are crusty and rude, it is because they recognize no superiors and therefore have no need of civility."

"And how do you manage to win souls to Christ if their hearts are shut to man?" Arthur asked.

"I go only where I am wanted," Mr. Brontë replied simply.

Charlotte had been buttering a slice of bread for her father, and when she finished preparing his plate she took up her knitting.

"You must learn to take their rudeness with good humor, Mr. Nicholls," she said quietly. "Take it with a grain of salt and you will discover beneath it all a good deal of kindliness and warmth. They *can* be a hospitable people." Her hands fell still and she looked up directly at Arthur. Her large brown eyes held his own, and he felt himself grow very still inside. "They are indeed stubborn in the face of strident authority but will yield like lambs to gentle persuasion."

Mr. Grant raised an eyebrow over his cup of tea. "Like lambs? Lambs, Miss Brontë? The man who can make them yield like lambs, now, that is a shepherd I have yet to meet in these parts."

Charlotte buried her gaze in her knitting and grew quiet. Arthur found himself watching her out of the corner of his eye.

"You'll have your hands full with the church school, Mr. Nicholls," Patrick Brontë continued.

"I look forward to the challenge, sir."

"It will be a challenge, indeed. They have a strong dislike of authority. And what little learning they have is steeped in superstition and heretical in nature."

"However, we are making progress on some fronts, Nicholls," Mr. Grant said. "We shall soon have a church in Oxenhope, thanks to my unyielding efforts. It's not a simple matter, raising subscriptions from these people. They're a tightfisted race."

Charlotte eyed Mr. Grant surreptitiously over the rims of her spectacles. More like extortion, she thought. The way he badgered everyone, going back again and again, rarely showing gratitude.

To Arthur he added, "Oxenhope's the village just up the hill to the south. The Methodists have a chapel there. They've quite overrun the place and gotten their claws into everyone. We sorely need a presence." He leaned forward with an air of secrecy. "I was counting heavily on the Greenwoods, but they contributed only a measly sum—I shan't tell you how much. It would embarrass the old man." He shook his head. "Very shabby."

"Do you hunt, sir?" Arthur asked, noticing the musket on the wall.

"Papa," Charlotte whispered, "Mr. Nicholls is speaking to you."

"Do I hunt?" Patrick repeated, swinging his dim gaze in Arthur's direction. "No, sir. But I served in Lord Palmerston's regiment at Oxford and have, by necessity and training, acquired a great appreciation for weaponry. I lived through the Luddite uprisings and we would not have been so foolish as to walk outdoors unarmed." He leaned back in his chair and spread open his jacket to reveal the pistol at his belt. "Habit, I suppose. I should feel quite exposed without it."

Charlotte glanced up at Arthur, anticipating his discomfort. Inevitably there would be a shocked reaction. He would ask if the pistol was loaded, which it was. But Arthur surprised her.

He nodded solemnly. "I suspect it serves you well in these parts."

"Indeed," Patrick said. "We are all warriors for Christ. We do not weaken even in the heat of battle, even with the enemy surrounding us. We are sustained even at the darkest hour by belief in our cause. Belief in ourselves."

"Amen."

"Amen."

During all this time, Mr. Smith's mouth had been full of Tabby's spice cake. But once he was sated and had washed the last bites down with copious quantities of tea, there was nothing to restrain him from joining the discussion.

"I tell you, the best way to serve the Yorkshiremen is to leave them alone. And they never forget a harm done to them. Remember that." He dabbed his mouth with his napkin and leaned back in his chair. "It's a backward place, and there's no high society to speak of. If you're a man of refinement, as I observe you are, Mr. Nicholls, you'll be begging to get out in no time."

"Don't let yourself be discouraged, Nicholls," Sutcliffe Sowden said. He was a tall, delicate man with a calm and friendly demeanor. "We have made great strides in the district and Mr. Brontë does a commendable job of dealing with them. He's your example to follow. You'll never meet a man more patient or impartial when it comes to arbitrating between the locals. He's greatly respected, by churchmen and dissenters alike."

And that statement opened up the floodgates. Charlotte happened to be refilling their cups; she glanced up and saw that Arthur had gone a deep red, and she wondered if perhaps he had bitten down on a bit of nutshell in his spice cake.

"I should not think it much of a compliment to be respected by the dissenters," he said sternly.

At this, Patrick's eyebrow rose. "May I assume from that statement that you are intolerant of dissent?"

"How can I possibly be tolerant of a schismatic sect that wishes to destroy the established church and bring down all of England? Because that's what will happen," he said heatedly.

Charlotte observed him keenly. His massive frame seemed to be threatened with upheaval, an eruption just waiting to blow.

"I see you have been influenced by the Oxford movement," Mr. Brontë said.

"I align myself with all those who seek to block the advance of liberalism in religious thought," he explained.

"You'll need to get along with the nonconformists if you want to be effective," Patrick said matter-of-factly. "This is a disaffected population, and the dissenters are flourishing here in the north. They outnumber us two to one."

"I intend to change those statistics, sir," he said confidently. "I know the Baptists and the Methodists have built their schools here in the district, and their attendance has grown. But as part of my duties I intend to expand our own church school and make it flourish. The dissenters are a radical influence, and they should be eradicated like the plague that they are."

Patrick smiled again at this, and said, "Well, Mr. Nicholls, I gather I need not ask you to serve on any arbitration committee with me."

"Indeed, sir, I would have to decline," he said proudly, and held his cup out to Charlotte for more tea.

Charlotte poured with a steady hand, which was admirable considering how she felt about this new curate's narrow-minded views. She was losing patience with the whole lot of them. She had listened to their complaints and their squabbles for years, and she wondered if she would ever be free of this life of petty-minded curates and tea taking. She finished filling his cup, picked up her knitting, and then, during the lag in conversation, she spoke up once again.

"I have a dear friend from school who's a dissenter," she said breezily, with a quick glance at Arthur. "Her name is Mary Taylor. She is not the type to be easily eradicated. Indeed, if I were to place bets, I'd put my money on her."

Everyone laughed except Arthur. Charlotte had the advantage of her knitting and did not have to meet his gaze.

Arthur was distant and cool to her from that day on, although he never lacked in courtesy. Charlotte thought it just as well. She considered him merely another narrow-minded curate.

Arthur adopted the same cool reserve with Mr. Smith, whose manners he found repulsive and little better than those of the locals he so detested. Unfortunately, this coolness was ineffective in deterring visits from Mr. Smith, who seemed to spend more time calling on the other curates than tending to the needs of his parishioners. Arthur, on the other hand, plunged into his responsibilities with a conscientiousness that would come to define him, and he had little time for idle social calls.

It was quickly observed that Arthur was a punctual man, and Mr. Smith always contrived to call at just the moment when Arthur was sitting down to tea in his room, obliging Mrs. Brown to serve him as well. Before he knew it, Joseph Grant would be on his heels with Sutcliffe Sowden in tow, and they would sit around the table gossiping like magpies while Arthur anxiously glanced at the clock on his mantel and worried about all that was not getting done that day.

He learned that the Brontë family was always a source of good gossip. It was a family that fascinated: an eccentric old father, a dazzlingly brilliant son wasting away for love of a married woman, and three daughters who were little more than ghosts, although the villagers thought them very proud.

Mr. Smith took particular delight in heaping scorn upon the young women.

"If they had a mother, you could be sure she'd be on us like flies on a carcass to marry one of them. But the old man knows better than to try to foist one of those girls on his curates," he said.

Arthur spoke up and surprised them. "Oh, I don't think that's the case at all. I suspect they wouldn't take any one of you sorry fellows, even if you might be so inclined. I haven't laid eyes on the other two except from a distance—"

"Ah, well, they're as shy as church mice," Joseph Grant said. "They scurry into their holes when they see us coming."

"That may be," Arthur continued, "but I can tell you that Miss Charlotte Brontë is a proud woman and thinks much more highly of herself than you do of her, and rightfully so. She strikes me as a very clever lady, her father's daughter through and through."

"Precisely my point, Nicholls. Who wants a clever woman for a wife? Who wants a woman who can think like a man? And an ugly one at that?"

"She is certainly not ugly," Arthur replied, a little more vehemently than he realized.

"She's stunted, poor creature."

"I rather think of her as delicate."

"Think of her? Do you indeed think of her, Mr. Nicholls? Do your thoughts turn to her at night when you're lying alone in your cold bed? Ah! Ladies! Ladies! Come right up! Don't be shy!" Mr. Smith cried. He sat up from his perpetual slouch and wagged a finger at Arthur. "Here's a man just waiting to be ensnared! Right here!"

Arthur laughed along with Joseph Grant and Sutcliffe Sowden, but he said no more about Charlotte Brontë's appeal.

Arthur's stern reserve belied a tender heart, and he was deeply sensitive to the sufferings of others. He had been raised with his cousin Mary Anna, a young woman of such sweet disposition that he sometimes thought she was not quite real. Born with a bone defect in her legs, she had been forced to wear leg irons. Even as an adult she would not be able to walk without a cane. Arthur had witnessed the way boys had tormented her and how she had lain across her mother's bed and wept; he had listened to his aunt condemn the cruelty of men in judging a woman, how they valued a pretty figure over a good heart. When he grew older, the other boys learned never to say an unkind word about Mary Anna, knowing that if they did Arthur would beat them to within an inch of their lives.

Arthur was not quite ready to defend Charlotte Brontë's name with his bare hands; nevertheless, she now had a champion behind the scenes, albeit a slightly cowardly one. The time would come for bravery, and he would prove himself more than equal to the task.

It would be a long time before he knew her as anything more than a broad-faced woman who slipped in and out of the parsonage rooms like a gray rustling shadow, arranging a chair out of place or whisking away of bit of needlework left lying about by one of her sisters. She was tiny and squinted without her spectacles, but when she drew close and looked up at him, a slight tremor swept through his stomach, like ripples from something dense and blazing deep inside her person. He was a practical man, uncomfortable with poetics and without an inkling of psychology, and it perplexed him that a woman so lacking in stature and physical charms could make herself felt so intensely.

A couple of months later, when rumors began to circulate that Charlotte might be engaged to her father's new curate, she was dumbfounded as to where the gossip might have started. Fortunately, a scandal broke around that time. One night in November, Mr. Smith absconded with all the proceeds they had collected to purchase an organ for the church in Stanbury. He fled to Canada, leaving behind a heap of debts and a penniless wife and two children. This kept tongues wagging for months, and the villagers forgot all about matchmaking between Arthur Bell Nicholls and the parson's daughter.

Chapter Four

"What shall I do without you, Mary?" Charlotte said with a stricken face. "When you're gone, I'll have only Ellen."

"I fret about that. I truly do," Mary replied. "I shouldn't like her to have such unmitigated influence over you. She's a dear, sweet, sensible girl, but she's got those dreadful Calvinists breathing in her ear." Mary Taylor gave a shudder. "You're far too susceptible to that sort of thing as it is . . . all that pious self-denying nonsense."

"We both strive for Christian perfection. But I'm not like her. If I were more like Ellen, I'd have no doubt as to the fate of my soul."

"But how can you possibly compare yourself to her? She's never had an original thought in her life."

Charlotte smiled. "I shall miss your blunt manners."

"I'm sure you will. Who else will speak the bitter truth to you?"

"The ugly truth."

Mary Taylor wrestled herself around onto her stomach and raised herself on her elbows. Charlotte lay beside her in bed. She had the appearance of a sarcophagus, deathlike and stiff, her eyes fixed on the ceiling and her dainty, impeccably manicured hands folded across her chest. Mary recalled how she had always slept like this at school when they were girls. When the lights were out, Charlotte would lie in the dark and talk of her visionary stories and the characters she saw drifting through her imagination. They would all lie breathless as they listened, shuddering at the horrors she drew so vividly with her voice and the power of her words. Mary had thought her wildly impractical at best; at worst, mad.

"Charlotte," she said, her eyes full of remorse, "I've never said this before and I must say it now. I've always regretted those words."

"What? When you told me I was ugly?"

"It was such a heartless thing to say to you."

"You always speak your mind, but you're not heartless, Polly. I learned that about you very quickly."

They grew silent, remembering those days as girls at Roe Head School. At fifteen Mary had been tall and full-figured, with thick, glossy hair. Miss Wooler, the headmistress, had once declared Mary Taylor "too beautiful to live." But she could be harsh and terribly insensitive, and there were times when her comments wounded deeply; then there would be long periods of silence between them.

"You were so frightfully clever. You dwarfed us all intellectually," Mary said.

"Not you."

"Yes, even me."

"I alienated everyone."

"Because we were young and silly. You knew things no one else knew. You could look at a painting and *see* things, and you could *tell* us what you saw, and you knew everything about the poets we read. You had opinions, Charlotte. Pray tell me what fifteen-year-old girl has opinions?"

"Why, Mary Taylor, you're the most opinionated creature on the face of the earth."

"Not about art."

Mary dropped her head onto her pillow. "I truly am sorry, Charlotte, for calling you ugly."

"But I was."

"It was cruel. And you were frightened. It was your first day. We were all frightened on our first day." She paused and then tittered, "I admit, your hair was frightful."

A grin crept over Charlotte's face. "I'd gotten up before dawn that morning so Emily could curl it with the tongs. She scorched it." She shook with quiet laughter. "And my clothes. What a sad little sight I was in my hand-me-downs."

"Well, I didn't fare any better than you did. Mama always made us wear everything down to its last thread. She used to make us cross-stitch our brand-new gloves so they wouldn't wear out."

Charlotte reached for Mary's hand and gave it a gentle squeeze.

"Let's not talk about those days. Let's talk about you. About your plans. So you've decided to be a shopkeeper in New Zealand rather than teach English to dull little boys in Germany."

"It's a general store. My brother's done quite well with it."

"Fearless Mary."

"What's there to fear in making a fortune? It says something about good old England that I have to go all the way to New Zealand to earn the money I know I'm capable of earning. Did you ever hear of a governess making a fortune?" Mary smiled. "I'm quite looking forward to the adventure. I sail in March."

"How long does it take for letters to reach New Zealand?"

"About six months."

"Good grief."

Mary hesitated, toying with her long braid as she lay propped on her elbows.

"Do you still hear from your professor in Brussels?" she asked gently.

Charlotte shifted her gaze back to the ceiling, to the shadows. "I haven't had a letter since last summer."

"You mustn't dwell on it anymore. It's in the past. You must get on with your life."

"But I shall go back, Mary. One day, I shall return. I don't know when or how, but I shall." Charlotte turned her head, and her dark eyes bore into Mary's. "I have you to thank for it all. The letters you wrote to me while you were studying there, about all the wonderful things you were doing. The great cathedrals, the paintings you saw. Something inside me swelled when I read those letters. I was so angry with my life at the time, so impatient to be free."

"And rightfully so. You're far too duty-bound. I think going to Brussels was the only thing you've ever done truly for yourself and yourself alone. Are you keeping up with your French?"

"I'm trying very hard. I memorize a half page of French text every week. I try to speak French with Emily, but she'll have none of it."

"I'll make sure that Joe keeps sending you the French newspapers."

"Oh, yes, please do."

"Have you completely abandoned your project for a school?"

"I've lost my enthusiasm for it. I feel something in me is tamed or broken. I would so love to have some active purpose in life, but I doubt I'll find that here. Haworth is such a lonely, quiet spot."

She turned her dark, solemn eyes to Mary and said, "New Zealand," trying to fathom the enormous distance. "Shall I never see you again?"

"Come with me."

Charlotte shook her head.

"You said yourself you wish for more variety. You need a chance to meet people and experience life."

"That is my wish, but apparently that is not my fate."

"Your fate is as you make it; it's not predetermined. You mustn't stay here. You fall into the deepest depressions at home. If you stay here, it will ruin your health. You'll never recover. Think of what you'll be five years from now if you stay here."

A dark cloud came over Charlotte's face, and Mary feared she had brought her to tears. "Oh, Charlotte, I am sorry. Please, don't cry."

Charlotte rolled over and blew out the candle. Then she settled back in the bed and grew still. They were engulfed in darkness.

"Nevertheless, Polly, I intend to stay."

———

Upon her return from Brussels, Charlotte had fired off a storm of letters to Constantin Heger, her beloved professor—the first ones solemn, eager, brimming with concern for his well-being and her enthusiastic plans for her school. The later ones, written when she despaired that she would lose him, revealed a pathetic, heartbroken woman incapable of self-control. In her mind she was paying homage to the man who had nurtured and cherished the qualities that few outside her family had valued in her—not beauty but probity of thought, imagination, genius. The letters, however, were much more than that. Writing in a language that was not her own, distanced by the miles, another woman emerged; her self-restraint broke down and from behind a thin veil of denial she shamelessly bared her heart to him.

Monsieur,

I know quite well that it's not my turn to write, but my friend Miss Wheelwright is going to Brussels and has agreed to carry this letter. . . .

I'm terribly afraid of forgetting French because I'm persuaded I'll see you again one day—I don't know how or when—but it must be because I wish it so much, and then I wouldn't want to stand there dumb before you—that would be too terribly sad to see you and not be able to speak to you. . . .

I would not be so depressed in spirit if I could write. In the past I could spend days, weeks, whole months writing. Do you know what I would like to do, monsieur? I would like to write a book and dedicate it to my literature master—to the only master I have ever had—to you.

I haven't begged you to write soon because I fear imposing on you—but you are too good to forget that I nonetheless wish it so—I wish it very much—but enough of that. Do as you wish, monsieur. If I should receive a letter from you and thought that you had written it out of pity—I would be deeply hurt. Once again good-bye,

monsieur. It hurts to say good-bye even in a letter. Oh, I'm sure I'll
see you again one day—it must be—as soon as I shall have earned
enough money to go to Brussels I'll go—and I shall see you even if
only for a brief moment.

Try as she might to repress her thoughts of him, she was helpless to
control her dreams. Intensely felt, thrilling dreams during which some
romantically charged crisis would throw them together—then there
would be the sense of being in his arms, loving him, being loved by him.
She would awake in tears.

His few, infrequent replies did little to stanch the hemorrhaging of
her heart. Eventually she received a kind but stiffly formal letter from
Madame, his wife, requesting Charlotte to write only once every six
months. Charlotte, always obedient, waited precisely to the date before
setting pen to paper again. Then she wrote as if she had been waiting to
exhale all that time.

. . . I tried to forget you—to be constantly thinking of someone you
fear you shall never see again and whom, nevertheless, you greatly
respect, is exhausting for the spirit, and when you have suffered that
kind of anxiety for a year or two, you'll do anything to restore your
peace of mind. I have done everything, I have kept busy, I have ab-
solutely forbidden myself the pleasure of speaking of you—even to
Emily, but I haven't been able to conquer either my regrets or my
impatience—it's so humiliating—to be incapable of controlling my
own thoughts, to be a slave to a regret, a memory, slave to a single
fixed idea that oppresses my spirit like a tyrant. Why can't I have
for you just as much friendship as you have for me—neither more
nor less? I would be so peaceful, so free—I could easily keep silent
for ten years. . . .

You will perceive by the defects in this letter that I am forgetting
the French language—yet I read all the French books I can get
and learn a daily portion by heart—but I have never heard French

spoken but once since I left Brussels—and then it sounded like music in my ears—every word was most precious to me because it reminded me of you—I love French for your sake with all my heart and soul.

Farewell my dear Master—may God protect you with special care and crown you with peculiar blessings.

C. Brontë

Eventually, Constantin Heger's letters ceased altogether.

Chapter Five

Charlotte had always known that her temperament was ill-suited to teaching; she loved the subject matter but had no patience for the riotous little subjects themselves. Many years ago, when Branwell was nineteen and Charlotte not yet twenty-one, she had come home at Christmas from her first months of teaching at Roe Head School and confided her despair to her brother. The two of them, bemoaning the drudge life of tutors and governesses, had concluded that there was only one way to escape such a fate: they would publish.

Since childhood all four siblings had been scribbling stories and poetry, interweaving characters, events, and ongoing narratives that resulted in shared imaginary worlds of extraordinary detail. These imaginary kingdoms, long ago christened Angria and Gondal and teeming with political intrigue, adventure, and high drama, held infinitely more appeal than the dull routine of life in bleak Haworth. Like all children, they had discovered that this realm of consciousness was one over which they had absolute control, and therein lay the secret to their happiness. By drawing back the veils and slipping into Glass Town, they were able to free themselves from outside circumstances—their poverty, their isolation, and, for the girls, their plainness—all those things that had bred insecurity, shyness, and debilitating self-consciousness.

Writing could be a path to exquisite joy. It offered a way to live contentedly in an infinitely dreary world that offered little hope for change. They would always be odd; they would always be poor. And so they held on to their kingdoms long after the age when childish fantasies are put aside. Ambition never entered into the game. Not for the women. Well, perhaps a little for Charlotte. But only because Branwell yearned for fame, and she followed adoringly in his steps.

So, that Christmas it was resolved: Charlotte and Branwell would turn their writing to profit—and why not? How often had they lamented the quality of the literary material coming out of London's print shops? Young, full of grand illusions, they believed in the originality of their work; but above all they clung firmly to the Romantic's notion of the imaginary world as an exalted realm, and the poet as a divinelike creature.

Over the holidays they launched a letter-writing campaign, seeking opinions on their stories and poems and advice on how to get their work into print. Charlotte sent several of her best efforts to England's poet laureate, Robert Southey, along with a rather flighty, florid letter introducing herself as an aspiring poetess.

The reply, two months coming, was crushing—although Charlotte took some satisfaction in the fact that the illustrious poet deemed her worthy of a reply; Branwell's queries (undoubtedly off-putting in his overestimation of his own talent) had bagged not a single response.

"You live in a visionary world," Southey wrote,

> and seem to imagine that this is my case also. You who so ardently desire "to be ever known" as a poetess, might have had your ardor in some degree abated by seeing a poet in the decline of life. You evidently possess, and in no inconsiderable degree, what Wordsworth calls the "faculty of verse." But there is a danger of which I would, with all kindness and earnestness, warn you. The daydreams in which you habitually indulge are likely to induce a distempered state of mind; and as all the ordinary uses of the world seem to you flat and unprofitable, you will be unfitted for them without becoming fitted for anything else. Literature cannot be the business of a woman's life, and it ought not to be. The more she is engaged in her proper duties, the less leisure will she have for it, even as an accomplishment and a recreation. To those

duties you have not yet been called, and when you are you will be less eager for celebrity. Write poetry for its own sake; not with a view to celebrity. So written, it is wholesome both for the heart and soul.

Ah, there it was. She should have known better. Shame on her. Charlotte immediately replied:

At the first perusal of your letter I felt only shame and regret that I had ever ventured to trouble you with my crude rhapsody; I felt a painful heat rise to my face when I thought of the quires of paper I had covered with what once gave me so much delight, but which now was only a source of confusion.

I know the first letter I wrote to you was all senseless trash from beginning to end; but I am not altogether the idle, dreaming being it would seem to denote. I am the eldest daughter of a clergyman who has sacrificed his small means so that I might be educated in Brussels. I thought it therefore my duty, when I left school, to become a governess. In that capacity I find enough to occupy my thoughts all day long, and my head and hands too, without having a moment's time for one dream of the imagination. In the evenings, I confess, I do think but I never trouble anyone else with my thoughts. I carefully avoid any appearance of preoccupation and eccentricity which might lead others in the household to suspect the nature of my pursuits.

I have endeavored not only to observe all the duties a woman ought to fulfill, but to feel deeply interested in them. I don't always succeed, for sometimes when I'm teaching or sewing I would rather be reading or writing; but I try to deny myself; and my father— who has since childhood counseled me in the same tone as you have done—has rewarded my privation with approbation.

Once more allow me to thank you with sincere gratitude. I trust I shall never more feel ambitious to see my name in print; if the wish should rise, I'll look at Southey's letter, and suppress it.

Throughout the years that followed Charlotte continued to ride the fence between ambition and self-denial, and it was a balancing act fraught with constant tension. She was no rebel. She, too, subscribed to the powerful convention that it was not becoming for a lady (certainly not a Christian lady) to seek glory or recognition; but she was equally convinced of her own intelligence and of her elevated position in the clan as Branwell's equal. There might have been a happy compromise if Branwell had succeeded. Ambition might have been appeased vicariously if only her brother had lived up to his side of the bargain. But he did not.

During the final months of that turbulent summer following Branwell's dismissal, she watched the once powerful men around her gradually fail, their authority eroded by blindness and drunkenness. Certainly she mourned (even resented) their failure, but out of loss rose a new possibility. A new role for herself.

Surely there was justification for ambition when all the men in your life let you down.

"Emmy," Charlotte began, looking up from the tea towel she was hemming, "do read something of your poetry to us this evening, dearest. That would cheer me out of my doldrums, I think."

Emily lay on her stomach on the hearthrug, feet in the air and chin in her hands, reading a book by candlelight. Keeper lay sprawled at her side. She resisted for a moment, then turned a suspicious look on Charlotte.

"My poetry is not what you would judge cheerful."

Charlotte hesitated before replying. "No, but it always fascinated me. It's been years since we've read any of our verse to one another. I've quite lost track of your Gondal characters—Henry, Juliet Augusteena, Catherine Navarre. I daresay they must have changed."

"No, not changed," Emily replied. "New adventures and new intrigues, but they're quite the same." She turned back to her book.

They listened for a moment to the wind's haunting sighs and moans.

Anne rose from the sofa to fold the bedsheet she'd been mending. "There. That's finished. Another hole patched."

Charlotte put down her sewing. "Here. Let me help."

She rose, stepped over the sleeping spaniel, and took one end of the sheet from Anne.

"Emily, have you ever considered publishing your poetry?" Charlotte asked.

"What did you say?" she replied, rolling onto her side. Keeper—distressed by the tone of her voice—lifted his head and followed her warily with his eyes.

"Publishing your verse. You might consider it." Charlotte's voice softened. "It's really quite exceptional."

Emily twisted herself around and sat up. "You've been reading my poetry?" she accused sharply.

"It was quite unintentional. I came across your notebook while I was changing the sheets on your bed."

"And you opened it and read it?"

"Yes, I did, dearest," she said soothingly. "It was wrong of me, but I was curious. We used to share so much—we don't anymore."

Emily closed her book and rose swiftly to her feet, spooking both dogs, who scrambled out of her way. Towering over Charlotte, she said, "My notebooks are private. You have no right. What did you do with it?"

"I put it back of course. Now, would you listen to what I have to say?" She reached for Emily's hand, but Emily pulled away.

"What? You want to publish my poetry for the sake of a few miserable shillings? To be ridiculed and mocked by fools?"

"Emily, dearest, I'm trying to tell you that what you've written is of considerable merit . . . and should you be interested in publishing—"

"You know perfectly well I don't give a tinker's damn for your ambitious schemes. You wanted us to go to Brussels, I went to Brussels. You wanted a school, I agreed to a school. If you want to publish poetry, then publish your own. But I would sooner walk stark naked through Haworth than lay Gondal before the world."

She stormed out of the room.

Charlotte had gone white and stood trembling in the wake of her sister's wrath.

"Oh goodness," she said to Anne. "It's going to be quite unpleasant around here for a few days."

Anne motioned to the sofa. "Come sit back down. It's all right. She'll get over it."

Charlotte's hands were trembling as she picked up her needle.

Anne asked, "Do you really think it merits publication?"

"She hasn't shared it with you?"

"No. Not in years."

"It was completely unlike anything I've ever read—certainly it's nothing like the sort of feeble, soppy poetry women generally write. Really, it was quite extraordinary, and powerful."

Anne thought quietly for a moment and then said, "You should trust your judgment, Tally."

"But she's so frightfully stubborn. She always opposes me. Even when I have her best interests at heart."

"You know how to win her over. You'll think of a way."

That night before she went to bed, Charlotte knocked on Emily's door. Her room stood at the top of the stairs above the entry hall; it was tiny—barely large enough for a small bed, a dresser, and a chair. It had once been their playroom and, later, Branwell's room. Then he went away and Emily made it undisputedly her own.

Charlotte opened the door a crack.

"May I come in?"

There was no answer. Charlotte opened the door wider.

Keeper, who was curled on the rug next to Emily's bed, let out a low rumbling growl.

"It's only me, boy. It's okay."

Charlotte stepped in and stood in the darkness. "Are you asleep?"

There was a rustle of sheets but no reply.

Moonlight fell into the room along the edges of the shutters. Charlotte could see her form curled in the narrow bed just beneath the window.

"Emmy, when I found your journal, I glanced at it just out of curiosity. I had no intention of prying. But after the first few lines, I couldn't put it down."

Charlotte groped her way to the chair; she gathered up the jumble of petticoats and shawls and sat down, piling it all on her lap.

"Your feelings are peculiar, Emily. Peculiar in a rare, beautiful way that very few people see—because you don't want to be seen," she said. "And your poetry is very much like you. I read the verses aloud to myself and I fancied I could hear a sort of wild melancholy and musicality. It was your love of nature and music, all of it wrapped in this clear, condensed, and very powerful language."

She paused. She heard Emily rustle in the darkness. Listening.

"What is so unique and special about you comes forth with such genuineness, and such vigor, I should like all the world to read it, because then they would see my sister for who and what she truly is. There is nothing there to incite ridicule, Emmy, only the very highest praise."

There was a long silence, broken only by the sound of the keening autumn wind.

Emily replied dryly, "Go away."

With that, she buried her head in her pillow and pulled the covers around her ears.

Charlotte sat in the darkness, gathering her thoughts. "When we were children we dreamed of being authors, and if we have done anything with our lives so far, it is this: we write. If our other dreams fail, our dreams of school and travel, it's of no importance. If none of us ever marries, it will be no great disappointment to any of us. But I should not like to regret that we once had a chance at this, and we let it slip by."

After a long silence, when there was no response, Charlotte whispered, "Well, good night then."

Anne had already changed in to her nightgown when Charlotte came to their room.

"Did she agree to it?"

"No."

When Charlotte crawled into bed, she found a notebook on her pillow.

"It's mine," Anne said shyly. "I thought, since Emily's poetry brought you such pleasure, you might like to read some of mine."

The next day Emily punished Charlotte with a good dose of frosty silence. She skirted the offending sister all morning, aloof and unyielding. After she had ironed a small pile of linens, she laced on her boots and disappeared until the afternoon with a book of German poetry in her skirt pocket.

"Miss Emily's in a tiff this morning, ain't she?" said Tabby, who heard little but noticed everything.

But Charlotte was determined, and she waited out the day in strategic silence. That evening they gathered for family prayers in their father's study, and then the three sisters retired to the dining room.

As Charlotte sat mending one of her father's nightshirts by the light of a sputtering candle, she glanced up through her round spectacles. "Anne, do we have enough muslin to make Papa a new nightshirt? Look at this . . ." She held the garment up to the candlelight. "It's threadbare—I daresay it's a veritable work of art—all this cross-stitching . . ."

Emily, sprawled on the hearthrug, spoke up for the first time all day. "That's because Sally Mosley treats our laundry like it was her husband. Haven't you ever noticed the way she mutters to herself when she's raking away on the washboard?"

Anne and Charlotte exchanged a glance.

Charlotte folded up the nightshirt and then, as though steeling herself, perched on the edge of the sofa with her hands folded in her lap.

"Anne, you gave me an idea, last night."

Playing the innocent, Anne said, "Oh? What was that?"

"What if we were to publish our poetry together?"

Charlotte turned to Emily, who had not so much as twitched. "Anne brought me some of her poems last night. I was quite impressed. And I started thinking . . . what if we published together? Each of us would contribute a certain number of poems—"

Emily muttered. "Publish if you wish. But I'll have none of it."

"Even as a means to secure our future?"

Emily frowned. "We have our railway shares."

"Hardly enough to live off after Papa dies. Truly, Emmy dearest, what do you imagine will happen to us after he goes?"

"I don't think about it."

"Yes, which is why I must."

Anne said, "Oh, Emmy, don't be so fierce. It would be nice to have a little extra to take a holiday together from time to time. I'd love to go back to Scarborough. I've only been when I had the charge of all the Misses Robinson, and I was never at liberty to do as I wished. I should so like to go with you. You would love the sea."

Charlotte said, "But I quite understand your reluctance to open yourself to the ridicule of fools, for that is certainly what will happen. It will happen to all of us. I say this in the spirit of honesty and openness because we must be true to one another and ourselves, for if not, who can we trust?"

At that moment, they were brought to their feet by a loud noise on the stairs, the sound of someone falling and glass breaking, followed by loud cursing.

"Charlotte!" came a pathetic cry.

They rushed out and found their father in his nightshirt sprawled in a heap at the foot of the stairs.

He was trying to pick himself up, but there was glass all around him and the smell of sweet sherry where he had dropped the bottle.

"I'm here, Papa," Charlotte said as she stepped cautiously around the broken glass and the puddle of sherry. "Anne, fetch the broom and a pail."

"Curse these eyes! Curse them! Wretched miserable eyes . . ."

Anne cleaned up the glass while Charlotte and Emily took him to his room and helped him find a clean nightshirt. Then they put him to bed. They returned to the dining room and sat in silence for a while. They were all shaken.

"Poor Papa," Anne whispered.

"Do you think anyone's noticed?"

"I don't know. I hope not. This village would crucify him."

"He's bored. That's why he drinks. He's bored and frustrated."

"Poor Papa."

The following morning, true to habit, Emily rose at seven and dressed in the dim light. After she had let out the dogs, she came back upstairs and found Anne and Charlotte in their room.

She closed the door and stood in the pale morning light clutching her shawl. Anne looked up from making the bed.

"We cannot use our real names."

Charlotte started, her fingers poised over the ties at her waist. "So you'll do it?"

"On the condition that we remain anonymous." Her features were fixed in that stern look of intimidation. "I should be horrified to be so exposed. To have our privacy violated."

"Yes, I understand, but—"

Anne said, "I suppose Charlotte could use her own name—"

"No. People would catch on."

Charlotte's face collapsed with disappointment. "Might you reconsider—"

"I'm quite firm about this, Charlotte. We cannot tell anyone. Not Papa, not Branwell. You certainly can't tell Ellen. She can't keep a secret. Nor Mary—"

"But Mary's on the other side of the world."

"The word would get back to her family. We would have to publish under pseudonyms and keep the entire business our secret."

Anne said, "How will we hide it from Papa?"

"He sees us writing all the time. He just doesn't have the foggiest no-tion what we're doing with it. Nor does he care." She shrugged. "He can't see anymore, anyway."

Emily turned her stern look on Charlotte. "You must swear to it."

After a long hesitation, Charlotte said, "All right, then."

"Go on, do it. Raise your hand."

"All right, I swear. To secrecy."

"Absolute and utter, without exception."

"Emily Jane, that's enough. Don't be so fierce."

"We could be whomever we wish to be," Anne said.

Charlotte pulled her dress over her head, and with her chin in her chest as she buttoned up her bodice she muttered, "Well, we could be men then, couldn't we?"

"I suppose we could."

"Or at least choose names that could be masculine."

"Like when we were children," Anne smiled wistfully. "When we were Parry and Ross and Wellington."

"But brothers. With the same family name."

There was a certain aura of romance about it, since the work had to be done under a cloak of secrecy. Throughout the short winter days and long evenings that followed, they scurried back and forth from kitchen to dining room to bedroom, trawling through old copybooks behind closed doors, reading aloud and advising one another, rewriting with a fresh critical eye. Clumsy, rambling pieces were restructured; others were pruned and polished. During those hours the dimly lighted parsonage hummed with energy. This was no tedious labor per-formed out of duty. This was a calling. The hours flew by. Time seemed to disappear. Industry brought with it fresh hope, and hope fueled their writing.

They left to Charlotte the tedious correspondence with publishers, and when at long last they found one who would take the work on con-dition that they assume the printing costs, they agreed to pay the expenses out of the small inheritance from their aunt, hoping to make a little from the sales and perhaps win some critical acclaim.

But more important, their little publishing effort drew them back to their passion for storytelling. The process of sifting through their stories of Angria and Gondal generated new ideas. Mature ideas, drawn from observations of real life, deepened by personal experience and passions profoundly felt. *What if?* they asked themselves and one another. *Why not?* they thought. So by the time the proofs for their small volume of poetry arrived from the printer the following spring, they had each plunged headlong into their first novel.

It was natural that Charlotte's novel should be born out of heartache and the need to live again moments that would never be matched in intensity of feeling. For years she had been writing the story in her head, in flashes of scenes and dialogue, and by the time she sat down to write, she knew exactly where the narrative would take her. She would revisit Brussels; she would refashion her own story of unrequited love in the way writers have that gives them the power to transform a painful reality; she would create for herself the one thing she so desperately desired: the condition of loving deeply and being loved in return.

If Arthur began to fall just a little in love with her that spring, it was because she had slipped into that mystifying state of grace where she could move untouched by all the drama swirling around her. Always light-footed, she seemed to Arthur to fairly float down the lane in front of his eyes, and when she greeted him in the hall of the parsonage or poured his cup of tea, her eyes seemed to conceal some hidden joy. He thought her detached and vaguely wild of spirit, like a half-tamed creature trapped in the body of a quaint little clergyman's daughter.

Chapter Six

That winter, correspondence flew back and forth between C. Brontë, Esquire, of Haworth and the London publishers of Aylott & Jones. Their father was blind and Branwell far too self-absorbed to realize what was going on under his very nose. His senses were often dulled by gin, and when sober, he was irritable and obnoxious, and the sisters shunned his presence. He would occasionally happen on them in the dining room in the afternoon or evening, scribbling away in their little copybooks, and he thought they were just as they had always been. It irked him that they took no interest in the epic poem he was writing about Morley Hall, or the piece he had published in the *Halifax Guardian*.

In February, Charlotte put on her heavy shawl, concealing the two paper-wrapped parcels that contained the fair copy of their poems, and quietly slipped down the hill in the cold to deliver it to the postmaster's cottage. When she returned, she found Emily and Anne waiting upstairs in the front bedroom, where they had lighted a fire.

"It's done," Charlotte whispered as she closed the door behind her.

"Lock the door," Emily said.

When Charlotte had done so, Emily whipped out the bottle of port she had been concealing behind her skirt.

"Look what I took from the cellar!"

"Oh, you are one for mischief!" But Charlotte's reproof was all bluff, and she wore a broad smile as she hung up her bonnet and smoothed down her hair.

Emily opened the bottle and poured each of them a little of the port, and they gathered in a circle before the fire and raised their glasses to one another.

"To the brothers Bell," Charlotte pronounced solemnly. "Ellis, Acton, and Currer."

"To the Bells!"

"May their humble efforts meet with some small degree of success."

They started at the sudden sound of a door opening. Branwell had emerged from his room, and they stood frozen with their glasses in their hands, waiting while he clambered down the stairs to the kitchen for his breakfast.

When he had gone, Emily pulled a stool up to the fire and sat, warming her feet and sipping her port. She was quiet and reflective, but she wore a look of satisfaction that was almost a smile.

"We lit a fire," Anne said apologetically.

"I think the expense is quite justified," Charlotte reassured her.

"Oh, I do hope it all comes to something."

"Even if it doesn't, we shall have our verse in print, and as we've seen, that is no small accomplishment."

"I had no idea it would be this difficult to find someone to publish us, even at our own expense."

"Well, it's done, and we have reason to be proud of ourselves." She held out her glass and Anne smiled and refilled it.

"I passed Mr. Nicholls coming out of the school," Charlotte said, "and I confess I was in such a spirited mood, I quite chatted the socks off him." She sipped her port, remembering the baffled look on his face. "He honestly did not know what to make of me."

"I think he rather likes you," Anne said.

"Likes me?" Charlotte laughed. "He thinks I'm an old maid. Of no interest to him whatsoever."

"Ellis, more port?" Anne said.

Emily twisted around on her stool, holding out her glass. Her face was flushed from the heat of the fire. She said, "I was thinking, we should move forward, just as we discussed. We must not stop here."

"You mean with our novels?" Charlotte said.

"Yes." She turned her gaze back to the fire and said quietly, "It really would be quite wonderful, wouldn't it, if we could earn our living like this? Doing what we've done this past year. We would all be at home together, and we could take care of Papa. We wouldn't need a school." She took a sip of her port and added, "I never liked the idea, really. I didn't like the idea of having strangers live here with us."

"Oh, this is much better," Charlotte said, trying to contain her enthusiasm.

"We owe you a good deal of gratitude, Charlotte," Anne pointed out. "You've managed all the business—finding us a publisher, and dealing with the printing, and the bank drafts. It was much more work than I had thought it would be."

"Yes, it's all worked out rather well, hasn't it." Charlotte spoke quietly, trying to conceal her sense of inner triumph.

They fell into a discussion of their novels—how they should submit them and to whom they might apply. Emily was concerned that the publishers might wish to meet them.

"Branwell knows these things," Emily said. "He was working on a novel last year. He knows all sorts of writers and artists in Halifax. Perhaps we could ask him—without letting on what we're up to."

"What Branwell knows, we can find out," Charlotte said flatly. "We managed on our own with our poems. We can do it with our novels. Aylott and Jones could give us some guidance. I'll write to them."

They heard their brother on the stairs, calling for Charlotte: "Where is everyone? Damnably quiet in this house. Where are all the women?"

Emily snatched the bottle and stashed it behind the bed.

Charlotte opened the door.

"There you are! Good Lord, what are you all doing up here? And you've got a fire going. Mustn't let the old man see that."

He had dressed in a hurry, and he had the irritable, anxious look of a man who had gone too long without a drink.

"What do you want, Branwell?"

"I need ten shillings."

"Ten shillings?" Charlotte started.

"I have business in Halifax . . . I need money for the train and my expenses," he shot back impatiently.

"It doesn't cost ten shillings to go to Halifax."

"I'm staying with Leyland for several days. I have to pay him something for my meals, and I have some other business—"

"I don't have that much money on me. And I certainly wouldn't hand it over without asking Papa, and he's out at a meeting with the trustees."

"Papa said I was to have it, he told me last night . . . and then he forgot."

"Then you'll have to wait until he returns."

Branwell hesitated, his forehead plunging into a deep frown. He reached into a pocket and withdrew a bundle of Lydia Robinson's letters that he carried with him everywhere. Then he dug back into his pocket and fished around, finally coming up with a few coins. He spread his palm, and his hands shook while he counted his pennies.

"Then just give me a shilling for now," he muttered in an unsteady voice. He was trying not to plead.

"I will not," Charlotte said flatly. It made her heart ache to see him like this. "You'll just spend it on drink."

He glared at her, his breathing quickening. His jaw tightened; then suddenly he drew back his fist and slammed it into the wall next to her head. Charlotte flinched, and Branwell bellowed in pain.

"Charlotte!" Emily cried. She thought he had struck her and came racing into the hall.

She found Charlotte on her knees, with Branwell writhing in pain. He was sitting on the floor with his head between his knees clutching his fist and trying not to cry.

"I've broken it, damn it," he wailed. "It's my writing hand!"

"Let me see it," Charlotte insisted.

"I'll go get a cold cloth," Anne said, and she ran downstairs.

Emily stood over them, hands on hips, unmoved. "Writing hand, my eye," she sniffed. "You can write with both hands, brother."

He threw her such a pathetic look that she softened, grudgingly, and knelt beside her sister. "What a stupid thing to do, Branwell."

"Show me your hand," Charlotte repeated. He held it out for her to examine. The knuckles were bloodied and beginning to swell. When she tried to get him to open his fist he flinched, then said in a low, plaintive voice, "Please, Tally, if you love me at all, you'll help me get a little money from Papa. He'll give it to you."

"Are you in debt again?"

"Just a little . . . to the Old Cock. The proprietor's a good sort, and I promised I'd pay him this week."

Anne came running up the stairs with a cloth and a bowl of snow, and the three sisters knelt on the floor, nursing their injured brother. This subdued him; this was what he needed most, a little sympathy and understanding.

He seemed quite pathetic when he looked up and said, "Charlotte, I would never touch a hair on your head. I would never hurt any of you. You all know that, don't you?" He began to weep.

He sat on the floor sobbing while they looked on. It was raw, hopeless misery, and there was nothing any of them could do.

Anne wrapped her arms around him and drew him to her. Her own eyes were brimming with tears, and with a throaty whisper she said, "Every night, in Papa's study, and before we go to sleep at night, and in the morning, we get down on our knees and beseech God to guide you out of this insanity . . . but it falls to you, Branwell, if you can only believe. You *must* believe. Christ Jesus will give you the power to overcome your temptations. You can put all this behind you."

Branwell broke away from her embrace and wiped his eyes with the back of his sleeve. "Annie, don't talk like that. You know how I abhor it."

"My dear brother," Anne went on, "now more than ever you need our Lord. Turn to Him. He'll lift you out of your despair."

"You poor deluded creature. You believe all that rubbish, don't you?" He struggled to his feet. "Well then, I see I can't get any help from you."

Without another word, he plodded down the stairs.

The girls watched from the window as he made his way down the lane toward the Black Bull Inn.

"I suppose he'll find someone to buy him a drink," Anne said with a shade of bitterness.

"He always does."

"Or he'll go to the druggist. He has enough for a few grains of opium."

"I thought he'd struck you," Emily murmured.

Charlotte turned and saw her sister's eyes, steeled in anger.

"He would never hurt any of us."

Anne put her arm around Emily. "Don't be angry with him. He's not himself. He's not the same brother anymore."

"You know, I felt badly at first, that we didn't include him in our publishing scheme," Emily said.

"You mustn't feel badly," Anne replied. "You know he would never consent to pay to publish his poetry. He's far too proud. That's the one thing Papa has always counseled him against. Papa thinks it's just money thrown away."

"And Branwell could not have kept our secret," Charlotte observed. "He would have blabbed to everyone."

"It's all right," Emily said, taking a deep breath. "I don't feel guilty about it anymore."

In the end, the reality was this: their brother had abandoned them years ago. He had become a part of the grand world reserved for the greater sex: the boxing clubs, the literary and musical societies and Masonic orders, the political campaigns and alehouses. He traveled freely and acted without restraint. The sisters had briefly ventured beyond the home, but now they had returned to domestic confines, to the private world of kitchen and parlor. They were on their own.

They watched until he was out of sight. Then they each took their glasses and very carefully poured the remaining port back into the bottle. Emily plugged it with the cork, and Anne shoveled ashes onto the flames to extinguish the fire.

Rather than discouraging their efforts, the turmoil at home galvanized the sisters, throwing them back on their imaginary worlds and driving them into the fortress of their own company. The very quietude that had chased Branwell from his home was, in reality, a ceaseless activity of the mind. In the evenings when the only sounds to be heard were the clock ticking on the stairs and the wind whistling in the chimney, they worked by the light of their candles, breaking silence only to exchange pages and offer advice, some of which was taken, some not. Their habit of pacing round and round the dining table helped to loosen their imaginations as well as their limbs. When visions came to them they would settle back down a their writing desks, pick up their pencils, and get on with telling their tales.

The first copies of *Poems* by Currer, Ellis, and Acton Bell—a slender volume bound in green cloth—arrived at the parsonage one morning early in May. The parcel, addressed to C. Brontë, Esquire, had been opened—the brown wrapping paper torn and the books loosely tied back up with string. If the culprit had been their brother, he showed no signs of being wise to their little undertaking. Nevertheless, it was a baffling incident, and they thought it best to hide the volumes in case Branwell got hold of one of them and recognized their poetry, which he was sure to do. So even in their own home their small claim to glory was concealed from public view, stored away beneath a stack of chemises in a drawer or locked in a small trunk, places where women were apt to conceal the secrets in their lives.

For all his failings, Patrick Brontë's son was greatly loved in the village. His boisterous presence always enlivened any company, and he never condescended to the lower sorts. So that summer when the news reached Haworth that Lydia Robinson's husband had finally died, Branwell became the object of great excitement and speculation. The poor fellow was beside himself with anticipation. On many an afternoon he stumbled down to the Bull and collapsed into his favorite chair, where he hoped to find a sympathetic ear—there being none to find at home.

"My legs have turned to jelly," he'd cry out with a weak laugh. "And look," he'd say, holding out a trembling hand for all to see, "look at that.

Damn, look at the state I'm in." Then he'd lift his glass with that same shaking hand and sink his mouth into the froth.

"Hasn't slept or eaten a bite for days," William Thomas murmured to the wheelwright as he mopped up a spill on his mahogany countertop. "Waitin' to hear his fate."

"Ye think she'll marry him?"

The innkeeper only shrugged philosophically.

On other days he came down to the Bull with a bounce in his step, brimming with optimism: "I'll hear from her today. I know it. Feel it in my bones. My fortune's about to change, gentlemen." He'd run a hand through his limp red curls and groan, "And damn it, it's about time, isn't it? I'm overdue on that score. But I don't have long to wait now. I wager you a year from now I'll be master of Thorp Green!" He'd raise his glass in a toast to his own future, and his eyes would flash brightly; William the innkeeper thought he looked a little mad. "When I think of how my poor lady suffered all those years with that eunuch of a husband. She was so starved for affection. Now, what does that say about the man? Does he think a woman like her can be neglected without consequence? It was damn criminal. If she turned to me for consolation, he only had himself to blame." His face would soften. "She was my muse. Ah, William"—or John or Hartley, whoever was there to listen and nod— "if you'd seen the effect my poetry had on her." Then a rapturous smile would bleed across his haggard face. "Good God, what a sweet woman she was. It broke her heart to have to part from me. But I'll hear from her now, and things will all be put right soon enough."

If he had an attentive audience, he would dig into his jacket pocket. "See that?" he would say as he unclenched his fist to reveal a pale ring of woven hair. "I had it made from a lock of her hair. I'd wear it, but I'm afraid I'll lose it." He would touch the pale trinket to his lips and slip it back into his pocket with the bundle of her letters.

Tabby remarked on the matter one day while Charlotte was at the kitchen table, going over the household accounts.

"So the young master's goin' to be married soon to 'is lady, I 'ear."

"Is it true, miss?" Martha asked in wide-eyed wonder. "Will 'e be livin' the life of a gentleman in a big house?"

"You hear wrong, both of you," Charlotte replied sourly.

"But my father says that now that Mr. Robinson is dead there's nothin' to stop—"

"Martha, your father only repeats what Branwell tells him, and he's got his head in the clouds right now."

For days Branwell's mood swung between elation and despair, until finally the long-anticipated message arrived. It had been a busy day at the parsonage, with tradesmen stopping by and the parish clerk taking tea in the kitchen. Martha was slow to get the door when the bell rang, so Charlotte answered it herself. It was young Johnny who ran messages for the owner of the Black Bull.

"There's a gentleman down waitin' for Mr. Branwell," he said, out of breath and bright with excitement.

"Did he give you a card?" Charlotte asked.

"No, miss, but he says he's come with a message from a lady, and that Branwell would know what it's about."

They were startled by a shout, and Charlotte looked around to see Branwell hovering on the stairs at the back of the hall.

"It's Lydia!" he cried gleefully. He came bounding down the stairs in his stockings and grabbed his coat from the hook.

"Oh, my shoes!" he shouted. "My shoes! Where are my shoes! Oh, what the deuce, shoes be damned! Come on, Johnny, my boy, take me to the man," he said. He dashed past the boy, raced across the small garden, and vaulted over the low stone wall into the cemetery.

"Wait, Branwell!" the boy cried as he clambered over the wall after him.

"Hurry up then," Branwell shouted back as he sprinted through the cemetery. When he reached the lane beside the church, he hopped onto one of the flat box graves, spread his arms to the heavens, and sent up a resounding "Hallelujah!" Then he leapt off and ran shoeless down the stone stairs toward the Black Bull Inn.

Charlotte found her father hunched over his desk with his head in his hands.

"I suppose you heard," she said.

He nodded his head.

Charlotte began to tidy up his desk. "I don't know whether to give any credence to the story or not," she said. "Branwell seems to think she'll marry him and then he won't have a worry in the world." She arranged his pipe on the pipe rack. He had dropped a scattering of tobacco on his desk, and she carefully scooped it back into the tin.

"God help me," Patrick muttered, "my heart has hardened toward that woman. She's ruined him." He lifted his clouded eyes to Charlotte. "You cannot know, daughter, what it's like for a father to stand by and watch a beloved child sucked into the power of someone like that. He won't listen to me. I have no control over him. We can only turn to God and beseech His aid. Come, Charlotte. Let's pray. Kneel down with me and pray. Let us pray for him to be delivered from this harlot."

Everyone at the Black Bull knew something was wrong that afternoon. Branwell closed himself in the back room with the visitor, but after the visitor had gone, Branwell did not emerge. Hartley Merrall was upstairs meeting with the other mill owners about the wool comber's strike, and when he came downstairs they asked him to look in on Branwell. Hartley found him on the floor curled up in a ball, bleating like a lamb.

Hartley got him to his feet and said he'd take him home. A powerful storm had moved in, with sharp gusts of wind and rain, and he had difficulty getting Branwell up the lane. Arthur, who was standing at the schoolroom door, saw them coming and ran to help.

"What happened?" Arthur asked as he slung Branwell's limp arm over his shoulder.

"Poor fellow's had a shock."

"It's not drink?"

"Hasn't had a drop." He shot a glance at Arthur. "Might've been a fit. Had 'em since he was a boy."

"What kind of fit?"

"Falls down an' goes all stiff. I seen him break a tooth once. Awful frightening to watch. Like the devil's got him."

"It's epilepsy. And it's neither of the devil nor is it divine," Arthur replied sharply.

"Well, us folks here don't call it anything. Out of politeness for the family."

"Very good," Arthur answered, a shade more gently.

They were nearing the gate to the parsonage when Arthur said, "I think it might be wise to take him around the back of the house to the kitchen, so as not to distress Mr. Brontë."

Hartley caught the look in Arthur's eye. "Yes, quite. Good idea."

Dripping with rain, they found Martha in the backyard scurrying to bring in the laundry. She let out a cry of distress at the sight of Branwell slumped between the two men, but Arthur quieted her down quickly enough.

"Hush, Martha. He's not hurt. Go get your mistress and do it quietly, do you hear?"

Dripping with rain, they waited in the scullery with the dogs anxiously whining at their feet until Charlotte appeared. She was too humiliated to offer Arthur anything but a curt nod of thanks.

"Leave me alone," Branwell mumbled, his face in the pillow. Charlotte was trying to get him out of his wet jacket. He refused to cooperate and rolled to the wall.

"You're shivering. You'll catch your death of cold."

"Good. I shall be only too pleased to have an easy way out of my misery."

She managed to peel his muddy socks from his feet without protest.

"Oh, Branwell." She shook her head. "Why didn't you wear your shoes? You've torn a hole ..."

He gave her a pathetic look. "Yes, Branwell's socks are ruined and they must be mended."

He turned back to his pillow and began to weep uncontrollably. Charlotte was afraid to leave him alone. She covered him with a blanket.

"What happened? Who did you meet?"

"What do you care? You don't care a tinker's damn for my happiness."

"I rather think that you enjoy your wretchedness."

"Enjoy it?" he said with an astounded look.

"You refuse to make any effort to improve your situation."

"I promise, you would never say such a thing if you had ever, for one moment, known the heartache of truly loving a good and worthy being whom you cannot and will never have!"

"No," she replied coolly. "No, those sentiments are quite . . . quite foreign to me, dear brother."

The door opened and Anne slipped into the room. Branwell's face softened as she sat down on the bed beside him.

"What happened?"

"I had a visit. William Allison."

"From Thorp Green?" Anne asked.

Branwell nodded.

"He's the Robinsons' coachman," Anne explained to Charlotte.

"She can't marry me now," he whimpered. "Not now or ever. That heartless husband of hers made sure of it. He made her swear at his deathbed that she would sever all ties with me. If she marries me, she won't inherit a thing. William said she's sick with remorse now, for what she's done to me and to him both. All she talks about is going off to a convent." Branwell wiped away a tear with the back of his hand.

There was a knock on the door, and Martha entered.

"My father's downstairs, sir," she said to Branwell. "He heard you were ailin' and wants to know if he can do anything . . ."

"Bless the man, God bless him." Branwell threw back the blanket and sat up. "Tell him I'll be right down. Tell him to wait."

When she had closed the door, Charlotte and Anne watched in astonishment as he pulled a small purse from his pocket and poured out a handful of gold coins.

"Where did you get all that?" Charlotte asked.

"Where do you think?" he said sullenly. "Do you think I'm lying when I say she loves me?" He took out a half sovereign and stuffed the purse back into his jacket. "Now, this, this will buy me a little forgetfulness."

John Brown was waiting in the kitchen, his sun-streaked hair damp from the rain, his shirt covered in a fine gray dust. He had been in his shed, working a block of stone, when Arthur Nicholls had stopped by and alerted him about the incident at the Black Bull.

As a child, Branwell had hung about the shed while John Brown chiseled names on tombstones, and in the graveyards while they buried the dead. For all his coarseness, John possessed finer instincts than those that were generally found among his vulgar companions, and Branwell liked him for his easygoing company, and his solid and manly advice. John believed that there was not a care in the world that couldn't be righted with a little hard currency, and he was more than happy to take Branwell's half sovereign into the village to change it, and return with a measure of gin and a small bottle of tincture of opium.

Branwell spent the rest of the day sitting on the ground in the shed with his back against a slab of cool marble, drinking from a flask while John Brown chipped away at a tombstone. By supper, he was too drunk to stand up, so Emily came out and helped him back home. He was sick in the night and woke up the household as he groped around in the dark for the washbasin, shattering the water pitcher. In the morning, they could smell the stench from the hall, and when they went in they found him in a deep, opium-induced sleep. They could not waken him, so they did their best to clean up after him, mopping the floor and clearing away the broken porcelain, washing his face and changing his sour shirt. Emily took up soup and bread and tea, but she had a hard time rousing him, and finally they left him alone.

Chapter Seven

The wind had blown Charlotte's hair loose, and she stood in the kitchen with her head down, fiddling with her combs, annoyed with her sisters for being gone so long.

"Miss Brontë . . ."

She whirled around. Arthur stood in the kitchen doorway, stiff and proud-looking, his hat in his hand. It was half past seven, and he had just emerged from her father's study.

"Good evening, Mr. Nicholls," she said frostily.

"I wondered if I might have a word with you?"

"Certainly."

Tabby was in her chair in the corner near the stove; she glanced up from her knitting and shot a sly look to Martha, who was measuring out tea. The curate had made quite a stink earlier in the week when he and all the Puseyite clergy in the district had boycotted a concert at the Haworth church—simply because the featured soloist, a celebrated tenor from Manchester, was a Baptist.

"May I inquire if you've had any success finding a surgeon for your father?"

"I've had some names brought to my attention," she answered.

"I see." He paused. "But as yet you've not fixed a date?"

"Mr. Nicholls," Charlotte said, making no effort to hide her impatience, "I know you're eager to take your holiday, but I'm sure you understand that my father is quite wary of having someone cut into his eyes unless he's completely confident of a successful outcome."

"It was not my intention to upset you," Arthur replied coolly. "I merely wished to inform my family when they might expect me. There are others involved, as I'm sure you are aware."

"You did not upset me, Mr. Nicholls," she answered with a pinched voice. "I am not upset."

"Of course not," he replied stiffly with a civil bow. "Good evening."

He smoothed back his jet-black hair before setting his hat on his head, then paused in mid-gesture and added in a sort of cool afterthought, to let her know that he was indifferent to her, "I thought I might take Flossy for a walk."

"He's gone for a walk on the moor with Anne," Charlotte replied. She felt guilty now, and gave him a strained smile. "But thank you for offering."

"So, Miss Anne's health is improved?"

"Yes, it has. Thank you."

"I'm glad to hear that." He added thoughtfully, "My cousin Mary in Ireland suffers from asthma as well. It is a terrible affliction."

"Yes, it is. But my sister bears these things with no complaint."

"And you are much improved as well?" he added. "You are well over your cold?"

"I am, sir."

"It's been a dreadful season," he observed solemnly, fastening his eyes on the hat he held in his hands. "Everyone in the village has been down with colds or influenza. But I'm relieved that you've all pulled through and your father is quite on the mend."

Out of pity for him, Tabby spoke up: "Ye're doin' well yerself Mr. Nicholls, sir? Ye're not ailin'?"

His smile was immediate and broke over his face with such gratitude for this kind word that Charlotte felt another pang of conscience. "Thank you for your concern, Tabby. I seem to have come through quite unscathed."

He wished them a good day, then turned and strode back down the hall and let himself out through the front door.

"Oh, that man does irritate me," Charlotte cried, flinging up her hands. "If he says one more word to me about his holiday in Ireland, I think I'll—"

"Ah, miss, the gentleman 'as 'is good side, now. You mustn't be so 'ard on 'im."

"His good side. What? He takes Flossy on walks?"

"An' it's a good thing 'e does," Tabby muttered. "That little dog's fat as a sheep."

Charlotte felt besieged. She shook her head and resigned herself to an imperfect order of things. "Martha, I'll just take my tea by myself. It's long past the hour. I'm tired of waiting." She looked around for her fan. "It's terribly thoughtless of them to be out so late."

Tabby paused to rest her hands. "It's a right fine summer evenin', good for walkin', and Miss Anne don't get out enough as it is."

"I do worry, though."

"They've got the dogs," Martha remarked as she poured boiling water into the teapot. "No 'arm will come to 'em."

"It would do ye good to get out a little more than what ye do," Tabby said. "When ye was younger, ye'd be outdoors with yer sketch pad till ye couldn't hardly see yer hand in front o' yer face, and no one could get you to come inside."

"I don't feel so carefree anymore, Tabby. There's so much here at home that needs attention, and I dare not go away for fear it'll all come crashing down." She had found her fan—beneath Emily's book of German poetry—and gathered up her skirts and sat down at the bench. "I'll eat in the kitchen, Martha."

"But, miss, it's unbearable 'ot in 'ere."

"Yes, it is, but I am not inclined to sit alone in the dining room this evening."

Charlotte sat fanning herself while Martha prepared bread and butter and arranged a little cold meat on a plate.

As Martha set the plate before her, Tabby mused, "I think the gentleman 'as 'is mind set on marriage."

"Marriage? Mr. Nicholls? Good grief. Now who would want to be marrying that man?"

"Rumor 'as it that 'e's got a lady waitin' back in Ireland."

"Oh, is that what they're saying?"

"Stands to reason, miss. Mr. Grant brought 'is bride back from 'is 'ome in Essex."

"Only because none of our Yorkshire families was good enough for him." She took a sip of her tea and added brightly, "Well, maybe Mr. Nicholls will get married and remain in Ireland, and relieve us all of his intolerable presence."

They had already said evening prayers and their father had gone up to bed when she heard her sisters come in. They were quiet and spoke in whispers, but the dogs made a racket in the kitchen, whining and padding around beneath the table while Emily mixed up some cold porridge to feed them. Charlotte put down her sewing and went into the kitchen.

"I suppose you'll want something to eat," Charlotte said.

"Oh no, we had tea with the Heatons at Ponden Hall," Anne replied. They were both windblown and full of high spirits.

"We went all the way to Wycoller," Emily said. Emily was a fearless walker of incredible stamina, and she would strike out into the high, treeless moors, across heath and gorse and streams, as far across the tops as she could go, returning only when the last tinge of light had left the sky. She rarely told them where she had gone or what she had seen, but she might show them a drawing she had made along the way. Once she came home with a wounded hawk, which she nursed back to health and named Nero.

"Look what we brought back from the Heatons' library." Anne pointed to a small stack of books on the chair. Then she pulled two oranges out of her skirt pockets and said with a smile, "And these too!"

"That's very kind of them," Charlotte said as she closed the kitchen door. Then, speaking in a whisper, she added, "Emily, dearest, I know it's very difficult to tie you down in such delightful weather, but I do wish you would finish your fair copy of your novel. Anne and I have both finished ours, and we can't submit ours without yours."

Emily gave no reply. She disappeared to the scullery with a bowl in each hand and the dogs at her feet. When she returned, she sat down next to Anne who had begun to peel the oranges.

"Sit down, Tally," Anne said sweetly. "Let's eat the oranges."

Charlotte sat down opposite them, trying mightily to conceal her frustration.

"Mr. Nicholls has become a terrible nuisance," she said. "He wants his holiday, which is rightfully due to him, but Papa won't let him go until after his eye surgery, which must be done soon. Next month at the latest. And I would so hope to have our manuscripts all ready to submit by then." She took the section of orange Anne offered her. Then she looked across the table to Emily and said, "How much longer will it take you to finish?"

Emily shrugged.

Charlotte said, "Well, I suppose Anne and I could submit our works without yours, but then—"

Anne cut in, alarmed: "Oh, Tally, we can't do that. We've agreed to publish together. Three brothers and three volumes."

Emily, sucking the juice from an orange section, turned to Anne with a sly look. "I don't think she wants to be associated with my novel."

Charlotte started. "Emily, that's false."

"You said it gave you nightmares."

"Well, it did. There are some very violent and lurid scenes."

"But nightmares? Come, Charlotte, that's so affected."

"They're all such lost souls—Heathcliff is so heartless and cruel."

"Quite." Emily finished off the last section of her orange and licked her fingers.

"And Cathy . . ." Charlotte added. "I just can't imagine what the readers will make of her. She's quite unlike any heroine in any book I've ever read."

"You prefer slavish, groveling sorts of women."

"I suppose I do."

"I should not like to be ruled by any man."

"Oh, I should. But he must have a good and kind heart beneath his fierce façade."

"Like your Monsieur Heger."

Charlotte was surprised to discover how painful it was to hear his name voiced again.

"Yes. Like Monsieur Heger."

"Do you still write to him?"

Charlotte shook her head. It was the first time in more than a year that Emily had made a reference to Heger. She knew the truth—had always known—but she kept Charlotte's secrets absolutely, like she kept her own.

The candle was burning down, throwing a flickering light on their faces. Outside, night had fallen and the shadows had deepened, cooling the air.

Emily said, "I've a new poem rolling around in my head. It's quite absorbed all my thoughts, and I can think of nothing else."

Then she yawned and began removing the combs and pins from her hair. The dogs had finished their dinner and crawled beneath the table and collapsed. Emily, looking down, gave Keeper a nudge with her bare foot.

"Come on, boy. To bed."

Charlotte said nothing more to coerce Emily to finish the last bit of tedious work to ready her novel for publication. She knew Emily could not be persuaded by reason or threat, or anything in between.

Several days later Charlotte found her sister sitting in the shade of the cherry tree, reading a book, with Keeper's huge head cradled in her lap.

"You are quite good at hiding, dearest. Where's Anne?"

"Gone to the market with Martha," Emily replied, her nose still in her book.

Charlotte waved the letter under her nose. "We have news. From Aylott and Jones."

Emily laid down her book and looked up.

"I'm afraid the sales have been disappointing. They've only sold two copies of the book."

"Two? That's all?"

Charlotte turned over a wicker laundry basket, tucked up her skirts, and sat down beside her sister. "However," she hurried to say, "it has finally been reviewed." She unfolded the clippings that had been enclosed in the letter. "By the *Athenaeum* and the *Critic*." She peered over her spectacles at her sister and said with a smile, "Don't be so glum, Emmy. The reviews are good. The *Critic*'s review is positively eulogistic."

"Is it?" Emily said quietly. Charlotte knew she was trying to hide how much it meant to her.

"Yes, truly, dearest. They call our poems genuine and fresh." She leaned forward, laid her hand on Emily's knee, and beamed up at her. "But the lion's share of praise goes to Ellis Bell, and that's as it should be."

Charlotte read the reviews aloud. The critics hailed Emily's poetry as "an inspiration which may yet find an audience in the outer world . . . a fine quaint spirit which may have things to speak that men will be glad to hear—and an evident power of wing . . ."

Charlotte glanced up from time to time to watch how Emily's face—always so sullen and grave—came alive at this praise. It was all the more meaningful because the critic knew nothing about her.

"And there's something else," Charlotte said as she passed the letter and the reviews to Emily. "There's a gentleman who wants our autographs. A Mr. Enoch from Warwick. He bought one of the only two copies sold."

Emily smiled broadly. "We have an admirer?"

"Yes, we do, and I think we should oblige Mr. Enoch as quickly as possible. He may very well be the only admirer we'll ever have."

That evening, after their father and the servants had gone up to bed, they took up a sheet of fine stationery and signed the names of Currer, Ellis, and Acton Bell. Then Emily took out her penknife, whittled her quill to a perfect point, and began the task of making a clean, legible copy of *Wuthering Heights*.

Although she would never admit as much to her sister, Charlotte had been deeply impressed by the powerful human drama of *Wuthering Heights,* the passionate love between Heathcliff and Cathy, its peculiar inevitability and mythic quality. She was familiar with many of Emily's Gondal poems and old narratives from which her sister had drawn her novel, but the final work had indeed haunted her—not merely because of its brutality and amorality, but because of its undeniable power. It had forced her to recognize the sad inadequacy of her own novel.

The Professor had been finished, but the work had left her deeply unsatisfied. For all the silent love she had carried for Heger and the never-voiced heartache of separation and loss, she had not come close to expressing the power of her feelings. She had taken up the voice of her male protagonist and given very little of herself to the French lacemaker, and all her passion was lost somewhere in between. She had painted a superficial portrait, a simple narrative of wish fulfillment, when what she had wanted to produce was something urgent, true, and personal. Instinctively, she was seeking a narrative—impassioned like poetry—that might paint the workings of memory and the unconscious mind, all the powerful formative forces of her whole experience fused into images, emerging symbolically in the fullness of the imagination.

That summer, throughout the long, warm evenings as she sat near the open window darning her father's socks or mending one of Emily's petticoats, her thoughts returned to images that had always given her so much pleasure: a grand Gothic hall in an isolated place, a subservient young woman and a master. But as the ideas gave birth to a story, a new kind of heroine emerged. This young woman would have passion and soul—she would be a governess perhaps, poor and plain like herself, but neither slavish nor meek in spirit. She would be inferior in rank to her master, but in every other way his equal. She would name her Jane Eyre.

Chapter Eight

Toward the end of August Charlotte accompanied her father on the forty-mile journey to Manchester to have his eyes examined. The surgeon declared the cataract sufficiently hardened to be removed, a procedure that would need to be done without anesthesia; they would administer only a little belladonna to desensitize the eye. Afterward, her father would be confined to bed in absolute darkness and stillness for at least a month.

They remained in Manchester, and Charlotte spent the next few days finding lodgings in town and hiring a nurse. By the end of the week she was sitting in a stifling-hot waiting room while the surgeon cut into her father's eye.

Finally the door opened, and an assistant ushered her into the back surgery. Her father was sitting up, both eyes bandaged. They had removed the high white neckcloth he habitually wore, and it seemed to Charlotte that they had stripped him of his pride and rectitude. As his sight had diminished, he had sat in the gloom of his study, increasingly irascible, impatient, and demanding, so that at times Charlotte had felt his presence like a weight upon her slight frame, tied to her at every moment of the day, keeping her as much a prisoner as he had become. Now, with his long pale neck exposed and his eyes swathed in gauze, she was alarmed by how vulnerable he seemed, how this powerful man had been reduced to a childlike helplessness.

"The operation was successful," the doctor announced with solemn reassurance. "His sight will soon return to normal. I must say, Miss

Brontë, your father was quite courageous. Truly, he was an exceptional patient. Very steady. Didn't so much as flinch."

"Remarkable," Patrick boomed, "what our surgeons are able to accomplish these days." Then, gesturing blindly in the air: "My cravat, Charlotte. Get me my cravat. If I sit like this for much longer I'll catch a cold for sure."

Charlotte found the long strip of white silk and wound it carefully around his neck. She helped him while he fumbled with his coat and guided him down the steps and outside, to the waiting carriage. He was more than six feet tall, and she came just above his elbow.

When the carriage jerked into motion, Charlotte reached for her father's hand and gripped it firmly.

"Everything's going to be fine now, Papa," she said with quiet relief.

"Oh, Charlotte," he said in a solemn voice, "would that it were so easy to remove sin from the heart as it is to remove a hardening of the eye. With a sharp scalpel and a little burning, and several weeks in confined penitence, we see clearly again—no sin hardening the heart, nothing to cloud the light of Christ."

She gave his hand a squeeze. Suddenly the anxiety that had weighed on her for days—anticipating his surgery, the fear of losing him, the troubles of caring for him in his blindness—swept through her with a rush of emotion, and tears flooded her eyes.

The nurse was quiet and efficient, and there was little for Charlotte to do except prepare their meals. She was not much of a cook, but she managed to put food on the table and no one complained. For most of the day she sat at the window, where a few rays of light filtered through the gap in the curtains. She would knit for a few moments, and then she would pause and stare into the darkness for long hours, until the light began to fade and it was time to prepare their tea. There were no distractions, no one to inconvenience her or make demands on her, and in the quiet hours she turned to her imagination. This was her most precious companion, her great comforter—a means to defy the harsh reality of her existence. In her imaginary world she could change the natural order of things; life could be keenly enjoyed and needs fully satisfied. Over the long days spent in a sunless and silent room while Charlotte waited for her father's eyes to heal, Jane Eyre would make herself seen and heard.

Charlotte had little control over what emerged. She believed in the supremacy of the unfettered imagination. The inspired poet never paused for reflection, did not think about unity; ideas came naturally. In that peculiar light of creation she returned to her childhood, to long-suppressed memories of their days at Cowan Bridge. To Maria and Elizabeth, her long-dead sisters.

Maria had been ten when she went away to Cowan Bridge. After their mother's death, Aunt Branwell had kept the house and ruled the servants, but Maria was the one whose counsel they heeded, whose model of goodness they followed. She was wise beyond her years and the most beloved of them all. It wrenched Charlotte's heart to see her go. Eight-year-old Charlotte had stood on the tiny garden plot in front of the parsonage watching Maria and Elizabeth wave good-bye from the back of a cart, Maria wearing her own pale brand of courage and a determination to accept any hardship Providence threw her way. Watching her, Charlotte thought of a lamb driven off to slaughter, a sweet-faced girl with long, skinny legs dressed in a straw bonnet and a thin blue cloth coat, gifts from the charity ladies in Haworth. She gripped a small, scuffed bag. No one would have guessed by looking at her how powerfully intellectual and talented she was.

Three weeks later, Charlotte was driven off to Cowan Bridge by her father, and then late in November little Em, who was only six, was sent away to join them.

She recalled her first meal the day of her arrival. A bowl of rice pudding was passed down to her. Charlotte took a mouthful and gagged.

The girl next to her gave her a sly look and whispered, "I know, it's sour. The milk's always sour here. But if you don't eat it they won't give you breakfast, and the bread's the only tolerable thing you'll get all day. The only thing that isn't rotten, I mean."

Charlotte looked down the table to her sister Maria.

If Maria swallows, I shall swallow, she thought, forcing another spoonful to her lips. Maria was chattering away to the girl next to her and didn't seem to be bothered by the disgusting concoction. The second spoonful stuck in Charlotte's throat. She watched another girl spit hers into a handkerchief; Charlotte did the same and emptied her handkerchief in the yard when they went outdoors.

This was a charity school, and Charlotte expected frugality; her own home was austere and sparsely furnished, and she had watched Aunt calculate the flour and meat down to the penny. But the parsonage was a clean, tidy place and their food was properly cooked. Here, despite all the tricks she pulled on herself, summoning up images of roast pigeon or treacle or holding her breath while she chewed, there was nothing she could do to keep the food down. The hot pot was not beef but only fat, gristle, and potatoes, boiled to the color of slate. There were always disgusting things floating in the porridge, hairs and unidentifiable bits you couldn't chew. One night, after the others were asleep, the girl in the bed next to Charlotte's whispered that she had seen the cook take the ladle out of the pig-swill tub and use it to measure out the milk. They were all hungry, and one girl was quite skilled at stealing bread, but this Charlotte refused to do.

Every Sunday they traipsed two miles through snow and wet fields with wooden pattens strapped to their thin-soled shoes to attend Reverend Wilson's morning service, often staying for the afternoon one as well. They sat shivering through long hours of prayer in the damp church, their lips blue and fingers numb. Their feet never dried out, and at night their toes were raw and stiff from the cold.

Beatings were to be expected, although there seemed to be no justice in them. Maria, sharp and clever as she was, often forgot to clean her nails or tie her pinafore, so she was frequently under the cane, even when she was very ill and had barely the strength to stand. This turned Charlotte's stomach; she burned with indignation and longed to cry out in rebellion.

She remembered watching her sister drag her thin legs over the side of the bed, reaching for her dress.

"But I deserved it, Charlotte."

"No, you didn't."

"But I did. I'm far too careless about my appearance, and that will not do in a governess. It's for my own good."

"You're ill, Maria. How can they expect—"

Maria began to cough, deep, rasping coughs that brought up blood and stained her handkerchief a sharp crimson red.

"I cannot bear seeing you treated like this."

"Don't be weak, Charlotte. It's silly to say you cannot bear what it is your fate to bear."

No one wanted to hear her complaints, not God nor Mr. Wilson, the director—they were, after all, one and the same. She would certainly never complain to her father.

Charlotte was a grave and industrious child, and her needlework was always meticulous, which seemed to please the teachers. She thought if she was quiet enough, and small and plain enough, they would not take notice of her, although she suspected that every hint of feeling was visible on her face. It would become her habit to look down so that people could not read her mind.

It required a steely fortitude to make it through the winter. Maria grew weaker and weaker, and in February she was sent home. With the changing winds of spring, a fever swept through the school. The girls fell ill with terrifying rapidity, and the doctor pressed Reverend Wilson to remove them from the premises to a healthier location. Grudgingly he consented; those who were still left standing would be whisked away to a town on the Lancashire coast. It was all done in great haste. As they waited on the front lawn for the carriages to be loaded, Charlotte saw Elizabeth, too weak to walk, emerge from the school on the arm of a strange, dour-faced woman. She was lifted into a gig and driven away. Charlotte, in a panic, broke away and found Miss Andrews to beg an explanation; she was told only that her sister was too ill to accompany them and had been sent home.

In Silverdale they were herded into a school with makeshift cots, but by then they were fewer than a dozen. The next afternoon their father arrived. They saw him marching toward them over a sandy dune, his black coat whipped by the wind, his features frozen with anger and fear so that it appeared he was wearing a mask. Emily thought they had done something wrong to anger him, but Charlotte knew he had come to save them. She flew into his arms.

On the way home their father told them that Maria had died of consumption. Elizabeth survived only ten more days, and then the family vault in the church was opened again and they lowered the tiny casket down into the gloom until it came to rest beside that of her mother and Maria.

After the burial service, as Charlotte walked back home behind her father, up the path through the cemetery with the icy wind flaying her cheeks, she realized that she was no longer concealed, tucked obscurely within the folds of the clan. God had thrust her into the forefront at the head of the dwindling band of children. He had done it intentionally. It had fallen to her, the puny one of the brood, to set an example at all times.

When at last Charlotte settled down with her stub of a pencil and small squares of paper and began Jane Eyre's story, she could barely keep up with her thoughts. She wrote in a white heat, stopping only to dash out to the butcher for a few chops and to boil some potatoes or butter some bread for their tea. Her father, ever the good patient, lay in silence. The nurse applied leeches to his temples, and then she knitted or dozed in her chair by his bed. No one asked Charlotte what she was doing with the empty, silent hours in the darkness.

After several weeks the bandages were removed, but there were another two weeks of confinement in a sunless and quiet room. Finally the time came to pack up and go home. Patrick's sight had been restored. By that time, Jane Eyre had fled her lover and Thornfield Hall. She had taken a carriage as far as her money had allowed her to go, and now she was on a strange road and Charlotte had no idea what would become of her.

Charlotte packed the manuscript pages into her trunk; at the train station in Manchester she consigned it to the porter, then took a seat next to her father in the crowded compartment. On the journey home, while her father gazed out the window, Charlotte realized she had not even had the time to read what she had written. She would return home and stash it away on a shelf in her closet with other unfinished stories and pick up the monotonous activities of her busy life.

It would be nearly a year before she would complete the novel, and she would never fully understand that, in an attempt to capture her love for a man, she had created a myth. Jane's lover would have Constantin Heger's weakness for chocolate and cigars, his dark features, and an athletic physique that had the power to arouse her, but there would also be symbols of the father—powerful, distant, sightless—(she would say to him, "I shall keep out of your way all day, as I have been accustomed to do: you may send for me in the evening, when you feel disposed to see me, and I'll come then; but at no other time"). There would be hints of the noble Zamorna of her childhood stories, her oldest and dearest hero, a tortured, complex man. With this rough material mined from memory and the subconscious she created Edward Rochester, a man of intelligence and sensitivities equal to her own, a man entirely beyond her social reach. He would be blinded at the end, but she would restore his sight; plain, small, and insignificant though she might seem, he would find that she could fascinate a man like him and win his heart.

Her subconscious had understood—if she did not—that the obstacles to happiness were not merely external; it would take more than a slyly manipulative wife to thwart their union. Jane would be foiled by a violent, horrific creature, a madwoman, barely human at all. Although scarcely articulate, Mrs. Rochester would embody all the darkness of Charlotte's psyche: fire, fear, blood, sensuality, the foreign and the exotic—all these things trapped and enclosed in a room in an attic in the past.

Chapter Nine

There was little at home that winter to excite Charlotte's enthusiasm. She wrote frequent letters to Ellen, commenting with wry humor on the dreary events of life in Haworth. Mr. Nicholls had returned from Ireland without a wife and seemed to have no prospects of obtaining one. Although he had been fully ordained that year and could have sought a living of his own, he appeared to be quite content to tend to the business of his church school and play second fiddle to her father. Patrick secretly scorned his curate's lack of ambition, but as Arthur was by all accounts conscientious and hardworking, Patrick refrained from voicing such cynical opinions and counted himself fortunate to keep Arthur in Haworth.

Branwell could be thanked for what little excitement enlivened their days—although it was generally of the unpleasant kind. His drinking debts continued to mount, and their father was getting unpleasant letters from the proprietors of taverns demanding settlement of Branwell's bills and threatening court action if he did not pay.

Branwell's letters to Lydia Robinson always came back unopened, but on occasion the lady would send him money through the mediator of her family physician. Branwell would fly off to Halifax for a bout of drinking with his friends and come home broke and ill, threatening to take his life. On occasion he would sober up and send off a few letters seeking employment as a tutor on the Continent, but these efforts were halfhearted and short-lived. He had always been of slight build, and they were so concerned with the state of his mind that they paid scant attention to his wasting body. He went days without eating and nights without sleeping, and after a while the opium gained ascendancy over whiskey and gin. For the price of a few pence he could find days of relief from his misery. Under the influence of its pleasurable effects, he would sometimes rise from his stupor and scribble out a few lines of poetry, thinking he had produced something brilliant that would make his fame. He would lie sprawled on the sofa in a trance and remain there for hours, until his father picked him up and carried him to bed.

Meanwhile, the manuscripts of *Wuthering Heights, The Professor,* and *Agnes Grey* slowly made their way around the London publishing houses. After a month or two, they would land back in Haworth, returned with a curt letter of rejection, whereupon Charlotte would tie them all up again in fresh wrapping paper, address the parcel to the next publisher on her list, bind it with the same knotted string, and trot down to the village to post it off again.

Their volume of poetry sank without a trace, having peaked at total sales of two. When Charlotte requested several of the unsold copies, Aylott & Jones was only too happy to unburden itself of the little book. Charlotte had the idea of sending copies to their favorite authors, to Wordsworth, Tennyson, and Thomas De Quincey; it was better than leaving them around the house. It was just one more thing they would have to hide.

Anne was sitting on a stool in the shade of the cherry tree, shelling peas, when Charlotte came through the back gate. She set down the bowl and hurried to meet her.

"Where have you been, Tally? We were ever so worried."

Charlotte offered up a weak smile. "I'm quite all right. I've been for a walk."

"Tabby said you had a letter. She said it upset you." Then, in a quiet voice, she added, "Was it from Brussels?"

"No, dearest. I never hear from my Brussels friends anymore."

Emily came out of the house, dusting the flour from her hands. "What happened?"

Charlotte reached into her pocket and pulled out the letter. "It's from a publisher."

Anne said, "If it's from a publisher, how bad can it be? We've already been rejected by nearly every publisher in London."

"Not by this one." She passed the letter to Anne with a forced smile. "Thomas Newby will publish you, but you must bear the costs, as before."

Emily leaned over Anne's shoulder and the two of them read the letter together. After a moment, Emily's face clouded with a look of consternation.

"It doesn't say anything about your book."

"No," Charlotte said. "They returned it to me. It does not interest them. They find that *Wuthering Heights* is sufficiently long to take up two volumes of the proposed three-volume set. *Agnes Grey* will make up the third volume."

A deep pink spread over Emily's face. This was an outcome they would never have predicted, that Charlotte's book would be refused and theirs would be published.

"They say here they want fifty pounds," Anne said. She looked to Emily. "We would have to sell more of our railway shares. Do we have that much?"

"I think we do. But do we want to?"

"Yes," Charlotte said firmly. "Yes, you do. We've tried nearly every publisher in London. We've been trying for a year. If this is what it takes, then you should do it."

As she untied her straw bonnet, the wind caught it. It sailed out of her hands, rolling across the dusty yard. Emily sprinted after it, but Keeper got there first and snatched it up in his mouth, giving it a fierce shake.

"Drop it, Keeper," Emily commanded. When he gave the bonnet another playful shake, she stunned him with an angry blow across the head. He dropped the bonnet and sat cowering at her feet, gazing up at her with dark, sorrowful eyes.

Emily dusted off the bonnet and brought it back to her sister.

The dog had slobbered on the ribbon and there were tooth marks in the straw brim. Charlotte wiped it off and then quietly turned and went inside.

The manuscript Newby had returned lay unopened in Charlotte's room for several days. When she finally decided to send it out again, she was in a defiant mood; she scratched through Newby's name in bold, inky strokes and wrote to the side of it: "Smith, Elder & Co., 65 Cornhill, London." Charlotte disliked untidiness in all its forms, and such carelessness was against her nature; but it seemed to her, disheartened as she was, that her Professor was not good for much more.

Mr. Williams's desk was situated in a cramped and close little corner of the London publishing house of Smith, Elder & Co., removed from the clerks and at some distance from the stove, making it hot in the summer and cold in the winter, but this seemingly inferior situation was in no way an indication of his status in the firm. His appearance was equally deceptive: stooped and gray before his years, with an air of shabby neglect about his dress, he shuffled around the tables of manuscripts and books with a hangdog look, as though the solemn and sober work of literature had somehow exerted a gravitational pull on his body so that every aspect of his person dragged, sagged, or drooped. In reality, he was an intellectually lively and remarkably sensitive man, with keen commercial and literary judgment—which was why he sat in his cramped little corner just outside George Smith's door, and why every manuscript came across his desk, and why every book they published required his stamp of approval.

It was a sluggish August day, and there were only a few clerks in the office. London had fairly emptied itself. Parliament was out of session, the upper classes had gone off to their Continental watering holes, and only the most industrious men of trade labored on. George Smith was one of these, and by virtue of his responsibilities as general manager, so was Mr. Williams. Mr. Williams had just finished reading a very intriguing manuscript, and he was still formulating his thoughts about it when George swung open his door and stepped out.

"Williams, are you still here?"

"Indeed sir, and I shall be for some time to come."

"Egods, man, it's hot out here. Why don't you open your window?"

"I'm quite comfortable, sir."

"You could take off your coat, you know."

"That would be unseemly, sir." Then, noticing that George Smith was standing there without his coat, he added, "I would not like to set a poor example for the young clerks, sir."

"Well, can you come in here? I need your advice."

"Certainly, sir."

George Smith's office was small but had the advantage of a sky-light, and the brightness of the room caused Williams to blink, so that he didn't notice the bolts of silks and satins stacked high on a pair of chairs.

"Here," George said, reaching for a bolt of midnight blue silk and un-furling it beneath Williams's eyes. "What do you think of this one?"

Williams peered at him over the rims of his spectacles. George Smith was a dashingly handsome young man. He had been blessed with one of those little whimsies of nature—a deeply dimpled smile—as well as lively eyes and a muscular build.

"For a waistcoat, sir?"

"Yes. The family's out of mourning now, Williams, and all of a sudden my mother finds that my wardrobe needs refurbishing."

"Has it been a year already, sir?"

"Hard to believe, isn't it?"

"Indeed, sir."

George had taken over the small publishing house after his father's death the year before. He had inherited some dishonest partners and crushing debt, but he was a hard worker and was proving to be a keen businessman.

"Sir," Williams said, with a twist of a smile, "do you really think I'm the one you should be asking? Perhaps you might wish to consult your mother or sisters?"

"They are the last ones I should wish to consult. They can never agree on anything. Come now, man, I trust you."

Williams eyed the bolts of cloth, unfurled a gray satin and held it up to the light.

George said, "My tailor tells me it's all in the reds now."

Williams replied thoughtfully, "Does he, now?" Then, after having briefly unrolled a few more bolts and inspected them with the same close scrutiny, he chose four from the batch and with a decisive air laid them aside.

"There, sir. That should do it."

George gave a momentary glance at the selection. With a smile of gratitude and relief he said, "Yes. That will do nicely. Thank you, Williams."

"On another matter, sir. A manuscript just came across my desk. A writer I know absolutely nothing about, but I thought I might bring it to your attention."

"Something we might be interested in?"

"Not so much the book itself—it's a rather slight novel—would make up only a single volume, I'd say—and I'm afraid the story lacks appeal. However"—Williams paused and gripped the back of a chair with both hands—"there is great literary power on the page."

George leaned back against his desk and folded his arms. Whenever Williams spoke up, George listened carefully. Williams had been writing theater reviews for the *Critic* before George had snatched him up to work for Smith, Elder; the man had extraordinary insight and an eye for talent.

"Yes, go on."

"I think perhaps with a different subject . . . if the author might be persuaded to make another attempt . . ."

"And you're just the man to do that, Williams."

"Should you like me to write to him?"

"Yes, do. And leave me the book. I'll take a look at it this evening. What's the title?"

"*The Professor.* Written by a Mr. Currer Bell. Appears to be a northerner, sir. From Yorkshire."

The letter Charlotte received from Mr. William Smith Williams, literary assistant to George Smith of Smith, Elder & Co., was two pages long. She knew when she broke open the seal that it was no mere rejection, and she hurried up to her room, closed the door, and read it with trembling hands. They had declined to publish *The Professor,* but the book had caught their attention. Mr. Williams had been able to look past the story's shortcomings and was able to discuss at length its merits and qualities, and believed he had discovered a writer of promise.

Charlotte sat down to write a reply that very day, explaining that she had nearly completed a longer work that might interest him. Three weeks later, she walked four miles to Keighley to the train station, where she posted the fair copy of the completed manuscript of *Jane Eyre.*

Sunday was George Smith's only day of rest, and his mother, who worried that he worked excessively long hours, jealously guarded what little time he spent at home. She was understandably upset when—at eight in the morning, while they were still having breakfast—the doorbell rang.

"It's Mr. Williams, sir," the servant announced. "The gentleman would like a word with you."

"Oh dear, George, not on a Sunday," Mrs. Smith exclaimed. "And before you've finished breakfast."

George swallowed a mouthful of sausage, dabbed his mouth with a napkin, and nodded to the servant.

"Show him in."

Mr. Williams entered hesitantly, clutching his hat and a parcel wrapped in brown paper under his arm. He nodded to Mrs. Smith, who was busy tucking a graying strand of hair into her white morning cap.

"Good morning, madam," he said. "I do apologize for the inconvenience."

"I suppose it must be important if you've come all the way to Bayswater on a Sunday morning," George said.

"Actually, sir, I spent the night at the office. Finishing this." He stepped forward with the bundle. "I urge you to read it at your earliest possible convenience."

George put down his napkin and reached for the parcel.

"Is this our new literary sensation?"

"It may well be, sir. Do you remember the name Currer Bell?"

"Was that *The Professor?*"

"Yes. That's the one. This is his new work. Quite a different story altogether. Title is *Jane Eyre.*"

George took it into his study after breakfast, thinking to read the first few chapters, perhaps skim through a few more. He settled down in his reading chair and picked up the manuscript. Before long, the servant knocked and entered.

"It's your groom, sir. He's brought your horse."

"Brought my horse?"

"Yes, sir. You were to ride today. You were to meet Mr. Sturbridge in the country."

"Not until noon."

"It is noon, sir."

"It can't be."

"I'm afraid it is, sir."

George took out his watch.

"By Jove, it is." He set aside the manuscript, went to his desk, and jotted off a quick note of apology to his friend, excusing himself due to urgent business. He gave it to the servant to deliver to the groom, then settled back down in his chair.

The rest of his day was given up in much the same manner. When the servant came to announce lunch, George asked for a sandwich and a glass of claret, and he read on until evening. He dined quickly and returned to his study. Sometime after eleven his mother slipped in and quietly went about replacing the candles; the ones on the mantel had gone out and George hadn't even noticed.

It was after one when he finished the book. On the way to bed, he noticed the light beneath his mother's door. He found her sitting up in bed, reading. She put down her book and turned to him with the brightly serene smile that had always been there to encourage him, even in their darkest hours.

"So, you've finished it?"

"Yes."

"My dear boy, I do hope it was worth it—you sacrificed your entire day."

"It was worth every minute."

"Are you going to publish it?"

"Most definitely. I intend to write Mr. Bell tomorrow and make him an offer."

He came across the room and leaned down to kiss her soft cheek, which smelled of lavender water.

"Good night, Mother."

"Good night, George."

At the door he hesitated and said over his shoulder, "It was a most extraordinary book. I think I've never read anything quite like it."

That week, Ellen Nussey came for a long-overdue and much-anticipated visit.

She was to arrive by the afternoon train, and Charlotte, dressed in light gingham and a straw bonnet newly trimmed in blue ribbon, set off to walk the four miles to the Keighley station. She had barely passed the last straggling cottages and struck off across a field when she heard her name called. She turned to see Emily running up the lane, skirts hiked up around her ankles; Emily squeezed through a stile in the drystone wall and tore across the field toward her.

Charlotte was alarmed, immediately thinking of her father or some episode with Branwell, and she turned back on the path.

Emily came flying up, completely out of breath, and drew a letter from her pocket.

"This came," she said, a hand on her heaving chest. "From Smith, Elder."

Charlotte took it from her and opened it. Emily watched her expression for signs of disappointment or elation, but she could detect neither.

"So? What did they say?"

Charlotte covered her mouth with her hand, then just as quickly drew it away and said in a faint voice, "They've offered me a hundred pounds for *Jane Eyre* and first refusal rights on my next two books." She looked up and glanced around the field. The cows had stopped grazing and were watching them with huge liquid eyes. "I think I should sit down now."

Charlotte sat on the moss-covered low stone wall while Emily read the letter. Her face had stretched itself into a ridiculously wide smile that she was quite helpless to control. Meanwhile, she was having wild visions of herself running at the cows and scattering them with shrieks of joy. Emily finished the letter and, in a rare display of affection, hooked her arm around her sister's neck and kissed her roughly on the cheek. Then she began offering advice about the terms, wondering if they might negotiate more than a hundred pounds. Eventually, Charlotte's brain—confused by an overabundance of happiness—resolved its befuddled state the only way it knew how: she burst into tears.

It took a while for Charlotte to regain her composure, and then she worried that she would be late arriving in Keighley. She entrusted the letter to Emily, who—before letting Charlotte out of her sight—reminded her that she could not so much as hint about their publishing to Ellen.

Ellen had arrived on the four o'clock train and was waiting patiently on a bench in the shade of the station, her blond curls a little damp around the edge of her pretty bonnet, her blue eyes betraying just a shade of disappointment. She carried a new parasol the shade of pale mint, although she knew the wind might well ravage it on the walk back to Haworth.

When they had first met at Roe Head, Charlotte had not cared much for her. Ellen was conformist to the core and slavishly mindful of the opinions of anyone with money or social influence. But she was also kindhearted and affectionate, and Charlotte craved affection. Ellen had arrived at school just days after Charlotte, and she had found fourteen-year-old Charlotte in the empty classroom, huddled behind the long drapes of the bay window sobbing her heart out while the other girls played outdoors. Ellen had gently coaxed her out of hiding, and together the two homesick girls had sat on the window seat and spilled their hearts to each other.

There was something disarmingly reassuring about Ellen, a genuine kindness that invited trust, but Charlotte had never known intimacy outside the intense bonds of her own uniquely gifted family. As children they had felt themselves branded by their poverty, and as a result, the feminine rituals of social calling had become a painful experience not to be endured. On the few occasions when their aunt had herded them to social tea drinkings in the finer homes on the outskirts of the village, the girls had suffered acutely from condescending glances and cutting re-marks. Their best dresses were often hand-me-downs passed on to them by the very families in whose parlors they would be obliged to sit for a stifling hour or two, staring across the tea table at mothers and daughters who would recognize Anne's dress or Emily's bonnet, something discarded, too old-fashioned to be worn by anyone but the parson's charity children.

And so they grew up, socially defective, isolated, but with a firm be-lief in their worth as individuals. Intellectually gifted, they withdrew into their own tight world, where all that mattered were books, paint-ings, and music. Every human unkindness preyed on their minds, but alone, within their mental world and the comfort of their family, they were giants, titans, genii.

Much to Charlotte's surprise, over the long summer break follow-ing her first year at Roe Head, Ellen had kept up a faithful correspondence. The next summer, Charlotte was invited for two weeks at Rydings, the Nusseys' grand old battlemented house with its rookery and fruit trees. It would be another year before Charlotte had the courage to reciprocate the offer.

"She sounds boring and snobbish," Emily had said. Emily didn't like having to entertain visitors.

"She can be snobbish, but honestly, Em, I find it refreshing sometimes, just to gossip about frivolous things."

Emily gave one of her contemptuous little grunts.

"Besides, Ellen likes me. And whenever someone likes me, I can't help but like them in return."

"I can't see why. You have Branwell and me and Anne. Why should you need anyone else?"

"Because I do."

"She won't like us. No one does. We're poor and we're all odd. Except Aunt, but no one pays any attention to her. You just wait. Papa will launch into one of his horrifying tales after dinner and scare the wits out of her. She'll never come back again."

But she did. Over the course of the years, they became comfortable with each other's qualities and faults; they were contrasts but they suited each other, and affection grew into love. Charlotte was capable of infinite love.

Ellen had already sent her luggage on with a carrier, and so they went directly to the Devonshire Arms for tea. Charlotte's spirits were high, and Ellen thought she had not seen her friend so cheerful in years.

"So, your dear brother Henry is engaged to be married," Charlotte said gaily.

"Are you not just a tiny bit jealous, Charlotte?"

"Jealous! Why, not a whit!"

"You could have been his bride, you know."

"Yes, and ten to one I shall never have the chance again." She waved her gloved hand in a carefree gesture. "But *n'importe*."

"He was truly very fond of you."

"Oh, Nell, Henry thinks he knows me, but he doesn't. I'd shock him—he'd think me too wildly romantic for his taste and he'd be constantly censuring me, and there you have it. That's not the kind of husband I need." She would not remind Nell of how irritable she could become when dissatisfaction set in, how insipid conversation with mediocre young men turned loose the ogre in her. And the idea of marrying one—like dear Henry . . . well, you might as well lock her up in the attic and throw away the key.

Ellen sipped her tea and with a wounded voice said, "He is a grave and quiet young man, but then clergymen often are."

Charlotte reached across the table and touched her arm. "Dearest Nell, Henry will make a wonderful husband, but I know I could never have for him that intense feeling that would make me willing to die for him."

"Do you still think you can find that kind of love?

"I doubt it, but I can't marry without it." Charlotte added, "I only regret that you and I will not be sisters-in-law."

This seemed to be what Ellen had wanted to hear. She smiled. "But we are sisters in spirit."

"Yes. And that is more meaningful than any binding laws."

She peered at Charlotte, whose eyes seemed unusually brilliant. There was something very beguiling about her today, a spritelike air and effervescence. "My dear, you must have some news to tell me."

"News?" Charlotte started as she set down her cup.

"Are you hiding something from me?"

"What would I be hiding?"

"Have you had attentions shown to you from a certain quarter?"

"You mean romantic news."

"Precisely."

"Where would I find romance in Haworth?"

"Your father's curate?"

Charlotte burst out in laughter. "You see romance in the strangest places, Ellen dear."

"What else would make you so lighthearted and cheerful?"

"A visit from you and a bright sunny day," she beamed.

They walked back to Haworth in the cool of the evening, both of them refreshed and relaxed. They fell into easy chatter about the many dramas in their families. Ellen's oldest brothers moved in aristocratic circles in London and were always good for a little court gossip, but the younger brothers seemed to be plagued with constant misfortune or poor health, one of them mentally ill, another an alcoholic. Ellen confided all these heartaches to Charlotte, and in return Charlotte openly confided Branwell's adultery and addictions. In the privacy of letters and on visits like this, the most humiliating and distressing incidents were aired, wept over, prayed for; anger was purged and hope renewed. The only topic they never discussed was Charlotte's writing, and so Charlotte kept her secret, and Ellen continued to search for romance in the air.

Chapter Ten

In the middle of October, London was just falling back into the rhythms of the social season. George Smith arrived early at his club, hoping to find a quiet spot where he could settle down with his newspapers and skim through the theater and book reviews.

Within half an hour every seat was taken and waiters with bar carts were rattling to and fro with their cargo of tinkling glass. George remained hidden behind his paper for fear of finding himself drawn into conversation and thereby losing a good quarter of an hour listening to Mr. Wheatstone grumble about how Certain Members helped themselves unfairly to the rice pudding or how that selfish Burton hogged all the newspapers.

But when he heard William Makepeace Thackeray's voice, George quickly folded the paper and rose to his feet.

"Mr. Thackeray, sir."

"Sit, sit, Mr. Smith," Thackeray said. He was a sizable man, endowed with height, bulk, and equally weighty opinions, generally of the cynical and contrary kind. Thackeray rarely took the time to read the works of new authors, and his opinions could be harsh. Nonetheless, George had confidently sent him an early copy of *Jane Eyre*.

George remained standing. "May I offer you a drink, sir?"

"No, no. I'm on my way in to dinner." Thackeray wagged a finger. "I do wish you had not sent me that new book of yours, *Jane Eyre*."

"And why is that, sir?"

"I lost an entire day reading when I should have been writing. I've got printers waiting for my next installment—and here you send me a book that is absolutely irresistible."

"I thought you might enjoy it."

"Enjoy it? Why, the man and woman are capital! Capital! I was exceedingly moved. Some of the love passages even made me cry—quite astonished my old servant when he came in with the coals, finding me blubbering into my handkerchief like a sentimental old fool. Who is this Currer Bell?"

"We know nothing about him at all. The manuscript arrived without any introduction."

"Oh, I'd wager it's a woman. It is a woman's writing. But a damn fine mind. Must have had a classical education to write like that. If it's a woman, she certainly knows her language better than most ladies."

Thackeray checked his watch, then stuffed it back into his waistcoat pocket. "I must go. Do give my respects to the author." Then, on impulse, he added softly, "I'd like to write a letter myself to Currer Bell. If you would be so kind as to forward it on to him."

"Currer Bell would be honored, sir."

"I don't know why I should bother, but I feel I must. I was exceedingly moved."

That very day in Haworth, Charlotte and Anne put on their cloaks and trotted down the icy lane to the postmaster's cottage to collect several heavy parcels, which turned out to be Charlotte's six copies of the three-volume set of *Jane Eyre*. It had a quiet reception by comparison to the excitement it was already causing in London literary circles, of which the sisters were as yet ignorant. They waited until the others had gone to bed, and then Charlotte ceremoniously presented each of her sisters with a copy of *Jane Eyre*. The three of them sat around the fire hugging their shawls, with their feet propped on the grate and the dogs sleeping on the rug. The house was deadly silent except for the sound of pages turning and the wind, which they didn't notice.

"It's very nicely done," Anne said. "They published it well, don't you think?"

Charlotte nodded.

No one had to say a word, but it was on all their minds that Newby had still not brought out *Agnes Grey* and *Wuthering Heights*. He seemed to be procrastinating, making promises and breaking them, and Emily kept writing polite inquiries, but there was nothing else they could do.

Charlotte settled the three volumes in the lap of her skirt and folded her tiny, finely shaped hands over them. A long, serene silence filled the air.

After a moment, Emily rose, set her volumes on the mantel, moved back her chair, and lay down on the rug with Keeper. Burrowing into the warmth of his body, her head pillowed against his chest, she tugged her shawl around her shoulders and curled up, gazing into the fire. The dog twitched a paw and slipped back into his dreams.

"I do like Jane, you know," Emily said. "I like her very much."

"I'm glad."

"I was thinking, if you write that story again, about the professor, you must make him true to life, the way he really was, and you must keep your own voice. Like you have in Jane."

"I've been thinking about reworking it."

"Yes, you should." Emily added thoughtfully, "What will you do with the other three copies of your book?"

Charlotte shrugged. "There's little I can do with them, given that no one knows I'm the author."

"You might be able to trust Mary Taylor with one, don't you think?"

"You wouldn't object?"

"Well, she is on the other side of the world. It would take six months to get there."

"This will come as quite a surprise to her. She thinks imagination is a rather useless faculty unless there is a moral to preach."

"You must swear her to secrecy."

"I shall instruct her to burn any letter with a reference to our work."

"Will she do it?"

"Mary? Oh yes. Without a doubt."

Anne asked innocently, "Do you think it will be reviewed?"

"I do hope so," Charlotte said.

"It will be," Emily pronounced flatly, and no one contradicted her.

From the *Westminster Review* of *Jane Eyre: An Autobiography:*

> Decidedly the best novel of the season . . . amply merits a second perusal. Whoever may be the author, we hope to see more such books from her pen; for that these volumes are from the pen of a lady, and a clever one, too we have not the shadow of a doubt.

From the *Era:*

> This is an extraordinary book. Although a work of fiction, it is no mere novel, for there is nothing but nature and truth about it. . . . The story is unlike all that we have read, with very few exceptions, and for power of thought and expression, we do not know its rival among modern productions. . . . All the serious novel writers of the day lose in comparison with Currer Bell.

G. H. Lewes in *Fraser's Magazine:*

> We wept over *Jane Eyre*. This, indeed, is a book after our own heart, and, if its merits have not forced it into notice by the time this paper comes before our readers, let us, in all earnestness, bid them lose not a day in sending for it. The writer is evidently a woman, and, unless we are deceived, new in the world of literature. But, man or woman young or old, be that as it may, no such book has gladdened our eyes

for a long while. . . . The story is not only of singular interest . . . but it fastens itself upon your attention, and will not
leave you. The book closed, the enchantment continues . . .
it is soul speaking to soul; it is an utterance from the depths
of a struggling, suffering, much-enduring spirit: *suspiria de
profundis!*

Since they were removed from clubs, salons, and dinner parties where
the well-read gathered, it was George Smith's stoop-shouldered, self-
effacing assistant who brought the excitement to their doorstep. Mr.
Williams kept up a stream of long, thoughtful letters, enclosing the latest reviews and posting them as instructed to Currer Bell in care of
C. Brontë, Esquire, Haworth. He was quite sure that C. Brontë and
Currer Bell were one and the same: he had the proof of their handwriting under his nose; but the author's identity remained an absolute
mystery.

   "My dear Mr. Bell," he wrote,

> *I can assure you that you cannot underestimate the extent of your
> growing celebrity. I was a theater critic for the* Spectator *before as-
> suming my present post with Mr. Smith, and it has been a long
> time since I've seen the creatures in such a frenzy. They are
> tumbling over themselves in a rush to crown you with their praise;*
> Jane Eyre *is quite the literary sensation, and everyone is speculat-
> ing about the identity of the mystery author. I received letters
> addressed to you from George Henry Lewes and another from
> Leigh Hunt, eminent critics with whom I am sure you are ac-
> quainted, letters which I will forward today. I am sure they are
> both eager to congratulate Currer Bell and welcome him to the lit-
> erary fold.*

Charlotte spent hours bent over her desk that winter, whittling away
one quill after another as she exuberantly composed some of the most

pleasurable letters she had ever written. She wrote of art and the mysterious sway of the creative process, of poetry and literature, of her brother Ellis's own unique genius. The only true intellectual companions she had known, with tastes like her own, had been Branwell and Constantin Heger, and they had both abandoned her. Now she had a new audience worthy of her keen intelligence, and she confidently voiced her convictions on these things. Her correspondents may have suspected her sex, but she addressed them as a man, and they replied to her as an equal.

Through all this, Charlotte felt as though she were riding a wave of muffled euphoria. All the long-hoped-for praise and worldly recognition had to be quietly folded up and tucked into the drawer of her small, portable writing desk or whispered about among the sisters in the kitchen or at night by firelight. Charlotte thought it was sadly ironic that such acclaim should come to her, and that she was not at liberty to enjoy its benefits. Yet, as she wrote to Mr. Williams, were her identity made known, she would suffer a painful self-consciousness that would destroy the peace of mind she needed to be able to write. All of England was abuzz about *Jane Eyre,* and yet its author continued to pass before their eyes unnoticed, a shadow in their midst.

Quite unexpectedly, around the first of December, a parcel arrived from Newby; it contained the authors' copies of *Wuthering Heights* and *Agnes Grey.* Emily and Anne were devastated to discover that he had rushed the books into print without bothering to make their final corrections, but this disappointment was soon lost in the deluge of disturbing reviews.

Critics attacked *Wuthering Heights* as a strange, wild story, which it was—and as lacking artistry, which it did not. More than anything, they were baffled by it, just as Emily was baffled by them.

Charlotte watched her read the reviews, then quietly shut them away in her writing-desk drawer.

"What kind of world do these people inhabit that they are so blind to human nature?" Emily said coldly. "There's nothing extraordinary at all about my characters. They are real and true."

There was little Charlotte could say. She could have predicted the public's reaction. "They're Londoners, Emily Jane. They live in a different world."

"Indeed—an intolerably false world. A very dull, stupid world."

Charlotte confided in Mary Taylor, far away on the other side of the world:

My dearest Mary—

I am enclosing the volumes of Emily and Anne's works—which they both send with fond wishes.

I regret to say that Wuthering Heights *has provoked the harshest condemnations. The reviews have wounded Emily to the quick. All the critics write of the exceptional power of her language but they cannot understand the use to which she has put it: hers is indeed a dark genius that dwells in realms quite distasteful to the civilized mind, and I fear the book has offended a great many people.*

There is some truth in what they say, but I cannot bear to see her wounded so. It breaks my heart, Mary, and she is far too proud to show her feelings. It is rather queer the way it has turned out for the three of us, now all of us published authors—I would never have anticipated such feelings would disturb our domestic tranquillity— beneath the surface of our tedious lives run deep currents of pride, tempered by a fierce need to protect one another. We must all three brave harsh winds that blow hot and cold, and I find it strange that we can be so disquieted by these blasts when we are so far removed from the storm. Our bonds of affection are so deeply rooted that we feel each other's heartache as if it were our own, and I can not take the same pleasure anymore in my own success.

As for my book, we have run through the second printing and a third will follow. It seems that they have adapted Jane Eyre *to the stage (a ghastly melodramatic version with the ridiculous subtitle of*

"The Secrets of Thornfield Hall"!). On the more serious side, there is a woman who would like to translate it into French. I confess I should be pleased to think it was being read in certain circles in Brussels, although I doubt any—save one—would guess that Currer Bell was the little English schoolmistress who had briefly lived among them.

By now they seem to have made the connection that the Bell brothers are all related, and Mr. Williams writes me that there is speculation that we are all one and the same author—a hypothesis that has not served me well, as now there are a few new reviews claiming to detect the same coarseness in Jane Eyre that they so condemned in Wuthering Heights. I'm quite astounded as I can see no similarity in our works at all.

I'm sorry to say that no one even bothered to review Agnes Grey—I don't honestly know which is worse, to be ignored or reviled. Yet, as usual, Anne is the most courageous of us all; she can be quite harsh on me if I whine too much and reminds us that there is much to be thankful for, not least of which is the check I just received for another hundred pounds. Anne is well into her second novel—the cautionary tale of a debauched young man—she does not want for inspiration. Emily and I are struggling with ideas. I have made three attempts at something new and abandoned them all. That is quite like Anne, I think, to just get on with it.

Burn this letter, as you promised.

To Ellen, she wrote:

My dearest Nell,

We are getting on here the same as usual—by that I mean Branwell continues to make our lives miserable. He is all self-pity with us and rage with Papa. I'm afraid we've all given up on him. It's much worse when he has money as he only spends it on drink or

*worse—which is why Papa gives him none, but then he wheedles it
out of Her, and we're back to where we began. Mr. Nicholls has
just returned from his annual holiday in Ireland and he, God
knows, is just the same. I cannot for my life see those interesting
germs of goodness in him that you seem to have discovered on your
last visit; I find him appallingly narrow-minded. I fear he is indebted to your imagination for his hidden treasures.*

*Since your visit we have seen no one, been nowhere, and done
nothing (to speak of) and yet we manage to be busy morning to
night. I wish we had some real news to make this worth your time to
read, but you must content yourself with my fond kisses instead.*

The "nothing" of which they could not speak and that kept them so
busy was all the more essential to their peace of mind because of the madness raging at home. As much as they would have liked to avoid their
brother, they were forced by the circumstance of his dependence to live
his miseries day in and day out. The family was slowly coming to terms
with his uselessness. He seemed to be one of those Darwinian experi-
ments destined for extinction: what could possibly be worse than a smor-
gasbord of talents coupled to an ultrasensitive nature without a lick of
self-discipline? Disappointments forced him into retreat; opposing winds
knocked him down and left him bitter, whining, incapable of moving on.
He had been given every privilege their meager means could afford;
adoring sisters and proud father had fed his ego and allowed him every
indulgence; and all had been squandered.

Oh, but what promise he had shown in his youth! Such exuberant
charm! "Send for young Patrick Brontë!" they would cry at the Black
Bull when a gentleman of distinction passed through, and little Johnny
Robinson would race up to the parsonage and beg for Branwell to come
down. Dazzled by his silver tongue, strangers never knew what hit them.
Was it the particularly potent ale they served at the Bull or was it that
carrot-headed little chap's zinging wit and intellectual precociousness?
They knew Genius when they saw it. They fully expected to see the day

when his name would be glorified far and wide, like Wordsworth and Tennyson. "Brontë!" they would say. "Of course, we knew him well! What brilliance! What a gift for storytelling!" They'd tell how he'd blow in on a summer day crooning a tune, his tongue itching to drink and jest; he'd sweep off his sweat-stained tall hat and what would fall out but some of his latest verse! And what about the time he fooled a Londoner into thinking he knew that Great City like the back of his hand, when in reality he'd merely memorized the maps? How he'd sit in his chair by the fire on stormy nights and bewitch them with long passages from Shakespeare, Shelley, or Byron. At the slightest encouragement he'd strip off his jacket, roll up his sleeves, and strike a sparring pose, faking punches as he sprang light-footed around the sawdust-covered floor, just a little exhibition to remind them how he'd boxed in his younger days. To prove he had some well-toned muscle attached to his five-foot-three-inch frame. That virility came in miniature as well.

But the sad truth was that none of this energy carried over to the canvas or into verse. He had been infinitely entertaining in his golden days, but now nearly everyone—even the locals at the Black Bull and his fellow artists in Halifax—found him a bore. It is indeed one of those small human tragedies—some might even say one of God's nasty little jokes—to fill a heart so full of desire, mold it so perfectly to a vocation, and then deny the man the courage equal to the task.

In truth, his struggle was not any different from Charlotte's: both of them had addled their brains with romantic stories of aristocratic heroes and heroines pining after forbidden love, and both struggled to resign themselves to the fact that life was not going to live up to their dreams. First, their family was neither high-bred nor glamorous; and second, adulterous love was messy. In real life the home wrecker who went off to live with the beloved suffered social alienation and, often, loss of fortune as well. But we mustn't judge Charlotte and Branwell too harshly for their fantasies. They lived in a time of straitjacket morality when the slightest quiver of the flesh gave cause for outrage. Denial of human desire was the battle cry of the day. God help those poor souls who had desire in abundance, who had what it took to love heatedly, passionately, to the death.

Branwell lived and died by his family's judgment, and his contempt flowed from a sense of utter helplessness. At home every glance, every innuendo, every silence carried a resounding echo of his failures. He hated feeling dependent upon them—his aging father and sickly sisters—and he spewed out his frustration in venomous rage. *Look at them!* he'd think as he caught glimpses of his sisters scurrying about the rooms, tending to their domestic trifles, scribbling out their poems—vainly attempting to get them published. He knew their secret. He'd noticed the brown-paper parcels—snatched from the postmaster in the lane and concealed behind skirts with fidgeting fingers before disappearing forever God-knows-where. They must have dipped into their little savings for the writing paper and postage. Illusion, all of it. Naïve dreams that would amount to nothing. Just last year Emily had come to his room to ask him to read something she had written, but he had refused.

"My dear sister, I can't even summon the courage to concentrate on my own poetry. Let alone yours."

"It's not verse. It's a story."

"It will just distract me."

"From what?"

"From what I should be doing, which is my own work." He locked his fingers behind his head and looked up at her with mournful eyes. "I'm thoroughly exhausted. The slightest excitement and my heart starts beating wildly. All this business has brought me so low."

"What a whining coward you are."

He roused himself to shout after her as she disappeared down the hallway. "You know it's useless, don't you? It's impossible to break into that business. You won't get anyone to publish it. Some poor underpaid lackey will just feed it to the printer's fire!"

He collapsed back against his pillow.

Good Lord, he thought with a mental scowl, *what could my virginal sis-*

ters, enclosed in their miniature lives, possibly have to say? What kind of stories could they tell? Surely the same sort of childish fantasies they have been writing since girlhood.

It was easy for them to nag him about trivial matters—Charlotte always on him for his appearance, chiding him to change his shirt, take a bath, shave. Emily with her stony looks and Anne with her smiles reeking of piety. But his father! To hell with clean linens—the old evangelical would have a son cleansed of sin! Every night just before the stroke of eight his father appeared at his door with prayer book in hand, summoning him to evening prayers in the study. Now, there was a standoff worthy of great theater. The erect old parson with his trademark scowl, bristling hair, and snowy neckcloth rising to his chin, waiting . . . waiting. Sometimes Branwell was still sleeping off the gin. But often he was just drunk enough to be nasty. His father would find him sitting on his bed chomping on a cold pipe (he could rarely afford tobacco), his writing desk propped on his knees while he sketched or wrote by the light of a single candle.

"Branwell, we're all assembled. Come downstairs and pray with us," he said one night.

"Great God! It's the good reverend!" Branwell cried in mock astonishment, whipping off his wire-rims and blinking up at his father. "Oh, so sad, old man. Why so sad? A degenerate son causing you problems? Well, take it to the Lord our Savior! Indeed, get thee downstairs to thy knees and save that reprobate's soul!"

The old reverend never so much as batted an eye through all the blasphemy, but inside his heart was breaking.

"You're weak. We're all weak, but I believe this is a peculiar sort of disease from which you suffer—"

"Disease?" Branwell interrupted. "Rubbish. What I suffer from is an infuriating family that refuses to understand what I'm going through."

"Men do not die of love."

"Well, you certainly won't. You're immune to that disease."

"If you would but turn to Christ for strength."

"Ah, yes!" He winched his brows together like a man pondering a grave problem. "Now, there's an intriguing idea for you! Take a poor soul they hammered to a cross a couple of thousand years ago and get him to sort out the mess! Brilliant, Father! Brilliant! That's the spirit!"

"He will, if you would only repent—"

"Repentance? Is that the recipe?" He screwed up his mouth again. "But repentance of what? I mean, good God, man, we could get bogged down here . . ."

There was no point going down that road. Branwell would declare that he did not regret for a moment the affair—that Lydia had taught him the realities of life: what real suffering is, what real love is.

"Our Savior will deliver us. . . . He alone has the power to transform our hearts—"

"Actually, I have my own little list here. . . . Just this morning I was thinking of all the miseries laid in our path. . . . Now I, for one, would like to be saved from Virgil's plagiarisms and Homer's repetitions—and what else? Oh yes—please, dear Lord, save us from Queen Elizabeth's brand of virginity and Pretty Mary's death! And none of us wish to go the way of Cromwell's nose and Charles the First's head!"

A shadow moved in the hall.

"Come, Papa," Emily said softly as she stepped into the room. She took her father's hand, gently drawing him away. "Come away. Leave him be."

Branwell rambled on with his ridiculous prayer, enjoying himself immensely, until Emily darted back in and hissed, "Shut up, Branwell."

But the old man would be back again the next evening.

What he dreaded most was finding his son curled in a shivering ball in a tangle of filthy sheets, staring up at him with the eyes of a man possessed by the devil. Through chattering teeth Branwell would threaten to kill himself if his father didn't give him a few coins to buy a drink or a little laudanum to relieve the pain.

On these nights the father would slowly, painfully get down on his stiff knees beside the bed, and with tears in his eyes he would beseech God for mercy.

Yet despite the scorn and mockery heaped upon his head, he was the last—the only one—who refused to give up on his son. With characteristic determination and insight far ahead of his time, he spent hours pouring over medical journals, seeking to understand the frightening disease that was consuming his child. In the margins of his own copy of *Modern Domestic Medicine,* next to the entry on insanity, he made detailed notes about delirium tremens and the effects of intoxication. Instinctively, he knew that his son's weaknesses—his epileptic fits, his susceptibility to intoxication—were the results of a peculiar disorder of the mind, possibly a hereditary predisposition. Deep in his heart he believed that his son was not so much a sinner as he was one who had been sinned against—by this Jezebel, Mrs. Robinson. By himself, a father too poor and too protective to give him the formal education he deserved. That winter the old parson nursed his son through hellish hours of delirium, witnessed the sweating and uncontrollable tremors of the body and the demonic hallucinations of the mind. He had prayed over a dying wife and two daughters, but he prayed more fervently now than he had ever prayed in his life, fearful that he might lose his son for all eternity.

"You humiliate us," Charlotte said to her brother one day, her eyes flashing with restrained fury. "I don't dare invite anyone to visit. Not with you in the house."

"Give me a few shillings and I'll be out of your hair in the time it takes me to pull on my boots."

"And from now on, if you want to eat," she continued, ignoring the halfhearted plea, "you can drag yourself down to the table on time."

She was fuming, ready to stamp her tiny foot at him the way she'd done when they were children and he had shown himself heartless and insensitive. He recalled the incident when he'd stolen her favorite character, Mary Percy, and killed her off. Charlotte—never one to concede defeat—had raced back to her writing desk, sharpened her quill, and worked out a plot twist to bring Mary back to life.

"I have no appetite," he moaned. "Just go away. Leave me be."

"Well, your appetite seems to make an appearance as soon as the dishes are done. It's unfair to Tabby, begging a meal from her that late at night. She can barely walk anymore. And I've told Martha she is no longer to bring breakfast to you in your room. They have enough to do without serving you hand and foot."

"You're heartless," he said in a wounded voice.

Charlotte complained to Emily, "Have you seen his sketches? They're dreadful—distraught women on their knees, and himself hanging from a noose. He feeds on his own misery—he wallows in it like a pig in its swill." She would begin to grow agitated, and then Anne would remind her that they had work to do.

With no resources of his own, his only opportunity for escape was to take himself off to nearby Halifax, a thriving wool town nestled in the Calder Valley. It boasted its own circle of notable poets, artists, and musicians, and his good friend the sculptor J. B. Leyland was one of them.

Leyland was a kindhearted soul with a soft touch and a weakness for drink. He was easily drawn to excess, and when inebriated, the two men got on like wildfire. Later they would awake in Leyland's rooms with gray plaster casts of dead men staring them in the face, not knowing how they'd gotten there but relieved to be indoors and not sprawled in a mucky cobbled alley behind the Old Cock. Leyland, overworked and in debt, was a perfect companion for Branwell's misery.

"Do you suppose she's forgotten me?" Branwell said one night as he leaned on the table and focused his weak, watery eyes on his companion.

He swayed, just slightly off balance; his elbow slipped off the table. Leyland grabbed for him and caught a handful of jacket.

"Steady there, man."

Branwell pulled himself up and tried to remember what he had been saying. All he could notice was his empty glass.

"What letter?" Leyland prompted.

Branwell reached for the bottle of wine and cautiously maneuvered the neck over his glass.

"Steady on . . ." Leyland muttered, watching him fill the glass.

"The letter . . . got a letter from their family doctor. Been a good friend to me, he has. Writes to me from time to time. But such damned depressing news. Tells me I should give up hope. But she can't have forgotten me—I know she loves me still."

"They're a fickle sex," Leyland slurred, stumbling over his consonants. "Can't be trusted."

"You should have seen me. I was the favorite of all the household."

"Don't doubt that . . ."

"I even started perfuming my handkerchiefs just to please her."

A muffled snort escaped Leyland's nose.

"She was so lonely and unhappy. Always making me presents—and telling Anne how fond of me she was. I knew what she wanted from me and I knew it was wrong, but by God, Leyland—to feel that power, to know that there's someone who lives every waking minute in anticipation of one glimpse of you—one word."

He stared grimly at his glass of wine.

"Now she's gone. It's all gone. My dreams, my health, my youth—"

"Don't be a fool. You're not even thirty yet."

"But I can't work. I've lost my appetite. My nights are dreadful. I still dwell on her voice, her person . . ."

Leyland, who had heard all this before, let his thoughts wander into the fog.

"She doesn't get my letters. They send them back unopened. Bastards. They hate me like hell. Now I'm stranded. Thoroughly stranded."

In some remote region of Leyland's brain, the fog lifted. "You mean to say the money's dried up?"

Branwell's head drooped lower. "I'm sure if I write to the good doctor—he'll make an appeal to her on my part. . . ."

"Lord, I hope so . . ."

Branwell began to slip into his moody worst. Tears swelled in his eyes. "It's the mind, Leyland. It's dried up. Frozen. Nothing rouses my imagination anymore."

"You'll find your way back," Leyland said, with more reassurance than he felt.

"I fear it's worse than that . . . it's not just about inspiration. I've never told anyone this before . . ."

"What?"

"It doesn't work anymore, Leyland. I can't find the words. My powers have greatly diminished. I can feel it. Nothing I do is any good."

Leyland could not bring himself to do anything but give a somber and sympathetic nod.

"All I know is that it's time for me to be something when I'm nothing. Nothing at all. My father can't have long to live and when he dies, my evening will become night."

There was a long, difficult silence.

"God, Leyland, she did love me once. We did have hope for a future together. And I swear to you, she loved me even better than I did her."

Even in his lucid moments he could not admit to himself that it was the loss of the lady's estate that had dealt the final blow to his dreams. He knew, deep down where truth swims in the murky subconscious, that without her money the only future for him lay in a lifetime of demeaning labor as a lowly tutor in the service of those more fortunate than himself.

"Let's order another bottle," Leyland said, lifting a sluggish arm to his friend's shoulder. "The night's on me."

"Too good of you. Such a bore. All this bother about bills."

"We'll manage."

"Bugger the bastards."

"Amen."

Despite the lamentable state of his mind, Branwell plodded on—scribbling a few lame verses from time to time, trying to squeeze from his damaged brain cells a handful of worthy words. All his life he had turned to his imagination for delivery from worldly cares; there lay his inner sanctum. Increasingly, he replied on opium; a few grains dissolved in alcohol—a tincture cheaper than gin—produced fabulous dreams.

And dreams were the stuff of which great poetry was made. Coleridge and De Quincey had proved as much, and he—Patrick Branwell Brontë, the great Romantic with a grief-stricken heart—he would imitate them.

The *Halifax Guardian,* a reputable newspaper with high standards, had published a number of his earlier poems, and so one fine spring day, his pocket jingling with a few shillings courtesy of a father grateful for the slightest effort, Branwell rode the train into Halifax with the intention of placing an ad for a position as a tutor on the Continent and—more important—submitting his latest labor for publication. It was an earlier poem he had reworked, transforming his grand passion into great art; he had dedicated it to Lydia and signed it by his pen name, the noble (and pretentious) Northangerland.

Just outside the *Guardian's* office he collided with January Searle, a critic and editor-at-large in the district. Searle was a dreaded figure, a self-important man with harsh opinions; the local writers cultivated his friendship, but they all despised him.

"Mr. Brontë!"

"Mr. Searle. Good day."

"A coincidence, running into you . . ."

"How's that, sir?"

"Because I've just finished this strange novel—surely you've heard about it—*Wuthering Heights*. Supposedly written by the brother of the author of that improbable melodrama *Jane Eyre*."

"Oh, I've heard of the books, sir. Caused quite a stir—"

"So you haven't read them?"

"Don't have time for that sort of thing, sir," he replied. "Been busy with my own work . . ."

Searle leaned closer and said in a low voice, "You sure you're being straight with me?"

"I beg your pardon?"

Searle eyed him closely. "You really don't know what I'm talking about?"

"I am indeed baffled, sir."

"You sometimes write under a pen name, is that correct?"

"I do. I publish my poetry under the name of Northangerland."

"Not Bell?"

"Bell?"

"So you're not the mysterious author of *Wuthering Heights*?"

Branwell screwed up his brow. "I am not."

"Well, I'd have sworn it was written by you. Thought I saw something of your brooding in it—all that business about love beyond the grave. Just the sort of strange fancy that a diseased genius such as yours might produce. And the setting appears to be Yorkshire, you know."

"You prick my curiosity, sir. I shall have to read it."

"You must! A devil of a hero. Byronic and quite Romantic. But shocking beyond words. I dare say I'm a little disappointed. Thought I'd unmasked one of the infamous Bell brothers." Searle touched his hat and sped away.

Branwell was a familiar face around the *Guardian,* and the editorial clerk found him unusually subdued that afternoon. He was in a hurry to do his business, and then he went quickly on his way, which was not like him at all.

The bookseller said, "Beg your pardon, sir, we got in only a few copies and sold them right away."

"*Wuthering Heights?*"

"Yes, sir—comes in a three-volume set with a shorter title. Don't recall the other one straight off. Name of a woman."

"*Jane Eyre?*"

"No, sir. That was published last September." The bookseller opened a ledger and squinted through his spectacles at the entries. "But I've got more on the way if you'd like to place your order. Be more than happy to hold—"

Branwell cut him off. "Who are the authors?"

"All three titles written by the Bells. Relatives I hear, and rumor has it they're—"

"The surnames," Branwell snapped. "What are the surnames?"

"The surnames? Rather unusual names, as I recall. It was Currer Bell wrote *Jane Eyre*—"

"Currer?"

"Yes, sir. Rather odd for a Christian name. More often a family name."

"And the others?"

He lowered his nose closer to the ledger. "Here we are. *Wuthering Heights* and *Agnes Grey* by Ellis and Acton Bell."

"Ellis and Acton."

"Would you like to leave your name, sir? We should have them in next week."

Immediately upon arriving at the Old Cock he sent off a note to Leyland.

My dear sir,

I have come to town on a small matter of business—and having tried your rooms and all your usual haunts, I am now at the Old Cock waiting for you. Haworth is overrun with men of Gothic ignorance and ill-breeding and I cannot return until I have drunk from the well of your sympathy—providing that I have not already drained it dry. Unspeakable sorrows overwhelm me at present, and although outdoors all is sunshine and blue sky, I am lost in darkness. For mercy's sake, come and see me, for I shall have a bad evening and night if I do not see you—I hardly know where to send the bearer of this note so as to enable him to catch you.

NORTHANGERLAND

Like many provincial inns, the Old Cock maintained a lending library for its patrons, and Branwell was told that he was indeed lucky to get his hands on one of the novels because there was a waiting list a foot long; Elijah Daniels was next up for *Wuthering Heights* but he hadn't come to claim the book yet, so Branwell was welcome to it without charge for a few hours.

He ordered a whiskey and settled in a chair by a window where the light was good enough to read by.

The prose was new and fresh to him, but within a few pages he recognized the raw materials of his sister's imagination. This was certainly not Charlotte's writing: this was no tale of slavish submission, of yearning for the sophisticated and the glamorous. Here was the creation of a wild, natural world populated by people of violent, raw emotions; he could easily see Emily living here—content, at peace, at home.

"My God," he muttered, his heart thumping.

Then he began to laugh.

That was the last thing he remembered. Sometime later he woke up with the Old Cock's owner staring down at him; worry was etched on her kindly, florid face. He'd had a sort of fit, she explained, just fell off his chair and went quite unconscious—although he'd barely touched his glass of whiskey. After it had passed she'd had him carried to the back room and laid out on a bench. Branwell begged her forgiveness, praying he'd done nothing to offend her, and as soon as he had the strength to walk he took himself out.

Leyland's landlady let him in, and Leyland found him wrapped in a grimy blanket, asleep on the floor.

"Not drunk," Branwell said, raising a gaunt hand to grip his friend's arm. "Had a little illness—you know what I mean—quite temporary. All right now. Not drunk . . . promise you. Just need to sleep."

That spring they noticed a change for the worse; he seemed entirely broken down and embittered. He borrowed money everywhere and owed everyone. He had run up such a bill at the Old Cock that the owner took her case to the authorities. A sheriff's officer from York came around one day with a warrant for Branwell's arrest.

He behaved appallingly, crouching in the chipping shed behind a chubby marble angel until Emily came to get him.

"You can come out. He's gone," she said sharply, hugging her shawl around her bony shoulders. "Thanks to you we'll be eating potatoes for the rest of the month."

He rose, shivering, his nose red from the cold. A hoarse cough shook his small frame.

"If it'd been up to me, I'd have let you go to prison."

"How can you say that?" he cried. "Can't you see how ill I am? I would've died."

Emily was struck with sudden remorse. The idea of Branwell in a rat-infested prison, shivering on a straw mat teeming with vermin. Her brother.

"Don't be a fool," she said gruffly. "We would never let them take you. Papa would sell our last stick of furniture rather than see those monsters take you away."

She put an arm around him to steady him. "Come inside now. It's safe."

There was no one else home that fine April morning. Martha had gone to the butcher's, their father had driven to Griffe Mill with Stephen Merrall, and Charlotte had taken Tabby to visit her nephew in the village. Later they all wondered at the seemingly insignificant circumstance that prevented a tragedy, how Anne, who was in the kitchen with the glue bottle mending a chipped teapot, had suddenly recalled that there was a broken china cat sitting on her dresser. How she had deliberated, thinking about the other chores that needed to be finished that morning, but had opted in favor of fetching the cat with the broken tail.

Branwell had not been out of his room all morning. Now, reluctant to disturb him, Anne climbed the stairs on tiptoe. Mounting the last few steps she noticed gray smoke seeping from the crack beneath the door of his room.

Her heart in her throat, she pounded on the door.

"Branwell!"

When there was no reply she threw open the door; a gray cloud wafted from the room, and through the veil of smoke she saw her brother on his bed against the wall, stretched out like a dead man on a funeral pyre.

His sheets, tumbling over the side of the mattress, had caught fire from a candle set on the floor.

"Oh Lord—oh mercy!"

Holding up her skirts, she dashed inside.

"Branwell! Get up!"

He lay in a drugged stupor, eyes wide open and staring, incapable of either speech or movement.

There seemed no way to reach him without breaching the wall of flames.

"Emily! Help!"

The washstand! she thought. But the washbasin stood empty. "Where's the pitcher?" she shouted at him. "What did you do with it?"

She spied it on the floor beneath the window, but it, too, was empty. Finally, in a panic, she flung it against the wall above his bed.

"Branwell!"

At the sound of shattering pottery and his sister's shouts he turned his head, bringing his glassy eyes to rest on her.

Just at that moment Emily flew into the room. With the seeming strength of a Titan she grabbed her brother by the collar of his nightshirt, heaved him off the flaming bed, and dragged him across the room to safety.

She yanked the burning sheets from the bed, hiked up her skirts, and kicked the flaming bundle into the corner. She was still stamping out the flames when Anne came back up from the scullery lugging a bucket of water.

Once the fire was out, Anne slumped to the floor, her back against the wall. Emily stood in front of her, protective, feral, the dripping bucket swinging from her hand.

"Are you all right?" she asked Anne.

"I think so. Are you hurt?"

"No."

But their hearts were pounding and every limb was shaking violently.

"I shouldn't have thrown the ewer. I was trying to wake him up."

"It's all right."

"It was Aunt Branwell's." She mustered a weak smile. "It'll just give me something else to glue together today."

Anne lowered her head between her knees and began to sob.

Emily was far from tears. She glanced around the room, at her sister weeping and her stupefied brother who was now sitting in the middle of the floor examining his ripped nightshirt with an idiotic look on his face. The room was a disaster: shards of the shattered ewer all over the bed, a sodden bundle of burned sheets in the corner, piles of waterlogged papers and books scattered across the floor; had the papers caught fire, they would have taken the entire house with them.

"You fool!" Emily seethed, wheeling around to face her brother. "You selfish, self-pitying fool!"

"It's no use," Anne said, looking up with a tear-streaked face. "He can't hear you."

"Damn you, Branwell!" She threw down the bucket and slapped him hard across the side of the head.

He flinched and turned horrified, baffled eyes on her.

"Emily Jane, don't!" Anne cried, stumbling to her feet.

Emily struck him again. He curled into a ball and covered his head with his hands to protect himself from the blows.

"You could have burned down our home! Is that what you want? You want us thrown out on the street and homeless?"

Anne began to scream, begging her to stop.

They had all grown up with a dread of fire, instilled in them by a father who had prayed over too many children who had burned to death. He allowed no curtains on the windows, only wooden shutters, and they had been taught to zealously tend all fires, oil lamps, and candles. That evening they sat with their father in his study and discussed how they were going to protect themselves from their brother. Patrick saw only one solution: Branwell needed to be under constant surveillance. His door would remain open at all times during the day, and at night he would sleep in his father's room. Patrick would lock them in at night and keep the key on himself so that Branwell would not wander.

"I am persuaded, children, that if I can keep him off drink long enough, these terrible deliriums will pass."

Charlotte was firmly against the plan. "But what shall you do? Stay awake with him all night?"

"If I must. We will face his demons together."

"He still manages to get himself drunk in the day, Papa. We can't keep him a prisoner."

"At least at night my household can sleep without fear."

"Hardly, Papa. We're more afraid for you than for ourselves."

"He can't harm me. He's weak and ill."

"And so shall you be if you spend your nights locked in a room with him."

But he was resolved.

The following morning, when her father left the house for a meeting, Charlotte found John Brown in the churchyard. She asked him to come quickly to the parsonage to remove the loaded pistol hanging in her father's bedroom; he was to take it up to the field, discharge the thing, then return it to the wall.

After that day, their father's declining health began to concern them as much as their brother's. In truth, the seventy-one-year-old parson had a remarkably strong constitution, although he would have his daughters believe otherwise; every attack of influenza or bronchitis sent him spiraling into a gloomy, mildly hysterical state of mind where he would convince himself that he was about to die and leave his children penniless. And now his spirits, too, were being worn down. They couldn't help but notice the strain on him, and they talked about what they might do to cheer him. It was Emily's idea to tell him about *Jane Eyre*.

The servants were out that afternoon and Emily was baking, a chore

she thoroughly enjoyed. She liked working at something that was physical and sensual, yet mechanical enough so that she could read while she
kneaded, and compose lines of poetry in her head.

"I think Papa should know," she said as she sprinkled flour over the
table.

Charlotte looked up from the account books. "Know what?"

"That you've written the best novel of the season." She scooped the
sticky dough out of the bowl and worked it into a ball. "Anne and I have
already discussed it."

Charlotte glanced at Anne, who looked up from the silver teaspoons
she was polishing and smiled in agreement. "We thought it might be just
the thing to cheer him."

"But he can't know about *our* books, Anne's and mine."

A breeze swept through the window, and Charlotte laid down her
pen and snatched the coal merchant's bill just as it flew into the air.

"I'm not sure I want him to read it," she said.

"Why?"

She closed the ledger and leaned forward on her elbows. She thought
for a moment, then replied, "I'm afraid that he'll find it second-rate. Just
some silly domestic novel."

Anne gasped, "Charlotte! What ever would make you think that?"

Charlotte said quietly, "Because I'm not his son."

They were a little stunned at her frank admission, although they
knew it was bitterly true.

Charlotte watched Emily knead and turn the dough, admiring the
smoothly powerful movements of her hands and lean arms, and after a
moment she added, "Deep down he will always regret that it wasn't
Branwell who earned all the accolades. We are his daughters, and it's just
not the same."

Emily said, "You should show him the reviews."

"Yes, I suppose that would help."

"He'll be proud of you, Charlotte. He ought to know what you've accomplished," Anne said.

"And besides," Emily pointed out, "we can't keep rushing around snatching all the mail and fending off all the questions from the postman about Currer Bell. It was easy when he was blind, but now it's a little like cat and mouse all the time."

"Oh, it hasn't been that difficult," Charlotte answered. "Even when things pass right under his nose. He is infinitely uncurious about our lives."

Anne added, "And we should be thankful for that. We've had enormous freedoms that other daughters don't have."

Charlotte asked her, "Would you like him to read *Agnes Grey*?"

"Then he'd know about Emily's book. The reviewers always link our books together."

"Then we'll just keep doing what we've always done—we glance through the papers before they get to him and pull out any reviews that might tip him off."

Emily said, "When I was in the village yesterday, I stopped in at Mr. Greenwood's and asked if he had *Wuthering Heights* and *Agnes Grey*. Do you know what he said?" She smacked the dough onto the table and threw her weight into the rolling pin. "He said he didn't have it and didn't plan to order it." Emily lowered her voice and fell into the Yorkshire dialect she imitated so well: " 'That *Wutherin' Heights* seems to be a strange sort of book. About a savage family up here in our parts. A bit of a novelty. Nothin' I'd recommend to ladies such as yourselves.' "

Anne said, "I am quite grateful now for our anonymity. I cannot imagine what our lives would be like if everyone knew we were the infamous Bell brothers. Although I confess there have been moments when I wished people knew I'd published a novel." She paused to smile sweetly. "Not out of vanity, but because people have such a mild opinion of me or, rather, they have no opinion at all, and I think I am quite capable of something forceful, something that would shock them out of their complacency. I have seen a good deal of shocking behavior in the great houses where I worked . . . really shocking things that are condoned in the upper classes, and yet no one seems to find the voice to speak out against them, or if you do, you're considered vulgar and coarse. I find that the harsher the critics are on Emily, the more resolute I am that my second novel be unfailingly true to life."

That was the first, the last, and the only time Anne expressed herself so freely and fully on her own writing, specifically on *The Tenant of Wildfell Hall.* Charlotte, who had never approved of Anne's choice of subject, had the good sense to keep her opinions to herself.

That evening, Charlotte stood at the door of her father's study, clutching the three compact volumes of *Jane Eyre.* The room was sacred ground, and even after all these years, she still trembled a little on the threshold, even more so when she came with a request or seeking his approval. When she was eighteen, she had fretted for days before getting up the courage to ask for an allowance. He'd only laughed and said, "Now, what would a woman be wanting her own money for?"

He was reading by the light of his candle, and he did not look up when she entered.

"Papa," she said, and then she suddenly lost her courage and her knees began to tremble.

"Yes, what is it, Charlotte?" Impatience shaded his voice.

"I've written a book."

"Have you, my dear?" He continued to read.

"It would please me very much if you'd take a look at it."

"You know I can't be troubled to read manuscripts. It's too hard on my eyes."

"It wouldn't be much of a strain, Papa." A hesitation. "It's in print."

Finally he glanced up, wearing an expression of mild scorn. "I do hope you haven't been involving yourself in any silly expenses, now."

"No, Papa, on the contrary. I've already made a little money from it."

His white brows arched and he lowered his head to peer over the rims of his spectacles.

"Made money, have you?"

"Yes, and I've brought you the reviews." She set the books in front of him and placed the reviews neatly on top. "The reviews are rather good."

He glanced down at *Jane Eyre*.

"All right. Leave it here. I'll take a look at it."

They were all too anxious to concentrate on their writing that evening. Anne, who had just received the printer's proofs for *The Tenant of Wildfell Hall*, put the pages aside and pulled out her knitting. Emily lay sprawled on her stomach on the floor with her feet in the air, reading *Mary Barton*, a gift to Currer Bell from the author. Charlotte was stitching a new apron, although the work was hard on her eyes. When the clock on the stairs struck nine, they heard the handle turn and looked up to see him standing in the doorway. He had changed dramatically over the past few months; the flinty old man with the ramrod-straight bearing had softened to something sadly fragile.

"Good night, children," he said. "Don't stay up too late."

Then, almost as an afterthought, he added, "Oh, and you might like to know that Charlotte's written a book. And it's a better one than I had expected."

After he had gone, Emily said, "Does he honestly think we don't know about it?"

"Of course he doesn't. It's just his sense of humor," Anne said.

"But that's too dry even for me."

"I'm sure he feels more than he shows," Anne said.

Emily glowered at the door where he had been standing; she would have liked to thrash him just then.

Anne returned to her writing and Charlotte went back to calmly whipping stitches, which was also something that she did quite well.

Patrick Brontë wound the clock on the landing. Then he went on up the stairs to his room. His son was sound asleep on the tester bed, curled up in a tight ball. When he was asleep, the father could still see in him traces of the innocent and lovable boy, the onetime prince, the child of promise. Patrick took great care not to wake him. He sat on a chair by the bed, and while he unbuttoned his shirt he thought about his daughter Charlotte and this book she had written. For some time he had noticed that they always seemed to be busy writing, but he had not given it much thought. As children they had written their little stories and occasionally brought them to him to read. He had been pleased that his daughters were occupied, but he had not once imagined that it would come to this.

He hung his trousers and waistcoat neatly on the chair, then unwound the high starched neckcloth and folded it on his dresser. He slipped on his nightshirt, blew out his candle, and knelt beside the bed to pray. His head was swimming with thoughts of his wretchedly failed son and his tiny, clever Charlotte, who had made him proud.

There was a coughing sound from the bed, and a rustle of sheets.

"Get up, old fool," Branwell slurred, his lips caked with dried saliva. "Nobody up there to hear you."

Chapter Eleven

Emily had caught Keeper sleeping on Charlotte's bed, and she whipped him and dragged him growling and snarling down the stairs, through the kitchen and out the back door. When her temper had cooled, she went looking for him and made atonement with a piece of dried beef. Now they were both sunning themselves in the field just above the parsonage. Keeper's fat belly rose and fell in a deep, heat-induced sleep, and occasionally his ear twitched away a fly. Emily lay on her back beside him with her hand shielding her eyes from the morning glare, following the shifting cloud shapes as they sailed across the sky in subtle variants of soft whites and grays. It was to her an achingly beautiful spectacle; it awed her that something could appeal so strongly to her senses and yet elude her touch. At moments like this, she did not want to be disturbed.

"There she is."

It was Anne's voice. His sleep interrupted, Keeper heaved a deep sigh.

"Emily, dearest, can you come down here? It's really quite important."

Emily groped for the dog at her side; his short-haired coat was smooth and warm. Out of the corner of her eye she saw him lift his head; he had heard their approach. Now they entered her line of sight, looking down at her, blocking the clouds.

"Emily dearest, we need to talk. Can you please come inside?"

She squinted up at them. Charlotte was wearing her agitated air.

"What's this about?" Emily grumbled, raising herself on an elbow.

"Emmy, I don't want to stand in the heat. Will you please come inside?" Charlotte was being very firm, very bossy, and Emily wasn't in the mood for bossy sisters.

Anne, always the reconciler, said, "I'll fetch a parasol. You tell her about Newby." And she went down the hill.

At the mention of her publisher, Emily sat up. "What about him?"

"He's done a most unscrupulous thing."

Neither Anne nor Emily were pleased with the way Newby conducted his business. It was clear that he'd brought out their novels only after Currer Bell had attained literary stardom and he'd realized he could profit by association with the name. Earlier that year, Charlotte had worked hard to persuade George Smith to publish her sisters' next novels, and then Emily and Anne had refused his offer and remained with Newby instead, leaving Charlotte miffed and with egg on her face. It was another example of Emily choosing to be contrary just for the sake of being contrary, and refusing to be managed by her sister, even when her sister proved to have the better judgment.

"Well, he's just pulled another of his deceitful little tricks, trying to make money."

"What has he done?"

"He did this: he took Anne's new novel and sold it to an American publisher—a serialized version, I believe—but he's advertised the book in a way that implies that the author is Currer Bell—the author of *Jane Eyre*. He's been telling everyone that we're all the same author. That there's only one of us, and that's me."

Emily swatted at the fly buzzing around her face. "That's nothing new," she replied, falling back into the cool grass and closing her eyes. "The critics have been speculating about that for months."

"Yes, the critics have, but our publishers know quite well that we are not the same people, that there are three of us. Mr. Williams and Mr. Smith know that there are three brothers who all write different books and that Currer Bell has only written one. So far. At least that's what they used to think . . ."

Charlotte paused to open the collar of her dress and fan herself.

"It's so hot," she said. She was losing her temper with Emily, and that was never the way to deal with her. She stood there trying to cool down until Anne came up the hill holding a parasol and an oilcloth under her arm. They spread the oilcloth on the grass, then pulled up their skirts and sat down.

"Can't you see where this is leading, Emily?" Charlotte began, trying to keep her voice low and calm. "Please do sit up and listen."

"I can hear quite well with my eyes closed," she mumbled.

"My publishers got wind of it all, and they think that I've written a new book and sold it to someone else. While I'm under contract to them. They're furious. They demand explanation."

"Well, what do you want me to do?"

"They need to know that there are three of us."

"So write to them again."

"Emily, they need to see us. They need to see three bodies."

Emily shot upright. "Oh, no," she warned, in a hotly defensive tone. "I'm not meeting anybody."

"This is critical. You need to meet Mr. Newby face to face."

"No, I don't. It's Anne's novel he's advertising falsely. Anne should go."

Anne spoke up quietly; she always waited for just the right time to be heard and inevitably trumped the game. "But I am going. I already told Charlotte. I think we must set Newby straight. He's been devious with us from the start, and I think a surprise visit from his authors is just what he needs. Besides, I've never been to London and I should very much like to go. I'm ready to leave today."

Emily glared at them. It irked her when Anne took Charlotte's side. "Then go. But you must swear to me that you will never refer to me by name. I shall remain your brother Ellis Bell." Her gray eyes fixed them with a sharp gaze; it was enough to send a chill through both sisters, even on a sweltering day.

"So you're not coming?" Anne asked.

"If you go, you don't need me."

"Then we'd better get bustling, Anne," Charlotte said briskly, and she rose and shook out her skirt.

She went directly to her father to make her case. The fact that he did not yet know that Anne had written a novel required Charlotte to shade the truth, which she was quite willing to do. A rational man, he saw the necessity of her making a visit to her publisher accompanied by Anne, and offered to pay their expenses, but Charlotte felt the cost should be her burden. She had already received two hundred pounds for her novel, and it gave her great satisfaction to have her own money to spend.

That very afternoon they sent off their luggage, and after tea they set out to walk the four miles to Keighley. The sky was the color of India ink and thunderclouds were advancing swiftly from the west, but Charlotte would not be deterred. They plodded through a good half hour of stinging rain along the way and arrived at the train station soaked to the skin. In Leeds, Charlotte gladly paid for first-class sleeper tickets on the night train to London, and they managed to dry out their muslin dresses and shawls, although Charlotte didn't sleep a wink.

They arrived at eight in the morning and without the remotest idea of where to find lodging. They took a cab to the Chapter Coffee House in Paternoster Row, where she and Emily had stayed on their way to Brussels. Charlotte remembered it as being past its prime then, and it had certainly not improved in the six years since.

The coffeeroom downstairs was still a dingy, worn-out place, with heavy beams and a low ceiling. Their room was no better: a washstand stood precariously on feeble legs, a dresser bore the scars of years of careless use, and the wallpaper was faded and peeling. The floor sloped toward two high, narrow windows that looked out onto a forest of soot-blackened chimneys. Charlotte suspected that the room had not been cleaned, or even used, in months. But it had the advantage of being situated in the heart of the old publishing district, and Cornhill was only a few minutes away.

Charlotte leaned toward the mirror above the washstand and studied the face framed by the deep hood of her summer bonnet. She had never liked her looks, and a sleepless night hadn't improved on her complexion, which tended toward ruddiness and now, after a thorough washing in cold water, seemed to glisten in the morning light. Her eyes were shot with red, and her tiny hands were already trembling.

"Oh, Annie," she said, tying on the bonnet, "I don't know how to reconcile myself to myself sometimes. Here we are, away from home, out in the big city on our way to meet our publishers—everything I've craved so keenly—but I can't enjoy it. You know I'll pay for all this pleasure with a splitting headache in a few hours."

Anne sat patiently waiting on the bed, already neatly done up. "You'll feel better after you've had breakfast. It will calm your nerves."

"I couldn't possibly eat anything."

"Yes, you can." She rose to take the ribbon out of Charlotte's hands and tied a neat knot beneath her chin. "There, how's that?"

Charlotte turned back to the mirror and glowered at her reflection. "We're such country bumpkins."

"Yes, we are, but we happen to be rather famous ones." She passed Charlotte's spectacles to her and said cheerfully, "Shall we go, Currer?"

Paternoster Row was a dark and narrow street with gloomy warehouses rising on both sides. More than a century ago, at the request of the eminent publishing houses situated there, posts had been driven into the flagstones at each end to prohibit horse-and-carriage traffic. A queer silence reigned here, not so much that of tranquillity as of decay. Charlotte and Emily gathered up their skirts, picking their way across the flagged street and the trickle of sewage, and hurried toward the bright, bustling thoroughfare of Cheapside.

On the corner they came upon a driver who was unloading kegs from his wagon, inconveniencing a carriage and provoking a good deal of shouting, so that Anne and Charlotte had to struggle through the crowd that was beginning to form. It was just the sort of thing Charlotte needed, a bit of riotous London to strip away her self-consciousness. From there on, the walk to Cornhill was like an adventure on the high seas; it was only a half mile, but it took them nearly an hour. There was in that festering capital all the excitement she had so keenly missed since Brussels. She had come here once before in the firm belief that her life was just beginning, and today she felt that she was picking up where she had left off. The four years in between Brussels and now were only dreary, empty spaces, an emotional wasteland where she had survived through the richness of her imagination.

No. 65 Cornhill was a large bookseller's shop, full of young clerks who glanced up curiously as the door opened and two provincial-looking women stepped inside. Charlotte immediately felt the heat of their stares—she knew how she and Anne must appear, in plain silk dresses remade countless times, and retrimmed bonnets. They stood there for a moment, pale-faced and unsure of themselves, setting off a few titters of laughter among the younger lads.

Determined to hide her nervousness and ignore the mocking stares, Charlotte stepped up to the counter. She caught the attention of a clerk and said in a quiet voice, "I'd like to see Mr. Smith, please."

The lad darted a look at her, wondering what business someone like her might have with Mr. George Smith, but he checked his inclination to ask questions and went off to fetch his employer.

Charlotte and Anne waited for some time on the bench before the boy reappeared.

With a faint air of condescension he said, "Mr. Smith regrets that he is very busy just now, ma'am. He'd like to know who's asking for him, if you please, ma'am."

Charlotte replied firmly, "I regret that I am not at liberty to give you our names. Just tell Mr. Smith we've come on private business." Charlotte then lowered her voice and added, with a hint of mystery, "I can assure you, Mr. Smith will want to see us."

When George Smith came out from the back of the shop, Charlotte thought it couldn't possibly be him. She had imagined someone older; certainly she had never dreamed he would be so fine-looking. He dismissed the boy with a sharp word, and she could tell he was impatient at being disturbed on this Saturday morning, but he stepped forward and addressed her in a kindly manner, and she liked him immediately because of this.

"Did you wish to see me, ma'am?"

"Are you Mr. George Smith?"

"I am."

He watched while she drew a letter out of her skirt pocket. It was the last letter he had written to Currer Bell.

At first, he was completely baffled; he did not suspect it was her. Currer Bell had always made it clear that they would never meet.

"Where did you get this?" he asked sharply.

She gave him one of her wry smiles. "Why, sir, it arrived in the post. Just like all your correspondence."

She saw that he still didn't understand. Later she would recall this moment with pleasure, watching him grapple with the vast disparity between how she appeared and how he had imagined her. With a confused look he turned the letter over in his hand and glanced again at her. Then, with delight, she saw the surprise when it dawned on George Smith that this child-sized woman with great honest eyes was the literary lion Currer Bell.

Charlotte offered her gloved hand and said, "I'm Miss Brontë, although you know me by another name as well."

Indicating her sister with a glance, she whispered, "And this is my brother Mr. Acton Bell."

He shook Anne's hand, and then he was the nervous one. The shop had gone quiet, and all the ears were straining to hear.

"Please, ladies, come into my office."

He hurried them past the gawking clerks, snapping orders along the way: one boy was sent to find Mr. Williams, another dispensed across the street to fetch coffee, a third told to bring an additional chair.

His office was not as grand as Charlotte had imagined, but there was the skylight and a bewitching clutter of manuscripts and hundreds of books. The grandest interior of the most splendid residence would not have suited her better than this cramped room. A second chair was brought in, books were piled up to make more space, and as soon as they had settled down and the door was closed, Charlotte launched into an apology, along with a vehement condemnation of that greedy and scurrilous Newby.

"He knows the truth, sir, I promise you. He has never been misled by either of my sisters or myself."

"There's a third sister?"

Charlotte went quite red and added quickly, "Ellis insists that he be known only by his published name, and I'm afraid I misspoke in referring to him as my sister."

George Smith smiled. "I understand."

"I wanted you to see with your very eyes that we are separate people, and I thought this was the only way you might believe me. I could not persuade Ellis to accompany us—he is by nature reclusive, and a visit to the city would be most distressing to him—but as you can see, there are at least two of us."

George said to Anne, "And so you are the author of this new novel?"

Anne smiled and with quiet dignity said, "I am indeed the author of *The Tenant of Wildfell Hall.*"

George heaved a sigh of relief and leaned back in his chair, surveying his two authors.

"Oh, this is fine!" he said, clapping his hands in boyish exuberance. "What a day!" He broke into a broad smile, showing deep dimples that completely transformed his face so that you couldn't help but smile in return, and Charlotte was completely captivated. "Oh, there is so much you must see while you're here. There's the opera tonight—you do like Italian opera, do you not?"

"I have never had the pleasure, sir," Charlotte said. She found it difficult to repress a smile in his presence.

"Oh, my goodness, well—that you must not miss. And then there's the exhibition. And you must allow me to honor you with a dinner party."

"We intend to stay in London only a few days, sir."

"Then we shall have the dinner tomorrow."

"But that's such short notice."

"It can be managed."

At that moment the door opened and Mr. Williams entered. Charlotte shook the hand of the stooped white-whiskered man and thought how different her life might have been were it not for his fateful intervention. But it was George Smith who captured her attention, and she felt immediately at ease with him. The boy arrived with refreshments, and after they were served and the boy dismissed, George stirred his coffee and made plans to entertain the great Currer Bell.

"There are so many people who are dying to meet you—very important men like Thackeray and Mr. Lewes. I shall have them both to dinner."

"Mr. Smith, please, before you make any more plans . . ." She hesitated, and her voice softened with regret. "We would very much love to meet all these great and influential persons, but they cannot know who we are."

George frowned and set down his cup.

"But I cannot get men like Thackeray on such short notice without telling him whom he will be meeting. I'm afraid I must let him in on our secret."

"Then I regret to say we must decline. You must understand, Mr. Smith, that this is not merely a whim or an affectation on my part. It has been my brother Ellis's condition from the beginning that we remain anonymous. And I must, out of loyalty, abide by his wishes. I gave him an oath."

George looked crestfallen, and Charlotte felt his disappointment as keenly as her own. She added gently, "Sir, you must know that I am a great admirer of these gentlemen. The thought of being in the same room with them and conversing with them is more temptation than I should have to bear." She folded her hands calmly and said, "Sir, even our own father has been ignorant of our success—until several months ago, when Ellis . . . and my sister Anne here both gave me permission to inform him that I was the author of *Jane Eyre*. He still does not know that they have both written books."

It was beginning to dawn on George that he had a most unusual author on his hands.

"But what am I to do? I can't let you leave without tasting a bit of your own celebrity, Miss Brontë. . . . I may call you Miss Brontë, may I not?"

"You may, sir, but only you and Mr. Williams, and only in private. It is our secret," Charlotte said, implying an intimacy that she was beginning to enjoy.

George was having a difficult time letting go of his plans to parade Currer Bell around town—particularly since the two authors were so ridiculously unlike the "coarse and vulgar" creatures the critics had begun to portray; indeed, he thought he had never met a woman as delicate and demure as Charlotte Brontë. He had read her letters to Mr. Williams, and he knew her to be not only of an exceptional intellect, but unwaveringly honest and bold in her opinions. Yet here she sat, her tiny hands folded over the gloves in the lap of her skirt, with just a whisper of an Irish accent and keenly observant dark eyes, the very epitome of a sweet-mannered clergyman's daughter. He thought the entire situation was too beautifully ironic to be ignored, but ignore it they must.

Bit by bit they inched toward agreement: the sisters were to be known only as the Misses Brown, visiting from the country. They would be collected at their lodgings and driven by carriage wherever they wished to go; they would dine at the home of Mr. Smith and come to tea at the home of Mr. Williams. And Mr. Smith would call on them that evening, with his mother and sisters.

From Cornhill, Charlotte and Anne took a cab directly to Newby's office in Cavendish Square. By that time, Charlotte's headache had come on with a vengeance and she was not inclined to be polite to him. In the cab on the way back to Paternoster Row, Anne commented that Mr. Newby had seemed a little terrified of her, which Charlotte thought was not a bad thing.

The room was hot and stuffy, even with the window open. Charlotte lay in bed in her camisole and petticoat, with a damp cloth over her eyes.

Not a sound came from the street below.

"What are you doing?" she murmured to her sister.

"Reading one of the books Mr. Smith gave to you."

"Us. He gave them to us."

"Stay quiet, Tally. You must get over this headache before tonight."

"You don't think he means for us to attend the opera with them, do you?"

"I think he does."

She groaned.

"Are you still nauseated?"

"Yes, very."

Anne rose, removed the cloth from Charlotte's head, dipped it in the basin of cool water, and wrung it out.

"We don't need to go if you're not well."

"Of course we do. It would be terribly impolite to refuse. And besides, you've never been to the opera. It would be a pity to miss it."

Anne laid the wet cloth gently over Charlotte's eyes. "I can live without it."

Charlotte groped for her hand and kissed it. "You'd give up anything for anyone, I do think."

Anne sat on the edge of the bed, still holding her sister's hand. "This is a very important time for you. I should not want to do anything to spoil it."

"You do realize how ridiculous we'll look in those dull dresses that come all the way up to our ears."

"Hush," Anne whispered. She gave Charlotte's hand a little squeeze and returned to her chair near the window.

After a moment, Charlotte peeled back the cloth and peered at her sister through heavy-lidded eyes. There was a twist of humor in her voice when she said, "To think we're as old as we are and we've never bared our shoulders."

"I should feel quite uncomfortable doing so."

"So should I."

"We must appear so odd to them."

Anne lowered her book and smiled. "We are who we are."

"I kept glancing down at my gloves while I was sitting in his office. I was trying to hide them. They're so worn, and I've tried everything to remove the stains."

"Well, you took care of that. We have new ones now. And new parasols."

"Goodness, what will Papa say to such frivolous purchases? Kid gloves!"

"They are not frivolous, Tally, and besides, you bought them with your money."

"It's our money. It's for all of us."

Anne rose again and refreshed the cloth; then she patted Charlotte's hand and said, "I'll go down and check the time."

"Yes, do. We want to be waiting when they arrive."

Charlotte lifted the cloth and caught Anne on her way out.

"He's a handsome man, isn't he?"

Anne smiled. "Very. Very handsome indeed."

Charlotte lay back into the pillow. "And we should try to sponge the wrinkles out of our dresses."

They sat in the bay window in the stale-smelling meeting room, all alone, watching the street below. It was summer and light still brightened the western sky, but there was nothing but shadow on Paternoster Row. The elderly waiter had brought up a lamp for them, and here they waited.

Squinting through her spectacles, Charlotte could make out a small party coming down the dark street.

"Might it be them?"

"Yes, yes, I think so—the ladies are wearing evening gowns."

"Oh, goodness—the carriage can't come into the Row. How inconvenient for them. How embarrassing!"

"It's all right."

"Look," Charlotte said, peering through the narrow window. "Look how elegant." She pressed her face closer, so that her breath fogged the cool pane. "What is she wearing in her hair?"

"It looks like a wreath."

Turning suddenly to Anne, she cried, "Take the flower out of my hair."

"But why?"

"It's all wrong."

"It's pretty."

"I look like a clown."

"No, you don't."

"Just take it out, please."

She had removed a faded silk flower from her bonnet and fastened it to her hair with a comb. Now she fumbled for it with nervous fingers.

Anne calmly removed the flower. "How's your head?"

"Throbbing."

"You'd better take another whiff of your smelling salts."

"Good grief, brother dear, where are you taking us?" Eliza exclaimed. She was a large dark-haired woman two years older than George. Yet she deferred to her brother in all matters and dutifully did his bidding, as they all did, although she reserved the right to make her opinions known. She released his arm to gather up her fragile tulle skirt and mountains of petticoats, treading cautiously along the flagstones in her blue satin slippers.

"What a miserable little place."

"This is quite well known, actually. Used to be a favorite haunt of authors back in its prime."

Sarah, who hung on her brother's other arm, was seventeen and had just come out this year. Like her sister, she had inherited her father's heavy, horsey features, but she had her brother's buoyant good nature. She glanced up at the sign for the Chapter Coffee House and said, "So we *are* meeting an author."

"No, little Sassy, they are the relations of a very important friend of mine. They are simple country ladies, and I expect you two to be on your most gracious behavior toward them."

Sarah pinched his arm. "Oh, please don't call me little Sassy, George, not in front of them."

Eliza gave a whimper and muttered, "My shoes are all soiled."

Inside, they followed an elderly servant up the broad, shallow staircase.

"This place is ancient," Sarah whispered to her sister, ogling the wainscoting and heavy beams. "It looks like it belongs somewhere in the wilds of Scotland."

The waiter led them into the low, long room and with his candle indicated the two women huddled across the room on the window seat.

"Misses Brown," George exclaimed, sweeping off his blocked silk hat and striding toward them.

Charlotte rose to greet him, and in the glow of his earnest admiration she forgot her plainness and her homemade dress, and her self-consciousness momentarily faded away.

Mr. Williams was waiting in the carriage for them. Once they had settled in, George rapped on the roof and they pulled away. Four women in petticoats gave cause for a little joking—George complained that he was drowning in organdy and lace—and Charlotte, feeling suddenly chatty, popped off with a self-mocking witticism about her high-necked dress. This provoked boisterous laughter from Sarah, who had a quick sense of humor.

Mr. Williams smiled kindly and leaned forward to whisper, "Miss Brown, you have earned the right to appear in public however you desire."

Eliza had remained distant, with a slightly condescending air, but she overheard the comment and darted a quizzical look at Charlotte. It dawned on her that whoever this plain little woman was, she was definitely important.

In the midst of all the mystery, tulle, and perfume, Charlotte found her tongue, and she fell into a witty banter with little Sassy and talked all the way to the opera.

Never again would Charlotte enjoy her celebrity as much as she did that night. She descended from the carriage on George Smith's arm, and together they climbed the red-carpeted stairs toward the lobby. Mr. Williams escorted Anne, and as they mounted the stairs beside her, Charlotte pressed George's arm with a trembling hand and whispered, "We're not accustomed to this kind of thing, you know. It's all very grand."

Heads turned to stare at the two provincial-looking ladies escorted by one of the most eligible bachelors in London. Gentlemen smiled and tipped their tall silk hats. Ladies dressed in sprawling gowns fanned themselves and glanced their way, arching their long, bare necks in attitudes of bored condescension. Young women whispered behind gloved hands, and their mothers cast sharp, appraising eyes on the queer little woman with George Smith. George paraded her through their midst with a proud smile, and it was only nervousness that kept Charlotte's giddiness in check.

George leaned down and whispered to her, "I would imagine everyone here has read *Jane Eyre,* or at least would pretend they had done so, and if they had any idea who you were, they'd be fawning all over you."

Charlotte beamed up at him and whispered in reply, "I regret I cannot give you that pleasure, sir."

"Oh, but I am enjoying our little secret, Miss Brown."

George astutely managed to avoid the clusters of his acquaintances, and he herded their party through the crowded lobby and toward the stairs to their box.

At the bottom of the great staircase, as his famous author paused to gather up her skirts, George Smith glanced down on the coils of her dark hair glistening in the light of the candelabras and an unexpected wave of tenderness swept through him. Then she looked up at him with sparkling dark eyes and took his arm. Her touch was as light as a leaf.

During the opera, when the lights were low and her face illuminated by the stage, he was able to observe her more easily. She had a disconcerting habit of looking down when she spoke, so that it was difficult to see her face, and he had the impression that she was ashamed of her physical appearance. But when attention was not on her, those fine eyes sharply observed everything around her. Now, glancing at her under the cover of darkness, he thought about the story of *Jane Eyre,* which had brought her such fame. Her book had been written with such passion, and the love between the man and the woman was so heartfelt and true. He thought there must have been a man somewhere in her past, a man she had loved deeply, and he suspected that her love had not been returned.

They departed on Tuesday morning, after a whirlwind of dinners and teas at the homes of George Smith and Mr. Williams and a rushed visit to the Royal Academy and the National Gallery, which delighted Anne and brought back bittersweet memories of Brussels to Charlotte. George drove them to the train early that morning, shook their hands, and sent them off laden with books, which was the only gift Currer Bell would accept from her publisher.

The train had already left the station when the door to their compartment opened and they were greeted noisily by an old clergy friend of their father's. He stumbled into their compartment, struggling with a small bag, which he heaved onto the overhead rack. He plopped down into the empty seat next to the window, complaining of the heat and the crowds, and declared himself blessed to have found a compartment with agreeable companions.

"First class is always preferable," he said, fanning himself with his round hat, "but it's not always practical, is it?" He breathed heavily on them for a while, dabbing at the sweat glistening beneath the white stubble on his cheeks. But no sooner had he caught his breath than he shot back up, dug around in his case overhead, withdrew a book, and sat down. It was *Jane Eyre.*

Without apologies, he settled his reading glasses on his nose and opened the book to a marked page.

Under the cover of her skirts, Anne poked Charlotte gently in the leg. Charlotte looked up from her own book, read Anne's glance, shifted her gaze to the cover of *Jane Eyre,* and it was all she could do to restrain herself from laughing.

They traveled for hours without a word between them, and Thomas

Crowther didn't so much as lift his eyes from the book, ignoring each stop, the flow of traffic in and out of the compartment, the swaying of the coach on the rails.

Finally, he laid down the book and removed his glasses to rub his weary eyes.

"By Jove, it just occurred to me," he said, shifting in his seat and settling his glasses back on his nose, "it was your father who lent this novel to me." He arched his eyes expectantly, only to be met by a disinterested silence and a mere nod.

"Have you ladies not yet read it?"

Anne deferred to Charlotte with a smile, and Charlotte replied, "Sir, we have little occasion to read novels."

"Oh, but I'm quite astonished, Miss Brontë, because the first part of the story is about this poor Jane's horrible abuse at a clergy daughters' school, and I lay any money on it that it's the same one you attended with your sisters." He shifted forward in his seat. "You know, I sent my daughters to that school too, and I'm acquainted with that old Calvinist Wilson, and I tell you, Mr. Currer Bell has got him just right."

"Indeed?"

"Well, I'm surprised you haven't read it yourself by now."

"So you think the portrait is true to life?"

"Oh," he exclaimed, "why, it's like he walked off the page, I tell you. Everyone recognizes him, you know—oh, it's caused quite a stir in our circles. Whoever the author is, he's done us all a service. Abominable place, that school, and Wilson deserves the calumny of having himself exposed like this. Although I didn't suffer the terrible losses that your family did, miss, there were many others who did—"

He came to a sudden pause, for lack of breath rather than lack of anything more to say, and Charlotte and Anne smiled kindly at him.

"Please, Mr. Crowther, don't let us disturb your reading. You seem to be enjoying it so much."

"Oh, my goodness, indeed I am. I'm just at the part where . . . well, I won't spoil the story for you," he said. He picked up the book and dis-

appeared again behind its cover. Gradually, as the train headed north-
ward, he succumbed to the heat and the movement. He nodded, awoke
with a jerk, then nodded again, until his chin finally came to rest on his
chest and he forwent the pleasure of reading for the greater pleasure of
sleeping.

Arthur came across the novel not long after that. It was passed to him—
furtively—by his good friend Sutcliffe Sowden, vicar of Hebden Bridge,
during a visit Arthur paid to him one afternoon at his lodgings. Sowden
waited until the landlady had cleared away their tea. Then he stood up,
withdrew the book from behind a row of theological volumes, and laid it
in front of Arthur with the air of a man lending a naughty book in a
men's club.

Arthur threw back his head and laughed his deep laugh. "You keep
it hidden? Goodness, man, you want me to read a book you're ashamed
to keep out in the open?"

"Just read it," Sowden said, jamming his hands into his pockets and
frowning down at his friend.

"And why should I?" Unlike Sowden, Arthur rarely read novels.

"Because everyone is reading it, and as opinionated as you are, you'll
not want to be left out of the debate, now, will you?"

"You're right on that point. What's it about?"

Sowden shrugged apologetically. "It's a love story."

"Ah! Just what I was hankering to read." Arthur picked up one of the
small green leather volumes and opened it with an air of skepticism. "So,
what's all the controversy? Besides the fact that all of London is in a tizzy
to discover the identity of the author."

Sowden thought deeply for a moment. "It's an extraordinary novel.
The critics have been quite ruthless, and I do see their point. But I
mustn't taint you with their prejudices before you have a chance to judge
it yourself."

"Come now, man, you can't tempt me like that. What are they
saying?"

"What are they *not* saying? Everyone seems to have such strong opinions about it. That it is coarse and offensive. Disgusting, even. And powerful. Magnificently eloquent."

Sowden became agitated, which was quite unlike him; he stood up and began to pace. "It's the heroine, this Jane. She's quite intense and honest and true."

"Honest. About what? Sowden, you're being obtuse."

Sowden blurted out, "About love. The way a woman feels those things." He snatched the book from Arthur's hands. "Here, let me read this to you. Just imagine a woman standing in front of you talking to you like this. She is inferior in rank but sterling true, and you have treated her most unfairly."

"Unfairly? How?"

"You have tricked her and teased her, and led her to believe you are to marry another woman when you know she is in love with you. Then later when you are to marry her, you are found out to be a most heartless rogue. You already have a wife, but she's mad and locked in the attic. So you beseech poor Jane to be your mistress. But I'm getting ahead of the story."

Arthur leaned back and gave a hearty laugh. "Yes, do read it to me. I'll know just what to expect the next time I find myself in such a situation."

Sowden read, his eyes boring into the page, his large hands slightly tremulous.

> "Do you think, because I am poor, obscure, plain, and little, I am soulless and heartless? You think wrong! I have as much soul as you—and full as much heart! And if God had gifted me with some beauty and much wealth, I should have made it as hard for you to leave me, as it is now for me to leave you . . ."

At first Arthur was inclined to laugh at the absurdity of Sowden's deep baritone rendering female sentiment, but Sowden was a gifted

reader, and after only a few words the woman's voice took hold of
Arthur. He felt the incandescent power of the words—only briefly—
but it was enough to silence his inclination to ridicule when Sowden
closed the book and returned it to him.

It was a long, steep walk from Hebden Bridge back to Haworth, and a
mighty storm blew in over the moors. First there were gusts of wind and
deep rolling clouds marshaling over the livid hills of heather; then came
torrents of rain. Arthur had to remove his hat to save it from the driving
wind, and he had to tuck the small volumes inside his waistcoat. After
an hour, when the pelting rain had soaked his coat, he moved the books
inside his shirt against his chest, and with his hat over his heart he
braced the wind the rest of the way home. He perspired heavily with
the exertion of the climb, up and down the rock-strewn paths, through
the stiles, past farms and out-barns, searching for landmarks to keep him
on the right path, seeing little else before him.

His thoughts wrestled with the woman's voice. Sowden's reading had
left him with the unsettling impression that he had briefly glimpsed
someone he knew but could not identify. He certainly did not think of
Charlotte. He saw Charlotte in the light of a dutiful and highly conscientious clergyman's daughter. A peculiar woman from a peculiar family,
intellectual, argumentative, and overly inclined to all things artistic perhaps, but certainly not a passionate little Jane Eyre. The girls were all
shy and reticent, hiding in the parlor and kitchen, appearing only when
their father wished or when duty required. He could not imagine any of
them writing those words.

When he reached his lodgings that evening, he removed his boots
and gave his coat to Mrs. Brown to dry by the fire, and then he went up
to his room and took out the books he had so carefully protected all the
way home. It was damp from his perspiration, and the leather was soft
and warm. He quickly changed into dry clothes and then sat down to
read. He remained in his room and read late into the evening and had
to ask Mrs. Brown for another candle when she came to clear away his
supper.

He read until the candles burned out, and in the morning, after he had finished teaching at the church school and performed a marriage, he hurried back to his room and pulled up his armchair to read by the light of day. He burrowed through the novel like this for several days, paying hurried visits to a sick weaver and a grieving mother, and the perfunctory visit each evening to Reverend Brontë in the parsonage, just across the lane.

Arthur may not have had a poetic imagination, but he was as susceptible as any intelligent reader to the spell of Charlotte's words. The woman's voice, full of rage and hunger and passion, seemed to go with him wherever he went. His heart swelled, and he became moody and irritable when Patrick Brontë launched into a tirade about church taxes, and he snatched up his hat, gave a hurried excuse, and rushed home to finish the book. When he came to the passage Sowden had read to him, he found his eyes had filled with tears.

Arthur was a man of considerable reserve, as disciplined with his emotions as he was with each minute of his carefully planned day, but he found in this plain, obscure governess a heart not unlike his own—a heart capable of great love. He even thought about writing a letter to Currer Bell and telling him how the story had moved him, but the thought flitted in and flitted out, to be lost among countless noble intentions that are never performed.

Chapter Twelve

It was a hot July day and Charlotte had intended to spend the morning on her correspondence, but when she heard her sisters clatter down the stairs and the dogs whining in the kitchen, a pang of longing for the outdoors tore at her chest. The morning sun angled through the east windows, warming the stone floor, and the garden was throbbing with birdsong. She quickly put away her writing desk and dashed into the hall as they were heading out the front door.

"Wait," she pleaded. "I'll come with you."

Emily whirled around. Every fiber in her body yearned to be out the door. "Hurry, then. If you dawdle we'll go without you."

Charlotte paused on the stairs and called, "Did you pack lunch?"

Anne said, "We have enough for you. Just hurry and change."

It had been weeks since they'd been on a ramble together. Charlotte always had something to do around the house or was busy replying to letters from friends and publishers. Now, with Keeper and Flossy trotting in the vanguard, the three of them headed up the lane, nearly colliding with a trio of boys who were racing toward the church school, shouting taunts at one another, their arms churning and jackets flapping. A cap flew off, and one boy dashed back to get it.

Charlotte stopped to pick it up and handed it to him. He snatched it out of her hand, muttered a breathless thanks, then sped into the school.

Charlotte watched him go with a bemused smile. "Poor child. Confined to a schoolroom on a day like this."

Emily and the dogs had already outdistanced them, and Charlotte and Anne fell into a single file on the path.

They came to a stile at the top of the field, and they gathered up their skirts to squeeze through. Emily was already far ahead on the path, her arms swinging freely in a carefree gait. She came to a muddy puddle and leapt over it, flashing a single flannel petticoat beneath a limp gingham dress that had gone out of style when she was twelve. On her head she wore a ratty straw cottage bonnet. The effect was one of absolute disregard for her appearance.

And yet, Emily was deeply content with her lot in life. She had at her doorstep the only thing of interest to her: the natural world of the moorlands. Her material needs were simple, and she was oblivious to the restraints and frustrations that consumed Charlotte. Like a creature perfectly adapted to its function, Emily accommodated her daily domestic routine to her vibrant inner life and the recreation of her visionary world. She kneaded bread with a book of German poetry propped on the kitchen table and created stories in her head while she swept the floor or made the beds. Others might find her life rather cold and sad, but Emily, who knew bliss, was not one whit to be pitied.

Charlotte—who had such a profound desire to please—had always been in awe of this inflexible and extraordinary sister. On this bright July morning, watching her disappear over the hill, Charlotte thought there was nothing on this earth as near and dear to her as Emily.

Anne was wheezing, and they paused to rest on a low stone wall.

"Did you tell Martha we were all going out?"

"Yes."

"I do hope Branwell doesn't pull anything foolish."

"She'll keep an eye on him," Anne reassured.

"Do you think he's heard the news about Mrs. Robinson planning to marry again?"

Anne exchanged frequent letters with the Robinson girls. They knew very little about Branwell's sufferings and cared even less. But they were very fond of their old governess and shared all the details about their family life with her, including the fact that their mother expected to marry a certain Sir George Scott—once old Lady Scott died.

"I don't believe so," Anne replied. "I certainly wouldn't tell him."

"No, certainly not. He's quite miserable enough as it is."

Anne's black-and-white spaniel had rounded back and now stood before them on the path, wagging his body excitedly, begging his mistress to hurry along.

"Yes, Flossy. We're coming." She stood, drawing a deep breath. "Let's go on now."

They struck on up the hill, following the narrow trail, winding between the great swells of tall grasses moving like waves with the shifting winds. The heath was in bloom, carpeting the treeless tops in undulating patterns of pinkish-purple flowers. Low stone walls cut across the slopes and the dells, dividing the pastures into a mosaic of coppers, browns, and greens that ravished the eye with color. Moorland sheep grazed everywhere.

When they reached the top of the knoll, they saw Emily waiting on the next rise, her bonnet in her hand and her loose hair whipping around her face. She turned and, seeing them, waved a wide arc with her arms, like a seaman flagging his crew at the discovery of a new world.

They stopped to rest at the Meeting of the Waters and ate their apples in the cool spray of the waterfall. As children they had played here often with Branwell. The moss-covered rocks, the leafy bracken, and rushing waters had set the scenes for their little plays; in these nooks, toy soldiers had been transformed into the heroes of their imagination, epic battles had been won and armadas sunk amid the tadpoles and the bees.

Charlotte stretched out on her back on cool moss. "Let's stay here," she said.

"Don't be such a lump," Emily sighed with exasperation. "We've barely left home."

"But I'm quite content." She turned her head to her sister. "And you, I see, are restless."

Anne said, "Whether we stay or move on, it matters not to me. It is a perfect day and we're together."

"There's a marsh not far from here. There must be wildflowers in bloom," Emily said.

" 'Not far,' " Charlotte laughed. "That means it's a good two hours away."

Anne rose to her feet, her bonnet hanging loose on her back as she scanned the distant horizon. "Or we might try to go as far as Dove Moor. I think that is my favorite place in all the world. It's so strange, a man might think himself on the moon."

Anne was in thrall to the lay of the land; its variations never ceased to amaze her, the knolls, cloughs, and crags, every rise and fall opening a new vista. Emily could easily lose herself in the smallest marvel of God's creation—the plumage of a linnet, or the fine veins of a bilberry leaf.

"Then on we shall go," Charlotte said, as she stood and shook out her skirts. "Lead on, Captain."

They gathered up the cloths from their lunch and set off toward the west with Emily in the lead. At their flanks trotted the two dogs. Emily could have led them to the ends of the earth and they would have followed; had she been a man, she would have taken them there.

The month of August came in wet and wild, with frequent thunderstorms that swelled the rivers and creeks. September broke through with a long stretch of hot and cloudless days, drying out the fields and elevating the general tenor of life in the village.

Arthur had hoped to steal a few hours of trout fishing up on the moors that day, but his visit to a widow in Gauger's Croft took longer than he had anticipated. The old lady suffered from arthritis and an inflammation of the eyes, so that she sat in her cramped, dark cottage all day long with her cat on her lap, smoking her pipe, waiting for her son to come home from the fields. Arthur thought her mind had begun to wander a little, from loneliness and old age. But today, her complaints were more spiritual than physical. She was afraid she was losing her faith, and the fact that she could no longer read her Bible distressed her. Arthur pulled a chair up beside her and opened the Bible to one of her favorite scriptures, but the passage seemed to trouble rather than soothe her. Arthur suspected that one of the Methodists had been to visit her and had planted all sorts of doubts in the old woman's mind. He did his best to reassure her that she had committed no unpardonable sins and was still living in the grace of God, but the more he tried to woo her out of her melancholy, the more despondent she became.

As the shadows darkened and Arthur's hopes of trout fishing began to fade, he felt his patience wane. When a neighbor stopped in, Arthur took advantage of the intrusion to jump to his feet, and with a warning to the old widow to steer clear of the dissenters, he picked up his prayer book and hat and fled for the door.

As he hurried through the dark, damp tunnel to Main Street, he was feeling glum and dissatisfied with himself. These villagers were a baffling people, full of peculiar notions and superstitions, with crude habits and customs they were unwilling to change. There were small-landed proprietors grown rich from their tenants and mills, who would not part with a penny's worth of education for their sons, even less for their daughters. They put their children to work in their own mills, and then they vilified Arthur when he condemned the practice from the pulpit.

For all the good Arthur had done through his work in the church school, by his efforts to entice even the poorest in his parish to his classrooms, there were some who bore grudges against him for one thing or another. They didn't like it that he tried to put an end to the cockfighting and campaigned to close the whist gambling houses. He was too conscientious and principled for their tastes, and it seemed he was always crusading against the superficial evils of the village.

But those who knew him well—and it was primarily the poorest in the village—held him in high esteem. The twelve-year-old girl to whose house he now directed his steps was one of those. Hannah Grace, who had once been one of his most earnest pupils, was dying of consumption. She lived with her parents and seven brothers and sisters in a two-room stone cottage wedged like an afterthought at the end of Lodge Street. Lodge Street was not much better than the slums of Gauger's Croft. The air smelled of wool grease and offal from the slaughterhouse across the way, and there was always a stench wafting in from the middens on the corner where they dumped their night soil and animal refuse. Arthur had never quite gotten used to the squalor and the smell of poverty, and he figured he probably never would. But not once had it stopped him from his duties. It was a constant reminder to him of the hard choices of the poor.

As he passed the Black Bull he heard a trumpet blast out a few notes. Upstairs, where the curtains were blowing in the breeze, the brass band was setting up for a rehearsal. There was the sound of laughter and Arthur smiled, thinking what a fine day it was, worthy of laughter, and that he might still be able to make it to the stream.

At the end of Lodge Street, he noticed a figure sitting on the steps of Hannah Grace's cottage; he thought it might be one of Hannah's brothers, but then he recognized the carroty hair and the spectacles. Branwell was slumped on the bottom step, staring into the depths of his hat. He gave a startled look as Arthur approached and then broke into a coughing fit that racked his thin frame; when the coughing ceased, he started to stand, but he was too exhausted and sat back down on the step and lifted his face in a weak smile.

"Nicholls," he said lightly. "My good man. They said you might be around."

Arthur was surprised at the sincerity of his tone; in the past Branwell had always greeted Arthur with the swaggering sarcasm that he reserved for anyone with a clerical collar, and he avoided their company like the pestilence he believed them to be.

"Good day to you, Mr. Brontë."

"Hannah's dying, isn't she?" he asked, his small, dark eyes shiny with tears.

Arthur was stunned. He had never known Branwell to visit the sick or the poor.

"Yes, I'm afraid she is."

"I'm quite fond of Hannah Grace. She was one of my little Sunday scholars back . . . in the days of my innocence and youth . . ." He struggled for breath, then continued: ". . . when I ventured to perform a few duties incumbent on a clergyman's son." He added in a tone of self-mockery, "Although I confess I did them poorly." He clapped his hat down on his head, grabbed the iron railing, and drew himself up on unsteady legs. "Don't know if I did any good for the poor child. Although"—another gasp for air—"she seemed quite pleased to see me."

"I'm sure she was," Arthur replied kindly. "It was very thoughtful of you to visit."

Branwell seemed surprised at Arthur's sympathetic tone; it struck a chord in his fragile soul, and the thought occurred to him that he had misjudged the curate all these years.

"Do you think so?" he asked eagerly. "I read her a psalm. Seemed to cheer her a little. Would have liked to pray with her." Then he added, his voice hoarse and trembling, "But I'm not good enough. How could I pray for her? I can't even pray for myself. I think I've quite forgotten how."

He was racked again by a cough so violent that his knees gave out, and he collapsed back onto the steps. The effort seemed too much for him, and he grabbed his chest while he struggled for breath.

"Perhaps you should go home," Arthur said, bending over him anxiously. Branwell rested his head against the railing.

"They never have a kind word for me, my man."

"Oh, but I'm sure they do."

"No," Branwell said with a tired shake of the head. "I told Charlotte . . . said I was coming to visit Hannah, and she . . . she only gave me this look, like I wasn't in my right mind. Why can't they give me credit when . . . I'm trying to do some good? I'm not . . . so selfish as they think."

This long confession seemed to drain the last bit of energy from his body.

"You are indeed quite ill, sir. I trust you've seen a doctor."

Branwell managed a sickly grin. "Wheelhouse? Been hovering over me all summer. Man's an incompetent booby."

Arthur tended to agree with him and did not press the subject.

"Come," Arthur said, lifting him to his feet. "I'll help you home."

Arthur remembered having helped him home a year ago, and he was slight then, but now Arthur could feel his ribs underneath the broadcloth coat.

Branwell was so short of breath that he had to pause every few feet on the way home. They met John Brown coming out of the Bull, and John took him up Church Lane to the parsonage. Arthur turned back toward Lodge Street and Hannah Grace's cottage. By then the light was fading from the sky.

"I'm afraid the end is near. Quite near, Mr. Brontë," Dr. Wheelhouse said gravely. Patrick sat behind his desk, with Charlotte standing by his side. Emily and Anne waited in the dining room.

"But I fancied I'd seen a change, for the better." Patrick said in disbelief.

Charlotte spoke up. "Papa refers to his attitude. He's been, well, kinder. More affectionate these past few days."

The doctor sighed, "Ah, indeed—that sort of change often signals the end."

"He's dying? My boy's dying?"

Charlotte could not bear the sound of anguish in her father's voice; she laid a hand on his shoulder.

"It appears to be a general wasting away," the doctor pursued. "Between his bronchitis and the drink . . ." He shook his head sadly—a practiced gesture indicating they should resign themselves. The matter was out of his hands.

The three sisters sat side by side on the sofa, hands and arms linked, finding solace in the nearness of one other.

Charlotte said, "Poor Papa. He's in there poring over his medical books. He thinks we've been quite blind."

"In what way?" Anne asked.

"He says Branwell's been showing all the symptoms of consumption when the doctor thought it was just bronchitis. He's seen it before, with Maria and Elizabeth, and he's being quite harsh on himself for not recognizing it earlier."

"Papa thinks it's consumption?" Emily asked.

"Yes."

Emily said, "So he's dying."

None of them was prepared for this; wasted and ill though he was, none of them believed he would die.

Emily's eyes grew watery and she suddenly bolted up, snatched a book from the table, and lapsed into the rocking chair.

A gloomy silence hung in the room.

Emily sniffed loudly, and Charlotte rose to offer her a handkerchief. Emily declined with a shake of the head, preferring to wipe her nose with the back of her sleeve. Without taking her eyes from the page, she said gruffly, "If I should ever fall ill, by God, I swear that man Wheelhouse will not touch me—you must promise me—he's repulsive—and his breath reeks."

And he had a disturbing manner of glancing at them, with a lascivious smile, when their father's back was turned.

Patrick Brontë had a horror of sickrooms; he had always left his sick children to be tended by the servants, or one another. But that Saturday he pulled a chair to the side of his son's bed and kept an unbroken vigil through the day and night. For years Branwell had opposed every attempt his father had made to restore his faith in God, but that night Patrick won the battle for his son's soul.

During the evening Branwell grew utterly calm. Serene. And his eyes looked with tenderness on his father, who knelt beside the bed.

"I did love you all dearly, but I loved you most of all, Papa," he whispered. "I know you did your best, and I pray God will forgive me for all the suffering I caused you. I have wasted my life, the life you gave me, and I am deeply ashamed."

There was no mention of Lydia, not even to John Brown when the sexton came to his bedside. In those final hours it seemed that Branwell had found his center again, his home, his family, and his God.

On Sunday morning when Charlotte entered the room, she heard her brother praying for the first time in years. He seemed untroubled, and as he prayed he looked with love on his father, white head bowed in his knotty old hands, muttering his long, eloquent prayers. It was a strange duet, father and son in whispered prayer after they had been locked in battle for so many years.

When the end finally came, it was too much for the old man and he cried out, "My son! My son!" All the father's stiffness and austerity were stripped away, and he gathered his dead child in his arms and rocked him, murmuring tender words of love they had never heard him express to any living human being. Witnessing her proud father so broken and helpless was more than Charlotte could bear. She stepped forward and laid a hand on his shoulder.

"Papa," she whispered gently. "Papa, he's gone now. He's at peace."

He would not be consoled. "Leave me alone," he cried. "This is my son, my *son!*"

That afternoon the servants prepared his body. Martha, who had shaved Mr. Brontë during his blindness, now performed the task on the dead, lathering up the boy's face and wielding the razor with smooth strokes and a steady hand, taking care to leave the red side whiskers long, the way he wore them in life. Old Tabby stripped off his clothes and tenderly sponged down his arms and chest, his hands and feet, muttering to Martha about how he was the closest thing to a skeleton she'd ever seen. When he was bathed, they buttoned him into a clean shirt and his best jacket, although his clothing hung loose on his wasted body.

Once the life had gone out of him and all the unhappiness had been released, he looked handsome again, like his old self. As Charlotte stood in shock over his pale corpse, the memories of his transgressions faded swiftly. The natural affections between brother and sister, once so strong, rushed into the void in her heart and drowned her in sympathy. That she had let him depart from this world without a parting sign of her love for him was a regret she could not bear to face. She took her guilt and fled to her bedroom, and for a week she shook with a fever that had no origin in any pathology.

They had the coffin finished by nightfall, and when they brought it upstairs Martha exclaimed that Thomas must have got his measurements wrong because the wooden box was barely big enough for a child.

That night, with Branwell laid out nicely in his coffin in the dining room, mild and serene in the golden glow of lamplight, a quiet descended on the parsonage. Gone were the loud drunkenness, the raised voices, the distressing sounds of a restless man searching for a way out of his misery in a locked room in a parsonage in the middle of the night. They all lay awake listening, but the only sounds that broke their grieving silence were an occasional cough, and the wind rattling the windowpanes, and the clock ticking away the hours on the landing.

Arthur wanted very much to be a comfort to them that week, but there didn't seem to be a place where he could fit in. He came by every day, but he found few people he cared to engage in conversation. There were artists and poets from Halifax and Bradford and plenty of dissenters, and village men from Branwell's circle of drinking friends at the Black Bull. Branwell's weaknesses were common enough to the Yorkshiremen—they were hard-drinking, entertaining types, talkers rather than doers. Arthur greeted them with stiff civility and then looked in on his parson.

Mr. Brontë kept to his study that week, receiving the vicars and incumbent clergymen from all the neighboring parishes who had known him these thirty-some years. It was an older, tight-knit crowd, and they passed the time reminiscing, soothing their sorrows with anecdotes of bygone days. Arthur was himself a big talker and was well known for his love of argument in the circle of his brethren, but on this occasion he held his tongue and showed himself perfectly mild-mannered.

He looked for Charlotte but never found her. On Wednesday he found Martha in the scullery with her arms in a tub of water, scouring a heavy pot, and asked if Charlotte was ill.

"Aye, she is," Martha snapped impatiently. "Took to her bed with one of her headaches the day her brother died an' hasn't been down since. Got a fever now. An' she's the one the reverend depends on so, an' the house full of people mornin' to night, an' the funeral tea tomorrow. Miss Emily helps me out in the kitchen, but she ain't no good with the visitors, an' Miss Anne's not much better. Those girls'd rather walk on fire than chitchat to folk."

She hung the pot on a hook and shook her head. "What kind of headache hurts that long. I can't understand it. If she's grievin' it ain't no more than anyone else."

Branwell's godfather came up from Bradford to perform the burial rites. Arthur merely assisted, along with Sutcliffe Sowden, the only clergyman Branwell had ever befriended. Throughout the service Arthur strained to catch a glimpse of Charlotte's face behind her black silk bonnet, but she was too small, and seemed swallowed up in the crowd.

Chapter Thirteen

September brought forth a few last gasps of glory—bright, sun-filled days with balmy breezes—but then the dreary autumn crept in, trailing a wind that smelled sharply of cold rain. The sky hung like a canopy of gloom that barely changed its countenance from dawn to dusk, and the earth was muted to a single tone of gray the color of stone. On some mornings the village was swallowed up by fog that lifted only at noon, and darkness fell all too soon. The cold weather confined them once again to the parsonage, their lives unfolding quietly within its walls, in rooms shorn of all but the most necessary comforts by a father with spartan tastes and an eye on heaven. Coals were used sparingly; fires were lit in the study and the dining room, but they burned brightly only after nightfall or when visitors came to call.

As the days marched by, each of the sisters wrestled with her brother's ghost, and shifted around the material remains of his sad life in an effort to put order in death where there had been none in life. Branwell's amateurish portrait of his sisters, which hung on the landing next to the clock, where it might catch the eye of visitors, was taken down. Patrick carefully rolled up the canvas and stored it away in the deep drawer at the bottom of his dresser beside treasured keepsakes from his dead wife and daughters. On her hands and knees, Martha scrubbed and oiled the wood floor in Branwell's bedroom. A freshly laundered counterpane was spread on the bed and every nook and cranny thoroughly dusted, so that when they were finished the room had the same austere sheen as the rest of the parsonage, and not a trace of shame remained. Emily, as self-appointed trustee of his literary estate, had long since gathered up all his personal papers, his scattered poems, the novel fragments and childhood stories, and quietly taken them to her room.

"What should we do with it all?" Charlotte asked one evening as they sat in the dining room. Still weak from the fever that had laid her low, she sat wrapped in a heavy shawl, her feet on a stool before the fire, looking through Branwell's notebooks, which Emily had placed on her lap.

They reflected on the question, each of them turning it around in her thoughts in her own way.

Anne said, "It only reminds me of how terribly unhappy he was." She leaned into the warmth of the fire. "But he's at peace now, and we can find strength in the knowledge that God is merciful and loving. There is no sin so great that He cannot forgive."

"He wasn't always unhappy," Emily said.

Emily rose to add a few lumps of coal to the fire. She pumped the bellows until the coal burst into flame, and in the sudden flash of light Charlotte scrutinized her sister's face. Her cheeks seemed to have lost some of their plumpness. She professed only to have a touch of bronchitis, but to Charlotte's ears her cough had the deep, hollow ring that suggested something more serious. Now the physical effort of working the bellows brought on a spasm of coughing. Emily returned to her chair, pressing a handkerchief to her mouth and avoiding Charlotte's sharp, inquisitive stare.

Charlotte resisted the urge to inquire about the state of her health. It would achieve nothing. Instead, she asked, "Has Papa seen any of this?"

"No. I took everything before he had a chance to go through his room."

This was the way they always handled their father, protecting him from anything that might upset him.

"What about the letters from Mrs. Robinson?" Charlotte asked.

Anne and Emily exchanged a look.

"There weren't any letters from Mrs. Robinson."

"The ones he carried around in his pocket."

"They weren't from her. They were all from Dr. Crosby. The Robinsons' family doctor."

"They were very kind letters. But they repeatedly urged him to forget the lady—"

"She was no lady."

"Well, whatever she was, she seems to have left poor Branwell high and dry, without a word all these years. It seems that all the news he ever got from Thorp Green came from this gentleman."

Charlotte thought of the desperate letters she had written to Heger and wondered what he had done with them. His letters to her were locked away in a japanned box at the bottom of her dresser; she could not bear to destroy them, although she never took them out anymore. After all these years, the slightest evocation of his memory still elicited a dull, aching sadness.

"Well, I suppose we should burn them, all the same," Charlotte said quietly.

Emily and Anne nodded.

Anne rose. "Where are they, Emmy? I'll fetch them."

When she came back downstairs, she untied the packet and one by one, slowly and with great care, fed each letter to the fire. The flames shot up around the edges and ate up the words until nothing was left but curled gray ashes that settled lightly upon the black dust. Then Anne picked up the poker and stirred the red-hot coals so that not even a feathered trace remained.

Emily rose and bid them good night. She nudged the dogs with her toe, and they stretched and followed her to the front door. She waited in the cold draft of the doorway while the dogs sniffed the hawthorn bushes. The icy wind felt like knives in her chest, and she muffled her cough with her shawl.

Their bedroom was cold, and Charlotte was quick to finish brushing her hair and scurry to bed.

She withdrew the brass warming pan, set it on the floor, and crawled between the sheets. "I'm very worried about her," she told Anne. "She seems so tired. And her cough sounds frightful."

Anne sat on the edge of the bed, pulling on long woolen socks. "But you mustn't allude to it—she gets very annoyed."

Anne fished behind her pillow for her nightcap and pulled it down over her ears, then crawled in next to her sister.

"I'm sure it's only an inflammation."

"The cold is always hard on us. You have a cough. Papa has a cough."

"We just need to stay inside and keep warm."

Charlotte raised herself on an elbow, cupped her hand around the candle on their bedside table, and blew out the flame.

"How is she taking his death?"

"Much as you would expect. Quite serenely."

There was a silence, and then Charlotte said, "Sometimes she frightens me, with the way she holds so lightly to life. She sees too much romance in death."

"She has her strange ideas, as do we all."

The thought of losing Emily terrified Charlotte. Without Emily, the light would go out of her world, although she could not say as much to the sister who lay beside her.

A sudden gust of wind wailed down the chimney like something alive and grieving, causing them to burrow down beneath the covers and cling to each other for warmth. They were quiet for a long moment, listening to the mournful wind.

"Good night, Genius Annie," Charlotte said sleepily.

"Good night, Genius Tally," Anne replied.

Genii they had all once been, named in a flight of imagination by their brother when they were children and believed anything to be possible, when they ruled supreme over their imaginary kingdoms, and life could be created or destroyed with the stroke of a pen.

They all pressed on with their work; Emily and Charlotte were finally well advanced in their next novels. As winter approached, the east wind blew wild and keen over the frozen hills, bringing a cold that chilled the stone flags and spread from the glass panes of the windows. Emily's cough worsened, but any questions about her health met only with flashes of annoyance from her intense gray eyes.

"Why do you worry yourself about my health?" she would say, looking up from a book with a slightly contemptuous air. "One's health is such a wearisome subject."

"You're not eating," Charlotte lamented.

"None of us have an appetite. None of us are in robust health. We never have been. We are all quite used to these little annoyances."

"But your cough sounds quite serious, dearest."

"It's nothing I can't bear—and I would bear it with pleasure if you'd stop pestering me."

And bear it she would. It had always been in her nature to bear up, to refuse any appearance of weakness. She would no more seek sympathy than she would go begging in the streets, and she would certainly not keep to her bed and play the invalid. She still rose punctually at seven, dressed, and made her way to the kitchen, where she sat before the fire to put up her hair. One morning as she wound a knot at the back of her head, the comb slipped from her grasp and fell into the grate. Seeing that Emily was too weak to get out of her chair, Martha rushed in with a poker to sweep it out of the fire, but by then the teeth had burned away.

"I'll fetch ye another comb, miss. Don't ye budge," Martha said, scurrying out before Emily could sound her opposition.

Tabby rose from her chair to stir the porridge on the stove. "Ye shouldn't be up," she scolded. "Ye should be in yer bed sippin' bran tea, with a warmin' pan under yer feet."

"Have you ever known me to lie in bed all day?"

"I've never known ye so pitiful thin," Tabby answered, "lookin' like a skeleton."

When Martha came down with another comb, they watched while she coiled her hair and secured it in the back with her comb. They could see how much that small effort took out of her; her breath came short and quick.

Tabby shook her head in bewilderment and muttered, "Ye're a strange one." She ladled a little of the porridge into a bowl and set it in front of Emily.

"Now, ye'll eat some o' that if ye want to get yer strength back."

Emily stared at it with a kind of bewilderment.

"I threw in a few currants and a little honey," Tabby said gruffly, "although I don't know why I troubled, seein' as how ye got no interest in feedin' anything 'cept that dog o' yers."

Tabby deliberated over the bent head, Emily the porridge.

Then the old servant turned back to her chores, flashing a look to Martha to leave her be.

Emily swallowed only a few spoonfuls and then set the bowl on the floor for Keeper, who had been poised and alert at her side. But Tabby felt herself the victor and bragged to Charlotte that morning that she'd coerced Miss Emily into eating three spoonfuls of porridge, although in truth it had been only two.

Charlotte quickly took the cheering news to her father. He shook his head gloomily. "The disease works like this. Don't be fooled."

"How can you be so sure it's consumption?"

"I've seen it before."

Charlotte preferred her own foolishness to his bleak pessimism, and the women saw this small success as a sign of improvement. Their steps were a little lighter that morning and smiles broke out in the kitchen, all for a few bites of porridge.

Emily's fierce stoicism was a thing of wonder to Charlotte, and she danced tenderly around her sister, fearful of ruffling her feathers and trying valiantly to keep her own fears from showing too keenly on her face.

The only interference Emily welcomed was the flood of books that continued to arrive at the parsonage, gifts from Charlotte's sympathetic publisher, who wrote discreetly that they hoped the books would offer a distraction for Ellis Bell while he recovered from his cold.

In her own letters to Mr. Williams, Charlotte poured out her despair. When Mr. Williams wrote recommending homeopathy for Ellis Bell, Charlotte showed Emily the letter.

"That's very good and kind of him," Emily said with halting breath. "Do tell him . . . that Ellis Bell is most grateful for his advice. But . . . your dear Mr. Williams is quite delusional. Homeopathy is just more quackery."

"Well, perhaps Ellis would consent to see a doctor."

"Ellis will not have a doctor near him." She glanced up from the book she was reading, her eyes flashing a sober warning. "Certainly not . . . that repulsive Wheelhouse."

"We'll send for Dr. Teale from Leeds."

"Absolutely not. And should you go . . . behind my back and send for him anyway, Ellis . . . will refuse to see him and the poor fool will slog all the way here in the snow for nothing . . . and undoubtedly charge Father an exorbitant fee for his trouble."

To have body or mind exposed was inconceivable to Emily, and Charlotte sometimes thought there was more than rational skepticism behind her resistance, that it must be grounded in some irrational fear. But it did no good to try to penetrate her thoughts or comprehend her strange ways.

"For my sake, please?"

Emily's eyes remained on her book.

"I cannot bear to see you so ill."

Emily turned a page.

"I could not bear to lose you." Charlotte's voice faltered.

"Oh, hush. Must you be so morose?"

"Perhaps if you saw the sister I see, you would be inclined to treat her a little less harshly."

Emily's breath was now coming in short, uneasy pants. "You see me . . . as you would like me to be."

"I see what you might become. An author who is just coming into her own—a woman who has just started to exert her extraordinary powers—"

"Come now, after I'm gone . . ." She paused to catch her breath. "Do you honestly think . . . anyone will ever notice . . . this obscure life of mine?"

"You have written a powerful novel."

"Which everyone . . . views . . . with horror."

"What of your poems?"

"My little rhymes." She coughed, a hoarse, racking sound. "Sold all of two copies."

"You could be a great essayist. Like the American Mr. Emerson."

"I shall gladly . . . leave . . . essays to Mr. Emerson and his ilk."

"Please, Emmy. Just a simple visit from a doctor. A good one from Leeds or Manchester. If he confirms it's nothing serious, then I promise I shall leave you in peace."

Emily's expression hardened. "No doctor."

"Must you always be so unyielding?" Charlotte cried.

"My fate is . . . in God's hands. I am . . . content to leave it there."

Then, suddenly softening when she saw the anguish in her sister's eyes, she said simply, "I'm not going to die."

Charlotte believed her.

One day when Martha was doing the washing, she came across a handkerchief coated with dried bloody phlegm. With a wooden stick she fished it out of the tub of boiling water, dropped it onto the washboard, and ran to find Charlotte. It was indeed Emily's—her initials were embroidered in faded thread in the corner.

"Ye need to tell the master," Tabby said.

"No. He worries endlessly about our health as it is. And still, it may prove to be only an inflammation."

"But ye need to find a way to help the girl, miss, since she won't help herself."

"I know that, Tabby," Charlotte snapped. "She forces me to neglect her, and I cannot bear it."

Tabby shook her head pitifully. "Always been a stubborn child. She was never so 'appy as when we was all scolding 'er at once, and 'er defying us. Always liked to bait us. She knew she'd win. She knew she'd get 'er way."

At this, Charlotte's face clouded, and she sat down on a stool in the laundry room and broke into tears.

Finally, deceptively, Charlotte resorted to consultations by correspondence. She sat down and wrote a detailed account of Emily's symptoms: the shallow panting, the sharp, stabbing pains in the side, the flesh wasting away before their eyes. If it was consumption, might she still be saved? Was there any hope? Were there cures that might be pressed upon an unwilling patient? The physicians in London and Leeds sent back their replies, full of weighty words that signified authority and knowledge, much of it as difficult to decipher as an oracle's utterings. One sent a prescription for a serum, which Charlotte quickly obtained from the chemist and left in a vial on Emily's bedside table, along with a note indicating instructions for its dosage. The vial, unopened, was shuffled around from bedroom to kitchen table to mantel, where it sat until Martha got tired of dusting around it and stored it away in their medicine chest.

Even as she grew steadily worse, Emily refused to alter her daily routine; she bore up without a word of complaint, and so the illness swept her along. The harder she fought it, the more quickly it advanced on her. She answered the burning pain in her side not with a gasp and a sharp cry, but with the stiffening of her jaw while she swept the hallway or cleared the dishes from the table. She pushed herself to the limit while the disease gnawed at her insides and spat her out. As the diarrhea worsened, she had to make her way on feeble legs a dozen times a day through rain and snow to the privy in the backyard. Once the wind was so fierce that it knocked her down and Martha found her sprawled helpless on the frozen ground. Sometimes the privy door froze shut, and she would have to stand in the cutting wind, shaking with fever, while one of her sisters pried it open. There was not one indignity that could strip away her supreme command of her spirit. As her body failed, her harsh indifference became a thing of wonder. Charlotte watched her for a sign of panic or despair, but Emily's cool eyes never betrayed so much as a flash of weakness.

By the time the tuberculosis had reached its latter stages, they had grown accustomed to the strange ritual of acting as if nothing were wrong with her. At dinner and tea, they orchestrated their conversations around the sound of her deep, hollow cough, which tore at their hearts. They looked on as she went about the few daily chores she could still perform, although she had become so emaciated that her wool shawl seemed like a crushing burden on her frail shoulders. She still rose and dressed every day, fed the dogs, and sat in the rocking chair sewing on buttons or darning socks. When she became too weak to sew, she read. When she could no longer hold up a book, Charlotte or Anne read to her. Keeper never left her side and padded anxiously behind wherever she went, with the kind of mute and mysterious comprehension of death that only animals possess.

Few people outside the parsonage and its regular visitors were aware of Emily's condition. Arthur had not laid eyes on her in months, and it was on Keeper's account that he was admitted to the heart of the home and saw with his own eyes that she was dying.

It was a wintry afternoon rendered even more miserable by a sharp wind and stinging sleet. Arthur had just come from a deathbed and was plodding up the snow-covered lane to find John Brown and give him instructions for yet another name to be engraved on the Sugden family tombstone. It wasn't the deaths that disturbed him so much, but the misery of the living, and he was pondering God's baffling will when he heard Keeper's bark—a relentless yelp that warned of strangers. With a good hold on his hat, he lifted his head and squinted through the driving sleet. A horse-drawn wagon had pulled up beside the chipping shed, and when Arthur approached he found that the drivers had stepped inside to take shelter from the wind. They stood glowering at him with their gloved hands thrust deep into the pockets of their heavy coats, stamping their sheepskin boots, their caps pulled down over their ears, their faces red and raw from the icy wind. Arthur could see that they were waiting for John, and he figured they were out of temper at not being able to make their delivery and get on their way. He had not even noticed their dogs until he heard the growling coming from the beneath the wagon. Out of the corner of his eye he saw Keeper stalk across the lane; then

Martha came running out of the back kitchen crying his name. Within a flash the three dogs were at one another, a fury of vicious snarls and growls in a flurry of fur and snow. With bared teeth they went for the eyes, the neck, and the chest, and Arthur could see that old Keeper was no match for the two of them, tough and weathered though he was.

"Hey there!" he shouted to the carriers. "Hey! Call off your dogs!" But they only watched from the shed, grinning from ear to ear like they were proud of how their dogs could draw blood. Martha had advanced into the lane, flapping her apron and shouting at Keeper to come away, and Charlotte was calling from the yard, but they knew there was nothing they could do. Arthur was so sickened by the men and their cruelty, and seeing the women helpless and the old dog being mauled, that he fairly lost his temper. He threw down his prayer book and let loose a string of curses at the carriers that quite shocked them all. He grabbed the feed bucket from the back of the wagon and marched into the fray. He knew he'd get bitten, and he only hoped he could distract the other dogs long enough to draw Keeper away. Arthur managed to beat off one of the dogs, but Keeper—his eyes swimming with blood—was fighting blind and had his teeth sunk well into the black jowls of the other. It was only when Arthur crept close enough to catch the old dog's attention that Keeper recognized a voice of authority and loosened his grip a little. By then the carriers had come out of the shed and stepped in to give him a hand. Arthur took Keeper by the collar and escorted him, bloodied and limping, back to the parsonage.

Arthur was given a hero's welcome in the kitchen, although the bulk of sympathy went to the old dog. Martha and Tabby and Charlotte worried over them, fussing about with pans of boiling water and clean rags. Arthur had a bad gash in his hand, but he was more concerned about a cut in Keeper's chest that wouldn't stop bleeding. Arthur knelt down on the floor with the dog and got him to lie still while he sponged away enough of the blood to find the wound.

"Here it is. Nothing so big that it won't heal. If he can keep it clean with his tongue, it'll be all right."

Keeper lifted his swollen head and licked the curate's hand.

"Well, now." Arthur smiled, patting the dog gently. "I'll take that as ample payment for my troubles."

They were all touchy and on the verge of tears these days, and Arthur's gesture of kindness was sorely needed in a home that had seen so much sorrow. Tabby turned away so that they wouldn't see her tears, and Martha would have thrown her arms around his neck and hugged him shamelessly were it not for the presence of Charlotte. They knew how she spoke so harshly of the curate, and they would not do anything to cross her.

Arthur was suddenly aware of their eyes on him; he rose and self-consciously smoothed back his wind-blown hair. "Well, ladies, I don't see anything else. Those wounds should heal up if you keep him still."

"You'll have a nice cup of tea before you go, Mr. Nicholls," Charlotte said unexpectedly.

Arthur's first reaction was to decline, and he almost had the words out of his mouth, but then he changed his mind. "I would be very grateful for a cup of tea just now, Miss Brontë." When he looked up, his face burst into that broad smile of his that lit up a room, but Charlotte had turned to the cabinet to get down the tea things and didn't notice.

"We are the ones who are grateful," Charlotte said quietly. "Emily would have been out there in the fray herself, were she well enough."

"I don't doubt that for a minute," Arthur said, shaking his head in a gesture of respectful awe. "I remember once watching Miss Emily traipse across a field right in front of the Heatons' bull, and that is one bad-tempered creature. Well, she crossed right under his nose. And he respectfully let her pass. She seemed to know he wouldn't harm her. She does indeed have a way with animals."

Arthur noticed then that Martha was wiping back tears, and he wondered what he'd just walked in on, because it couldn't be just about the old dog.

Charlotte said, "I apologize for serving you in the kitchen, but Papa is over at Oxenhope for a meeting."

"Here's your hat . . . an' your prayer book, sir," Martha said, setting both on the table behind him. "I'm sorry, but the cover got a little wet from the snow," she added timidly.

It was just the kind of thing that would put him out of sorts: a damaged prayer book, a tarnished chalice, a hat worn during service—any little thing that might imply disrespect to the church. But he only glanced at it and said, "It's a prayer book. It can be replaced. This old warrior here is one of a kind."

A strange sound cut through his talk, a rapid, rasping breath. He turned to find Emily paused in the doorway, lost in the folds of a heavy shawl. Her face had the appearance he had come to recognize in consumptives, the skin clinging to the bones, with no flesh to give contour or shape, so that she was hardly recognizable.

Arthur pushed back the bench and rose to his feet. "He's all right, Miss Emily. He'll be as good as new in a few days."

Emily fixed him with a dim and indifferent gaze, as if she didn't recognize him. Keeper, detecting her presence, lifted his head. With great effort, he got to his feet and limped painfully toward her, wagging his tail. Slowly, weighing every movement against the reserve of strength left in her body, she turned and shuffled out of the room with Keeper trailing behind her.

Charlotte set a pitcher of milk on the table and then turned away.

"I do believe her inflammation is subsiding," she said, "and all these symptoms will presently be leaving her, and she'll be gaining back her strength. I am not so gloomy as my father; he has seen this affliction in our family before, and he warns me that I must not hope—but I cannot renounce hope. I cannot. I cannot."

She spoke with a steady, mild voice, but she was trembling so much that when she turned toward him with cup and saucer, it rattled in her hand. He reached for it and took it from her, and this time he caught her eye. For once she did not avoid his gaze or cut him with an impatient and curt remark. It was not so much his countenance as it was his entire bearing that spoke of a tenderness, a willingness to shoulder the burden of her particular grief, an offer of understanding; it broke through her taut and stiff reserve and softened her like a beam of sunlight on a harsh winter day.

In the hours leading up to her death that Tuesday in December, as she sat in her chair before the fire, too weak to even lift her head, Emily admitted at last to her mortality. With a breath that rattled up through the hole in her lungs, she whispered that she would see a doctor, if they would be so good as to call him. Charlotte immediately dashed off a note and Martha hurried down to the Bull to find a messenger, but they all knew it was too late. Her father lifted her in his arms and carried her up the stairs to her room, laying her gently in her narrow bed positioned beneath the window that looked over the valley and the moors rising to the east. It was past noon and the sun had already moved to the south, but she turned her head so that her gray eyes fixed on the weak wintry light spilling into the room. There was scant consciousness left in her mind, but in the last terrible moments of suffering she was dimly aware of her family and the servants around her, and Keeper curled on the rug beside her bed, and the pressure of Charlotte's hand in her hand, the fine, delicate fingers intertwined firmly with her own.

Just three days before Christmas, they buried Emily in the family vault beneath the aisle in the church, beside her brother and her mother, her sisters and her aunt. Keeper accompanied them into the church, into the family pew, and lay at their feet while Arthur conducted the service. After the funeral tea when the few guests had gone home, the old dog padded upstairs to her bedroom and lay there, whining softly, until nightfall. When the moon rose high in the cold December sky and she didn't return, he set up a pitiful howl that was carried off into the night on the keening wind.

As Charlotte lay next to Anne, listening to the dog's wail, she wondered how it was possible to feel so empty and still be alive. Finally she rose, lit her candle, and turned for consolation not to the Lord's Word but to Emily's writing, to the final lines of *Wuthering Heights*.

> I sought, and soon discovered, the three head-stones on the slope next the moor—the middle one gray, and half buried in the heath—Edgar Linton's only harmonized by the turf, and moss creeping up its foot—Heathcliff's still bare.
>
> I lingered round them, under that benign sky; watched the moths fluttering among the heath and hare-bells; listened to the soft wind breathing through the grass; and wondered how any one could ever imagine unquiet slumbers for the sleepers in that quiet earth.

Chapter Fourteen

By the time Christmas Day arrived, Arthur needed relief from the gloomy atmosphere of Church Lane. It was not only the parsonage that was affected but his own lodging as well. Branwell's death had touched off a tremor of marital discontent, for Mrs. Brown had never approved of the way her husband had encouraged the young man's drinking habits—in a parson's son, of all people—and she poured a good deal of blame on John Brown's plate every night along with his meat and potatoes. The sexton had begun to find his suppers unpalatable and now took them down at the Black Bull, coming home late and drunk. Martha, desolate over Emily's death, dashed across the lane several times a day to seek consolation from her mother and sisters. The good-natured gossip and laughter were gone, and the kitchen of Sexton House was a glum place, with the women always swollen-eyed or in tears. Even the Haworth Band had slipped quietly past the Brontës' windows on their Christmas Eve caroling tour, thinking the parson would take little joy in songs celebrating the birth of a child when he had just lost two of his own.

Arthur was a man of deep and strong attachments that found their expression not in words but in loyalty, duty, and care. He had been deeply concerned about the reclusive old reverend sitting in silence in the cold gloom of his parlor following his son's death, and at the end of every day, even when exhausted to the point of collapse by his wide-reaching parish duties, Arthur made it a point to call on him. He listened to the father pour out his confusion, his disappointments and regrets, and Arthur in his loyalty buried all these confidences in his heart; never a word was leaked outside the walls of the parsonage. Arthur had come to accept that his role in the family was as a sort of inferior appendage, one that performed a host of needed functions but was never accepted as a worthy or an equal. It was expected that he bend and sway with the winds that blew through their lives, but the inner workings of his heart were of no concern to them. Without a family of his own, Arthur had often wished to unburden his heart to this clergyman he so respected and admired, but for all his virtues Patrick Brontë remained a vain, self-centered man who could not see a farthing beyond the issues and concerns that occupied his own thoughts. He was ignorant of how Arthur had grieved for the family, how he had knelt on the hard stone of the cold church late at night and prayed so fervently, first for the redemption of the son, then that God might spare the daughter; how the sight of Charlotte weeping as her sister's body was lowered into the vault wrenched the heart from his chest.

Arthur had been invited to Christmas dinner at the home of his friend Joseph Grant and his wife, Sarah, and immediately after the Christmas service he set off for Oxenhope in the whirling snow, head cleaving the wind, the pockets of his heavy coat weighted with oranges for his host. Joseph Grant had proved himself to be a shameless pragmatist who saw no need to spend much time in the service of the poor if they could be of no service to him. He had turned all this snobbism to good cause and had raised enough money from the wealthy landowners to build a church in Oxenhope, of which he now had the living.

His wife, Sarah, imported from Essex, was stout, dimpled, and refreshingly good-humored. She was also petty-minded, with an immense capacity for small talk, and perfectly submissive to her husband in thought, word, and deed. Lacking any facility for forming her own judgments, she had a habit, whenever he spoke, of chiming in at every pause, repeating his comments with the brainless mimicry of a parrot.

Arthur and his friend Sutcliffe Sowden shared many a chuckle at their expense, but Arthur did indeed envy them their happiness. The

Grants welcomed Arthur and all the bachelor clergymen to their home with genuine warmth, and Sarah esteemed it her sacred duty to play matchmaker to the unmarried curates. With each parting she would take Arthur aside in the passage and whisper, "We will find you a good wife, Mr. Nicholls. You may trust me on that."

That Christmas Day, Arthur warmed himself before a cheerful fire with a mug of spiced ale in his hand and laughed more easily than he had done in months. Sarah Grant had taken great pains with the vicarage, decorating it lavishly with garlands of holly and candelabras, and throwing spices on the fire to scent the rooms. They sang joyous carols and feasted on roast goose and applesauce, followed by Christmas pudding and coffee, and Mrs. Grant presided over it all with a great cheerful bustle that brought her normally florid complexion to a feverish radiance. Arthur could not imagine Charlotte Brontë bringing this kind of warmth and affection to any man's life, and yet, for all her cold and proud ways, his thoughts were forever fixed on her.

Arthur was pressed to stay the night, and after the other guests had departed, the conversation turned again to the sobering tragedies in Haworth.

"Oh, it is sad," Sarah said as she sat stroking her cat, "Mr. Brontë losing both his children within a few months."

"He trusts in God," Arthur replied, "and God has sustained him. They are all quite calm. Although I confess it's the younger sister who gives most cause for concern now."

"You mean Miss Anne?"

"She's very weak and has lost a good deal of weight."

Sarah started. "Oh goodness, you don't mean to say that she's consumptive as well?"

"I can't say. I dare not ask." He hesitated and then added, "Miss Brontë is most distressed, but she contains her grief most admirably. I have always had the impression that she was more attached to Miss Emily than Miss Anne."

Joseph Grant raised a lazy eyebrow. "I had to sit next to that girl once at a Whitsuntide tea—one of the most awkward moments I've ever experienced."

"Do you mean Miss Emily, dearest?"

"Indeed I do. Try as I might, I couldn't get a word out of her. I had the distinct impression she was looking down her nose at me. Most rude. I made sure I never got stuck sitting next to her again."

"I don't believe anyone really knew her—outside her family," Arthur said.

"I doubt there was anything to know."

"I respectfully disagree with you, Mrs. Grant. She was proud and reclusive, but I think she was quite an exceptional young lady."

"Ah, as usual. Arthur comes to the defense of the Misses Brontë," Joseph teased.

"Exceptional in what regard?" his wife asked.

Arthur could not say—it was an impression he'd often had, on the rare occasions when he had exchanged a word with her. "I've heard the Heatons of Ponden Hall speak of her with admiration. Apparently she read a good deal and borrowed from their library."

"But you, Mr. Nicholls? What shall you say in her defense?"

He was thinking of the times he had walked through the garden gate to the strains of piano music. Several times as he'd glanced through the parlor window he had caught a glimpse of Emily from the back, her lean figure bent over the keyboard and her elbows bobbing in the air, but she had always vanished by the time the door was opened. Upon entering the parlor he would find the small cabinet piano shut up and sheets of music hastily swept into a pile on the chair.

He said simply, and with a trace of sadness, "She played the piano with great feeling."

"Ah, well, that is to be expected from any educated young woman, is it not?"

"If I speak simply, it does not imply that her talent was mediocre. I was never graced with a performance, but I heard snatches here and there and it was quite impressive. She studied in Brussels, you know, and was quite fond of the German composers. I once had the privilege of catching a few strains of an aria from Handel's *Messiah*. It was a summer day and the window was open, and I recognized it and stopped to listen." He paused, remembering how Keeper had heard the crunch of his steps on the gravel walk and started whining, and the music had abruptly stopped. "What little I heard was no less than brilliant."

Mrs. Grant suddenly leaned forward with a gossipy gleam in her eye. "Mr. Grant tells me you allowed that dog of theirs into the church for the service."

Her husband scowled. "I was ready to have a word with the old parson when I heard that he intended to do it, but Arthur here dissuaded me."

"Mr. Nicholls!" she scolded with a wide grin. "That is so unlike you!"

"I daresay the dog was better behaved than many of our parishioners," Arthur smiled. "Didn't make a sound throughout the service."

"Oh, listen to him, Mr. Grant. Where are all his scruples about the dignity of the church?"

"Scruples aside, I certainly kept my distance from the beast," Joseph frowned. "I remember when he nearly took a chunk out of my backside."

"Oh yes, dogs are terribly unpredictable, we find. They can be quite ferocious." She stroked her cat lovingly. "Well, I shall leave you two to sort out the truly important matters." She gently set the puss on the floor and rose, smoothing her skirt. As she passed her husband, she laid a hand on his shoulder and said with a bright smile, "We need to find him a wife."

Chapter Fifteen

Charlotte had been at the upstairs window with her opera glasses for nearly twenty minutes when she finally caught sight of the gig coming up the road from Keighley. Even at a distance she could recognize it by the peculiar lope of the old bay, drawing the only conveyance Haworth had to offer; she had paid to have it pick up Ellen at the train station in Keighley and deliver her to the parsonage, a luxury she had never been able to offer her friend in the past.

Charlotte snatched up her shawl and hurried downstairs to wait outside at the gate. The roads were hard and icy, and Charlotte had been worried that the weather might have prevented her friend from visiting.

Ellen alighted from the gig, her eyes big pools of worry.

"She's very thin," Charlotte cried over the wind. "It will be a shock. But you mustn't say anything. She's trying so hard to be brave."

Ellen followed Charlotte upstairs to the guest room, which had last been Branwell's. She removed her bonnet and glanced around, thinking how lonely it must be now, with all of them gone but Charlotte and Anne. After the driver had deposited her trunk and been dismissed, she turned around and saw how bravely Charlotte was fighting back the tears.

"I'm so glad you've come."

Ellen took her friend in her arms, and Charlotte broke down in sobs.

Ellen caressed the soft brown hair. "I wish you'd sent for me earlier," she whispered.

"Emily wouldn't have it. You know how she is."

"Yes, I know."

"But Anne was so eager for you to come. She considers you a true friend, not just mine but hers as well." Charlotte dabbed at her nose with a handkerchief.

"And so I am."

"She is so quiet about losing Emily. She never says a word, but you can see it in her face."

"Will she see a doctor?"

Charlotte nodded. "Oh, yes. We've written to a specialist in Leeds, and he's coming out tomorrow to examine her. She talks freely about her condition, and that's a great relief to us."

"How is your father?"

Charlotte shook her head. "Not well. And he worries so. Every day he asks about my health. I must be strong, for both of them."

"And I am here to help you."

Charlotte squeezed her hand. "Oh, dear, you're still so cold from your journey. Come, we must get you downstairs to the fire."

Anne was sitting in the parlor, in the chair where Emily once sat, but she was cheerful and in good spirits. Charlotte had warned Ellen on the stairs, "Don't be fooled into believing she's not very ill." Anne had begun to waste away, like the others, and Charlotte could now recognize the signs of gradual decline.

Ellen noticed small but distinct changes in the home: the fire in the dining room burned brightly, and Ellen knew it must have been stoked all day long, for the room was comfortable and warm. At tea, they were served Martha's special spice cake and thick slices of cold meats; there was a choice of marmalade or blueberry preserves. Anne had little appetite, but she clearly enjoyed herself, and there was a festiveness to the occasion that was not entirely forced.

Finally, Anne looked up with a smile, and with a quick glance at Charlotte she said, "We have something to share with you."

"Yes," Charlotte confirmed. "But you must swear to secrecy."

Ellen's eyes lighted on Charlotte. "You're getting married."

"I am not getting married," Charlotte stated calmly, "but you must swear not to reveal to anyone what we say today—not to Ann or Mercy, not to your brothers. Even though you will be sorely tempted at times."

Ellen nodded solemnly. "I swear."

Charlotte neatly folded her napkin and rose. Drawing a fob of keys from her skirt pocket, she unlocked a cabinet and took down a small stack of books, which she set on the table before her friend.

"It was Emily's wish that we remain anonymous. It was the only condition under which she agreed to publish. She was most insistent, and I could not break her trust. But now . . ."

Anne explained, "Mine is *Agnes Grey*. It's the last volume in the set with Emily's *Wuthering Heights*. And there's a copy of my second novel as well. We know you have *Jane Eyre*, but we did not think you had my books and Emily's, and we did want you to have them."

Dear Ellen, kept in the dark for so long, quite literally beamed with delight. Her hand shot to her mouth to conceal a gasp.

"Oh, my!" she thrilled, awash in emotion, remembering all of Charlotte's strident denials, yet conscious of the great privilege to be let in on the secret at last. Her eyes darted back and forth between the sisters.

"But you insisted it was not true!"

"We had no choice, Nell," Charlotte pleaded. "You must forgive us."

"We tried very hard not to lie outright," Anne hurried to add. "Charlotte and I were both very careful with what we wrote to you."

"She's right, Nell. Go back and read my letters to you. If you have them still."

"Oh, I do!" She turned to Anne. "So you're Acton Bell?"

Anne answered with a flushed smile, "I am."

She turned to Charlotte. "And you are Currer."

Charlotte gave a sheepish nod.

"I was right, all along," she said with a beam of smug satisfaction. "I was sure you wrote *Jane Eyre*. I knew it had to be you. I could tell from the stories you used to tell me about that awful school." Her smile widened. "And how could you think I wouldn't recognize your writing, Charlotte, after all the letters you've written to me over the years? It was your voice in that book."

"You will forgive me, I know. I had no choice."

"Joe Taylor is convinced you're Currer Bell."

"Yes, I know. He visited us last year. Some trumped-up excuse about asking my opinion about schools in Brussels, but it was really just a fishing expedition."

"Does Mary know?" Ellen asked.

Ellen had always been jealous of Charlotte's friendship with Mary Taylor, and Charlotte replied evasively: "I've written to her, but of course the letters take months to reach New Zealand."

"What about Branwell? Did he ever know?"

Charlotte shook her head sadly. "We never told him. We thought it would only make him more wretched than he was. Although, I confess there were times when he made certain comments that I found curious. I sometimes imagined he was looking at me as though I had betrayed him."

"You mustn't harass yourself so," Anne said to comfort her.

"And your father?"

"Papa didn't know until last spring. He was the only one we let in on the secret."

"But there was so much scandal! What did he say to that?"

"I give him only a carefully diluted account of everything. He gets just enough information to please him and no more, certainly nothing that would upset him. I should not like to see his peace of mind disturbed on my account."

Anne said, "We keep our lives as authors very much to ourselves and out of his sight."

"We don't bring it up to him more than once a month."

Ellen said, "Well, that's no different than it ever was. You've always sheltered him from the storms in your lives."

Charlotte added, "Anne and I have decided that we still wish our authorship to remain anonymous. Our anonymity has brought us the freedom to speak truthfully, and we should not wish to lose it. So you must keep our secret."

"Oh, I shall!" Then the thrill of it took hold of Ellen and she bubbled with delight. "Oh, you've done it, haven't you?" she said, pressing her hands to her chest. "This was always your dream. To live off your literary labors. To be independent."

The evening was quiet, as were all the evenings at Haworth parsonage in the winter, when daylight was so rare and darkness so deep. Anne grew feverish and her cough worsened, but the shadow of Emily's death and the specter of another were kept in abeyance by an abundance of candles, a brightly burning fire, and the presence of a friend.

That evening Charlotte invited Ellen to read to them.

"But you don't like the way I read," Ellen said sweetly, pausing to look up from her embroidering. She turned to Anne, hoping to draw a smile. "Once, when we were in school together, I tried to read a little poetry to her and she plugged up her ears."

Anne did indeed break a smile, and Charlotte laughed.

"Here," Charlotte said, thrusting the first volume of *Mary Barton* into Ellen's lap. "My publisher sent it to me. It was published anonymously, but the author has been revealed. A lady from Manchester by the name of Elizabeth Gaskell."

"Please, Ellen. Do indulge us," Anne said. "I'm sure Charlotte would like a rest."

"I would not do it justice," Ellen murmured with a shade of self-consciousness.

Charlotte reached for Ellen's hand and pressed it warmly. "You are such a comfort to us. No one, however lofty of intellect, no matter how artistic her reading, no one can ever be what you are to me."

With that, Ellen's inhibitions faded, and she put aside her embroidery and drew a candle near. Yet in the back of her mind lay the fact that her friend Charlotte was the notorious Currer Bell, who had written that "naughty" *Jane Eyre*. She could not forget that she was sharing an intimate moment with one of the great literary figures of the day, and her reading was unusually animated by a resonant glee.

Anne was not surprised when Dr. Teale kindly patted her hand, put away his stethoscope, and then retired to the parlor to consult with Charlotte and her father. Anne had always been perceived as the least capable in all things, and that perception would never change. As the youngest in a family of highly gifted and willful individuals, she had been forced to allow others to think and act for her. Now she would only know her fate secondhand. While she waited, she marched slowly around the dining room with her arm linked through Ellen's, putting on such a brave, cheerful face and chatting so gaily that Ellen was fooled into believing that she was not the least bit in despair.

In reality, her heart was pounding hard in her chest and her legs were weak from fear. She heard the parlor door open, and Dr. Teale was shown out. Charlotte and her father entered the dining room.

Her violet-gray eyes scrutinized their faces; she had no difficulty reading their minds. Her father sat down on the sofa, and with an expression of undisguised pity he reached out to her and drew her down beside him.

"My *dear* little Anne . . ." he began, but his voice broke and he could say no more.

It was delivered as she had expected; she had been condemned to death as gently as possible. Anne gripped her father's gnarled hand tightly in her own, and in that brief heart-pounding moment she knew what awaited her. She had witnessed her sister's long agony and knew what she would have to endure, the long days spent in no other use than suffering.

"Is there any chance that I might recover?"

Charlotte sat down next to her sister and took her other hand. "There is always hope. And Dr. Teale has been quite clear that with proper care it is possible to arrest the progress of the disease."

"Well, then, whatever you ask of me, I shall do it," Anne replied brightly, as though there were something exhilarating in the idea of facing off with death.

Anne became the model invalid, patiently submitting to the most revolting and torturous remedies. The greater her pain, the greater her bravery and cheerfulness. It was her way of proving her worth, of distinguishing herself and earning her family's approval. She slept in Emily's room now, at the doctor's recommendation, to avoid transmitting the disease to Charlotte. Anne didn't like sleeping alone, and she was terribly lonely at night. In those moments of forced solitude, she expressed her well-hidden despair in poetry that no one would read until after her death. When she wept, she turned her face to the pillow, taking care that no one should hear.

During the following months, Charlotte was able to fall back into that comfortable role of managing the lives around her; they were all content with her intervening hand, and thankful for it. She found a hundred little details to tend to throughout the day; she wrote letters to specialists asking second, even third opinions; she prepared pitch plasters and bran tea, and dressed the blisters on Anne's side, a result of overheated glass cups applied by overzealous doctors. She served up nauseating doses of cod-liver oil and carbonate of iron, believing she had some control over fate, refusing to accept that she would be the last, the only one to survive.

In the spring, Anne's symptoms seemed to lessen, and she expressed a desire to visit Scarborough, believing that the sea air and pleasant surroundings would be beneficial. Charlotte fought tooth and nail against the idea, citing a hundred excuses but keeping to herself the one that most terrified her: that death would come suddenly when they least expected it, and they would be far away from home.

Finally, Anne prevailed, having won her father's intervention and Dr. Teale's approval; Ellen agreed to come, too. On the day before their departure, Anne sent a note around to Arthur asking him to call upon her that evening.

After supper she told Charlotte what she had done.

"Mr. Nicholls? What ever for, dearest?"

"I would like to speak to him."

"Well then, just step into the parlor. He's there every evening."

"We cannot speak freely in Papa's presence; you know that. And I cannot entertain him alone, so of course you will be present, but I would ask you to allow me to converse with him without . . ." Anne paused and the color rose to her cheeks.

"Without what?"

"I know his narrow-mindedness offends your spirit of tolerance, and I know Papa likes to make fun of him, but he is a kind, sensible man and we all lean heavily on him. He may not be spectacular in the pulpit, but he is no less worthy of our respect because of it."

Charlotte was set to reply, the words itching on her tongue, but Anne stopped her with a gesture.

"Allow me to finish, Tally." She drew a painful breath and added, "Our family is greatly hobbled, and we have yet another abyss to cross, and Mr. Nicholls is a steady light in that darkness. Do not under-estimate him."

Anne's head fell back against the chair; she had exhausted herself. Through closed eyes she said, "When he is here I would like to direct the conversation myself, if you please, Charlotte. I don't see anything wrong in that."

Arthur came by that evening with a handful of yellow gorse and blue-bells for Anne, effusing about the splendid meadows in bloom above Hardcastle Crags. In the past Charlotte might have been niggardly in her appreciation, but now she thanked him warmly and begged him to take a chair.

Arthur set his hat on the floor and glanced stiffly at Charlotte. Un-usually for her, she had nothing to say. She stood near the door, clutch-ing the flowers in her hand, looking strangely meek.

Arthur turned to Anne, and Charlotte noticed how his reserve seemed to melt.

"Do you know the walk along Hardcastle Crags, Miss Anne?"

"I do, sir. We have picnicked in that area in the past. You walk there frequently, do you not?"

"I do. To visit my friend Mr. Sowden."

"Hebben Bridge is a long walk, sir."

"And he is a loyal friend," Arthur replied simply. "Your father tells me you are off tomorrow to Scarborough."

"Yes, both Charlotte and I, with our friend Ellen."

Again he turned to Charlotte for a reply, but she gave him an awkward smile and said nothing.

He turned back to Anne. "A delightful party. Will you stay long?"

"I think not. But we will stop a night in York to visit York Minster, which I have seen but would like to visit again."

"And you have arranged for pleasant lodgings in Scarborough?"

"Yes. We have an excellent situation with a view of the sea."

"Ah, capital, Miss Anne! A well-deserved treat after a long, dreary winter. I expect to see you back in greatly improved health."

"Yes, I do intend to return, Mr. Nicholls, if it would please God to spare me. I long to do some good in the world before I leave it. I have many schemes in my head for the future."

"Schemes?" Arthur said with interest. "What kinds of schemes?"

Anne replied shyly, "Oh, nothing that would ever come to your attention. They are humble plans, but still I should not like them all to come to nothing, and myself to have lived to so little purpose."

"You should never say that, Miss Anne," he told her in his soft Irish voice. "You have lived the life that God has given you." He paused and then added in a gently reassuring tone, one that Charlotte had never heard him use before, "It is a sign of wisdom to recognize those things we cannot change about ourselves and our fate. You, Miss Anne, you have lived your life in devotion and constancy in His love, and He asks no more than that."

"And how would you know this about me, sir?"

"I am not as unobservant as you may think."

Anne smiled. "Then I need not tell you why I have asked you to call."

Arthur leaned back in his chair and stroked his side whiskers in a pretense of deep divination. "Might it have to do with a certain black-and-white spaniel?"

"It might."

"The same little spaniel that comes daily to my rooms and accompanies me on my visits in the parish? I believe he goes by the name of Flossy, is that right?"

Anne smiled. "You will continue your attentions in my absence, will you not?"

"I assure you that you will return to find him lacking nothing except your own irreplaceable affection."

Charlotte had been biting her tongue all throughout this exchange; she had never seen Anne speak more than a few words to Arthur Nicholls, but it occurred to her that there existed between the two of them an unspoken sympathy. For these few minutes, Charlotte had been made to feel quite disposable, and it stirred a curious emotion in her heart, something she could not recognize.

In a gracious gesture, Anne held out her skeletal hand. "Thank you so much for coming."

Arthur rose, took her hand, and shook it.

"Good-bye," he said warmly. "God grant you a safe journey and a speedy recovery."

Charlotte accompanied him into the passageway. He settled his hat on his head and opened the door without addressing a word to her. Out of politeness, Charlotte spoke up.

"Thank you for calling," she said.

When he turned, she saw that his face had completely softened. It was not the Mr. Nicholls she knew; he wore an expression of utter vulnerability, and his eyes were swimming with tears.

"You have my deepest sympathy," he muttered. Without waiting for a reply, he hurried outside.

When Charlotte returned to the dining room she found Anne prettily flushed, with a book in her hands.

Charlotte sat down with her mending basket on her knees and pulled out one of her father's socks. She stretched the wool tight to examine it for holes and gave a melancholy sigh. "There's so little to do anymore. We were always making for Branwell. He went through his shirts so quickly." Then she laid down the sock and looked up at her sister. "What schemes?"

Anne lifted her eyes from her book with a baffled look on her face.

"The schemes you were talking about to Mr. Nicholls."

Anne said, "Novels, of course, Charlotte. What else would it be?"

"Oh," Charlotte said, and she picked up the sock again.

Anne smiled quietly to herself. Of all those close to her, it had been Arthur who had offered some small tribute to her worth. Nothing grand had ever been expected of her, and there was nothing to disappoint where there were so few expectations. But Anne had finally come to recognize her own qualities: she had learned how to grow, to allow experience, good and bad, to shape her intelligence and her writing. She had succeeded as a governess and a novelist, but Emily really hadn't cared, and Charlotte had unfairly measured her little sister's accomplishments against her own genius and prejudices, and found them unworthy of recognition.

In York they wheeled her around town in a bath chair, and with her own earnings she bought two bonnets and a new dress in a pale sprigged muslin. Ellen declared it the prettiest dress Anne had ever owned. Watching her admire her reflection in the mirror and shake out the softly flounced skirt, Charlotte brightened a little, imagining a day when Anne had recovered, and would wear her white dresses again.

Everywhere they turned they found strong arms willing to lift her out of a carriage or carry her across the railway lines, and her joy seemed to cast a sweetness on every inconvenience, great or small. Scarborough was Anne's favorite place in all the world; the town cheered her immensely. She drove a donkey cart on the beach and took the baths; she walked the bridge and sat on a bench at sunset, watching the sea.

On Monday morning, just a few days after their arrival, as she sat in her armchair looking out over the bay, she felt death coming on—a "change," she called it. She wanted to spare Charlotte the trauma of transporting her body back to Haworth for burial, and she wondered if there might be time to make it home if they left that very morning. A doctor was summoned, but he only confirmed what Anne knew.

They eased her onto the sofa, and Charlotte hovered over her, tears running down her face, nervously fidgeting first with the lap blanket and then the pillow under Anne's head, in an effort to make her sister comfortable.

"Take courage, Charlotte," Anne said. "You will not be alone. Ellen will be a sister to you, and God will not abandon you." She quieted her sister's busy hands and whispered, "Thank you for bringing me here. I am happy, and God has blessed me with a gentle death."

At that moment, the clock in the parlor chimed the hour and the chambermaid called to them through the half-open door that dinner was being served in the dining room. When Charlotte turned back to Anne, she was dead.

She was buried at Scarborough in St. Mary's churchyard on a cliff overlooking the bay, wearing the pretty green-sprigged dress she had purchased a few days before. Only Charlotte and Ellen were there to mourn, along with Miss Wooler, their old schoolmistress from Roe Head, who was summering in her house in North Bay.

Charlotte's father wrote, urging Charlotte to remain with Ellen in Scarborough for the sake of her own health, but the town was far too gay to suit her mood. They moved farther down the coast, to a quiet fishing village where the waves crashed and thundered against the cliffs and seagulls haunted the empty beach.

From there, far away from the throng, Charlotte resumed her correspondence with Mr. Williams in London:

> *Had I never believed in a future life before, my sisters' fate would assure me of it. There must be Heaven or we must despair, for life seems bitter, brief, blank. To me, these two have left in their memories a noble legacy. Were I quite solitary in the world—bereft even of Papa—there is something in the past I can love intensely and honor deeply, and it is something which cannot change—*

which cannot decay—which immortality guarantees from corruption.

A year ago, had a prophet warned me how I should stand in June 1849—how stripped and bereaved—had he foretold the autumn, the winter, the spring of sickness and suffering to be gone through, I should have thought—this can never be endured. It is over, Branwell—Emily—Anne are gone like dreams, gone as Maria and Elizabeth went twenty years ago. I have buried them one by one, and thus far God has upheld me.

The fact is, my work is my best companion—hereafter I look for no great earthly comfort except what congenial occupation can give.

Then, with her emotions still raw, she picked up the pen again and returned to *Shirley*.

Chapter Sixteen

Charlotte tilted the tall looking glass to catch her full reflection. The black silk dress trimmed in velvet had seemed smart enough back in Haworth, but here in London none of her clothes seemed quite right. She had poured over patterns with Ellen and gone through two dressmakers, worrying herself sick over fashions and fittings, always questioning her own judgment and never fully trusting that of anyone else. Every attempt at a more fashionable style would eventually send her scurrying back to safety behind the familiar neat and tidy look.

Whatever she did, she always felt herself lacking.

She stepped back from the mirror and turned to the side. The folds of the full skirt swung gracefully with her step, and the close-fitting corsage showed off her tiny waist to advantage. The high bodice was cut slightly loose, to give the illusion of breasts; other women padded their bosoms, but Charlotte would not. In a nervous gesture of which she was unaware, her hand crept to her neck, to the jet mourning brooch, her sole adornment. To anyone who met her, it served as a solemn reminder of the events that had shaped her life during the past year.

Returning home from Scarborough that summer had proved to be a test of bravery in the face of intolerable pain. In the past, home had been a haven. Now there were too many empty rooms. Every evening after Martha and Tabby had retired upstairs to their room at the back of the house, and Arthur had come and gone, with the dogs settled down before the fire, a profound silence filled the parsonage. She would try to imagine them sitting with her, Emily on her stool before the fire, Anne in her chair, but all she could see was the deep vault and the dark earth where they now lay. Her only prop was a faith that seemed miserably inadequate to her grief. "I cannot avoid this," she would say to herself as she squinted through her spectacles at some trivial piece of handiwork, her vision often blurred by tears. "I must endure it," she would say, and then suddenly, with no provocation, the guilt and pain would start to rise.

She found escape in her characters, Shirley and Caroline. At the beginning they bore traces of Ellen and, especially, Mary; with Emily and Anne gone, they became a way to give life to companions now in the grave. Motherless herself, she created a mother for Caroline—albeit clumsily. Against a background of political change and social struggle, she explored the complex psychological landscape of Woman's needs, her impotence and powerlessness.

In *Shirley*, she probed the injustices that enraged and embittered her. She exposed the silliness of men of the church, the pathetic alienation of spinsters—a future she feared would be her own. Throughout the novel ran a current of hostility and alienation between men and women, an image of her own painful relationships. Nothing was resolved at the end. There were no proposals for radical change because Charlotte had no solutions, not for her own life nor anyone else's. In the end, she simply married off Caroline and Shirley to imperfect men, leaving them to struggle on in an imperfect society.

With the publication of *Shirley*, her fame only grew brighter. Charlotte thought the book somewhat sad and bitter, but her publisher had expressed himself satisfied, and now the reviewers had taken hold of the work. If they found less to excite, they also found less to condemn.

George Smith and his mother had quickly written to invite her to their home in Bayswater. Charlotte had preferred to face her critics in London rather than rattle around in an empty parsonage in the dead of winter. She told herself that her father was accustomed to solitude. Certainly he grieved, but for all he knew, they were still there, all three sisters, marching around the table so quietly that he never heard them, solemnly whispering their stories, no more intrusive on his life than a shadow.

Mrs. Smith and her daughters had been let in on the secret that the timid country clergyman's daughter was the notorious author of *Jane Eyre,* and they had been scrupulously attentive since her arrival. They put her up in an elegantly appointed room with richly colored chintz curtains and upholstered chairs, where she awoke in the dark of morning to the sound of a maid scratching around in the grate starting a fire. A fire in the morning! A warm room in which to dress! Each evening, she returned to find costly wax candles lighted beside her tester bed and on the washstand—such luxuries! There were extravagant dishes of venison, turbot with asparagus, and *meringues à la crème,* although Charlotte ate like a bird. Theater, exhibitions, and sightseeing excursions were planned for her entertainment, but the excitement wore her down. They gave a dinner party for her to meet her idol, the great Thackeray, and she trembled in his presence and dared not speak a word.

Charlotte stepped up closer to the mirror to check her delicate silver-and-jet earrings, and a pale, haggard face stared back. The whirl of events had left her unable to sleep at night, and now she felt a headache coming on. With nervous hands she tidied up the dressing table, neatly arranging her brush and comb, her tortoiseshell jewelry box, making sure that everything was in its proper place before she went down.

The morning room always bore a faint trace of rosewater mingled with smoke from the crackling wood fire. The city seemed remote, emitting only a low, sustained note, as though from a distant organ. It was a pleasant, peaceful room, with the furniture comfortably arranged, and Charlotte had hoped to have a few moments alone before breakfast, but George's mother was already at her desk. Charlotte had found her to be faultlessly even-tempered, rather stern perhaps, but by no means unkind. She possessed the serenity and self-assurance Charlotte had observed in women who had borne many children by men they loved, and who loved them in return. She had observed this serenity in Monsieur Heger's wife. It was a nature Charlotte envied and grudgingly admired.

"Good morning, Miss Brontë," Mrs. Smith said brightly, with a quick glance at the dark circles under Charlotte's eyes. "Did you sleep well?"

"Quite well, thank you," Charlotte said with a forced smile.

"Last night was bitterly cold. I do hope your room was warm enough."

"Yes, it was, thank you," Charlotte nodded. "Much warmer than that to which I am accustomed."

"Is it too warm, my dear?" she asked pleasantly. "Is it stuffy?"

"Not at all. I'm most comfortable, ma'am. Truly I am."

"Very well, then," she said and returned to her correspondence, sorting through papers and opening envelopes with a cheery briskness.

Charlotte glanced about the room for the newspapers, which were always laid out for her to read, but this morning the table was conspicuously bare. *Shirley* was to be reviewed that day in the *Edinburgh Review,* and Charlotte immediately suspected that they had hidden it. In that case, the review must have been bad.

"Forgive me for disturbing you, ma'am . . ."

Mrs. Smith met her gaze with a solemn, wide-eyed look. "Oh, my dear, you're not disturbing me in the least. We know you prefer a quiet morning."

"Has the paper arrived?"

"What paper is that, my dear?"

"The *Edinburgh Review.*"

"Oh!" she exclaimed innocently. "Oh, it's not here?"

"I believe Mr. Lewes's review of *Shirley* was to appear today, was it not?"

"Perhaps it's been mislaid," she replied, then quickly went back to her paperwork, avoiding Charlotte's prying gaze.

"I would very much like to read it," Charlotte said after a long hesitation.

Mrs. Smith sat back with a sigh. "Miss Brontë, I confess that George asked me to keep it from you. He was afraid it would upset you, and he didn't want your day marred by unpleasantness. Perhaps you might like to read it this evening, after George returns."

There it was, Charlotte thought. Another poor review. She struggled to put on a brave face. "It is most kind of you, but I would prefer to read it now."

Mrs. Smith rang for the parlor maid, who then returned, slightly out of breath, with the paper on a silver tray.

George Henry Lewes had been one of those critics whose wild enthusiasm for *Jane Eyre* had prompted him to initiate correspondence with Currer Bell through her publishers, but his zeal often took the form of bombastic lectures on her failures. He had urged her to cultivate the mild-mannered, highly polished style of Jane Austen to counteract her tendency to melodrama and her overcolored imagination. Charlotte felt it was very much like urging a fish to fly, and in her replies she passionately defended the Romantic ideals to which she and Emily had clung, and her conviction that clarity and common sense did not always yield the heart's truth.

But what had given her most cause for concern was his claim to have solved the mystery of her identity, and his careless refusal—despite her pleas—to judge her strictly as an author, not as a woman.

Now, as she adjusted her spectacles and unfolded the large tabloid sheets with tremulous hands, she thought he must have been brutal indeed to write something that her publisher deemed should be hidden from her.

"We take Currer Bell to be one of the most remarkable of female writers—that she is a woman, we never had a moment's doubt," he wrote.

> Yet, a more masculine book has never been written! *Shirley* exhibits ever more of Currer Bell's Yorkshire coarseness and rudeness than its predecessor; it is the very antipode to "ladylike"—which is all the more shocking since we know it to be a fact that the authoress is the daughter of a clergyman! Woman, yes—but not, we suspect, mother. For this proof, we cite the preposterous story she weaves around the heroine Caroline, who, it is revealed, was senselessly abandoned as a child by her mother. Currer Bell! If under your

heart had ever stirred a child, if to your bosom a babe had ever been pressed, never could you have imagined such a falsehood as that! . . . *Shirley* is not quite so true as *Jane Eyre;* and it is not so fascinating. The characters are almost all disagreeable and exhibit intolerable rudeness of manner. Unmistakable power is stamped on various parts of it, but it is often misapplied. Currer Bell has much yet to learn, especially, the discipline of her own tumultuous energies . . .

For a long while Charlotte struggled to remain hidden, screened behind the broadsheets. She was helpless to check the tears that flushed down her face, gathering in her mouth, at her chin, dripping silently onto her black silk gown. There was something absurdly ironic about the moment, the force of her feelings, the loneliness and lovelessness bursting forth at a time and place when they must at all cost be suppressed. She could not put down the paper. Mrs. Smith would look up. And then she would be exposed—vulnerable, sensitive, so pathetically womanish.

She thought, *If I just sit here long enough and allow all this to pass, and my tears to dry . . .*

There was the sound of rustling skirts and the tread of steps on the carpet.

"Miss Brontë?"

Mrs. Smith moved aside a cushion and settled her broad self noisily onto the sofa. "Now, now," she said matter-of-factly, "you must not allow them to excite you so."

Charlotte lowered the paper and quickly folded it away.

"I do apologize. I've been quite rude, haven't I?" Charlotte mumbled as she fished a handkerchief from her sleeve.

"Nonsense."

"This is precisely what you were trying to spare me." She dabbed at her eyes and cast a look up at Mrs. Smith that was so appealing, so wanting of affection, that it was impossible to remain unmoved.

"My dear, it is Mr. Lewes who owes you an apology. It was most thoughtless of him to write some of those things, although I do believe he does not intend it so—George tells me he is a great admirer of yours. But he is a rather pedantic young man, quite full of himself like all these brilliant literary men, and I fear he would be stunned to think he has wounded you so."

A deep shudder shook Charlotte's tiny frame. "When my sisters were alive, we would laugh over this kind of thing."

At the mention of her sisters, Mrs. Smith understood that the tears were about much more than a review of her book.

George's mother was not the caressing kind, and when she reached to pat Charlotte's knee it was roughly, rather like whacking a cushion, but the intentions were heartfelt.

"Now, now, dry those tears and let's have an end to all this."

But the emotions had taken their toll, and Charlotte's head was pounding. She raised a hand to her temple; her face had drained of all color.

"I'm afraid I'm not feeling well," she whispered. "I think I should like to retire to my room."

"By all means. Indeed, you do look weary, Miss Brontë." Mrs. Smith rose as Charlotte slid from the sofa and headed for the stairs. "I'll send the maid up to draw your curtains."

Mrs. Smith had to ring twice for the maid before the girl arrived, wide-eyed and out of breath.

"It's Miss Brontë," the maid apologized. "I found her in the upstairs hall, wandering around in a terrible state. She said she was confused by all the doors and couldn't find her room. I showed her to her room, ma'am, but she looked frightfully pale, like she might faint."

Mrs. Smith hurried upstairs and stood listening for a moment at the door. When she heard the unmistakable sound of retching, she knocked lightly and entered. Charlotte was bent over the washstand, heaving violently with each convulsion. Mrs. Smith closed the door and strode across the room, slipping an arm around Charlotte and untangling the strands of dark hair that had fallen into her face.

"Here, here, let me help you," she commanded gruffly. "I've nursed four children through worse than this, and a dying husband."

She snatched a towel from the rack beside the washstand, dampened it with water from the pitcher, and pressed it to Charlotte's head.

"Take a deep breath, my dear. There. There. That's better."

When the nausea was calmed, she ordered Charlotte out of her dress and into bed. Once the curtains were drawn and the maid had gone, Charlotte opened her eyes to see Mrs. Smith approaching with a basin of water. She pulled up a chair beside the bed.

"I beg you not to tell Mr. Smith about this," Charlotte murmured. "I should not like to upset him."

"I shall tell him only that you were overtired and needed to rest." She wrung out a cloth and laid it over Charlotte's forehead. "Now lie still and try to sleep."

"My dress . . ." Charlotte murmured.

"I've sent it down to have it sponged clean."

"You are very kind."

"My compliments to your dressmaker."

Charlotte's eyes fluttered open. "Do you approve?"

"It's very becoming . . . done up very nicely," she replied. "Simple and elegant."

"You must not bother yourself with me," Charlotte said. "I'm quite accustomed to being alone."

"Indeed, my dear, too accustomed. You should be alone as little as possible."

Charlotte fell still, and after a moment she felt the clasp of cool, damp skin as Mrs. Smith placed a hand in hers, and gave it a brisk, reassuring squeeze.

George Smith blew into the entry hall on a gust of wintry wind, shaking the damp drizzle off his hat before he passed it to the manservant.

"Where are they?" he asked as he shed his heavy coat and untwined the wool scarf from his neck.

"Upstairs in the drawing room, sir."

"Did my flowers come?"

"Yes, sir."

"Good."

George knew the effect the Lewes review would have on Charlotte, with the heartless references to her spinsterhood and lack of maternal instinct, and the merciless harping on the lack of delicacy in her writing; he anticipated a rough evening ahead. But as he climbed the stairs, he could hear the soft murmur of easy conversation and laughter coming from the drawing room. To his surprise, when he opened the door he found his mother and Charlotte sitting beside the fire, happily chatting away in the manner of old friends.

"There he is!" his mother exclaimed, laying down her needlepoint as he strode across the room. "And he's in time for supper!" She arched her neck and presented her cheek in feigned coolness. "We had hoped to see you at tea."

Charlotte rose to stand beside the fire, her warm brown eyes brimming with an easy gaiety that took George by surprise.

"Listen to her," George said as he leaned down to plant a kiss on his mother's cheek. "I can never please her."

"You are my witness, Miss Brontë. You know he's never on time for breakfast, nor for any meal for that matter."

He had not missed Charlotte's bright gaze all this time, shining up at him with the warmth of gratitude.

"Thank you for the yellow roses, sir," she said. "It was much too kind. And I fear they were had under false pretenses. As you can see, I am in exceedingly fine spirits."

"What have you done to her, Mother? I think I've never seen Currer Bell so relaxed."

"I've done as you ordered. Let her rest," his mother replied as she gathered up her thread and tucked it into her basket. "We canceled all our excursions for the day. It is so wretchedly cold, and truthfully, we've spent a very pleasant and quiet afternoon."

"I hope she didn't tire you out with her old-lady gossip," George said to Charlotte.

"On the contrary, your mother's gossip is very enlightening."

"Oh? How so?"

"I told her all about the scandal around Mr. Lewes and his wife."

George turned an alarmed look on his mother. All of London society knew that Lewes's wife had been living openly with Leigh Hunt, Lewes's close friend and editorial partner; she had even borne Hunt's children. But such scandal was only whispered between intimate friends, never mentioned in polite company.

"No need to look so shocked, my dear boy. She has every right to know. Particularly since Mr. Lewes is so quick to judge Miss Brontë's novels, and then lives so scandalously. And his own novels were such abject failures. Really, they were quite awful."

George turned to Charlotte. "So you read Mr. Lewes's review."

"Yes, and I'm quite recovered now."

"Good," he smiled.

"And Mr. Thackeray called," Charlotte continued. "He saw the review and came by to cheer me. It was ever so kind of him."

"We'll have no more talk of reviews this evening, George," his mother ruled, casting a stern warning glance over the rims of her spectacles. "We will converse only on cheerful topics."

George Smith found his author intriguing to watch that evening, the waiflike creature in the black of deep mourning, her fairylike hands folded at her waist. There was an exquisite sensitivity at work in those intelligent eyes. Even when she was silent, those eyes were never passive; they watched carefully, noticing everything. She seemed to be reading your feelings and attitudes, at times even your soul.

Over dinner, the conversation flowed freely with the claret and port, from soup to roast saddle of mutton and cheese. George would glance at her, and he would wonder at his extraordinary fortune; here at his table sat London's most sought-after literary phenomenon. She was his. This tiny lady—the great Jane Eyre.

Returning to her room that evening, Charlotte sat up writing letters to Ellen and her father. Shrewdly, she held up different masks to each of them. To her father she was the connoisseur of art; she wrote of the paintings at the National Gallery, of seeing the great actor Macready perform *Macbeth*. Rarely, if at all, did she mention George Smith. "I get on quietly," she wrote. "Most people know me, I think, but they are far too well-bred to show that they know me, so that there is none of that bustle or that sense of publicity I dislike." Then, as an afterthought, she added, "I met Thackeray."

To sociable Ellen she spoke of London society and the people she had met, painting herself as the epitome of a country clergyman's daughter, as if she feared losing her austere little soul if she were to enjoy herself too much. "Mrs. Smith watched me narrowly—when I was surrounded by gentlemen—she never took her eye from me—I liked the surveillance—both when it kept guard over me among many or only with her cherished and valued son—she soon, I am convinced, saw in what light I viewed both her George and all the rest." She added poignantly, "She treats me as if she likes me. As for the others, I do not know what they thought of me, but I believe most desired more to admire and more to blame."

When she had sealed the letters and undressed, she crawled into the deep bed, which had been carefully turned down by the maid. Before she blew out her candle, she glanced around the pretty green room with the chintz curtains, momentarily fancying herself in a family such as this.

Her heart wanted desperately to cling to George Smith, but she could not paint herself into the portrait, could not imagine her queer little body linked to his athletic six-foot frame. He was eight years younger than she, bright-spirited and sweet-tempered. He would have a pretty wife with a fortune and social graces, certainly not a stunted clergyman's daughter, regardless of how great her fame.

Chapter Seventeen

They waited until the end of her visit to introduce her to the London literary critics. Charlotte knew how much it meant to her publisher, and she would not have disappointed him for the world, regardless of how much she dreaded the confrontation. The opinions of these men carried enormous weight, and it was a necessary trial she would have to endure to disprove the rumors that Currer Bell was godless and immoral.

She sat in George's office in bonnet and gloves, perched stiffly on a chair with her teacup and saucer in her lap, watching George and Mr. Williams as they paced the small space, excitedly discussing plans for the dinner party at the end of the week.

"They're all coming," George said proudly. "Quite speedy replies. Mr. Chorley of the *Athenaeum* replied within the hour."

"And the *Examiner*?" Mr. Williams asked.

"Confirmed."

"And the gentleman from the *Times*?" Charlotte asked.

George fixed her with a meaningful glance. "I haven't sent out his invitation. I wished to consult you first."

Just that week the *Times* had published an excessively sarcastic notice of *Shirley* that had shaken Charlotte even more than Lewes's remarks.

"He must be invited," Charlotte said brightly. "It would be impolite to exclude him. Besides, I should be disappointed only to meet my friends. I should like to meet my foes as well. I should like to see what manner of creatures they are."

"And Mr. Lewes?"

She paused to take a sip of her tea, which had gone cold. Her hand trembled, and the cup rattled on the saucer as she lowered it to her lap.

"I should very much like to meet him as well."

George knew how the harsh judgment of some of these men had wounded her and her sisters, and he was amazed at her toughness of mind.

"You need not look so surprised," Charlotte said, meeting their looks with steady eyes. "I am ready for the challenge."

"Do you realize how unusual it is to get these men to agree to sit in the same room together?" Williams asked. "Chorley and Lewes can't tolerate each other. And Forster's feuding with all of them. But not one of them would turn down an invitation to meet you, even if it meant sitting down with the devil himself."

Charlotte took another sip of her cold tea and replied with a twist of humor, "Very aptly said, Mr. Williams, since there are some of them who do indeed take me to be the devil."

After she had gone, George sank into a chair and propped his feet up on a pile of manuscripts. "I admire her ever so much, Williams. She suffers terribly before these dinner parties, you know. Frightful headaches and nervous spells. But she has the heart of a lion."

On her last night in town, London's most eminent critics rolled up one by one in front of George Smith's home, bringing to an end the feverish excitement that had reigned that day in the editorial offices of the city's great newspapers. Despite the gossip, some of them were still not convinced of her sex. They didn't know what to expect, if they would enter the drawing room to find a dazzling and witty beauty or an unmannered Yorkshire weaver. Some of them still clung to the suspicion that Currer Bell had written *Wuthering Heights*.

In order to steel her nerves, Mrs. Smith had forced a copious tea on Charlotte, and Charlotte had waited out the afternoon with quiet resignation, installed on the sofa near the crackling wood fire, knitting infant's boots for Mrs. Smith's charity basket.

That evening as the drawing room door was thrown open and the great and powerful were announced, George remained firmly at her side; his mother stood at a distance, keeping to her role of watchful chaperone. One by one Charlotte braved the onslaught, all the while praying that her nerves would not fail her and she would not speak stupidly. John Forster of the *Examiner* bounded into the room, peered down at her from beneath his bushy black brows, and began pumping her hand with a fresh overeagerness that took her by surprise. Lewes surprised her even more. There was a vivacity in the man and an irrepressible sense of fun that permeated all his conversation. He bore a haunting resemblance to Emily—the wistful pale eyes, the full mouth—and she thought she could not hate him, whatever he might say or do. Only Chorley shocked her. More than six feet tall, he strutted in with his patent boots, his enormous velvet lapels, his satin scarf puffed out like the crop of a pigeon, and extended his gloved fingers with the statement "Henry Fothergill Chorley, madam. Art and music critic and editor for the *Athenaeum* since 1830." He then struck an affected pose with his hand inside his waistcoat, looking down his short, turned-up nose at her with an expression of undeniable self-satisfaction. Charlotte was stupefied, having never met an authentic dandy, believing Queen Victoria had snuffed them out in the previous decade.

Nevertheless, this group accounted for the most prolific geniuses of the day, having between them published enough literary essays, novels, plays, and biographies to paper every inch of George's grand Bayswater residence. The conversation was nothing if not brilliant, and they were all, even swaggering Chorley, squeakily civil to her. She was a literary sensation, and they would all go away that evening wearing Charlotte Brontë in their cap as they wore Browning, Dickens, Tennyson, Carlyle, and every other poet or artist worth celebrating.

On the way down to the dining room, with Charlotte on his arm, George leaned over to whisper reassuringly in her ear, "You seem quite composed this evening."

She gave his arm a slight squeeze and drew herself up on her tiptoes to whisper in his ear, "I'm determined to enjoy myself. After all, it is my last night."

He covered her hand with his own, pressing it warmly. "You will be back here often, I insist upon it. My home is always open to you."

But as George escorted her to her chair near the head of the table, when she realized that she would be surrounded by strangers, she was seized by panic. Without warning, she gathered up her skirts and turned away.

"Charlotte?" he whispered to her, catching her elbow. "Where are you going?"

Ignoring his baffled look, she slipped out of his grasp and quickly marched to the other end of the table, to where his mother sat. The servant stepped up and drew out the chair next to Mrs. Smith. Charlotte sat down, flushing brightly as she arranged her skirts.

Mrs. Smith whispered to her, "But, my dear, you are the guest of honor. Your place is beside George."

Charlotte was mortified by her own timidity. She only shook her head and kept her eyes averted.

"It's quite all right, my dear." Mrs. Smith found Charlotte's knee and gave it a pat. "If you feel more comfortable beside me . . ."

The dinner was a two-hour procession of dishes accompanied by countless bottles of champagne and claret. Mr. Sutherland from the *Times,* a raspy-voiced man with a pocked face, took up the topic of Dickens's *Martin Chuzzlewit* with the roast goose and didn't drop him until they had been served the plovers' eggs in aspic jelly.

Gradually, thanks to the wine and the reassuring presence of Mrs. Smith, Charlotte's self-consciousness began to vanish and they began to draw her out with their questions. Pausing first to compose her thoughts, she answered simply but always clearly and without a trace of self-doubt. These men, so accustomed to London's fashion of intellectual affectation, its verbal banter and wit, found themselves disarmed by her earnestness.

By the time they had finished the *macédoine de fruits* and started on the cherry ice, they had all drunk a good deal. There had been a little sniping between Forster and Lewes, and they had all fairly well drowned Thackeray in abuse.

"You are a great admirer of Mr. Thackeray's, if I recall, Miss Brontë," Mr. Forster said.

"Indeed, I am. He honors the Truth." She paused. "In all but his portrayal of women. Only there do I fault him."

"But his women are perfect models of modesty, Miss Brontë," Forster declared.

"Indeed. Therein lies his error."

"Now, having met you, knowing you to be a faultlessly well-bred lady," Chorley simpered, a little too unctuously, "I cannot imagine that you would have all our women behave like Jane Eyre."

"Because she speaks frankly of her feelings?"

Forster replied, "The sentiment she expresses is not one we would wish our women to emulate in literature."

"Would you condemn the expression of these sentiments in real life?"

"Between a well-bred man and woman, most certainly!" Chorley cried.

"Hypocrite," Lewes muttered, emptying his glass.

Chorley ignored this and ranted on: "It is the purpose of our literature to purify human passions and teach the importance of virtue. We cannot allow our literature to trample on our conventions."

Sutherland, who had been falling asleep, roused himself to speak. "Indeed, I found there to be a coarse frankness of dialogue between the man and the woman."

Charlotte gazed around the table at them, her eyes blazing. "Perhaps you confuse virtue and convention, gentlemen. Conventionality is not morality, and self-righteousness is not religion."

Lewes, who had become a little tipsy, was clearly in Charlotte's camp. He leaned forward and glared down the table at the others, raised his brandy snifter, and cried, "Well said, Currer Bell! Well said!"

"Oh, but I assure you, if I said all that I think on the matter of women and how we are seen through this warped glass—by even the cleverest, and most intelligent men, like yourselves—I'm quite sure I'd be stoned."

"Come, come now, Miss Brontë, I cannot believe that you would have our literature strewn with vulgar and coarse heroines!"

"But there is my point, sir—that you confuse coarseness with honesty. Why, I have never—even from childhood—believed your heroines to be natural or true. Your good woman is a queer cross between a painted doll and an angel, and your bad woman is always a temptress. If I should be obliged to copy these characters, I would simply not write at all."

She shrugged, then calmly added, "I paint women as I see them, and they are honest and real. If the public refuses to acknowledge this reality, I can quietly put down my pen and trouble them no more. From obscurity I came; to obscurity I can return."

There was a deep, stunned silence. None of the men dared to meet her gaze.

Breaking the chill, Forster leaned across the table and pleaded, "Miss Brontë, we beseech you to do no such thing. For poor George's sake."

There was relieved laughter, and the conversation droned away through coffee and the end of dinner.

Lewes was the last to depart. As he stood in the hall putting on his coat, he tottered forward and said, "You and I should be friends, Miss Brontë. We have much in common. We've both written naughty books."

George had never witnessed his author's wrath until that moment, and it was a glorious thing to behold. She stared up at the pale little Lewes, her eyes fired and her voice trembling with rage. "Mr. Lewes, I have not read your novels, but I would imagine that there is as great a difference between your work and mine as there is between your personal conduct and mine. And I can assure you, I am quite as well informed on your personal life as you are on mine. Although I would not commit the grave and thoughtless indiscretion of making allusion to it in the press."

He seemed at once chastised, and he furrowed his brow and said gently, "But we are friends, are we not?"

"We were once," she replied sternly.

"Are we not now?" he pleaded.

A moment of rigid silence passed; then, softening, she extended her hand to shake. "I'm sure we shall be friends again one day."

"I'm not quite sure what they made of me," Charlotte said when she and George were alone. She was visibly exhausted. A strand of hair had fallen loose, and with her head down she absentmindedly fished for a comb; it was an unguarded gesture, revealing a softness and vulnerability George had not seen before.

"I think a few of them might be afraid of you," George smiled.

"Afraid of me?"

"Because you've shown yourself to be independent of their judgment. They'll respect you for it, albeit a little grudgingly."

"That's just as well," she replied. "I think I shall be less afraid of their condemnation in the future. It's a liberating feeling."

"And perhaps in the future you'll be less afraid to sit at my side."

She dropped her eyes. "I do so regret having disappointed you. I was only concerned about appearances."

"No one is going to find it improper for a poor publisher to lean upon the prop of his famous author."

Her eyes flashed a smile. "I would be proud to consider myself your prop."

"Charlotte, I want you to know that I'm not blind to how difficult this is for you. I only hope that these two weeks of activity have brought you a little distraction from your grief."

He had called her by her Christian name. It sounded so very natural, not at all forced or improper. "Oh, they have," she replied earnestly. "And I am ever so grateful."

As she started up the stairs, he teased, "Don't wait too long to return. You'll forget your way around the house and get lost again."

She gave him a tired smile. "Good night, George."

"Good night, Charlotte."

He watched her, thinking she looked smaller than ever as she disappeared quietly and noiselessly up the stairs. Just like a bird, as Rochester had called her. He thought of her returning to her empty parsonage in bleak and snowbound Yorkshire. There was something heart-wrenching in the idea that this little creature would be entombed in such a place, moving about it like a spirit herself. Especially when he thought how that slight, still frame concealed such a strong, fiery force, which neither tragedy nor harsh condemnation had been able to extinguish or freeze.

After her departure, a good deal of gossip about Currer Bell spread through London; some people spoke of her visit years later, telling the tales to their daughters once their daughters had reached a suitable age to read the scandalous book. They had wanted something eccentric and striking, a figure worthy of the author of *Jane Eyre*. Instead, she appeared to them like an austere little Joan of Arc (Thackeray said this to George), rebuking them with one glance from her great honest eyes. She clearly did not suit the wordly circles of London's literary elite with its noisy dinner parties, its fashionable opinions and easy morals. They neglected to see that it was the high-principled woman in mourning who commanded the life she led; the simple dress and sleekly knotted hair spoke of her strong sense of rectitude, her determination to do the right thing. Always. Even at the cost of her own heart.

Chapter Eighteen

A freezing mist hung in the air as Arthur trudged through the winding ginnels of Gauger's Croft, past yards where chickens and pigs scavenged in the rotting refuse. With every step he ruminated on the epic misery of this place, on the multitude of suffering hiding behind every door of these dank, dark cottages. There was an overwhelming sense of oppression in these northern textile villages. It was not the poverty of the destitute or the beggar. It was a poverty of brutal labor, of women, children, and men swallowed up in the clanking of the mechanical loom—ceaselessly spinning and weaving until they were broken, ill, or dead. Diseases gorged themselves on this kind of poverty; consumption and fevers crept in and settled down, striking and sparing with an incomprehensible rationale, then moving on as mysteriously as they appeared.

Through the gray gloom, Arthur caught sight of the new Haworth physician advancing toward him.

"Sir, are you coming from the Barraclough house by any chance?" Arthur asked when the doctor drew near.

"Indeed," Dr. Hall replied sadly. "The man passed away not more than an hour ago."

"I've been out at the Stancliffe farm. They didn't have a conveyance to spare and I had to walk, or I would have been there."

The physician clapped him on the back and said, "We've not got wings, Nicholls, and God knows we're not angels. Don't be so hard on yourself."

"It wasn't cholera, was it?"

"Good grief, no. His lungs failed him. He was a weaver. It gets them all in the end. What made you think it was cholera?"

"Mr. Brontë seems to think we haven't seen the end of it."

"Nicholls, my friend, you've got to take that old man's predictions with a grain of salt. He sees mayhem around every corner."

"Perhaps, sir, given his recent tragedies, his worries are justified."

"Well, let me assure you, I haven't had a case of cholera since last summer. So put your mind at ease on that matter. God knows there's enough disease here without that one." He touched his hat and hurried away.

That evening when Arthur stopped by the parsonage and learned that Mr. Brontë had not risen from his bed all day, he reacted with alarm.

"In bed? What are his symptoms, Martha?" Arthur asked as she took his hat and gloves. "Is it the fever?"

"Nay, sir," Martha replied. "It's his bronchitis. It's gotten worse." She added quietly, "And his spirits are low, sir. What with Miss Brontë bein' in London, an' the house so empty now."

Arthur found the old man propped up in bed with a flotilla of pillows at his back, swaddled in a neckcloth up to his ears and a clean white nightcap pulled down over his silver-bristled head. He sat perfectly erect, staring glumly into the shadows. A cold draft from the window worked its way through the shutters, causing the candle flame by his bed to dip and dance.

"Come in, Nicholls," he said, turning pitiful eyes on his curate. "Dr. Hall was just here."

"How are you feeling?" Arthur said as he dragged a chair to the bed.

"Not well. Not well at all. I'm so very weak, and it galls me. And I do so worry about Charlotte. London's such a wretchedly unhealthy place, and she's so fragile." He placed a gnarled hand over his heart and sighed. "I shall sink if God takes my beloved Charlotte from me."

A hoarse cough tore through his chest, and he sank back exhausted into his nest of pillows.

"Is there something I can get you?"

Patrick gestured to the table. "A serum. Over there," he wheezed.

Arthur rose and went to the table, searching in the dim light for a vial amid the books and papers. His attention was arrested by a trio of small volumes. He paused, picked up the top one, and turned back to Patrick.

"What's this?" Arthur said with a startled look. "*Jane Eyre?* Goodness gracious, I hope you don't leave this out where your daughter might read it."

This provoked a coughing fit so violent that Arthur dropped the book and hurried back to old man's bedside. Patrick had gone red in the face, and Arthur poured him a glass of water from the carafe by his bed and thrust it into his hand.

After the fit had calmed, Patrick lapsed back with his hand on his heaving chest, fixing Arthur with a narrow look.

"Have you read *Jane Eyre?*" Patrick croaked.

But before Arthur could reply, Patrick waved a gnarled finger and commanded, "Just bring me the book."

When Arthur did so, Patrick said, "Take at look at the cover. Read it to me."

" '*Jane Eyre: An Autobiography*.' "

"By?"

" 'Edited by Currer Bell.' "

"It's a pseudonym, you know."

"Yes, I've heard as much," Arthur said with a touch of impatience. "I *have* read the book, sir."

"You've read it, then? Good, good! I didn't think you to be the literary sort."

Arthur stiffened but let the barbed comment pass without reply. Patrick reached for the bedpost and drew himself upright. With a gleam in his eyes he said, "You know, Nicholls, mine are no ordinary children. You've remarked that yourself." He jabbed at the book. "Look again at the name. Note the initials, if you please."

In a flash, even without Patrick's prompt, Arthur understood.

"Currer Bell stands for Charlotte Brontë," Arthur said in a low voice, not quite believing himself as he spoke. The beaming look of pride on the old man's face was confirmation enough.

"She's in London visiting her publisher as we speak. It was her wish to remain anonymous, but the word is out in London now, and it would spoil my pleasure to have you hear it from someone else."

Arthur was too stupefied to respond. Patrick leaned closer to boast, "They've paid her five hundred pounds, Nicholls. Five hundred pounds! And another five hundred for her second novel, *Shirley*!"

"As I recall, there were other Bell brothers, were there not?" Arthur asked.

Patrick nodded. "Ellis Bell and Acton Bell."

"Why bless my soul," he said with awe. "It was Emily and Anne."

Arthur thought back to all the moments he had watched them in the simple activities of their daily lives, how he had strained to understand their whispered conversations, observed their unconventional ways. Sometimes timid, sometimes sullen, they had seemed to him strange and unknowable. There had always been something remarkable about them, something he could not put his finger on. Unexpectedly, his eyes began to burn. He remembered Anne's obscure comment, about schemes she had planned for the future, and he wondered if this was what she meant.

"God rest their souls," Arthur said quietly. As he looked up, he saw tears streaming down the old reverend's face. He was staring gloomily at the wall again, lost in his memories.

Inside the cover, Arthur found a batch of newspaper clippings. He unfolded one and saw that it was a review.

"Read it," Patrick muttered. "Read it aloud to me."

For the next half hour, Arthur read to the old clergyman, first the reviews—which were only the positive ones. Then, at Patrick's request, he began the first chapter of *Jane Eyre*.

> "There was no possibility of taking a walk that day. We had
> been wandering, indeed, in the leafless shrubbery an hour

in the morning; but since dinner (Mrs. Reed, when there was no company, dined early) the cold winter wind had brought with it clouds so somber, and a rain so penetrating, that further outdoor exercise was now out of the question.

I was glad of it; I never liked long walks, especially on chilly afternoons: dreadful to me was the coming home in the raw twilight, with nipped fingers and toes, and a heart saddened by the chidings of Bessie, the nurse, and humbled by the consciousness of my physical inferiority to Eliza, John, and Georgiana Reed. . . ."

After a while Patrick began to doze, then snore, but Arthur continued to read. Only when the clock struck nine and Martha looked in did he close the book.

"Do you need another candle, sir?" she whispered.

"No. He's asleep. I'll be going now."

Arthur blew out the flame and followed Martha down the stairs.

As she handed him his hat, he said, "Martha, tell Mr. Brontë I've borrowed his book."

"Oh," Martha said, suspiciously eyeing the small volumes he was slipping into the pocket of his greatcoat, "I'll be sure to tell him, sir. He's very particular about his books."

Arthur stayed up late into the night reading *Jane Eyre* a second time. He found himself pausing to reflect on certain passages, attempting to weed out fact from fiction. He was interested not so much in the workings of Charlotte's mind as the inclinations of her heart. He did not want to think there had actually been a Rochester somewhere in Charlotte's past, that a man had wreaked such havoc on her heart. Rochester had affairs with French cabaret singers; he kept abominable secrets and seduced his governess. Somehow, this kind of hero didn't fit into Arthur's knowledge of Charlotte's life. For years he had watched her mingle with the most prosaic order of men, with curates, schoolmasters, and parish clerks; there was not a Rochester among them.

It took Arthur the better part of a week to finish his second reading of *Jane Eyre,* and then he came to the parsonage begging for Charlotte's other book.

"Can't have it, my man," Patrick said from his throne of pillows.

"And why not?"

"It's loaned out."

"Loaned out?" Arthur frowned. "To whom?"

"My old friend Morgan in Bradford."

Arthur scowled darkly. "And when will you get it back?"

"End of the week."

Arthur looked so wretched that Patrick began to laugh, which brought on a coughing fit.

At last the old man was free to boast about his daughter, and when Charlotte's letters came, Patrick was quick to share them with his curate. "She's met Thackeray!" he crowed several days later, slipping on his spectacles while Arthur leaned over the grate to warm his hands. "And Harriet Martineau." Darting a look over the rims of his spectacles, he added, "Very celebrated lady. Writes essays on political theory. Brilliant."

Arthur gave a careless shrug. He didn't read many essays on political theory; nor was he the sort to be starstruck.

Plunging his nose back into the letter, Patrick mumbled, "She quite objects to all this notoriety, you know, but can't avoid it. Dinner parties in her honor, that sort of thing." He turned over the single sheet. "She talks about the theater here somewhere . . . let's see, where is it . . ." Finally, frustrated by his poor eyesight and the frugal light afforded by his candle, he waved the letter at Arthur. "Oh bother. Here, you read it to me, Nicholls."

For Arthur it was a bittersweet thing to be brought at last into the bosom of this proud, strange family, to be made privy to Charlotte's travels, her reflections, her experiences. Each time a letter was given to him to read, he unfolded the pages with a mixture of dread and delight. He searched between the lines for intimations of a romantic attachment and found none, although Mr. Brontë insinuated otherwise. He spoke often and quite convincingly of the young publisher's attentions toward Charlotte.

"If she marries him, I'll have to give up my home and go into lodgings," he said with a grieved air. "It would kill me, Nicholls, having her go off to London, leaving me sick and old and alone. But how could I object to such a marriage?"

Arthur wore his best granite-like expression and refused to reply.

"A sound businessman, that George Smith. They've got a successful import-export firm, along with the publishing arm. He publishes Ruskin, you know."

A vague jealousy crept into Arthur's heart, and he anxiously waited for Charlotte's return.

Charlotte arrived back in Haworth only a few days before the first anniversary of Emily's death. They observed the day in gloomy silence—indeed, there was little to distinguish it from any other day. The seismic shift in their lives had effected only a slight shift in the order of things. She took breakfast and tea with her father and dined alone; if there were no letters or callers, no domestic business that required his attention, she might not see him until prayers at half past eight that evening. The dark hours were whiled away in a desolate silence, her father in his parlor with his pipe and glass of port, she in the dining room with her knitting.

How badly she craved companionship on these winter nights with the wind haunting the chimney. Her thoughts dwelled on her London friends, and every morning she waited impatiently for the post, hoping for a letter from George. At night on her knees she prayed, "Dear God, please don't let me think of them too often, too much, too fondly."

On Sundays when her father preached, she sat alone in the cold box pew where they had once all sat crammed together, snug and warm on wintry Sabbath mornings. Now her eyes remained locked on the prayer book in her lap or fixed dully on the steady, familiar figures in the pulpit. Christmas that year was the bleakest she had ever known.

After Christmas, Ellen came to visit. With Ellen there was no strain of keeping up appearances. They knew each other intimately, faults and habits, hopes and broken dreams. They sewed doll clothing and hemmed pinafores for the poor children in the village. They talked silliness and grumbled to each other, and made each other laugh. Ellen always brought with her a semblance of the way things used to be when Charlotte's brother and sisters were still alive.

"I haven't been able to sleep in this house since they died," Charlotte whispered to her one night in bed as they snuggled together for warmth. "Except when you're here."

"Do you have nightmares?"

"Yes. It doesn't seem to get any better. If I sleep at all I sleep lightly, and then I dream. When I wake up, my thoughts are worse than my dreams. I feel haunted—I keep remembering the way they looked when they died."

"You mustn't be so morbid."

"I can't help it, Nell. If I could change my thoughts, I would. You know I would."

"Why don't you have Martha sleep with you?"

"Then Tabby would have to sleep by herself. And Tabby's so old now. She shouldn't be left in her room alone."

"Well, I'm here now."

"Yes. I always sleep soundly when you're here."

"So go to sleep and don't dream."

And she did.

By the end of January, when Reverend Morgan had still not returned *Shirley*, Arthur began a campaign of harassment that nearly drove Patrick out of his wits.

"Be so good as to send him a note, would you?" Arthur pleaded one morning in the vestry.

"I'll do no such thing," Patrick answered tartly. "That gentleman is an old friend. He can have all the time he needs."

"Well, if I had that gentleman's salary I'd do myself the pleasure of buying my own copies of Currer Bell's works," Arthur shot back as he hastily hung his surplice in the wardrobe. "But I do not have his means and therefore am obliged to borrow what I would gladly purchase for myself, if I had the means."

Arthur shrugged on his coat, dusted off his hat, and strode out.

"What a peevish fellow," Patrick scoffed when he recounted the incident to Charlotte after church. "Sounds like he wants me to feel sorry for him. Ha!" Charlotte was setting the table for dinner, and she had to ask her father to get down the soup tureen from the china cabinet. Emily had been tall enough to reach these things.

"I suppose they'll all be reading it soon enough," she said with a note of dismay. In *Shirley* she had portrayed the curates in a particularly foolish and irreverent light, and she winced at the thought of their reading it.

"No doubt about it. There's no hiding now, my dear."

"Do you think they'll recognize themselves?" she asked as she smoothed out a wrinkle in the tablecloth.

"I daresay they will," he answered with a wry chuckle.

Toward the end of the week Martha came in huffing and puffing, babbling about how Mr. Nicholls had closed himself in his room the night before and had some kind of fit.

"What on earth are you talking about, Martha?" Charlotte gasped. "Is he all right?"

"Oh, yes, miss. He was laughin' over some book yer father'd given him. Mother said he was stampin' on the floor an' clappin' his hands so loud she thought he'd gone wrong in the head."

Charlotte went straight to her father. "Has Mr. Nicholls got a copy of *Shirley*?"

"I gave it to him last night."

"Oh!" Charlotte exclaimed. She started to leave, then said, "Apparently he's enjoying it thoroughly."

"Nicholls? Doesn't surprise me a bit. Has a good Irish sense of humor."

"I didn't realize," she murmured.

"You have to dig a little, but it's there."

She got a good taste of it that week from behind closed doors. Every evening Arthur stopped by the parsonage to read his favorite passages aloud to Mr. Brontë, and Charlotte sat in the dining room with her armchair pulled up to the fire, sewing and listening to his deep, infectious laugh. Despite herself, it never failed to put a smile on her face. As long as he was there on the other side of the hall, laughing, she felt a little lighter and a bit less lonely.

One evening as she came up from the pantry with a jar of marmalade for breakfast, she found Arthur in the entry hall on his way out. Anne's fat little spaniel had nudged open the dining room door and now stood on his hind feet with his paws on Arthur's leg while Arthur lavished caresses on him.

"Flossy, get down," Charlotte scolded.

"Good evening, Miss Brontë," he said as he straightened, suddenly flustered by her appearance.

"Good evening, Mr. Nicholls."

Encouraged by the warmth in her voice, he blurted out, "Fine book, Miss Brontë. Delightful. I enjoyed it immensely. The Yorkshire folk are quite proud of you." Then he blushed beet red.

"I take that as a great compliment coming from you, Mr. Nicholls."

"Do you now?"

"Indeed."

"That scene with the curates at tea was capital! Capital!" he said, breaking into a smile. "And the part where the dog chases Grant up the stairs . . . I nearly fell off my chair laughing!"

"You mean Mr. Donne," Charlotte corrected. "The character's name is Donne."

Arthur's grin stretched wider. "Well, it was Keeper that took a bite out of Joseph Grant's backside, if I remember correctly."

"Mr. Nicholls, these characters are wrought from my imagination."

He belted out a full laugh. "Ah, say what you will, but you've got us all in there, warts and all, and I think I'm a better man for it."

Charlotte found herself glowing. "I doubt Mr. Grant will be quite so amused."

"Mr. Grant's sulking, but he'll get over it."

"Has he read it?"

"He has. Got it before I did. His wife has it now."

"Oh, goodness," Charlotte said, trying to keep a solemn face. "I suppose he knows I'm the odious Currer Bell."

"His wife heard it at the market in Bradford."

Charlotte reacted with surprise. "You didn't tell him?"

Arthur stiffened. "I'm no gossipmonger, Miss Brontë. I told no one."

Typically, he had taken offense, but she had no wish to argue with him this evening. She answered him gently, teasingly, "That's the last thing I would fault you with. You're as tight-lipped as they come."

He nodded, softening only slightly, not quite sure how to respond.

Soothingly, she added, "I understand that my father let you in on the secret, and I would have found it perfectly normal for you to tell your friends."

"I knew they'd all find out soon enough."

"You didn't even tell Mr. Sowden?"

"Mr. Sowden heard it from the Merrall brothers. Not from me."

"My goodness," Charlotte exclaimed, "you are a marvel."

"And you are being sarcastic," he answered, his mouth twitching with a repressed grin.

"Not a whit!"

"Then if you're going to flatter me, pray do it truthfully. Say something I can believe."

"What? That you are 'sane and rational, diligent and charitable'?" she teased, which was how she had described him in her novel.

Arthur laughed, and Charlotte flashed her crooked smile. The crusty irritability that had always poisoned their relationship was suddenly gone. Swept away.

Arthur said gently, "Miss Brontë, I know how you cherish your privacy. I presume that if you kept your secret for this long, there must be a reason. Given how famous your books are, I would be ashamed to think that through any indiscretion of mine, I had caused you the least bit of discomfort."

Charlotte was momentarily taken aback; she immediately thought of Lewes and his rush to print everything he had discovered about her. What a different breed of man this was standing before her.

"That's very thoughtful of you," she said quietly.

They were startled by her father's cough on the other side of the door.

Arthur hurried to button up his greatcoat. "Good night, Miss Brontë."

"Good night, Mr. Nicholls," she said. Arthur opened the door and stepped out into the cold February night.

The following week, Charlotte's anonymity was dealt its final blow. One morning she was in the kitchen when Martha returned from the market, red in the face from having run all the way up the lane with her heavy basket. She slung it onto the kitchen table, puffing and blowing, and cried, "Oh, miss! I've heard such news!"

"Goodness, Martha! Calm down! What have you heard?"

She collapsed onto the bench and panted, "Why, they're sayin' ye've been an' written two books—the grandest books that ever was seen! Father heard it at Halifax and Mr. Greenwood heard it at Bradford! They're goin' to have a meeting at the Mechanics' Institute to settle about orderin' 'em!"

They had the meeting that evening, and Martha reported back that once they received the books, the members would be required to cast lots; whoever got a volume would be allowed to keep it for only two days, and overdue fines would be calculated at the exorbitant rate of a shilling per day.

"Oh, miss!" Martha exclaimed. "There was such a crowd o' folk, ye wouldn't believe! They was all pushin' an' shovin' to get to the front to sign up even before we got the books!"

"What silliness," Charlotte said without lifting her eyes from her sewing.

"It's not silliness, miss," Martha said excitedly. "Ye're famous, miss!"

"Don't be a goose," Charlotte said with a surly frown. "It's late. Be off now. To bed."

At the end of the month, a notice appeared in the Bradford *Observer*.

"It is understood that the only daughter of the Rev. P. Brontë, incumbent of Haworth, is the authoress of *Jane Eyre* and *Shirley,* two of the most popular novels of the day, which have appeared under the name of 'Currer Bell.' "

She stood in the parlor, reading the notice to her father, and her palms began to sweat.

Chapter Nineteen

Charlotte was helpless to hold back the swelling tide of curiosity. That spring, celebrity seekers turned up from all over the region hoping to catch a glimpse of the infamous author of *Jane Eyre*. Although the remoteness of Haworth and Main Street's steep incline deterred the fainthearted, it was an indication of her novels' popularity that so many made the journey across the rugged hills. Once at the top of the village, they would stop at the Black Bull or the White Horse Inn, hoping to draw a little information from the taciturn locals, who more often than not answered their curious questions with hostile stares. The visitors would fortify themselves with a pint of ale and then set up Church Lane to gawk at the lonely gray parsonage and wonder at the inhabitants cloistered inside.

As Charlotte's circle of correspondents grew, her mornings were occupied writing letters. The few attempts she made to start another novel only led to depression, but letters were another thing. In her letters, she was at ease and at her best. Invisible and far away, she could engage in discussions with authors and readers who would form their impressions of her based strictly on her thoughts and her words. Her fame now extended across the ocean. She heard from Americans in remote mountainous regions and Canadian professors of literature. Unannounced callers showed up on the parsonage doorstep: a vicar from a township so obscure that Patrick couldn't find it on the map, a Penzance cousin they had never met before.

Arthur was appalled when, during one Sunday service, he noticed two strange young men ogling Charlotte from one of the free pews. His suspicions were confirmed when the service was over and they hung back, twisting their hats in their hands, and then made a rush toward her as she came down the aisle. Arthur barreled through the crowd and pounced on them like a hawk on a titmouse, shielding her with his voluminous snowy robes and detaining them long enough to allow her to slip behind him and escape through the south door and up the path to home.

"Who were they?" Charlotte asked her father that afternoon at tea.

"A couple of so-called poets from Bradford," he said. "One of them has written a book of verse, and he had come seeking Currer Bell's sage advice."

"I see. And what did my defender do?"

"The lad tried to give the manuscript to Nicholls to give to you, but Nicholls wouldn't take it. He was quite put out with them. Told them it was sacrilegious to come to church with such falseness in their hearts."

Charlotte tittered and said, "That's our boy."

There were new friends to be made that year, women writers like Harriet Martineau and Elizabeth Gaskell, but making new acquaintances was a daunting challenge for Charlotte. She would resist unless literally besieged, which is precisely what Sir James Kay-Shuttleworth and his young wife did. He was a baronet, a distinguished physician renowned for social reform, and when Charlotte stubbornly rejected their repeated invitations to visit Gawthorpe Hall, their magnificent castellated seventeeth-century pile just ten miles across the moors in Lancashire, the kind lord and lady swooped down on the parsonage one spring afternoon in their grand carriage and—encouraged by her father—gently abducted her.

Arthur disapproved, and he said as much when Patrick told him where Charlotte had gone.

"She was very reluctant to go," Patrick said.

"To her credit," Arthur stated, his jaw set.

Patrick scowled. "Well, I heartily approved."

"It's overbearing. Imposing themselves on her like that. Quite typical of their class."

"Sir James used to be secretary to the Council on Education. Done a tremendous amount of work on behalf of the poor. A very fine, courtly gentleman and precisely the kind of acquaintance she needs to cultivate. There's no one here worth knowing, Nicholls. Not a single gentleman with any prospects at all."

Arthur wisely dropped the subject, and they turned their attention to the work at hand, their petition to the sanitation board and a new roof for the schoolhouse. Arthur thought with dismay about how prosaic this life must seem to Charlotte, and any dreams he had once entertained seemed more remote than ever.

All that year, Charlotte's life swung like a pendulum between the anxiety of drawing rooms full of strangers and the silent gloom of the parsonage. Both were torture. The more she struggled for some kind of balance, the higher the pendulum would swing. Every time she left Haworth to visit her new friends in London, Windermere, or Manchester, the homecoming would be so painful that she would resolve never to leave home again.

That spring, Sir James insisted on the exclusive right to introduce her to London society at the height of the season, with its rounds of balls and soirées. "I shall have you to Hampton Court and Windsor, Miss Brontë. The royal family are great admirers of yours," he claimed during her visit, hammering away at Charlotte's resistance. He would send his carriage to collect her and bring her to Gawthorpe Hall; then they would leisurely travel down to London together, stopping along the way at the homes of his friends and family to show her off. Charlotte balked at the mere thought of such an ordeal, but her father wouldn't hear of a refusal.

"I detest that kind of thing. You know I do," she said, standing before his desk one morning with her hands clenched at her waist. She dreaded having to defy him; it made her stomach twist in knots.

"You will go, Charlotte. I wish it so."

"I shall not be lionized, Papa," she replied with quiet firmness. "George Smith and his mother were very respectful of my wishes, and everything was done very quietly and in good taste when I stayed with them. Sir James has no intention of being half so moderate in his expectations of me."

"You were in mourning last fall. That was quite different. By May you'll be out of mourning."

"Papa, I'd rather walk on burning coals."

"I won't be contradicted, daughter," he threatened. He took up his magnifying glass and resumed reading the newspaper. "Now leave me. I have work to do, and all this arguing is making my blood pressure rise."

The only bit of brightness in the picture was the prospect of a shopping expedition to Leeds with Ellen to purchase a new wardrobe. Now that she had a little money of her own and was free to wear something other than black, Charlotte quite enjoyed a day of visiting milliners and bootmakers, indulging in French kid gloves and store-bought camisoles, new fans and colorful parasols. Brussels had taught her the importance of finely tailored gowns, and she had acquired a simple, Quaker-like elegance that suited her. Even out of mourning she kept to the more somber tones, like dove-tinted mauve and moss green. Yet the small things baffled her, like the choice between a black or a white lace mantle, or whether a pink silk lining in her bonnet would seem too frivolous.

The hairpiece was Ellen's idea, a plait of brown merino wool that would give a little volume to her thin hair. They returned to their room at the inn in Leeds that afternoon, and Charlotte sat on a chair while Ellen wound the braid around the top of her head.

"Your father is absolutely right to insist," Ellen mumbled as she drew a hairpin from her mouth and jabbed it into Charlotte's skull. "He's doing it for your own good. You sink into depression at home. You must get away." She held up a mirror for Charlotte to inspect the hairpiece. "There. How does that look?"

Hesitantly, Charlotte explored the crown of hair with her fingers.

"It's all the fashion now," Ellen said.

Once Charlotte had examined her reflection from all angles, a smile swept over her broad face. "It does look rather nice, doesn't it?"

Ellen collapsed onto the bed. Then, with a sudden exclamation, she shot up and went to her cloak on the coat rack. Fishing in a pocket, she pulled out a packet tied with ribbon. "Here. George's letters."

Charlotte took the packet from her with a quiet smile and slipped it into her skirt pocket. She had been sending George's letters on to Ellen to read.

"So, now you'll stop boring me with all your silly hints," Charlotte said. "You see in what light he views me."

"I see that you're on first-name basis," Ellen said slyly. "And I think I detect a certain undercurrent there, even if you prefer to ignore it."

"Ellen, I'm eight years older and without the slightest claim to beauty."

Ellen leaned forward and snatched the hand mirror away from Charlotte. "I wish there were no mirrors in the world. Then you'd stop going on that way about yourself."

"I don't need mirrors, Nell. I see myself reflected in the eyes of others."

For once, fate worked in Charlotte's favor. Just a few days before she was due to leave, the hard-driven Sir James suffered a total nervous collapse. When George learned that Charlotte's visit to London had been canceled, he instructed his mother to invite her to stay in their grand new residence near the highly desirable Hyde Park Gardens. Within the week, Charlotte found herself back in the Smiths' home, bent over books of fabric samples with Mrs. Smith and her three daughters, listening to them debate between a blue floral and a bird of paradise design for the chintz morning room curtains.

It was May, and everything about London was different and splendid. George bent his schedule to accompany her wherever she wished to go. They took open carriage rides along Rotten Row at the fashionable hour when all London society came out to be seen. Hidden behind the deep hood of her spring bonnet, so tiny she might have been mistaken for a child, she gazed upon the scenes she had so often imagined as a little girl. Ladies in veiled riding hats and flowing green habits vied for the crowd's attention; red-coated hussars on horseback paraded along the lanes, stealing the hearts of a score of marriageable girls up from the country. Powerful and ambitious men demonstrated their skill driving matched pairs of spirited horses. It was London's dazzling vanity fair, and none of it was lost on her quick eye.

George pointed out the people worth noting, discreetly whispering names in her ear, adding little anecdotes that put a smile on her face. Charlotte was cautious never to breathe a word of this in her letters to her father or Ellen; it would have shocked them to know how much these jaunts pleased her.

That year the Royal Academy had a fine exhibit, with a Landseer portrait of her hero the Duke of Wellington and a new work by John Martin—which she did mention to her father. George teased her mercilessly about her idol worship of Wellington; especially to please her, he arranged a Sunday stroll when he knew the old man would be coming out of chapel. After walking past the duke, he spun her around and trotted her across the street, and they were able to cut back up a path and pass him again in the gardens. Then they collapsed on a bench to catch their breath, both of them laughing like childish pranksters. In George's company, bathed in his playful attentions, Charlotte reclaimed the vivacity she had buried with Heger.

Thackeray called one Saturday morning and stayed for two hours, and she went to his home to dine the following evening. That dinner was the only failed moment of her visit. She arrived in her chaste high-collared dress to find a room full of sophisticated society ladies, many in low-cut gowns with softly cleaved bosoms, and she was soon wishing she were at the Zoological Gardens among the lions and leopards. One particularly striking young beauty diverted George's gaze throughout the evening, and Charlotte—who was painfully observant of these things—

found herself sinking into a chilly silence, quite incapable of making conversation except with the quiet governess who was supervising Thackeray's young daughters. The evening was a disaster—the room dim and smoky from the oil lamps, Charlotte constrained and unbrilliant, the others breathlessly expectant. As soon as Charlotte left, Thackeray took up his hat and sneaked out to his club, abandoning his disappointed guests to gossip about how poor Charlotte's braided hairpiece was so obviously false. Years later, some would recall it as the dullest evening of their life.

She and George argued over only one thing: her portrait. He proposed the idea one evening after the opera. Neither of them were inclined to sleep, and his mother—who had slept through most of the performance—now sat snoring in her armchair, with her chin resting comfortably on her chest.

George sat with his legs stretched out, necktie dangling from one hand and a glass of brandy in the other.

"Richmond is the artist who did Harriet Martineau's portrait. The one you admired at her home. And I will bear the expense myself."

"I can't let you do that."

"Yes, you can."

"I see no need to have my portrait made. Who would want such a thing in their home?"

He belted out such a laugh that it startled his mother from her sleep. She muttered something nonsensical and immediately dozed off again.

"See," Charlotte said, with her taut little smile that both scolded and sparred. "She agrees with me."

"Mother doesn't have a vote in this one," he replied, swirling the amber liquid in his glass. "I won't let you squirm your way out."

"Truthfully, my dear father would be the only person who would derive any pleasure from such a portrait, and after he's gone, what would I possibly do with it?"

George slung his necktie onto the table, then sat up and crossed his legs. There was a thoughtful pause before he spoke. "And if I told you I wanted it for myself? That I wanted a portrait of my famous authoress, whose genius rescued my business when I feared it might fail and whose courage has been an inspiration to me personally. What would you say to that?"

Charlotte braved the intensity of his blue eyes, holding that sweet moment as long as possible. "Would it really displease you so if I were to refuse?" she asked softly.

"It would."

"All right then."

An impassive butler greeted them at the door, led them up a narrow staircase, and deposited them in a small alcove, where they waited while Richmond finished another sitting. During those few moments, Charlotte's courage nearly failed her. Watching her, George could see the struggle being waged behind those intense hazel-brown eyes. She withdrew her gloves and fidgeted with them in her lap, glancing anxiously toward the wide double doors. She looked as if she might bolt at any second, and George reached for her hand to calm her. She started, as if jolted by an electric shock. Her palms were hot and moist.

"He'll be out in a minute," George said soothingly, trying to think of something that might distract her.

But at that moment the door flew open and Richmond stood there. He was a good-looking man of middle age, slender, with fine-boned, aristocratic features.

"Ah!" he said as Charlotte rose to greet him. "Miss Brontë! This is indeed an honor! A very great honor!"

He led them into his studio, and as she slipped her spectacles into her pocket and untied her bonnet, she gave herself a stern little lecture and vowed not to let her nerves get the better of her.

She turned to find Richmond scrutinizing her with that intense objectifying look she had seen in the eyes of artists. She managed a smile and then removed her bonnet.

"What is that thing?" Richmond asked, striding toward her with his hands thrust deep into the pockets of his smock.

"What?" Charlotte asked nervously.

"On your head," he replied, his eyes boring down on her with a perplexed frown.

Her hand shot to the braided crown of hair.

"Your fur hat. Could you remove it?" he asked.

She turned a mortified look on George and immediately broke into tears.

"It's a hairpiece," George whispered to him. "Rather difficult to remove, I should think."

"Ah!" Richmond said. "I see." He cleared his throat. "Well, not to worry, Miss Brontë, we can work around it."

But he could see the nervous state she was in, and he summoned the maid, who took Charlotte away.

"I say, she's a sensitive little thing, isn't she?" Richmond said.

"Very. Particularly about her appearance."

"Ah, well, in that case, I think it best that she not see the work in progress. She can view it when it's finished."

"I am in perfect agreement, sir."

Charlotte returned a short while later, the hairpiece gone, looking pale and exhausted. She managed a brave, timid smile and offered a heartfelt apology.

She returned the following day for a final sitting. When he had finished, Richmond beckoned her to come forward and see the work. Subtle shading had improved the square jaw and broad nose and softened the irregular mouth, but the focus was on her intensely expressive eyes. In those dark pools he had captured her sweetness and melancholy, and hinted at the well of anxiety beneath the gentle façade. It was Charlotte, and yet not like her at all. Little did he know that, with his talent for quiet flattery, he had evoked a whisper of her sister Anne, who had always been the prettiest of the three.

George had a unique effect on Charlotte. With his boyish exuberance and charm, he was able to draw smiles and wit from her like a magnet, and somewhere along the continuum of her visit she laid down her defenses. Strolling down the street side by side with her hand wound through his arm, she would press her shoulder against him. Facing each other in the carriage, she would lean forward, place her hands on his knees, look up into his eyes, and talk away with sparkling frankness. They never lacked for words, and their silences were full of unspoken complicity. She fell in love with him not only for himself, but for how he made her feel when she was with him. She was loose and alive inside. If he had been so inclined, she would have allowed him to kiss her.

They returned one afternoon from an excursion and found George's mother and his youngest sister in the drawing room, Mrs. Smith busy with her embroidery and Isabella sprawled on her stomach before the window, copying illustrations of horses into her sketch pad.

"George, come and see what I've drawn," Isabella said brightly as she sat back on her heels.

But George was murmuring in a low voice to Charlotte, who broke away from him with a scolding glance and crossed the room toward the little girl. "What have you drawn, Bella? May I see?"

"Mother," George announced, "I've asked Charlotte to come up to Scotland with me next month when I go to fetch Alick home from school."

Charlotte twirled around in midstride and said lightly, "He's only joking."

"I daresay he is," Mrs. Smith chimed in.

"I am certainly not joking."

When his mother heard that tone of voice, her head shot up.

"Bella, dearest, take your sketch pad up to the nursery," she said as she swiftly put away her needlework.

"But Mama . . ." Bella whined.

"Bella?" she said sternly. The girl gathered up her pencils and chalks and sulked out.

George, busy checking his watch against the clock on the mantel, ignored the brewing tempest at his back. When he had pocketed the watch, he said, "I thought we'd take a little side trip up to the Highlands. Charlotte, you could meet us in Glasgow in two weeks' time, and from there . . ." He went on, planning the itinerary, dropping the names of Scottish watering places Charlotte had visited only in her dreams.

Charlotte had taken refuge in the chair opposite his mother. When George finished, she turned a raised eyebrow to his mother and said, "I do think your son is serious."

"Of course I am," he enthused. "Tarbet is on Loch Lomond—there's a perfectly decent inn there—and Oban is a lovely resort town. We'd be traveling through some of Scotland's most beautiful regions—"

Charlotte raised both hands in protest. "George, do stop. It's out of the question. I hardly think it's advisable for us to go gallivanting around the country together. That would certainly set tongues wagging."

"George, don't tempt her," his mother said sternly. "Her instincts are impeccable. You can imagine the gossip that would set off."

"There's nothing improper about it. Eliza's coming along—"

His mother interrupted. "Eliza is only two years older than you."

"—and Alick would be with us on the way back." George wagged a playful finger at Charlotte. "Mark my words, you'll not find a better chaperone in all of London than my seventeen-year-old brother. He's like a leech."

"George," his mother said sternly, "have you lost your senses?"

Hearing the rising alarm in her voice, George chose not to pursue the argument, although both women could see they had upset him by siding against him. After dinner, Charlotte put on her spectacles and tried to mollify him by reading a few poems in French by Lamartine. But he remained sullen, slumped in his armchair with his legs stretched out before him, one boot toe tapping away to the rhythm of invisible thoughts.

His mother knew him well enough to expect him in her bedroom that evening, and she sat dozing with a book on her stomach, waiting for the sound of his knock on her door.

"I'll have my way on this one, Mother, so don't oppose me," he stated calmly as he picked up a chair and plunked it down next to her bed. "I can't imagine a place more to her liking than Scotland would be."

His mother removed her reading glasses and turned a worried frown on him.

"Be frank with me, George. What are your intentions with regards to Miss Brontë?"

"My intentions?"

"You're not entertaining the idea of pursuing this woman, are you?"

"No."

"You hesitated just then."

He paused and lowered his voice soothingly. "Mother, dear, you know my weakness for pretty faces."

"I also know your weakness for clever people."

"I find her fascinating, but not in that way."

"But she might misread your attentions. You certainly don't treat her like a sister."

"I don't think of her as a sister. She's my author, and she's an extraordinary woman. Her mind, her personality—all of it intrigues me. But she has absolutely no physical charms. There's nothing in that regard to tempt me in the slightest."

"I'm relieved to hear that. But I do worry about how she might misconstrue all these wild plans of yours. She's such a sensitive creature."

"Yes, but she's also far too wise to think I could ever be in love with her." He leaned forward with his elbows on his knees and his hands folded, a thoughtful look on his face. "I see it this way. It's a gift I want to give her. The gift of my company on a simple excursion that would bring her an immense amount of pleasure. She needs to live, Mother. She has such a love of life, and she's had so little opportunity to experience it." He paused and added, "I think it might help bring out her next novel. She's struggling to find a story, and I'd like to see her return to that romantic vein again. Scotland might be just the inspiration."

"It's very kind and generous of you, my dear boy, but that's not the way the gossipmongers will see it."

"I see it as good business, Mother. To keep my author happy."

She hesitated. "Well, then, if it would please you."

"Then I'd like you to do something for me. Tomorrow, after I've gone to the office, I want you to use your influence to persuade her. Without your approval she won't agree, and that would greatly disappoint me."

Chapter Twenty

Ellen's home in Birstall served as a halfway house for Charlotte, a way of easing herself out of the whirl of London before descending into the tomblike silence of Haworth. In the past, when there had been so many Nusseys tumbling over one another, Brookroyd House had been a little overwhelming. The cramped Georgian stone house was filled with a staggering jumble of heirlooms and small treasures, patterned quilts, chintzes, and needlepoint. It was difficult to find a place to sit that wasn't cluttered with another body, a cat, or a sewing basket. The more fortunate ones had grown up and moved away, and Brookroyd had become a house of unmarried women and a wayside for the more troublesome brothers, who came around from time to time to stir things up. The drama felt warmly familiar, reminding Charlotte of the domestic upheavals, great and small, that had once occupied her own days.

Come warm weather, they escaped to the garden. In the mornings, while Ellen trimmed back the sprawling hollyhocks and weeded the potager, Charlotte would tag along, chattering away freely, her breathlessly long sentences dotted with expressions of deep affection like "my darling Nell" and "my dear, dear Nell." In the afternoons they sat in the leafy shade of an old beech tree and pitted cherries, and later, in the pitch black of a moonless night, they would stroll the gravel walks arm in arm, dissecting human nature and their own hearts.

Charlotte arrived at Brookroyd late and exhausted, and she didn't tell Ellen about her planned excursion to Scotland until the next morning. She knew she could count on Ellen for sound maidenly advice. Ellen's judgment hinged on the strictures of morality. Even romance must abide by the rules.

"You mean to say he sent his mother to argue his case?" Ellen said in wide-eyed wonder. "And she did his bidding?"

"Oh, the mother may be master of the house, but the son is clearly master of his mother," Charlotte said benignly, looking up from her embroidery hoop. "She quite pleaded with me. She said George would be very upset if I didn't go. George's father was a Scotsman, you know. He's quite proud of his native land."

Charlotte did not tell her dear friend how little persuasion it had taken, how she had lain awake all night, burning with resentment at having to deny herself the sweet opportunity laid at her feet. Because it was the right, the moral thing to do. Then she had gone down the next morning to discover that George had crushed his mother's objections and rescued her dreams.

"You mustn't go." Ominously, Ellen's voice dipped to the low register. "It's highly improper."

"It might be, if things were other than they are."

"What do you mean?"

"That I'm quite protected from him on two fronts: my age and my looks."

"Oh, Charlotte, you're fooling yourself. I've read his letters. I think he's captivated by you, my dear, and should you find yourself alone with him out in some wild mountainous region with no one to protect you . . ." Ellen was getting a little carried away, and Charlotte was tempted to smile.

"George and I understand each other perfectly. And we respect each other sincerely. We really do suit, in all ways except those that would excite romance. I don't fear his attentions in the least. I would go anywhere in the world with him." She added, a shade defiantly, "Even to China, if it would make him happy."

"What does your father say?"

Charlotte grew suddenly quiet, dropping her nose back into her needlework.

"Have you told him?"

"You know he is best kept in the dark about things that might upset him."

"You mean you intend to hide it from him?"

"Of course not. But I intend to present him with the situation at the right moment and in a certain light, to be sure to gain his approval."

Charlotte reached into her work basket and retrieved a small skein of gold thread. "Oh, Ellen, I am so weary of being sensible and ladylike."

"Charlotte!"

"And I am so longing to go."

Charlotte began carefully unwinding the skein, drawing out the fine gold thread.

"I think you feel more for him than you say you do, and I'm afraid he might take advantage of your tender feelings."

"Come now," Charlotte scowled as she held the needle to the light. "George is not a rake."

"No, but he's very worldly, and I think your judgment may be a little clouded."

Charlotte fell into a long, reflective silence while she threaded the needle.

"What are you working on?" Ellen asked, her attention drawn to the folds of heavy white silk in Charlotte's lap.

"It's an altar hanging." There was a shade of dejection in her voice. "I was growing tired of hearing Mr. Nicholls complain about our worn and faded altar hangings." She lowered the embroidery hoop to show Ellen. "It's my own design. A burning bush, in silver and gold thread against the white."

"It's lovely."

Charlotte straightened her spectacles and raised the hoop to her eyes. With her nose nearly touching the silk, she began whipping tiny, perfectly even stitches. "I think he'll be pleased," she said, but it was evident that her thoughts were not remotely inclined toward Arthur Bell Nicholls.

In the end, Charlotte and her conscience struck a compromise. She spent a mere two days in Edinburgh with George and his sister and relinquished the pleasure of an extended excursion into the wild romantic Highlands. But those two days would be remembered like no other time in her life. Away from his mother's watchful eyes, buoyant with the freedom of anonymity, Charlotte felt her heart suddenly take wing.

George planned every moment of those two days with Charlotte's pleasure in mind. The local driver he hired was a hard-featured man with a dry sense of humor and a gift for storytelling, and he knew every nook and alley of Edinburgh worth noting. As they rode around the city, Charlotte chattered away to him like an old soul, enthralled by his rich Scottish burr as much as his erudition; while he pointed out the sights, they talked about Scott's Waverly novels, about Scottish history and legends. George could barely keep up with the two of them; he sat back in the open cab enjoying the summer day, greatly relieved to see Charlotte so relaxed.

There would be no adventure in the Highlands, but George was adamant that she should see the literary shrines of Abbotsford and Melrose Abbey, even though it meant rising in the pitch dark to be on the road at the break of dawn. Abbotsford, the fantastic baronial castle built by Sir Walter Scott, was nearly a four-hour drive from Edinburgh, through magnificent wooded valleys. Once in the carriage, Eliza removed her bonnet, settled into her corner with her shawl behind her head, and slept most of the way, but Charlotte hung at the open window, determined not to waste a single precious moment.

They jostled along in silence, swaying with the coach as it wended its way through the valley. After a long while, George folded his newspaper.

"Are you ready to eat something?" he said quietly. "We have fresh buns the inn packed for us."

Charlotte drew her head back inside. "In a little while," she smiled. A strand of hair had blown loose and she tucked it into her bonnet. "It might amuse you to know that when my brother and I were young, we were slavish imitators of Scott. It was all very childish, but it was a source of pure enjoyment to us, re-creating those wild adventures, all those stories of revenge and power and love." A dreamy look came over her, softening her face and distancing her eyes.

"Have you any inclination to return to that kind of story again?"

She answered with a firm shake of the head. "I don't believe in fairy tales anymore." Then, sweetly, she turned her eyes on him and said, "I've never enjoyed myself so much, George. I don't know how to thank you."

He raised a hand in protest. "I will not hear any more professions of gratitude. This is quite as much fun for me as it is for you. I haven't been to Abbotsford since I was Alick's age." He shifted his weight and grew suddenly thoughtful. "He has an advantage over me, Alick does. He's much more studious than I was. I was quite unruly in school."

"Unruly?" Charlotte prodded.

"I was expelled. That's when Father put me to work as an apprentice in the firm." He gave her a dimpled smile. "We exported ladies' bonnets to India. It was a thoroughly practical education." He straightened his broad shoulders and drew a deep breath before confiding, "But it puts me at a disadvantage. Sometimes I find myself quite overwhelmed by the company I keep."

"You have a great intellectual capacity, George. There is nothing to stop you from acquiring knowledge."

"I don't have the time. I don't have a spare minute in my day."

"Then hold on tenaciously to what you have, and remember, when you're surrounded by the Ruskins and the Leweses and—"

"—and the Brontës—"

She flapped her tiny hand at him. "Remember that it is not that they have any greater capacity than you do. Perhaps through circumstances of fate they have acquired an erudition superior to yours, but Nature is a wonderful school—my sister Emily is a brilliant example of this—and you can arrive at a knowledge unsophisticated but genuine."

"That's what I find so remarkable about you," he said with a broad smile. "Any other woman would have flattered me. Told me I was perfect the way I am." He added with a shade of regret, "I wish we could have visited the Highlands together."

She leaned forward and placed her featherlight hand on his knee. "I have no regrets. These few days have surpassed anything I've ever known."

She shifted her gaze back to the window. "This country inspires such romance, doesn't it? It tempts one to do something wild and unpredictable."

"Like what?"

"Like . . ." She hesitated, her eyes flashing brightly. "Like hopping down from the carriage and setting off through the hills on foot!"

"Then I'll stop the driver right now!" George teased, reaching for his walking stick to tap on the roof.

"George! Don't you dare!" she cried with a twinkling smile.

The carriage hit a hole, tossing them to one side. Protectively, George reached out to brace Charlotte with one hand and his sister with the other. Eliza stirred in her sleep, and her bonnet slipped from her loose fingers to the floor. George retrieved it, and when he laid it on the seat he said, "I shouldn't have let you leave London. I knew you'd change your mind. I should have kept you captive until it was time to go, and then abducted you."

"An abduction! Straight out of Walter Scott!" Charlotte teased.

He spread his hands. "If it makes you happy . . ."

"Truly, a longer excursion would have been very difficult. I've been gone from home far too long. Papa's all alone now except for the servants."

"You've said he keeps himself very busy."

"Oh, he does. He's always knee-deep in all sorts of petitions and reforms. He still preaches on Sundays, and he's very much in demand as a speaker. And he has frequent visitors." She gave George a wry smile. "Mostly of the clerical sort."

"But what about you? What will you do down there in the winter?"

"You know very well what I'll be doing. I'll be writing my next book. I can't run away forever."

"Why don't you move into London?"

"And leave my father?"

"You'd bring him with you. After a few more novels, you'll be earning enough to live very comfortably."

"I couldn't do that."

"But you would greatly benefit from the company of friends so nearby. And you *have* friends in London, Charlotte."

She shook her head. "I could never induce my father to leave. I don't believe he has slept away from home once in nearly ten years. His entire life has been devoted to his parish."

"Do you intend to bury yourself up there in Haworth for the rest of your life?"

"I have no choice."

With a lighthearted smile George turned to admire a bit of scenery floating by the window. To him, the suggestion was nothing more than a passing whim, but it seemed to Charlotte that something had happened, something subtle and perhaps imagined, but it was enough to leave her with a gnawing sense of loss, like someone cut off from hope and set adrift with no dreams left in sight.

They returned late and Charlotte spent a sleepless night grappling with her emotions. She was more than a little in love with him, and their growing intimacy had given rise to a sense of possibility. But George was as unsuited to her soul as she was to his body, and Charlotte was profoundly aware of this. She thought there must be something dreadfully wrong with her that such a man would leave her so unfulfilled. He was a man graced with everything she lacked. A businessman, straightforward and uncomplicated, fascinated by a woman of psychological complexity. There, that was the end of it. There was nothing more to it. "You mustn't make demands on him," she warned herself. "Not if you want to keep him, or have any little portion of his affections. Don't expect too much of him or he'll feel you to be troublesome, and then it will be all over. Deny yourself and your needs, and be still."

Arriving at Ellen's directly from Scotland, she came undone. The stimulus of place and people had proved too much for her, and she landed at Brookroyd pale, trembling, and slightly feverish. After several days she roused herself enough to write George a cheery, playful letter in the voice of her author-self, Currer Bell, who always, at a distance, spoke more assertively than Charlotte Brontë. In it she attempted to place their relationship in the context of their vastly dissimilar lives. She wrote:

> *You are to keep a fraction of yourself—if it be only the end of your little finger—for Currer Bell, and that fraction he will neither let gentleman nor lady—author or artist—take possession of—or so much as meddle with. He reduces his claim to a minute point— and that point he monopolizes.*

"Oh, miss! Oh ye're home!" Martha cried. She stood at the front door of the parsonage drying her hands on her apron, and in the same breath she shouted over her shoulder, "Tabby, the mistress is 'ome!"

Charlotte was trying to fend off the dogs while directing the footman shuffling up the garden path with her trunk on his back. "Please to take it to the top of the stairs," she said to him while she herded Keeper back into the house. Old Tabby came hobbling out of the kitchen and added to the fracas with a sob. "Aye, miss, we've been worried sick about ye!"

Charlotte hurried forward to give the old woman a reassuring hug. "Tabby, what is all this nonsense?" she scolded tenderly. "Where's Papa?"

"Across the lane in the chippin' shed."

Charlotte handed her bonnet to Martha and hurried through the kitchen to the backyard.

Her father was coming across the lane from the shed, scattering the chickens with his walking stick as he swung open the gate. He was seventy-three now and his knees were failing him, but he still bore himself perfectly erect with the dignified air of an old warrior. Charlotte was ready to be annoyed with him until she saw the tears swelling in his eyes.

"Oh, my dear daughter. I'm so relieved!" he said as he drew her into a crushing embrace.

She squirmed loose and tilted back her head to look up at him. "I was in the cab down at the foot of Bridgehouse Hill when I saw Mr. Greenwood with his walking staff. He saw me and waved me down. He said you were quite beside yourself with worry about me, and that he was setting off to Brookroyd to get news of me!"

"Don't be annoyed, Charlotte. God knows how worried we've been, ever since I got Miss Nussey's letter. She said that as soon as you got back from Scotland you took straight to bed. I didn't know if it was one of your bilious attacks or something more serious."

He scanned her face with a worried frown. He had grown increasingly careless in his appearance; his shirts were frayed at the edges, and he never wore a proper necktie anymore. She stood on her toes and gave him a kiss on his bristled cheek.

"She's unduly vexed you, Papa. I was exhausted, and I have a slight cold. That's all. I needed to rest."

"You look pale. Is everything all right?"

"Everything is quite all right." She took him by the arm and led him back inside. "Come. Let me pour you a nice cup of tea to calm you down."

Early that evening, after she had settled him quietly in his study with his slippers, pipe, and a glass of port, she sat in the kitchen with Tabby and Martha, going over the household accounts. Charlotte had grown soft-hearted with the servants and long ago ceased questioning the occasional excesses. She suspected Tabby of pocketing a little soap and candles for her nephew now and then, and she imagined that some of their sugar and flour ended up in Martha's mother's larder. All she could do was voice a mild exclamation from time to time about how much sugar they went through in a month, although they rarely made fruit pies anymore. No one could make fruit pies as good as Emily's.

"You musn't let Papa work himself into such a fever pitch of excitement," she said to Martha, looking up from a bill in her hands. "It's not good for his blood pressure."

"Master gets hisself that way without no help from us."

"But you mustn't encourage him. You know how prone he is to look on the dark side of things. He can always find some way to torment himself. He's quite good at it."

As Charlotte set the bill aside, her glance took in both of them: Tabby in her chair in the corner pitting a bowl of cherries and Martha at the table sorting out the tradesmen's bills.

"It seems he was worried about more than my health."

Martha kept her head low and swatted at a fly. Tabby didn't hear, or pretended as much.

"He'd quite got it into his head that I had run off to Scotland to get married, or at least was on the verge of it."

A look passed between the servants. "Is it true, miss?" Tabby asked.

"Absolutely not." She leaned down to pick up some cherry stones that had rolled to the floor. "I'm quite annoyed with Ellen. She must have put that idea in his head." She dropped the stones into the pile on Tabby's lap and said, "Time to light the lamp, Martha. I can't see well enough to finish these accounts."

"Aye, miss," Martha said, and she rose from the bench to fetch the lamp.

In August, Richmond's portrait of Charlotte arrived, along with an engraving of the Duke of Wellington, a gift from George to Charlotte's father. Both had been beautifully framed at George's expense, and that same day John Brown came around with his ladder to hang them. The entire household had gathered in the dining room, and they were in the thick of discussion, each with an opinion as to the most favorable lighting and position, when Flossy came wagging into the hall, his curly hair matted and wet, and his tongue lolling half way to the floor.

Charlotte spied him and clapped her hands, herding the dog back into the kitchen, where she found Arthur standing in the doorway in his rumpled linen jacket and straw hat, clutching a string of trout.

"Good day, miss. Sorry about Flossy, there," he said. "Thought you might like a few of these for your dinner." He raised the string to show off his catch. The sun had burnished his fair skin, setting off the sky blue of his twinkling eyes. Without his clerical garb he had the air of an amiable country gentleman, and there flashed before Charlotte's eyes the memory of that encounter years ago when she had come upon him knee-deep in the stream, trout tickling with the village boys. The smell of the moors on a breezy summer day clung to his clothing, and she felt a peculiar longing as she imagined him rambling through the moors with Flossy, chasing up birds and watching the clouds sweep across the sky.

"What shall I do with them?" Arthur asked, noting her blank-faced silence.

Charlotte came to her senses. "Why, that's very kind of you, Mr. Nicholls," she said. "Let me fetch Martha."

A moment later she returned with the servant. Martha gave a little exclamatory cry and came bustling around the table toward Arthur. "Why, what good-lookin' trout, sir. This'll make for a pleasant change."

As she slapped them down on a sheet of newspaper and opened the knife drawer, the sound of voices in the other room drew Arthur's attention.

"Am I interrupting something?"

"Oh, not really," Charlotte replied with a dismissive shake of her head.

Martha gave a grunt of dissent. "The mistress had her portrait made in London, sir. Have to be somebody important to have yer portrait made by a famous artist, that's what I say." She finished sharpening the knife and, with swift strokes of the blade, began gutting the trout. "I think it's a good and proper likeness of the mistress. Tabby don't know what she's talkin' about. Anyway, she's half blind."

At that moment Tabby hobbled in, shaking her head and muttering under her breath, "Makes her look old." She saw Arthur and repeated her cry: "Makes her look old, I say."

"You remember me young, that's all, Tabby," Charlotte said loudly.

"But the portrait of the master is a good 'un."

"It's not Papa, Tabby. It's the Duke of Wellington."

Tabby only scowled and put up her hands as if to ward off any dissenting thought.

"You're welcome to come throw your opinion into the arena," Charlotte told Arthur.

"I'll call this evening," he said with a tip of his hat. "When I'm not smelling of fish."

That evening they stood gazing up at her portrait above the fireplace. The summer sun had slipped below the hills, and Charlotte struck a match to light the lamp.

"What do you think, Nicholls?" Patrick asked. Without waiting for a reply, he went on: "You need to see it in the daylight, without the glare from the lamp." Patrick stepped up and peered at it closely through his spectacles. "Wonderfully good and lifelike without flattering her, don't you think? A very correct likeness." His voice dipping in a sudden tone of remorse, he added, "Although there is one who could have appreciated it with more skill and taste than mine, but that person is gone now. And I must take the blame for that."

There was a moment of uncomfortable silence. Then, controlled, he went on: "It improves upon acquaintance. I like it more this evening than I did this morning. I fancy I see strong indications of her genius there." He raised his hand to silence Charlotte's rebuke. "Don't deny me my opinion, daughter. It may be that I'm partial and too enthusiastic, but that's my prerogative as your father."

Charlotte had been observing Arthur keenly. The granite-like face remained immovable while he gently fingered the rim of his hat. "Very fine. Very fine indeed," he said in a subdued voice.

A pang of disappointment tweaked her heart. She had hoped for a meaningful comment, a sign of critical appreciation, but there was none. Only this dull platitude. He turned to Charlotte. "I've neglected to thank you properly for the altar cloth. It was beautifully done."

"You're very welcome. I thought the white would come in useful."

"Indeed. It's already been put to good use. We've had three marriages this week."

As they moved toward the door, Patrick said, "That's the one duty I'm glad to relinqish to you, Nicholls. Marriage is pure folly, wouldn't you agree? A few days of madness followed by years of suffering. Marriage is for the weak. The wise remain single." He clapped Arthur on the back jovially and said with a burst of laughter, "A course you seem destined to follow, my friend."

Arthur stiffened. He turned toward Charlotte. "Well, good night, Miss Brontë."

"I'll see you to the door."

"Such a beautiful night," she declared in the doorway, glancing up at the stars shining brightly in the eastern sky.

He paused on the gravel walk and turned, his imposing figure in tall black hat and black garb blurred by the falling shadows.

He reflected thoughtfully for a moment and then said, "I may be mistaken, but I thought I saw a resemblance to Anne in your portrait."

Charlotte felt tears rise to her eyes. She said, "I thought so, too."

"Did you now?"

"Yes. It was the first thing I thought when I saw it."

"Rather remarkable that he could capture it. Such a subtle family resemblance. Quite impossible to define." Then, gazing up at the sky, he added, "Yes, a spectacular night. There is great beauty in God's gift of life. May we rejoice in it."

After he had gone, Charlotte remained in the garden. She walked around Emily's flower bed, now overgrown with grasses, and sat on the moss-covered stone wall below a thorn tree for a long while, listening in the darkness; there was an occasional churlish voice coming from the path that cut through the churchyard, the sound of boots in the cobbled lane, the cry of a lone owl, the wind.

She could not bear to go back inside and sit alone in silence.

From that evening on, Arthur understood what it meant to be falling in love. It was a miserable state of mind, he discovered, and he was completely blindsided by his feelings. The sound of her footsteps and the rustle of her skirt on the stairs were enough to provoke a sudden weakness in the knees and pounding of the heart, as if he'd just dashed all the way to the brow of Cockhill Moor. Whenever she attended one of his services he had to be quite severe with himself; he dared not glance toward her pew during the sermon for fear of losing his train of thought and going absolutely blank.

Chapter Twenty-one

Summer slipped quietly away, and most days London lay softly shrouded in a chilly mist. Thackeray found George Smith waiting for him at the club that afternoon, sipping his brandy and water and leafing through the *Times*. George had acquired a certain eminence in the literary world now, and the waiters—who knew these things—tended to him with a shade of obsequiousness beneath their placid masks.

They each lit a cigar and sat in contented silence, watching the gray smoke coil over their heads, glad to be out of the drizzle and in the relaxed warmth of their club.

"And how is your angry little lady of genius?" Thackeray asked in his droll manner, which Charlotte had found so difficult to understand.

"You provoke her, Thackeray. And I believe you do it quite intentionally."

"Of course it's intentional. The woman rouses my antagonism. All that idealistic cant about my mission as an author. I quite appalled her when I told her I was going off to America with Barnum and Bailey's to give my lecture series. She thought it undignified. So I proceeded to tell her I would be dressing up like a clown. I can be quite contrary, you know. Of course I take my work seriously. But writing is a business to me, not some higher calling. I write to pay the bills. I have two daughters to raise and I am determined to leave them with a good dowry. That is the extent of it, Smith."

George thought he should say something in Charlotte's defense, but his club always put him in an entirely different frame of mind from that which operated at Cornhill or at home. He studied his cigar, admiring the shape and feel of it.

"You must know how she admires you," he said at last. "She once said to me that one good word from you is worth pages of praise from any ordinary judge."

"Ah, but she's such a strange creature—staring up at me with those intense eyes of hers and hanging on every word I say, and then when she gets me alone she proceeds to tell me I have feet of clay because I pander to the upper classes." He scowled at the end of his cigar, then took a puff and leaned back to exhale. "I find she judges us London folk prematurely. We're not entirely without scruples."

"Indeed, she can be disarmingly frank."

"I shall never forget that fiery little lecture she gave me after I'd introduced her to my mother as Jane Eyre. She quite intimidated me, you know." Thackeray paused to muse. "She will defend her book quite boldly but is outraged when anyone tries to identify her with her character. I sometimes think she didn't fully understand what she had written until after it had been published. I think she revealed more about herself than she wanted to admit."

"Revealed what?"

"Why, all that story about resisting the temptation of an adulterous love."

George reflected on this for a moment and thought it better to steer the conversation away from the possibility of Charlotte Brontë's adulterous affairs, an idea he found entirely absurd.

"I sometimes wonder how she manages to write at all up there in that bleak little village of hers," George said. "Several of us in Cornhill correspond with her frequently. And my mother sends off a letter from time to time. To keep her spirits up."

"I'm afraid you can't count on me there. Ah, now, don't take me wrong, George. I have great respect for her integrity and her love of truth. She has an unspoiled quality and a simplicity that I greatly admire. But I'm sure you see why she and I can't be great friends. There's a fire raging in that little woman—and it doesn't suit me. She has had a story with a man and a great grief that has gone badly with her."

George, who had often suspected the same thing himself, thought it best to maintain a respectful silence.

After a moment, Thackeray asked with a sharp-eyed glance, "So I can assume there is no truth in those rumors about a possible match between you and your authoress?"

George threw back his head and laughed. "Not a grain of it. It would be pure conceit on my part to even consider myself worthy of her."

It was a gentleman's response, and George—businessman though he might be—was nothing if not a gentleman.

Several months later Sutcliffe Sowden stood by the narrow window of his vicarage in Hebden Bridge, admiring the minutely detailed illustration of a goshawk in Bewick's *History of British Birds*. Arthur had just presented the two volumes to him as a Christmas present.

"I thought it was time you had your own copy of Bewick," Arthur smiled.

"It's far too extravagant, Nicholls. I should be quite annoyed at you."

Arthur had taken on an additional private pupil to pay for it, a fact he did not find necessary to share with his friend.

"Came across it at a bookseller's in Leeds. I was looking for one of those dry philosophical things you seem to covet and there it was, sitting on a shelf right before my eyes. Calling out to me."

"Well, I should box your ears for it, but I won't. I shall cherish it. Now I shan't have to borrow Mr. Brontë's books."

"Precisely. And I shan't have to haul them back and forth over the tops."

"How is the old man?"

"Lonely," Arthur said. He unbuttoned his coat and turned to the fire to warm his hands. "This is the first Christmas he's ever spent without his family."

"Where did Miss Brontë go?"

"Brookroyd. To the home of her friend Ellen."

"Rather hard-hearted of her, don't you think? Going off and leaving the old man at Christmas."

"Ah, Sowden, you mustn't judge her harshly. She can't bear to be at home this time of year. Miss Emily passed away just before Christmas, you know."

"Well, you were the paragon of Christian charity, forgoing Sarah Grant's roast goose and Christmas pudding to keep him company. Especially knowing how frugal the old man is with his table. I suppose you had the same old joint and boiled potatoes."

Arthur gave a noncommittal shrug.

"Well, your presence was sorely missed in Oxenhope. It was far too quiet. Not a single argument. Everyone agreed with everyone. Very dull. Even Mrs. Grant commented on how tame we all were. 'Oh, where is that dear mule-headed Mr. Nicholls when we need him?' That's what she said."

Arthur filled his pipe with tobacco and lighted it. After a few puffs, he said, "In truth, I was glad of the opportunity to get the old man alone."

Sutcliffe Sowden placed the book on the side table. He could tell where Arthur's thoughts were heading. He picked up a carafe of port and poured them each a glass.

"The timing's all wrong," Arthur said.

"So you didn't ask for her hand?"

"Didn't even come close to it."

"Don't look so forlorn, my friend," Sowden said as he handed him a glass. "God will make your path clear."

"I may sound a little blasphemous here, but I tell you, Sowden, understanding God's will is like reading a first-year primer compared to guessing the minds of women. If I detected the slightest bit of encouragement it would help." He took a sip of his port. "But then, I don't know why she would encourage me. I don't think I've shown myself attentive in that way. I don't know." He scowled. "I watched Grant make after that Hodgson girl before he married Sarah. I thought he made an absolute idiot out of himself." He glanced up hopefully at his friend. "Perhaps I should just come out with it. Write her a letter."

Sowden barked out a laugh. "Egads, man, she's Currer Bell. How do you write a love letter to Currer Bell? I should be quite terrified."

"Precisely."

"I'm afraid I'm entirely useless in these matters. Couldn't tell you the first thing about how to go about making love to a woman. Why, the mere idea sends shivers down my spine."

"I'm being a bore, aren't I?"

"Absolutely not. I have no objections to listening to you moan. Just don't expect any commonsensical advice."

"Listening is good enough."

"You're entirely right, come to think of it. God help the poor soul who would try to convince you that you're on the wrong path about anything. Most hardheaded man I've ever met."

Arthur raised his glass of port and bowed his head in acknowledgement. "Thank you. Thank you."

Sutcliffe Sowden was as sexually innocent as Arthur, but the vicar of Hebden Bridge was Arthur's only true friend, so it was to Sowden that he bared his heart. They often shared their muddled thoughts about women, harping at length about the confusion provoked by something as simple as a lingering glance, while the real confusion of sexual desire and what to do with it hunkered silently in the obscure, frightened corners of their minds. As clergymen, they upheld the values of their age; they wished to be seen as moral men, respectable, pure, and wholesome. There was no room for the freedoms of that other class of bachelordom, the army officers who indulged in exotic experimentation with mistresses in India or Europe. On occasion they may have feigned a little envy of their licentious brethren. But for the most part, the idea of facing a woman in the flesh provoked only fear. Palm-sweating, jelly-kneed fear.

Once, in the name of science, Sowden had shared with Arthur a small publication describing Eastern practices of teaching young men arrived at the age of puberty the proper conduct of their instruments. "A woman must be prepared for intercourse if she is to derive satisfaction from it," the author wrote.

"By Jove, we're an ignorant breed," Arthur had bellowed while Sowden secreted the pamphlet away inside the cover of some dull, dusty volume and slid it back on the shelf not far from his copy of the naughty *Jane Eyre*.

Sowden hadn't seemed particularly concerned. "God will make these things clear to man in the hour of his need."

"I should hope so," Arthur had grumbled wryly.

In his university days, Arthur had been exposed to the occasional titillating read—short pornographic novels full of endless orgies with inexhaustible women, and books of prints portraying Indian figures in a multitude of imaginative and somewhat bestial acts. Apart from a few passing twinges of guilt, Arthur had found them enlightening. He had come away with a sense that the real truth about human desire fell somewhere between the pornographic and the perfectly pure. In short, he believed in—or, rather hoped for—the existence of physical love.

Having warmed himself sufficiently, Arthur sank into an armchair with his pipe and port.

"I can't put it off much longer, Sowden." He gave his friend a mournful look. "I might lose her forever."

Sowden sank into the chair opposite and studied his friend carefully. "Then make your move, man. What do you have to lose?"

Arthur reflected for a long while, staring blankly into the fire. "Perhaps I should wait until she finishes her novel. I know it's weighing on her. Even her father seems a little impatient with her. I can't imagine that a marriage proposal would be welcome right now."

"You're making excuses for yourself."

"Perhaps I am."

Defeated, Arthur sank even deeper into the chair.

To her dismay, Charlotte found herself incapable of moving forward with her third novel. She played with ideas and narratives while she dusted bookshelves, swept the hallway, and fed the dogs. She struggled with what she wanted to say and how to say it. She found no inspiration anywhere. On an occasional bright day, bundled in cloak, bonnet, and gloves, she would wander a short distance out onto the moors. But the landscape that had once enthralled her now seemed a wilderness. She would return shortly, saddened and chilled to the bone. Then her father would hound her for days afterward about her health, noting ominously the slightest cough or sniffle.

She wrote to Mr. Williams:

> *My sister Emily had a particular love for the moors, and there is not a knoll of heather, not a branch of fern, not a fluttering lark but reminds me of her. The distant prospects were Anne's delight, and when I look round, she is in the blue tints, the pale mists, the waves and shadows of the horizon. In the hill-country silence their poetry comes by lines and stanzas into my mind: once I loved it— now I dare not read it.*

After a lifetime of losing herself in imaginary worlds, she found that writing had somehow lost its power to take her out of the real world. Instead, she found herself probing corners of her heart and soul, and wherever she shined her inquisitive light, she came upon wounds and sores that had never healed.

Subjects of social interest, as she had attempted in *Shirley,* held no appeal for her.

"I cannot write books handling the topics of the day," she wrote to George that winter. "It is of no use trying. Nor can I write a book for its moral. To manage great matters rightly, as Harriet Beecher Stowe did with *Uncle Tom's Cabin,* they must be long and practically studied— their bearings known intimately and their evils felt genuinely."

With Ellen, who had never been privy to her life as an author, she corresponded very little. When Ellen complained of her silence, Charlotte replied:

I am silent because I have literally nothing to say. I might indeed repeat over and over again that my life is a pale blank and often a very weary burden, and that the future sometimes appalls me; but what end could be answered by such repetition except to weary you and enervate myself?

The evils that now and then wring a groan from my heart lie in my position, not that I am a single woman and likely to remain a single woman, but because I am a lonely woman and likely to be lonely. But it cannot be helped and therefore imperatively must be borne, and borne with as few words about it as may be.

As for the "twaddle about my marrying" which you hear—if I knew the details I should have a better chance of guessing the quarter from which such gossip comes—as it is, I am quite at a loss. Whom am I to marry? I think I have scarcely seen a single man with whom such a union would be possible since I left London. Doubtless there are men whom if I chose to encourage I might marry—but no matrimonial lot is even remotely offered me which seems to me truly desirable: and even if that were the case—there would be many obstacles—the least allusion to such a thing is most offensive to Papa.

I have heard nothing from Cornhill in a long while. They are silent. There has been bitter disappointment at my having no work ready for this season. Papa, too, cannot hide his chagrin.

The lilacs and laburnums were in bloom in the garden, throwing off a sweet scent that Charlotte had breathed in all week long as she sat at the window sewing. There had been a deep pile of new white muslin frocks to finish off, and now they were all done and neatly folded, ready to be distributed to poor children to wear in the Whitsuntide procession the following day.

There was always a tremendous amount of work to be done. The festivities began with a reception at the parsonage for the patrons and teachers. At the appointed time, the parson and his curates would emerge and make their way to the bottom of the packed lane, where the Sunday scholars, their teachers, and the brass band had gathered. Drums would roll, the church bells would ring out, and hundreds of the faithful would begin their slow, solemn advance through village and field.

In the past, her father had been at the helm. He was always a sight to see—the old warrior priest with his tall hat, walking staff, and that stupendous white cravat, striding out vigorously with the ferocious sense of righteousness that had served him well these many years amid these truculent souls. But now he went with them only to the bottom of the village, and when he returned he complained of weakness. Charlotte would serve him a little wine, and he would rest in his study until they returned.

Afterward came what Emily had once called a monster tea drinking, and the women certainly thought of it in that respect. Everything had to be done on a massive scale to serve the faithful in all three villages within the Haworth parish. In preparation for the day, every bench in the village had been pressed into service and set up in a mowed field above the village. Upon their return there were pints of ale waiting for the parched musicians, and for the children there were currant buns and sweetened tea.

The formal tea for the wealthy and the influential was held inside the schoolhouse, on tables set with snowy-white linens and bone china, with silver spoons and brass urns that had been polished to a shine. It was one of the few events of the year when Charlotte emerged in view of the entire village. It had always been her duty to preside at her father's table, pouring and passing cups to the Merralls, the Greenwoods, and the Taylors. Her table was renowned for its neatness; there was never so much as a smudge on a cup, and the spoons were laid out in martial order.

Charlotte was bundling up the last of the clothing when Martha entered.

"You can tell your father these are ready to take to the church."

"Yes, miss. Did you want to cut any lilacs for the table, miss?"

"I suppose so. A few."

"Shall we wait until tomorrow?"

"We're always so busy in the morning, Martha, with the reception here. I think I'll just cut them and take them over now. They'll keep overnight in water."

The schoolroom was unrecognizable. Every corner had been soaped, scoured, and whitewashed. The school desks had been stacked to the side, replaced by rows of long tables. Scores of women in work aprons were cleaning off benches and setting out their best tea things, while others hung garlands of evergreens and flowers cut from their cottage gardens.

Charlotte lowered the armful of branches onto the table and looked up to see florid-faced Mrs. Grant beside her.

"How lovely! Lilacs! Oh, how we wish we had something growing at home, but we can't get anything started." Charlotte noticed that her stout little figure had grown stouter: she was expecting.

"Good day, Mrs. Grant."

"Our table's right next to yours. I'm so glad. We never see much of you. Or at least I don't. It seems I never get out of Oxenhope anymore. Of course Joseph brings me news of you, but it's not the same, is it? As sitting down to tea together." She wrinkled up her nose and glanced over her shoulder to make sure no one was listening. "I know it's difficult for you in this dreary little place. It is for us, too. Such a want of elegance and good society. That's why this sort of thing is so good for them, put-ting on their best clothes and coming to a proper tea. Having to behave like civilized folk for a change." She laughed gaily at this.

Charlotte asked, "Have you seen Mr. Nicholls? Papa wanted a word with him."

"Oh, he's over there, with Miss Dixon."

"Miss Dixon?" Charlotte squinted; she was not wearing her spectacles.

"The new mistress for the first class. She's come from Manchester." She leaned close to Charlotte again and whispered behind her hand. "Although I wouldn't disturb him right now. I don't think that would make him happy." She smiled cheerily. "They're hanging the canaries."

"Canaries?"

"Miss Dixon thought it would be a lovely touch, to have them suspended from the ceiling and singing during the tea."

"Canaries? Hanging from the ceiling?"

"Miss Dixon is very fond of canaries. She has five cages. She's donating them just for tomorrow. Arthur's been busy with them all morning."

"Goodness. I'd think he'd have more pressing things to do," Charlotte muttered. She began trimming the lilacs. "Well, I'll speak to him later."

"It would be so nice for him if they were to marry. She's a very nice girl." Sarah Grant smoothed out her apron and glanced at the pair in the corner. "Arthur's such a good man." She turned back to Charlotte and said in a conspiratorial whisper, "We need to find him a wife."

Charlotte met Miss Dixon the next day at the parsonage reception. She struck Charlotte as a practical young woman, with a firm voice and a steady gaze, the sort that could be counted on to keep her wits about her in a crisis and raise sensible children. To any eye other than Charlotte's, the woman's attraction to Arthur would pass unnoticed. But Charlotte, observing keenly through her spectacles, caught the slight change in her expression when Arthur offered to fetch her a glass of wine, and the way she followed him with her eyes ever so briefly. It was noticeable like a breeze moving quietly among leaves.

"Nicholls, I say, we've been talking about the reforms we've accomplished, and Mr. Greenwood here reminded me of your battle with the washerwomen."

It was her father, who had caught Arthur on the way back from the refreshment table.

"Ah, have you now?" He handed Miss Dixon her wine, attempting to avoid Patrick, but the room was too crowded and there was nowhere to flee.

"We have to be thankful for the small victories, don't we, Nicholls? Still can't get clean water in the village, but at least we've no longer got sheets flying from the tombstones, thanks to you."

"Indeed," Arthur replied stiffly. He turned to Miss Dixon. "It was one of those vulgarizing local customs that had gone unchecked for years. Quite a battle, but I was victorious in the end." He shot a quick, sparring glance at Patrick over the rim of his glass. "Although I daresay the battle was a lonely one."

"Quite an upheaval, that was," John Brown laughed. "Our women don't take lightly to bein' told to change their ways."

Mr. Heaton said, "I recall 'ow I saw old widow Burder tryin' to sneak up the lane early one mornin' with her basket o' sheets—headin' straight for the churchyard despite Mr. Nicholls 'ere just 'avin' announced from the pulpit that dryin' sheets on the tombstones was prohibited. She caught sight of Mr. Nicholls and she turned round slick as a whistle and tottered right back down the lane—heavin' an' pantin' like a ghost was after her."

The churchwarden said to Arthur, "Did you not write a poem on the subject?"

Arthur chuckled. "No sir, not I."

Patrick turned sharply on Greenwood and peered over the rims of his spectacles. "It was *I* who wrote the poem."

"Well, then let's hear it."

Hartley Merrall stepped into the group with his plate piled high with macaroons. "Don't be bashful now, sir—go on, let's hear it."

Someone laughed, "Bashful? Mr. Brontë?"

The other guests were turning their attention toward the parson. "By all means, Mr. Brontë. Let's have a recitation."

"Yes, let's hear it!"

Patrick paused, waiting until they grew silent; then he began reciting in his grand and dramatic manner.

"The Parson, an old man, but hotter than cold . . ."

He boomed on through the titters and smiles, thoroughly enjoying the audience. When he came to the part about Arthur, he turned to his curate with a comic flourish.

> "His Curate, who follows—with all due regard—
> Though Foild by the Church, has reform'd the Churchyard.
> The females all routed have fled with their clothes

To Stackyards, and backyards, and where no one knows . . ."

Charlotte contrived to steal a glance at Arthur over the rim of her cup. Arthur was staring into the air with his granite-like expression, but all of a sudden his eyes—most uncontrollably—flitted to catch Charlotte's gaze. He turned a frightful color of red and glanced away again.

"And loudly have sworn by the suds which they swim in,
They'll wring off his head, for his warring with women,
Whilst their husbands combine and roar out in their fury,
They'll Lynch him at once, without trial by Jury . . ."

At that moment the church bells began to peal, signaling the call to line up for the procession. There was a hearty applause, and the guests, believing Mr. Brontë had finished, began to set down their plates and leave the room.

"Wait!" he cried. "There's more!"

"Papa," Charlotte cautioned in a low voice, with a light touch on his arm. She recalled the last lines, their casual cruelty.

But he would not stop. For effect, he removed his spectacles and spoke solemnly, with a funereal tone:

"But saddest of all, the fair maidens declare,
Of marriage or love, he must ever despair."

There were a few low chuckles. Greenwood and Michael Merrall clapped Arthur on the back. Arthur attempted a smile but his eyes swelled with humiliation.

Miss Dixon blushed deeply, her gaze drawn to the worn carpet. Not a word passed between them. She set down her glass and turned to the door.

Arthur glowered at Patrick on the way out.

That evening, as Charlotte was folding his newspapers and tidying up his desk, she said to her father, "You may very well be wrong about Mr. Nicholls, Papa."

"How's that, my dear?"

"About marrying. I think he has his sights set on Miss Dixon. She certainly has her sights on him, and she is quite the type to snare her man."

Patrick peeled off his wire spectacles and glared sternly at her from beneath his thick black brows. He looked very tired. He had come home, changed into his slippers, and fallen asleep in his chair.

"Miss Dixon? The new schoolmistress?"

"The one."

"That would be inconvenient. If he marries he'll need to find his own living somewhere. Couldn't possibly keep a wife on his paltry income. I should not like to lose Nicholls. I'd be hard-pressed to find a man as capable."

"So you admit your curate has some qualities."

"Of course he has qualities," he frowned. "But I shall not inflate his vanity with false flattery."

He rose stiffly from his chair and took the candle from his desk.

She watched from the hallway while he climbed the stairs to the landing and paused to wind the grandfather clock.

"I can tell you this much: Nicholls is much more valuable to me than to any poor deceived woman." He closed the clock case. "We've gotten used to each other, and I should find it very annoying to have to break in a new curate as old as I am." He shook his head grimly. "After seven years, I expected a bit more loyalty than this."

Charlotte thought that Arthur's happiness should be a consideration, but her father saw people—particularly women and inferiors—in terms of solutions to his problems, not as individuals with tastes and affections of their own. She would not express her opinion. He was working himself into a state, and she needed to appease him.

"Papa, you tired yourself out with that walk today. Get on up to bed."

"It's a sad thing to lose your strength," he said morosely as he raised his candle to light the stairs. "A sad thing. I don't recognize myself any-more."

"It's quite cool tonight. Shall I have Martha bring up some coals?"

"Nonsense. I won't have a fire in my bedroom in May. Sheer extrava-gance."

"Good night then, Papa."

That night as she lay in bed, her thoughts dwelled on Arthur. He had become a quiet, seamless presence in their lives. So much of the re-sponsibility for her father's parish had been left to his capable hands. From the first day he had assumed all the duties of the incumbent—the funerals, weddings, and baptisms, the additional load of Sunday services in Stanbury that were held in the schoolhouse built by him, the running of their own Haworth church school, the visits to the poor—and all of these operations had flourished under his hand. He had shouldered it all without so much as a murmur of complaint.

The thought of his leaving weighed on her that night, and when dawn broke she had still not gone to sleep.

That summer Charlotte had ample opportunity to watch for any blos-soming romance as she tended the garden in the front, hoping to bring forth a few blooms from the rocky soil. But neither soil nor schoolhouse yielded anything of interest. Arthur seemed intent on showing Miss Dixon his most rocklike and intimidating countenance. Whenever they passed in the lane, he nodded politely and bowled on by. Miss Dixon, on the other hand, seemed to slow her step, and once Charlotte caught her glancing at him over her shoulder. Charlotte was wearing her spectacles that day, and she was sure of what she had seen.

Thus it came as a shock to her when her father appeared at the back door one afternoon as she was helping Martha remove sheets from the line.

"I don't know what to think of that man," he said sourly as he squinted into the sunlight. Charlotte placed the folded sheet in the bas-ket and turned to him.

"I can only assume from your tone of voice that you're referring to your curate," Charlotte said wryly.

"He takes his vacation in a few weeks and he's been dropping hints that he may not come back."

"How odd."

"It's quite unlike him, going all moody and womanish like this. After all these years, all of a sudden he's unhappy. Says he's thinking about going back to farming in Ireland. Farming! Can you imagine? Proud as he is!"

"He couldn't possibly mean it."

"I have no patience for the man. Needs to toughen up."

Charlotte said, "To be honest, I thought he'd been looking a little peaked these days."

Patrick looked toward Martha. "Have you noticed Mr. Nicholls behaving oddly?"

"Why, yes, sir. hasn't seemed hisself lately."

"Is he ill?"

"Well, not in body, sir. Strong as an ox, he is. But there's somethin' eatin' at him. Mama's noticed it. His spirits is low."

"Has Miss Dixon turned him down?" Charlotte asked.

"No, miss. I'm sure of it. I think she'd welcome his attentions. But he hasn't paid suit to her. I'd know it straightaway."

"Do you think it's a woman in Ireland?" Charlotte asked.

Martha's dark eyes flashed excitedly. "Could be, miss. I've often heard rumored he has a sweetheart back home."

"Why in blue blazes do you women think that whenever a man's unhappy there's always a woman involved?" Patrick bellowed.

"Because generally there is," Charlotte said.

Martha giggled behind a sheet, and Patrick stomped inside.

Chapter Twenty-two

S he had begun the novel evasively, with a game of screens and mirrors and an aloof, benumbed heroine that even Charlotte didn't like very much. But Lucy was no accident. Charlotte intended her thusly. She would refuse Lucy Snowe even the most muted optimism; she would equip her mentally and psychologically for sorrow and loss.

A mere spectator in life, more dead than alive, Lucy Snowe resembled no contemporary heroine. Unable to be truthful about herself, Lucy diverted the reader by narrating a story about a child, Polly, a tiny doll-like creature of extreme sensitivity. Polly was still vulnerable and alive; she still cried when she was abandoned by her father and pattered about after the young man Graham Bretton, eager for his attention and love. It was Charlotte as a child, when she could still feel, worshipping her once-adored brother.

But after a while, it became clear that Lucy's nature was not as it appeared to be. Hers was a singularly constructed personality, a cauldron of anxiety, guilt, sorrow, and an enormous capacity to love, all of it sealed behind an imperturbable, tomblike calm.

Lucy had not one drop of faith in the future, but neither would she shrink like a coward before Fate. She would assert a choice, through the small window Fate had left open; she would bravely set off to Villette, an imaginary city resembling Brussels, on a journey of self-discovery.

It was inevitable that George work his way into Charlotte's novel after all of the shared ambivalence they felt toward each other, the impressions he made upon her and the longing he inspired in her. But she knew

better than to fabricate a falsehood, even in her fiction; she saw herself—
and him—too clearly. George's vanity would not be sacrificed for love of
a woman with neither beauty nor station, regardless of the bond between
them. He would have society's approval and play by the conventional
rules. *Villette* would not revive the myth of *Jane Eyre,* the illusion of a
great love that completes us and resolves all of life's problems. Lucy
could not have the handsome, charming hero, Dr. John; Charlotte would
betroth him to the beautiful Polly.

If Charlotte was suited for anyone on earth, it would always and only
be Heger. At long last she brought him successfully to life as the schoolmaster Paul Emanuel, and on the pages of *Villette* she shaped the relationship that had shaped her life. He had wielded such tyrannical power
over her with his dark scowls, his irrational and tempestuous moods, his
soaring intellect and explosive passions. Deeply flawed, he was also profoundly human. *He* could read her eyes, her gestures, her unspoken language. She had never been a shadow with him; he had brought her into
the light and seen and loved her for what she was. In his eyes, she had
been a whole woman.

All that year writing *Villette,* Charlotte suffered psychologically and
physically. The work forced her to confront the truth about her past and
come to terms with the harsh reality of what was left of her life. It provoked headaches and depression, wrenching pains in her neck and
numbness in her back and arms, blurred vision and eyestrain. At times
as she dipped her pen in the ink, she felt her breathing suddenly con-
strict as if a mighty fist were squeezing the air from her lungs; at other
times the tension produced a viselike tightening of her stomach. Her entire body rebelled against the memories she had revived and the scrutiny
of truth.

She finished the novel one morning in November. She had worked
all through the night and her fingers were cold and cramped. She put
down her pen and stopped the inkwell, then, with head bowed and
mitten-clad hands folded in prayer, she whispered thanks to God. Gath-

ering her shawl close around her shoulders, she rose and knocked on the door of her father's study.

"It's done, Papa. It's finished."

She stood before him light as air.

He folded his newspaper and came around the desk to take her hands in his.

"Well done, daughter," he said kissing her on the cheek. "Well done. Are you happy with it?"

"I've tried to do my best."

That morning she buttoned on her boots and took the dogs as far as Haworth Moor. Rain-sodden clouds hugged the treeless hills, and the distant views were lost in gray fog. For the first time in years she was able to breathe in the beauty and freedom of her beloved moors. She recognized them like long-absent friends.

On the way back, passing down a narrow, high-walled snicket she caught sight of a black-clad figure approaching through the mist. Flossy recognized him first, bounding ahead.

"Miss Brontë," Arthur said as they came upon each other. "It's much too cold for you to be out. There's nothing wrong, I hope."

"Not at all, Mr. Nicholls."

"Then you're well."

"Quite well."

Meeting her unexpectedly like this seemed to both fluster and please him. He smiled nervously. "You do indeed appear in good spirits."

"I'm sure it's the exercise. I've had a brisk walk."

"Ah, yes. A good brisk walk does a body good."

Arthur generally doted on the dogs, and they were circling at his feet, whining for attention. But he seemed oblivious to them; he stood blocking the narrow path, wearing a strained and tentative look. Charlotte had begun to notice this strange behavior, but she was not inclined to examine it too closely.

"And your book is coming along well?"

"I finished it. Just this morning."

"You've finished! This is quite good news. Indeed, very good news!"

"Why, thank you." Impulsively, in the fog of her own happiness, she blurted out, "Perhaps you'd like to come to tea this afternoon?"

"Today? Why . . . uh, yes, I would be delighted. A sort of celebration."

"Yes, if you wish." She smiled kindly at him. "It's just tea, Mr. Nicholls."

"Of course, of course!"

He hesitated as though he would like to say more. There was an awkward silence, and then he came to his senses all of a sudden, stepping out of her way so that she might pass.

"Good day, Miss Brontë."

"Good day, Mr. Nicholls."

At tea that afternoon Charlotte was talkative and engaging. Arthur was uncharacteristically mild-mannered and quiet. When she passed him a cup he took it meekly, with a furtive but piercing glance. Arthur had never before struck her as meek or mild-mannered. She hoped he had not misunderstood her lightheartedness. If she had suspicions she dismissed them. At this moment she was riding on a swell of pure joy. He happened to be there, and she swept him along with her.

That evening Arthur dashed off a short note to Sowden:

> She's finished her novel. I daresay I have no more excuses. It's now or never. I'm in a wretched state. I lose all composure in her presence. Fear I'm making a great fool out of myself. How odd that after all these years it's finally hit me like a ton of bricks. (I am not good at simile, but this one—although overused—is quite accurate.) Next Monday I shall pop the question. God give me strength! BURN THIS AFTER READING.

Three days later Charlotte finished the fair copy of *Villette* and posted it to Cornhill. Then she rewarded herself with a visit to Ellen. Arthur was deeply chagrined to discover she had gone. Also, as he confessed to Sowden, somewhat relieved.

Having earlier submitted the first two volumes of *Villette*—of which both George and Mr. Williams had warmly approved—Charlotte was confident that the finished book would provoke little controversy and find greater approbation than her previous work. Most of all, she was relieved that George had seemed pleased with the character of Dr. John. Yet she waited anxiously for a response.

"I can hardly tell you how much I hunger to have some opinion besides my own," she wrote him,

> *and how I have sometimes desponded and almost despaired because there was no one to whom to read a line—or of whom to ask a counsel. Jane Eyre was not written under such circumstances, nor were two-thirds of Shirley. I got so miserable about it, I could bear no allusion to the book—but it is finished now, and I eagerly await your verdict. Remember to be an honest critic and tell Mr. Williams to be unsparing—not that I am likely to alter anything—.*

George could not help but recognize himself in the character of Dr. John Graham Bretton, and his mother in the figure of Mrs. Bretton. At first, his vanity had been flattered by the portrayal. But then, in the third volume, he sensed a certain contempt creeping into Lucy's attitude toward the doctor. He made no mention of it to anyone, but it wounded him deeply.

There were a startling number of incidents that he recognized as having been drawn directly from their shared moments: the visit to the theater where a fire broke out, the intimate evenings in his home; only now did he realize to what degree her work was autobiographical.

He had always assumed that Charlotte would play the romantic card and at the conclusion throw cold little Lucy Snowe into the arms of the genial doctor. So when he finally had the third volume in hand and began to read, he was greatly disturbed.

"Good grief, Mother. She completely switches the narrative."

He'd come wandering into her bedroom that night with the manuscript in his hand.

"Oh dear. Is it too awfully confusing?"

"It certainly throws off the reader. She starts off building up the relationship between Lucy and Dr. John—"

"Dr. John. That's your character."

"Well, yes. Thinly disguised. What I find so unacceptable is that the
entire last volume develops the love story between Lucy and her irritable
old professor."

"Is he old? I thought the professor was a young man."

"I'm speaking figuratively, Mother. Yes, he is a young man. But my
point is that Dr. John almost entirely disappears from the story, and the
reader will want her to marry Dr. John. Not that dark and stormy little
Frenchman. And then she sends him off on a voyage at the end and he
disappears at sea."

"Dr. John?"

"No, the Frenchman. Paul Emanuel."

"He dies?"

"We are to assume as much. Drowns in a shipwreck."

"How dreary. What happens to Lucy?"

"She opens a little school and seems quite content."

His mother peered at him over the rims of her glasses. "And what
happens to Dr. John?"

"Oh, he marries this little doll of a creature. Not a very interesting
character at all. Indeed. A completely failed character." *So,* he had
thought upon finishing the novel, *this is the manner of woman of which you
deem me worthy.*

"What a pity," his mother replied. "I thought her characters were generally quite fascinating."

"Charlotte has difficulty portraying pretty women who are clever and
sociable."

"Well, dear, she writes what she knows, I suppose, doesn't she?"

"I wanted romance. This is hardly romantic."

When Charlotte returned from Brookroyd ten days later and there had still been no response from George, she sent off an anxious letter, asking if he had some occasion for disappointment. In response she received a check for five hundred pounds indicating acceptance of the work, although the sum was two hundred less than she had anticipated.

"Five hundred? That's all?" her father scowled. He made an attempt to restrain his disappointment, for her sake. Charlotte felt it keenly, nonetheless, and his disapproval festered in her thoughts the way it always did.

Still, from Cornhill there was no reply.

When several more days went by without a letter, she panicked. She told her father she was going down to London to find out what was the matter.

"There's something horribly wrong," she said anxiously. "He has never kept me waiting more than a week."

She had her bags packed and ready to go that morning when a letter came.

"He says he would have preferred a different resolution."

She stood by the window in her father's parlor reading the letter by the pale winter light. She would not permit him to read it.

"He's quite vague. Something in the third volume sticks confoundedly in his throat, but he makes quite a mystery out of it."

Charlotte immediately wrote a reply. George's next letter was only slightly more substantial.

"He writes that he finds Polly an odd, fascinating little puss but he's not in love with her."

"In love with her? Are those the words he uses?"

"He means as a publisher he's not in love with the character."

"That's an odd way to put it."

She immediately sent off a reply: "I understand that the spirit of Romance would have indicated another course, far more flowery and inviting, but this would have been unlike Real Life, inconsistent with Truth—at variance with Probability. How would you have seen the ending, given the characters as they are? What other conclusion might be possible? I see none."

George's reply was terse: "I shall answer no more questions about *Villette*."

When he saw that she would not change her mind, George gave the manuscript to Mr. Williams to read. The following day they sat in George's cluttered office.

"Flawed as it is, I think it will receive wide praise," Williams said. "And there is nothing controversial that would cause censure."

"I agree. But I would like to see a more satisfying resolution."

"You would have preferred Lucy to marry Dr. John."

"That's what our readers will want. They'll want to see her win the hero."

"I don't think Miss Brontë sees herself in that light," Williams said in the quiet voice of one murmuring a delicate truth.

"How she sees herself should have no bearing on what the reader wants. If Jane Eyre can snare Rochester, I see no reason why we can't have Lucy Snowe win the heart of Dr. John. This is a character we're talking about, Williams. Not Miss Brontë's life."

They fell silent. Rain tapped gently on the skylight.

George knew quite well how insensitive he had sounded just then.

"I'm a businessman, Williams," he mumbled. "I try to bring the public what they want." He sat up and with an air of finality gathered up the manuscript and returned it to Williams. "Here. Let's get it into print. Quickly. The public wants more of Currer Bell and they shall have him."

Arthur had stopped trying to track Charlotte's whereabouts, had indeed given up hoping for any kind of favorable timing for his proposal. When she returned from Brookroyd he was taken up nearly every evening with a flurry of duties, and then there was a visitor at the parsonage, a tall, well-dressed young man whom Arthur had seen a number of times over the years. Arthur became extremely nervous and convinced himself that it was a suitor.

"That fine young gentleman is Mr. Joe Taylor. Mary Taylor's brother," Martha's mother replied when he inquired.

"I see. And who is Mary Taylor?"

"The mistress's old school friend. She lives . . ." She turned to her husband, who had fallen asleep before the fire with his stocking-clad feet propped on the fender. "John," she cried, poking him with a knitting needle. "Where'd that spunky Miss Taylor move to? Not America . . ."

"New Zealand," he mumbled.

Arthur sat staring gloomily into the flames. His palms were sweating. He didn't dare ask more.

Mrs. Brown resumed her knitting. After a moment she added, "Aye, that Mr. Taylor's a nuisance these days, Martha says. Comes beggin' the mistress's advice on ma-tri-monial matters." She spoke the word slowly, feeling her way through the syllables.

Arthur's heart skipped a beat. He tried to keep his voice light. "Do you mean Miss Brontë is to marry the gentleman?"

Mrs. Brown screwed up her face. "Him? He's not good enough for *her*," she declared.

Arthur remained in the little parlor for a good half hour without muttering another word. They were accustomed to his taciturn silence. Mrs. Brown was glad he'd come out of his room that evening and thought this was a sign that he was on the mend.

"Charlotte, I'd like to have Nicholls to tea this afternoon."

"If you wish." She waited while he spooned potatoes onto his plate, then took the bowl from his hands.

"He's quite put himself out these past few weeks. A workhorse if ever I've seen one."

"I'll send Martha out for some meat pies. And we have some of her sponge cake in the cellar."

"Good. Good. He's very fond of Martha's sponge cake."

She smiled to herself. He never admitted to treating anyone badly, but he would make these small signs of atonement.

Arthur's legs felt like lead as he climbed the lane to the parsonage and let himself in through the garden gate. From the moment Martha answered the door and he caught a glimpse of Charlotte in the passageway, he began to unravel.

They sat in Patrick's parlor as they had so many times over the past three years, just the three of them; Charlotte poured tea, two fingers pressed gently on the porcelain lid, with the little finger arched as she tipped the pot. The gesture mesmerized him. As she performed the small domestic ritual he followed from the corner of his eye the graceful movements of her hands until she folded them quietly in her lap. A swan settling down upon the surface of a perfectly still lake.

He was keenly self-conscious and ate practically nothing, taking only a small piece of Martha's sponge cake. It stuck in his throat and he had to wash it down with tea. He could not recall what they talked about.

After tea Charlotte left them alone, and for more than an hour the two clergymen discussed parish matters. There was little to provoke disagreement. Both bemoaned the illnesses and deaths caused by Haworth's tainted water supply; recounted their ceaseless efforts to persuade the wealthy to pay to improve the lot of the poor; vented their despair at learning that the Merralls and Thomases, who lived in fine Georgian houses with fresh water and privies, had secretly petitioned for exemption from the proposed taxes to pay for water and sewage reform; talked about the need to find a new burial yard—there being no more room for new graves in the old one.

Those brief minutes when he took up his hat and bade good night to his parson were the longest minutes of Arthur's life. It flashed into his head that this must be what a condemned man endures moments before his execution.

The parlor door shut behind him, leaving him standing in the dark passageway gripping his hat. His jaw was trembling.

He tapped lightly on the door. There was a hesitation, and he imagined he heard the rustle of her skirts as she rose.

She opened the door.

He stepped inside and closed the door behind him. Too loudly. He flinched at the sound and turned to face her.

Her eyes told him that she knew why he had come. That he had been so transparent in his intentions only exacerbated his nervousness. He had imagined this moment a million times and had rehearsed the words he would say, but it all flew right out of his head.

"Miss Brontë," he croaked. Parched lips, parched throat—that was how his wretched body betrayed him at this moment when he needed steadiness. He clung to the brim of his hat, digging his fingers into the soft felt like a man in a tempest clawing at the earth to keep from being carried away by turbulence. He grew light-headed. He thought he might faint. "Dear God," he muttered to himself, "don't let me faint."

"I . . . I . . . oh dear. I must begin somewhere, and I don't know quite where. I . . . Miss Brontë, I have . . ." He scowled, and a look of utter dismay swept across his face. If she would but help him out, encourage him with a tender smile. But her eyes seemed to bore straight into his heart, and what she saw there inspired only pity.

He drew a deep breath and exhaled the words: "I can no longer bear to remain silent. I . . . I have cared for you for too long. My sentiments are not . . . my sentiments are of the most"—he was going to say "pure" but caught himself in time—"of the truest, most ardent, most fiercely devoted . . ." He stopped himself. He had ruined the brim of his hat. Crushed it. He dropped his hands to his sides.

"I am asking you to marry me, to be my wife. I grant this may come as a shock to you. A declaration of this sort is generally preceded by . . ." He faltered. "By a good deal of . . . of fanfare, and frenzy. I, more than anyone, wish it might have been otherwise. For I have . . . I have loved you deeply and truly for longer than you know."

She heard him out with an expression of deepest empathy. He saw that she was not in love with him. Miss Dixon had been in love with him, and Charlotte did not look at him with Miss Dixon's eyes. But neither was she cruel or proud to him. She knew suffering. Her novels had reassured him of that.

"Oh, Mr. Nicholls," she sighed. "I confess, I have not been inclined to give much thought to the matter."

"Yes, I understand. Of course. But you will, will you not? You will think upon it, give it some thought?"

"I . . ."

"Allow me at least the privilege of speaking to you again on this subject, for there is so much more I should like to say, but I find myself quite senseless at the moment. An absolute idiot. And before stepping into this room I was a sane, rational man."

"Have you spoken to my father?"

He drew a deep breath. "I dared not."

"Oh dear. That was most unwise."

"I know what his answer will be unless you petition him on my behalf. I beg of you to give me reason to hope. For the moment I ask for nothing else."

"You must go. I should not like Papa to find us like this."

"Can I have reason to hope?"

"Please, Mr. Nicholls. Leave. Quickly. You shall have my reply in the morning."

Of course she would not marry him; she did not love him. Yet his proposal had moved her deeply. A man she had known for years, ordinarily so statuelike, making such a spectacle out of himself—trembling, stirred, and overcome. My God, he loved her. A man didn't look like that, didn't take that kind of risk unless he truly loved. She stood in shock for a long moment and then went to find her father in his study.

Her father was already suspicious. He had heard Arthur go into the dining room. It had been awhile later when the front door closed.

"What did he want? What was he up to?"

"He asked for my hand in marriage."

There was a moment of silence as his eyes darkened and his face drew deeply from some hidden well of irrational rage, and then the exclamations began, low and rumbling, seething with contempt. Charlotte had expected sarcasm, mockery, even cruelty, but not this vilification—not this branding of his high-principled curate as deceitful, vile, and traitorous. He went on and on, his wrath gathering bile and indignation like a livid storm feeding on the elements. She thought he had quite lost his sanity.

"What duplicity! Slithering about here like a sly, cunning snake, worming his way into our family! We trusted him, and he has betrayed us! That's typical of his sort of lowly, conniving Irishman. They get what they want by deceit and lies. You know why he wants you, don't you? For your money. Why, do you realize what this means? I can't trust him! My own curate! He's useless to me now! Totally useless!

"How can he possibly think himself worthy of you! Him! He has nothing. No money, no property, no situation. He's a lowly curate, and a mediocre one at that! Why, there's nothing exceptional about the man! Nothing! He's an intellectual pygmy! To believe himself worthy of my daughter! Worthy of *my* daughter!"

She withstood his rage with outward calm. Meek, subservient, she flinched inwardly at the blows to Arthur's dignity and seethed at the injustice done to his name. Few people knew the degree of rage of which her father was capable. Blood swelled his neck and his temples; he had the look of a man pulsing with hatred.

If it were not for her father's poor health—the constant fear of rising blood pressure—she would have spoken up to defend Arthur's honor and his goodness. Instead, she listened, clutching the candle in her hand and trying to keep her own temper under control.

He did not even ask if she had any feelings for Arthur. It never occurred to him that she might care.

"I shall write him a reply in the morning."

"A clear refusal that he cannot possibly misinterpret. He's a thick-skulled man, Charlotte. You shall make it clear that there is no hope. Not a dram. Ever."

"I shall make it quite clear."

"And that he must never repeat these overtures."

She gave a barely perceptible nod.

"You will show me the letter before you send it to him."

"That won't be necessary."

"You will show me the letter!" he bellowed. "If it is not firm enough I shall add my own thoughts at the bottom!"

Charlotte wanted to throw something at him.

She spun on her heels and left the room.

"Charlotte!" he cried. But she was racing up the stairs to her room. She slammed the door and turned the key.

Chapter Twenty-three

My dear Miss Brontë,

I sense that there was another hand behind your letter—or perhaps eyes over your shoulder—as you wrote it.

The news has traveled quickly. John Brown met me with murderous glances this morning when I came back from teaching my class. His wife seems frightened of me, or perhaps she is only reluctant to show any kindness to me for fear of his temper.

And yet, if they vilify me, it is for expressing the most sincere, tender, and profound attachment.

I know you well enough to avoid any hint of affectation in my letters to you; besides, I would not be capable of it. Being neither poet nor artist, I have nothing but the most ordinary ability to express something that is to me quite extraordinary.

It is not easy to bare one's soul with the pen knowing that the words will be scrutinized, balanced, and weighed by one who has earned the highest order of praise in the art of words. Therefore, I will make every effort to keep my prose simple and straightforward—although there is nothing simple about my feelings toward you.

Until recently I have played only a small role in your life, and at times my very presence has been uncongenial to you. I am quite aware of your antipathy toward certain of my views, specifically my intolerance for dissenting religious factions. Those matters have *often been a sticking point between the two of us: that I prefer to maintain a social distance from dissenters may appear to you to be extreme and narrow-minded, but I should deem myself an insufferable hypocrite should I pretend to take pleasure in the company of those who seek the destruction of God's Holy Church.*

Yet, by some miracle, some Grace of God, over the past few years I began to sense a change in you. I waited for the slightest encouragement—sometimes I thought I caught a glimpse of it. A soft word, a willingness to engage me in pleasant conversation, a certain sensitivity toward my feelings. You seemed less inclined to the old mockery and contentiousness of the past. On occasion, you even thought to share some humorous anecdote with me. To any ordinary acquaintance, these are mere signs of civility—but to one in love, they kindled a tiny flame of hope in my heart.

The trials and tribulations you have suffered made you only more precious in my sight. So many times these past few years I have watched you come and go. When you departed, I would lose hope of ever having you. When you returned, hope would return. I know that homecoming is no longer joyous to you, as it was in the past. And yet, for me, your presence is the light that brightens even the darkest days.

I am at a loss as how to proceed. My affection for you will not waver. It is not a small thing to feel so deeply.

I remain your devoted friend
Arthur Bell Nicholls

Haworth, December 15th

Dear Nell,

I enclose a note which has left on my mind a feeling of deep concern.

This note—you will see—is from Mr. Nicholls. I know not

whether you have ever observed him specially when staying here recently—your perception in these matters is generally quick enough—too quick I have sometimes thought. Yet as you never said anything, I restrained my own dim misgivings. What Papa has seen or guessed I will not inquire—though I may conjecture. He has minutely noticed all Mr. Nicholls's low spirits—all his threats of expatriation—all his symptoms of impaired health—noticed them with little sympathy and much indirect sarcasm. On Monday evening Mr. N was here to tea. I vaguely felt—without clearly seeing—as without seeing I have felt for some time—the meaning of his constant looks and strange, feverish restraint. After tea I withdrew to the dining room as usual. As usual Mr. N sat with Papa till between eight and nine o'clock. I then heard him open the parlor door as if going. I expected the clash of the front door—He stopped in the passage, he tapped, like lightning it flashed on me what was coming. He entered—he stood before me. What his words were—you can guess, his manner—you can hardly realize—nor can I forget it. Shaking from head to foot, looking deadly pale, speaking low, vehemently yet with difficulty—he made me for the first time feel what it costs a man to declare affection where he doubts response.

I think I half-led, half-put him out of the room. When he was gone I immediately went to Papa and told him what had taken place. Agitation and Anger disproportionate to the occasion ensued—if I had loved Mr. N and had heard such epithets applied to him as were used—it would have transported me past my patience—as it was my blood boiled with a sense of injustice—but Papa worked himself into a state not to be trifled with—the veins of his temples started up like whipcord—and his eyes became suddenly bloodshot—I made haste to promise that Mr. Nicholls should on the morrow have a distinct refusal.

I wrote yesterday and got this note. There is no need to add to this statement any comment—Papa's vehement antipathy to the

bare thought of anyone thinking of me as a wife—and Mr.
Nicholls's distress—both give me pain. Attachment to Mr. N—
you are aware I never entertained—but the poignant pity inspired
by his state on Monday evening—by the hurried revelation of his
sufferings for many months—is something galling and irksome.
That he cared something for me—and wanted me to care for
him—I have long suspected—but I did not know the degree or
strength of his feelings.

"Good grief, man, what's happened?"

Sutcliffe Sowden found Arthur huddled in a dark corner of a public house in Hebden Bridge. A nearly empty glass of ale sat before him on the beer-stained table.

"My landlady said you were here. Why didn't you go in and wait for me at home? By Jove, you're blue in the face. Where's your hat? Come on. Get up. Come over here by the fire."

The fire had been allowed to burn out and Sowden called to the server.

"We don't burn a fire midday, Reverend," he was told by the woman who came out from behind the bar.

"Then I'll pay you for your wood. This man's ill."

When they had settled near the fireplace, Arthur reached inside his coat and withdrew two letters. He handed them to Sowden.

"One is from her. The other from her father. You will see for yourself which is which."

When he had read them, Sowden looked up at Arthur in astonishment.

"I find this shocking. Shocking. To think how diligently you've served him over the years and then have him accuse you so cruelly and unjustly."

Arthur looked miserable. His eyes were bloodshot and the color had drained from his face. "I know quite well that as clergymen we have the precious trust of the families we serve," he said soberly, "and that Mr.

Brontë feels I have betrayed that trust. A respectable suitor would have made his intentions clear from the outset. But what was I to do, Sowden? I was damned if I did and damned if I didn't. I didn't come here looking to marry one of his daughters. I didn't even plan to stay here, to tell you the truth. Besides, I know quite well his opinion of me. My only hope was to turn to her directly."

"Look, he can't mean these things. You know how fathers are. It's his pride. And Mr. Brontë is a very proud man. He only wants the best for his child. Just give him time to come to his senses."

"It's not him—it's not his letter that so distresses me. It's hers. You see? Even without loving me she is kind and good to me, not proud like him. Even though she says she can't return my feelings, she must have a grain of affection for me, somewhere, don't you think?"

"I don't know. I'm not good at this sort of thing, Nicholls. Women rarely say what they really mean."

"If she would only stand up to him, there might be a chance."

"Oh, now, I wouldn't count on that happening. She's a dutiful daughter. You wouldn't have her defy him, would you?"

The glimmer of light in his eyes vanished. "No." He shook his head. "Most definitely not."

Arthur buried his face in his hands. His strong, square features seemed incongruous with the misery that flowed from his eyes when he lifted them to Sowden's.

"I can't stay here. I can't go on like I did. The very thought of seeing her—I just come undone, Sowden. I can't help it. I can't go back to the way I was before."

"What will you do?"

"I shall resign. I'll go away. Far away. Someplace where there is nothing to remind me of her."

"Where?"

"I'll apply for a missionary post. Africa."

"Oh, good grief, man, not Africa. Don't be absurd. That's a death sentence for sure. No one survives Africa."

"All the better for me."

"My cousin is in the Australian colonies. Rather likes it there. Of course he ministers to the colonials. Doesn't set foot in the bush."

Haworth, 18 December

Ellen dear,

You ask how Papa demeans himself to Mr. N. I only wish you were here to see Papa in his present mood: you would know something of him. He just treats him with a hardness not to be bent—and a contempt not to be propitiated.

The two have had no interview as yet: all has been done by letter. Papa wrote—I must say—a most cruel note to Mr. Nicholls on Wednesday. In his state of mind and health (for the poor man is horrifying Martha's mother by entirely rejecting his meals) I felt that the blow must be parried, and I thought it right to accompany the pitiless dispatch by a line to the effect that—while Mr. N must never expect me to reciprocate the feeling he had expressed—yet at the same time I wished to disclaim participating in sentiments calculated to give him pain; and I exhorted him to maintain his courage and spirits. On receiving the two letters, he set off from home—I believe to visit his friend Mr. Sowden in Hebden Bridge. Yesterday came the enclosed brief epistle.

You must understand that a good share of Papa's anger arises from the idea—not altogether groundless—that Mr. N has behaved with disingenuousness in so long concealing his aim—forging that Irish fiction et cetera. I am afraid also that Papa thinks a little too much about his want of money; he says the match would be a degradation—that I should be throwing myself away—that he expects me, if I marry at all, to do very differently; in short, his manner of viewing the subject is on the whole far from being one in which I can sympathize. My own objections arise from the sense of incongruity in feelings, tastes—principles.

"Charlotte! Charlotte!"

She came to the top of the stairs and leaned over the railing.

"Come down here! I've had another letter from that man! You must see this!"

Charlotte came tripping down the stairs, holding her skirts. Martha came to the kitchen door with a knife in her hands, smelling of onions and hoping for drama.

"Go back to work," Charlotte scolded as she scurried past into the dining room.

Her father stopped his pacing to wave a letter under her nose.

"Look at this! This is quite typical of him. Deceitful to the last."

"May I read it please?" Charlotte held out her hand. Her eyes flashed in annoyance.

"He's changed his mind! He resigned and now he's changed his mind. That vile scoundrel will not let—"

She held up a hand. "Please, Papa, may I read it."

It was brief, a few lines. A softness floated over her countenance as she read; her father didn't notice.

She looked up. "This is a good sign, Papa. If he wants to withdraw his resignation, it means there's a chance for things to return to normal."

"It means no such thing! It means he's going to lurk around the parsonage scheming and behaving like the underhanded rascal that he is."

"That's quite unjust. Mr. Nicholls never once conducted himself with disrespect toward me."

"Well, I won't do it. He's resigned and he must go. Unless he gives me a solemn oath—in writing—that he will never again broach this obnoxious subject either to me or to you! That is the only condition upon which I will have him back."

"That's most unfair."

"Unfair? Unfair?! Why, it will be proof that his sentiments are false and calculated for his own gain. If he renounces you in order to take back his post, you will have your proof of his shallowness."

But Arthur would not cede to her father's blackmail. He simply did not respond to the demands. Charlotte felt sadly triumphant. At least he had not betrayed his love for her—worthless as that may have been to everyone except himself.

Dear Ellen,

You ask about Mr. N. He has never accepted the conditions Papa demanded to withdraw his resignation, so I feel it will all end in his departure. Nobody pities him but me. Martha is bitter against him; John Brown says he should like to shoot him. *He continues restless and ill—he carefully performs the occasional duty—but does not come near the church to preach, procuring a substitute every Sunday.*

I am surprised that you take Papa's side. You who were always seeing a match there, and now that it has come to pass you think it would be below my station. Indeed, our tastes and interests are oceans apart—he is quite indifferent to those things I cherish, and I cannot pretend that he is at my level in intellectual matters. But Dear Nell—without loving him—I don't like to think of him suffering in solitude, and wish him anywhere so that he were happier. He and Papa have never met or spoken yet.

In the midst of this turmoil Charlotte received an invitation from Mrs. Smith to visit. Smith, Elder was preparing for a speedy publication of *Villette,* and George urged her to come to London to tackle the proofs. Her father encouraged her to accept. Charlotte supposed it was simply to get her out of the way.

A week later, Charlotte found herself at the Smiths' splendid new house in Gloucester Terrace, sitting in her room with the proof sheets spread out on her desk. A crisis at work kept George at the office until late in the evenings, and she had a good deal of time to herself. She spent her afternoons visiting asylums, prisons, and orphanages and avoided society. It was a program greatly to her liking, motivated by the hope of finding in those wretched halls an inspiration for her next book, although George's mother and sisters thought her tastes a bit too gloomy. She saw Harriet Martineau but did not even tell Sir James Kay-Shuttleworth that she was in London.

She kept herself busy enough and might have put all the business about Arthur out of her head were it not for the frequent letters from her father with accounts of Arthur's miseries.

Charlotte was not eager to leave London. She was disappointed that George could find so little time for her, but she could see that the crisis at Cornhill was grave.

"You mustn't be alarmed, dear," Mrs. Smith reassured her with a brave face. "Just the inevitable consequences of that unfortunate business with his partner. George has inherited a rather untidy financial situation and he insists on setting it straight without resorting to drastic measures, if you know what I mean. But it will all get sorted out. I have the utmost faith in my boy."

Sometimes George left home at nine in the morning and spent the entire night in his office dictating lengthy business letters to his clerks to be dispatched the next morning to accounts in India or Hong Kong. He would appear at breakfast pale and worn, trying his best to conceal his worries. He had even been forced to abandon his habitual early morning rides in Rotten Row. George's sisters and mother tended to his every need with solemn concern, in the way of women who depend upon the men they love for their survival. Their devotion moved Charlotte deeply, but the bond of family was one from which she was excluded. Although their courtesy to her never wavered, she felt herself more isolated than ever before.

But there was something else, an uneasiness that preyed on her mind. She was nagged by the thought that George was avoiding her or, at the very best, that he was secretly relieved to have a legitimate excuse to stay away. Their candid conversations had been replaced by dry talk about business. Charlotte wondered if he had been disturbed by the way she had portrayed him—and her feelings for him—in *Villette*, but she could not be sure of it. More and more, she became convinced that their friendship was not the true one she had first imagined, where sympathies were real and would outlast circumstances. It was an intimacy predicated on expediency. Were she to fail him as an author, the friendship would cease.

She stayed until the end of January, to see *Villette* published and make sure gift copies were sent to Ellen and other friends. On the way back she stopped in Manchester to spend several days with her new friend the author Elizabeth Gaskell and her family. Elizabeth's little girls were beautiful, boisterous miniatures of their good-natured mother, of whom Charlotte was growing increasingly fond. It was the kind of genial domestic scene that contrasted so sharply with her own sad family life, and she returned home in a despondent frame of mind. It was February and the ground was frozen black and hard.

Barely had she disentangled herself from Tabby's embrace and untied her bonnet when her father launched into a tirade about Arthur. He tailed her into the dining room and hovered over her while she knelt down to greet the dogs, and while Martha lit the coals in the grate, he recounted how Arthur had sent off his application to the missionary society.

"Put him in quite a pickle, as he was forced to request a recommendation from me."

"I'm sure you spoke fairly of him, Papa."

"Fair! I was indulgent! Sang his praises and breathed not a word of his perfidy. I should like to see him gone. I wish him no ill but, rather, good and wish that every woman may avoid him forever unless she should be determined on her own misery. All the wealth of the Australian gold mines would not make him and any wife he might have happy."

"So he intends to serve in Australia."

"Indeed. It's all settled."

"I see." She spoke in a subdued voice. It struck her how intensely unhappy he must be to cut ties with England and voyage so far away. She had a brief flash of Arthur on a ship in a storm sailing to the colonies: the ending she had envisioned for Paul Emanuel in *Villette*. But that was fiction. The thought of Arthur drowning in an attempt to escape his unhappiness was not how she wanted things to end.

"I'll bring you a nice cup of tea, miss," Martha said as she brushed the coal dust from her hands. She lingered, hoping to catch more of the conversation, but Charlotte sent her back to the kitchen and then settled herself on a stool before the fire to warm her hands. Her father stood beside her in his worn-out coat and his slippers, chewing on his cold pipe and bristling with rancor.

"You know we had the bishop and the school inspector here."

"Did it go well?"

"I do wish you had been home. I was quite overwhelmed, Charlotte. But the visit went well—that is, until the end when they were all here for tea. I addressed that man, that odious reprobate, I spoke to him with civility, but he sat there during tea throwing dark looks at me, doing his best to look glum and dejected, and then he dared to speak sharply to me! I cannot forgive him this sort of treatment in public!"

"I am sorry, Papa. That is regrettable," Charlotte said quietly, "since he is a good man at bottom—"

"Good? Good?!"

"Well, it is a sad thing that Nature has not put goodness into a more attractive form."

"Into the bargain he managed to get up a most pertinacious and needless dispute with the school inspector."

"Oh my," she sighed. "Up to his old tricks again."

"I count the days until he is gone and I can live my life in peace."

"When does he leave?"

"At the end of May. We shall be rid of him forever."

"Here's Martha. Oh, good, she's put out the biscuits I brought from London. We'll have a nice tea, Papa, without any more talk of Mr. Nicholls. Come now. Sit down. You mustn't excite yourself any further."

When her father retired to his study, Charlotte immediately wrote a letter to Ellen, urging, "You must come quickly, dear Ellen. Please try to arrange your schedule. There are matters I must confide to you—I need not tell you the subject. The situation here at home is most trying. Try to stay long enough to be here when the reviews of *Villette* come out."

Charlotte sat on the bed in her nightgown and a heavy shawl, her knees tucked under her chin, while Ellen brushed her hair in the way that always calmed her, with long, soothing strokes. It was an intimate ritual they had shared since their schoolgirl days.

"You can do much better than poor Mr. Nicholls, you know. Really, you would be throwing yourself away. You're Currer Bell. You cannot marry just any old goose."

"I have my own objections, of course I do. But this isn't what concerns Papa. He only sees the situation in terms of himself. His pride would be offended. Not mine. His."

"Charlotte, if he came from an old family, with a good name, it wouldn't be so bad. But to be poor and with nothing else? You'd be taking a step down in society."

"May I remind you that Papa's family has no claims to distinction. He comes from a poor Irish farming family, just like Arthur does. Doesn't it strike you as hypocritical? All our lives, the wealthy landowners here have looked down on us because we were so poor. And now he treats Mr. Nicholls with contempt for the same reason."

Charlotte heaved her shoulders in a sigh. She lifted a soft brown coil of hair and ran her fingers through it. "I think I'm losing my hair."

Ellen rapped her skull with the brush. "You are *not* losing your hair. You don't have feelings for him, do you?"

"I don't love him in the least. But if you had seen him the night he proposed to me—. I can't forget his face, it still lingers in my mind—this man I have known for years, always so stern and hard-featured, crumbling before my eyes. I've never seen a man look like that, and I promise you, it's not easily forgotten. I believe he does love me—I believe he loves me truly and deeply."

It was the first time she had expressed these sentiments aloud, and the words were difficult to speak. She had received other proposals of marriage in her younger years—Ellen's brother Henry and that lively little curate from Dublin who'd followed up his one visit to the parsonage with a letter asking for her hand—but neither man had loved her truly and deeply, or even loved her at all.

"But you don't feel the same," Ellen said.

"No," she said sadly. "I do not."

"All the better. It would be quite unfortunate if you did."

There was a certain complacency in Ellen's manner and a touch of self-importance. The sort of attitude that drew lines to keep others out. Ellen had drawn a circle around Charlotte, Charlotte's father, and herself. Arthur was excluded, exiled to the land of the unworthies.

Arthur was too numb to feel the puzzled stares of the churchwardens who sat around the table in the upstairs meeting room of the Black Bull. Michael Merrall wore a grieved expression, and William Thomas tugged at his beard the way he did when something perturbed him. Wind hammered the rain against the windows.

Arthur was saying, "I have for some time felt a strong inclination to assist in ministering to the thousands of our fellow countrymen in the colonies. These men have been in a great measure deprived of the means of grace. I would hope to remedy that by my service in the missionary society."

It was clear to all of them that he had memorized his short speech. He fell into silence and stared sullenly at an invisible spot on the smoke-darkened wall.

"Tell us why you're going. Truthfully, sir. What has happened?"

Arthur spoke quietly. "I can no longer remain here."

"Has anyone asked you to go? Are you being forced out?"

"There are some who would wish it so."

"Speak plainly, sir. There's been a terrible quarrel between the two of you. Is it Mr. Brontë's fault?"

He shook his head firmly. "It is my own fault. Only mine."

"Do you blame Mr. Brontë?"

"I do not. If anyone is to blame in the matter, it is I."

"Are you leaving willingly?"

Arthur shook his head, and his eyes swelled with tears. "I do not leave willingly. It saddens me greatly."

Amid all this turmoil, *Villette* was published. On the whole, the reviews were positive, as Charlotte had predicted. Mr. Williams clipped them from the London newspapers and posted them to her.

From the *Literary Gazette:*

> This book would have made her famous, had she not been so already. It retrieves all the ground she lost in *Shirley,* and it will engage a wider circle of admirers than *Jane Eyre,* for it has all the best qualities of that remarkable book, untarnished, or but slightly so, by its defects. Viewed as a whole, there is so obvious an advance in refinement without loss of power, that it would be invidious to qualify the admiration with which *Villette* has inspired us by dwelling upon minor faults.

G. H. Lewes reviewed it for the *Leader.* Charlotte thought he showed himself exceedingly generous:

> Here, at any rate, is an *original* book. Every page, every paragraph, is sharp with *individuality.* It is Currer Bell speaking to you, not the Circulating Library reverberating echoes. How *she* has looked at life, with a saddened, yet not vanquished soul; what *she* has thought, and felt, not what she thinks others will expect her to have thought and felt; *this* it is we read of here, and this it is which makes her writing welcome above almost every other writing. It has held us spell-bound."

Critics called it "powerful" and spoke of its "well-observed, pictur-esque characters" depicted in a "masterly way," of descriptions of nature "as good as Turner to the mind's eye," of its "delightful freshness, force-ful sentiments." "Brain and heart are both held in suspense by the fasci-nating power of the writer," said one. The *Athenaeum* thought that M. Paul, that "snappish, choleric, vain, childlike and noble-hearted arbiter" of Lucy Snowe's destiny, was a "brilliantly distinct character." Detractors complained of its morbidity and improbabilities, and at the same time lauded its "redeeming beauties and surges of passion."

When a batch of newspaper clippings arrived from Cornhill, Charlotte would wait until the evening to bring it to her father, and she and Ellen would settle in his parlor for tea. Ellen thus was included in the tight cir-cle of Currer Bell's intimates—which was quite another thing from being Charlotte Brontë's friend. With her father's eyesight deteriorating once again, Charlotte simply edited out any negative passages as she read the reviews to him. It was the way she had always dealt with him.

She was understandably vexed when Mr. Grant swooped down on them one evening during tea, sounding the alarm of a caustic review in the *Guardian*.

"Have you not seen it, Miss Brontë?"

"I have not, sir."

"Well then, you must inquire immediately. Perhaps your publisher has withheld it in order to avoid wounding you."

"Mr. Grant, I am indeed indebted to my publishers for all I know of the favorable notices. The hostile notices I leave to the care of my friends, and they never fail to disappoint me. Come, please, sir, do sit down and have a cup of tea and tell us what you know."

"Well, I've not seen the review myself, but Mrs. Grant's cousin who resides in London read it and was most shocked. Here, I have her letter." He reached into his hat, withdrew a note, and unfolded it. Charlotte threw an uneasy glance at her father, who sat rigid with his mouth frozen in a downward thrust.

"She was kind enough to copy the phrases of interest. She says the reviewer calls the book stern and masculine and says that your—or, rather, Currer Bell's—vocation is in depicting 'suppressed emotion and unreturned affection' . . ."

At this Charlotte recoiled inwardly. She felt her cheeks grow warm, but she was intent on keeping her smile pleasant and cool.

". . . and, let's see—where is it—oh, yes, he complains of a 'cynical and bitter spirit' and a lack of refinement. And this—this most outrageous insult of all: he says, 'Lucy Snowe herself is Jane Eyre over again; both are reflections of Currer Bell; and for the reasons above given, though we admire the abilities of these young ladies, we should respectfully decline (ungallant critics that we are) the honor of their intimate acquaintance.' "

He folded the letter and tucked it back into his hat, his chest pumped with indignation.

"This is an unmanly insult, Miss Brontë," he huffed, "and I shall be glad to write a scorching—yes, scorching—letter to the editor on your behalf."

Charlotte could feel Ellen's embarrassment, and a quick glance at her father noted the restrained anger in his jaw. She rushed in soothingly: "Mr. Grant, please, do let me pour you a cup of tea. We have an extra cup right here. Do sit down."

He pulled up a chair and Charlotte said, "That was ever so considerate of you to alert me to this notice, sir, but I assure you, I know the critic in question, and he has every right to lisp his opinion of Currer Bell's female characters. I do forgive him very freely—but I assure you I am not in the least perturbed at not meeting his standard for an intimate acquaintance. Now, your tea. I trust you'll find it sweet enough."

They had found her weakness—this issue about loving and being loved in return—but she had bared her soul bravely and willingly for all of them to see, because she believed it was important to reveal the truth about women's hearts. So it was devastating when a woman with whom she had forged a fragile friendship revealed herself so utterly insensitive.

When Charlotte had stayed at Harriet Martineau's home in Ambleside, she had observed with admiration the woman's vigor and strength, watched her rise every morning at four and swim in the freezing lake waters before taking to her desk. As painful as it had been, she had listened with quiet tolerance to Miss Martineau's atheistic views. For her own edification, Charlotte had sincerely implored Miss Martineau to be a truthful critic of her work. So when she received Miss Martineau's letter she was expecting candid opinions, from one writer to another; but she did not anticipate this: "The merits are downright wonderful. As for the faults, I do deeply regret that your mind seems to be full of the subject of one passion—love. I think there is unconscionably too much of it (giving an untrue picture of life), and speaking with the frankness you desire, *I do not like its kind.*"

Then, the very next day, she received from Cornhill a packet containing a review in the *Daily News,* also written by Harriet Martineau:

> The book is almost intolerably painful. All the female characters, in all their thoughts and lives, are full of one thing, or are regarded by the reader in the light of that one thought—love . . . so dominant is this idea—so incessant is the writer's tendency to describe the need of being loved, that the heroine, who tells her own story, leaves the reader at last under the uncomfortable impression of her having loved two men at the same time. . . . It is not thus in real life. There are substantial, heartfelt interests for women of all ages, and under ordinary circumstances, quite apart from love.

After weeks of tortured reflection, Charlotte wrote a brief reply:

> *My dear Miss Martineau,*
>
> *In compliance with your wishes, I return to you your letter. I have marked with red ink the passage which struck me dumb.*
> *I know what love is as I understand it; and if man or woman*

should be ashamed of feeling such love, then is there nothing right, noble, faithful, truthful, unselfish on this earth, as I comprehend rectitude, nobleness, fidelity, truth, and disinterestedness.

The differences of feeling between us are very strong and marked, very wide and irreconcilable. It appears very plain to me that you and I had better not try to be friends. My wish is that you should quietly forget me.

Yours sincerely,
C. Brontë

Chapter Twenty-four

*V*illette's success kept Charlotte's spirits high that spring. The reviews continued to pour in, nearly all of them eulogizing in part, and with most criticism directed toward the book rather than her personal character. But in the absence of the old irritating speculation about her gender and identity, she was now forced to endure a different, even more cruel scrutiny—the kind that Mr. Grant had seized upon so enthusiastically. She had boldly dared to examine the psychology of a woman's unhappiness—and everyone knew that this woman was herself.

As it became evident that *Villette* was based on her years of study in Brussels, readers were curious to draw the connections between her novel and her life. In literary salons and over London dinner tables, through correspondence moving from one house to another across the country, those who had made her acquaintance began to speculate about her past and, above all, the identity of Monsieur Paul Emanuel.

To Lily Gaskell she had offered glimpses into her life in Brussels, but to no one had she ever whispered an intimation of love. It was quite unnecessary, since it was all there in the novel for everyone to read.

She could not know—indeed, it was a blessing that she would never know—how transparent she had made herself.

"Lily, you know George Smith. Is it true that he was the inspiration for Graham Bretton?"

"I'm sure he was."

"Is the portrait true to life?"

"Very much like him."

"What about that fiery little professor? He scolds her so abominably. Should you have fallen in love with him?"

"Well, one can see how Lucy Snowe did, when he alone had the power to see anything of her heart."

"I do feel almost a sense of reverence for one who is capable of so much deep feeling."

"Is she as sad in person?"

Elizabeth Gaskell put aside her embroidery and looked up at the Winkworth sisters. "I think she works off a great deal of her sadness into her writing and out of her life. I hope to have her to visit this summer. You will get a glimpse of her yourself." She added with a smile. "Be forewarned. She does have a wicked sense of humor."

Inevitably, men read her differently.

After finishing *Villette,* Thackeray sent off a note to the beautiful socialite with whom he had recently fallen in love:

> *It amuses me to read the author's naïve confession of being in love with two men at the same time; and her readiness to fall in love at any time. The poor little woman of genius! The fiery little eager, brave, tremulous, homely faced creature! I can read a great deal of her life as I fancy in her book, and see that rather than have fame, rather than any other earthly good or mayhap heavenly one, she wants some Tomkins or another to love her and be in love with. But you see she is a little bit of a creature without a penny worth of good looks, thirty years old I should think, buried in the country, and eating up her own heart there, and no Tomkins will come. You girls with pretty faces and red boots (and what not) will get dozens of young fellows fluttering about you—whereas here is a genius, a noble heart longing to mate itself and destined to wither away into old maidenhood with no chance to fulfill the burning desire.*

Heger hung like a shadow in Charlotte's thoughts during these months. Writing him into Paul Emanuel had not erased the pain, although that had dulled over the years. There had been profound satisfaction in reshaping her life so that she might have him and then ultimately free herself from him through his death. She hoped that she might be able to move on without him in the next book, but she had her doubts. She could not imagine the face of a lover that did not look like him and sound like him, and make her feel the way she had felt with him.

Easter arrived and Charlotte was kept busy entertaining visiting parsons and presiding over refreshments and local teas. She had been relieved to hear that Arthur had withdrawn his application to the missionary society and had found himself a curacy, but she did not know where. He and her father never spoke anymore. Arthur had withdrawn ever deeper into a solitary life. He still performed his duties, the marriages and burials, but in such a frozen and gloomy manner that the villagers and his fellow curates took notice and began to shun him. If Mr. Grant or any other clergyman called hoping to cheer him, he would scarcely speak; try as they might to gain his confidence, he would tell them nothing. His stubborn silence alienated his friends but inspired Charlotte's respect, and she fervently wished that her father would show the same restraint. Flossy still went to his lodgings, and he would come out and take the dog on lonely walks into the moors. He would cross the tops to see Sutcliffe Sowden, but that was all. No one else seemed to like him anymore.

"He looks ill and miserable," she wrote to Ellen.

> *I think he will be better as soon as he fairly gets away from Haworth. He has grown so gloomy and moody that all his parishioners who once held him in esteem are beginning to lose their respect for him. We never meet nor speak, nor dare I look at him—silent pity is all I can give him—and as he knows nothing about that, it does no comfort. It has all grown to such a cankerous stage. Papa has a*

perfect antipathy to him, and he, I fear, to Papa. Martha says she
hates him now—but she is easily agitated by Papa and her father.
I think he might almost be dying and no one in this house would
speak a friendly word to him. Alas! I do not know him well enough
to be sure that there is truth and true affection in his heart—or only
rançor and corroding disappointment at the bottom of his chagrin.
In this state of things I must be, and I am, entirely passive. I may
be losing the purest gem—and to me far the most precious life can
give—genuine attachment, or I may be escaping the yoke of a mo-
rose temper. With these doubts lurking in my mind, my conscience
will not suffer me to take one step in opposition to Papa's will—
blended as that will is with the most bitter and unreasonable prej-
udices. So I just leave the matter where we must leave all important
matters.

The wind, sweetened with the smell of moorland grasses, whipped at
Arthur's back as he made his way along the rocky path toward home. He
had been out to visit Mrs. Binns, who had never regained her health
after the birth of her sixth child, and Arthur suspected she would not
survive. The family had always been kind to him, and he had wanted to
see her and pray with her one last time. Night had already fallen when
he left the farm, but the moors were flooded with silver moonlight so
that he could see far beyond the rays cast by his lantern.

Lacking the means to keep a horse, Arthur walked out of necessity,
but he was a man of strong constitution with the endurance to tread the
ragged land, and he relished the physical challenge. Even on cold days
he would dawdle, taking time to marvel at the exposed roots of some
massive elder, or an intriguing outcrop of purplish rock, or the shifting
shadows cast by clouds racing over the frozen moortops. He found in
these moments a deep fulfillment quite outside the realm of his religion.
He had no inclinations toward botany, nor art, nor poetry; he did not
have the education to examine the world scientifically or contemplate it
through verse. He was quite simply a simple man in awe of creation, and

that God had not graced him with a particular talent by which to interpret it all did not mean that it was any less wonderful to him.

He had often pondered sharing these small delights with a wife. Had he accepted a living elsewhere, in a more civilized part of the country, he would perhaps have been married by now. But for reasons he could not clearly articulate he had remained here, and as the years had passed, he had grown firmly attached to this place.

And to Charlotte.

He passed down the narrow snicket between moss-grown walls and followed the path through the graveyard to the church. In his despondency he had been lax in supervising the altar preparations. Such negligence was uncharacteristic of him. The following morning, on Whitsunday, he would take his last communion service in Haworth, and he intended to perform it with all due reverence and dignity. Arthur firmly believed that the form of things mattered and that if the form broke down, the heart would be vulnerable to temptation.

The massive wooden door groaned as it opened and Arthur raised his lantern, casting light into the dank gloom of the old church. He glanced up into the vast empty shadows, remembering his arrival eight years ago. A swell of sadness rose to his throat, but he shook it off and crossed the cold stone floor toward the vestry.

"Good evenin', Reverend. I didn't mean to frighten ye, sir. I have the fair linen here, ready for tomorrow, all spotless and ironed without a wrinkle, the way ye like it."

It was Mary Burwin from the Altar Guild, one of the devout churchwomen who laundered his surplices and kept the silver vessels polished. She had disliked him intensely the first year; he had been critical of the way she and the others had performed their duties—had scolded them for wine stains on the altar linens and for tarnished chalices, and for waiting so late to prepare the altar that folks were already taking their seats while they bustled around dusting and setting out candles. But those days were long gone; they understood each other now, and deep affection had grown over the years.

"It's the red frontal for tomorrow, isn't it, sir? The one Miss Brontë embroidered with the gold cross?"

"Yes, Mrs. Burwin. Thank you."

She unrolled the end and held it up to the lantern to show him. The gold threads shone in the soft, glowing light.

"It's a beauty, this hangin', isn't it, sir? Worthy of a great church. But then Miss Brontë's stitches can't be bested." She rolled it back up and placed it in the cupboard with the silver. "Shall I lock it up, sir?"

When there was no reply, she turned. He seemed to have frozen, staring into the shadows, his eyes fixed but clouded.

"Sir? Do ye want it left open?"

He blinked. His eyes were full of tears.

"Oh, sir," she said quietly, patting his arm with a work-callused hand. "We're so sorry to see ye go. Truly, we are."

"I see everything is in order," he said stiffly. "I need not have worried that God's holy gifts would not be prepared properly."

"No, sir, ye need not worry yer head 'bout those things anymore. Ye taught us well, and we're greatly beholden to ye."

"You are a good servant to the Lord, Mary Burwin. A good servant."

At these words of praise—all the more meaningful because they were so rare—Mary's sere old face softened and tears stung her eyes.

Taking up his lantern he turned to go, and as he passed through the door, she called after him, "And don't ye worry, sir. I'll be in here early in the mornin'."

An unusual stillness marked the congregation that morning. Everyone noted his heavy voice as Arthur delivered the sermon, and the heaviness reverberated throughout the silence.

He descended to the altar to receive their alms, leading them through the confession and absolution of their sins. He knelt, he rose; he raised the chalice in the prayer of consecration. His voice broke. The congregation heard it, and all movement ceased.

"Hear us, O merciful Father, we most humbly beseech Thee . . ."

He struggled on, his rocklike countenance in a battle with forces he could not hold back.

"... who in the same night that he was betrayed, took bread ..."

Again the voice broke; he faltered, then lost control. Josh Redman was assisting; he stepped up to Arthur and murmured words of encouragement. Arthur struggled on but his voice was barely a whisper.

The communicants solemnly filed up and knelt before him. Charlotte had come alone this morning, without her father, intending to show Arthur by her solitary presence some token of regard. She had not thought it would be this difficult for him.

She knelt before him; he stood pale, shaking, voiceless. Never had she seen a battle more sternly fought with feelings than the one she witnessed that morning. His hands trembled as he held the cup to her lips to drink. She did not dare raise her eyes to him, could not speak to him or comfort him. She crossed herself, rose, and returned to kneel at her pew.

In the stillness, a sob broke from the back of the church. Then another. All around her, women were weeping. Charlotte—concealed behind her bonnet—wept quietly.

On her way out, she caught a glimpse of him surrounded by a small crowd of well-wishers. Mary Burwin stood nearby with a cluster of ladies from the Altar Guild, and there was not a dry eye in the lot. Charlotte avoided them; she slipped outside and hurried up the path to her home.

Charlotte had hoped her father wouldn't hear about it, but he did. Undoubtedly John Brown or Josh Redman reported the incident because he brought it up at tea. He reacted with anger, thought Arthur's conduct disgraceful. Called him an "unmanly driveler." Charlotte had not expected compassion from him. She held her tongue.

Charlotte came to the kitchen with an envelope heavy with coin.

"Take this over to Miss Dixon at the school, Martha. Tell her it's for the testimonial."

"Miss Dixon's gone, miss."

"Gone?"

"Left yesterday. Got a job teachin' in Skipton, I'm told."

"I see. Well then, take it to the headmaster."

With a glance toward the door, Martha cleaned her hands on the apron and whispered, "Is it for Mr. Nicholls?"

"Never you mind, Martha. Just take it."

"I hear they're gettin' him a gold watch."

"Go and come back quickly."

"That's real charitable of ye, miss."

"Well, I should hope so, since no one else in this house seems to have any charity in their hearts for the man. Now hurry. And don't tell a soul. Do you hear me? Not a soul."

On his last evening in Haworth, Arthur called at the parsonage to hand over the deeds of the school to Patrick and to bid them farewell. When he came out of the parlor, he found the door to the dining room open. Inside, the rugs were rolled up, the furniture moved to the center of the room; Martha and her younger sister Eliza were washing down the walls. Martha was on her knees, ringing out a rag in a pail of water, when she saw him standing in the doorway.

"The mistress is upstairs, Reverend," she whispered.

He nodded stiffly. The look of disappointment on his face tugged at Martha's heart.

He lingered and seemed to wish to draw out the moment. "I see you're up to a thorough spring cleaning."

"No, this is somethin' special, sir. Mrs. Gaskell's comin' for a visit, sir. She's a famous author like our mistress."

"I see. Well, good-bye then, Martha. Eliza."

"Good-bye, sir."

"May God . . ." His voice broke. The two women stared at him, a little in awe of this ox of a man so broken by love.

He turned and was gone.

Martha rose and dried her hands on her apron. "I'm goin' to fetch the mistress."

She slipped out of her wooden clogs and ran barefoot up the stairs. She found Charlotte in the front bedroom window, peering down at the garden below.

"Miss . . ."

"I know, Martha," Charlotte said.

"He's gone, miss. Gone for good."

Charlotte spun around, dashed past Martha, and down the stairs. Martha thought she'd never seen Miss Brontë hurry so.

There were questions Charlotte wanted to ask him—where he was going, what he would do. She couldn't have him leave thinking that she felt the same way her father did.

When she stepped outside and saw him leaning against the garden gate, her heart went out to him. He had paused there, unable to walk away, his head down, sobbing as though his heart would break. She went straight to him and stood at his side, looking up into his face. Suddenly, all those questions she had been burning to ask were swept from her thoughts.

"Mr. Nicholls, oh my dear fellow . . ."

His look was an appeal for hope and encouragement.

"My dear sir, you must not think me heartless. Your suffering . . . your constancy. I am not blind."

He found his voice. "I have so much I would have liked to say . . . had I just been given a few hours with you . . ."

"I am so sorry."

"Would you give me leave to write to you?"

"Oh, sir, there can be no exchange between us."

"But you will not return my letters, you would not be so cruel."

"My father—"

"I will find a way."

"Where are you going?"

"I will come back for you."

There was the sound of a shutter opening, and Charlotte started.

"You must go," she urged him.

"I will return."

He went out the gate and walked down the lane with a heavy step.

There was nothing more she could do. He was gone. Gone. That was the end of it.

She returned to her room upstairs and closed the door. Sitting on her bed, her hands clasped in her lap, she saw his face before her eyes. She recognized that look and knew what he was feeling. She had felt those same overwhelming emotions for Heger. That same kind of love. That same agony on parting, fearing she might never see him again.

A week later, Charlotte fell ill with influenza. She ran a high fever and a doctor was called from Leeds. She was in bed for nearly two weeks with severe headaches, too ill even to answer her own correspondence. To the more important letters from George Smith and Elizabeth Gaskell, she dictated replies through her father; Lily Gaskell's visit, for which she had been so eagerly preparing, had to be postponed.

They all suspected that her illness had something to do with Arthur's departure.

Then one night, when the servants had gone to their room and Patrick was on his way up to bed, Charlotte heard him cry out. Still weak, she wrapped her shawl around her shoulders and dragged herself from her bed to the stairs.

"Charlotte!" he cried. There was panic in his voice.

"What's wrong, Papa?" she cried.

He stood on the staircase with his candle in his hand and his face stricken with terror.

"I can't see!" he cried.

"But you have your candle."

"I can't see it! Has it gone out?"

"No, Papa, it's not gone out."

"It's gone all black on me, Charlotte! Everything's gone black! I'm blind! I've gone blind!"

She got him to bed—ill and weak as she was—then went outdoors, climbed the stairs to the servants' room, and woke Martha.

"Go get Dr. Hall. Run. I think Papa's had a stroke."

Dr. Hall conferred with Charlotte downstairs, alone. "The paralysis seems to have hit the optic nerve."

"Will he ever regain his sight?"

"I can't tell you. He may or he may not."

"God give us strength," she whispered.

"There's no way of knowing. He could get better."

"We mustn't tell him it was a stroke," Charlotte warned. "It will only upset him."

The following day the light began to return. Patrick said it was as if a thick curtain was gradually drawn up, leaving yet a dark veil. Within a few more days he could find his way around the house. Still, his vision was greatly dimmed and his spirits oppressed. Of course, Charlotte would not do anything to disturb his peace of mind. Arthur's name would not be uttered again.

Chapter Twenty-five

Tabby in her deafness seemed to understand more of Charlotte's heart than anyone else that summer. With her wobbling head and palsied hand, she would hijack the postman in the garden or the lane and deliver the post straight to Charlotte. Then she would hobble slowly back to her chair in the corner of the kitchen and not move until the day was done.

So Arthur's letters began to arrive that summer, and Charlotte handled the business the same way she handled all business with her father: discreetly.

"What about the new curate? Is he interesting?" Ellen asked.

"Not in the slightest," Charlotte sighed. "Papa's already grumbling."

It was a glorious July day of hot sun and vast blue sky. Ellen had just arrived, and they had gone straight to Sladen Beck to see the waterfall. They sat on the mossy bank with their petticoats tucked between their legs and their bonnets dangling down their backs.

"Ellen, I'm afraid I may be making a terrible mistake."

"In what way?"

"I may be throwing away something very precious, something that may not ever come along again."

"I presume you mean Mr. Nicholls."

"Yes."

"But your father is against the marriage."

"I'm thirty-seven years old. What other chances will I have to marry?"

"My dear, you are your father's only stay in his declining age. Your first duty is to him. You must abide by his wishes. If it is our lot to remain single, then we must endure it."

"And what shall I do when Papa's gone? What would be left for me? With no one to love and no one to care for."

"Oh, my dear Charlotte, you won't be alone. We could take a cottage together. By the sea. We could go to Filey, on the cliffs, where Miss Wooler has her cottage. You would write and I could keep house for you."

"So, that's it. We shall be old maids together, till the end."

"If it be God's will."

A long silence followed, with only the sounds of cascading water and the wind in the grasses.

"I had a letter from him."

"From Mr. Nicholls?" Ellen's voice was heavy with disapproval.

"He heard from Mr. Grant about Papa's stroke—and that I was ill. He was quite anxious about us."

"You didn't answer, did you?"

Charlotte shook her head. "No."

"You had no business opening the letter. You should have returned it."

Charlotte remained silent.

"You're not possibly taking this courtship seriously, are you?"

"I should like to have a chance to become better acquainted with him."

"But you know him! And you've had nothing but scorn for him for years."

Charlotte hesitated before confessing, softly, "I've not always been fair to him. I have too often exaggerated his faults and ignored his virtues. You know how harshly critical I can be." She added, with wry grin, "Particularly of curates."

"What are you saying?"

"I'd like to correspond with him."

"You would deceive your father?"

"Only until I can be sure of my feelings."

"Charlotte! I hardly recognize you anymore! After all these years of abiding by your conscience, you would put your own interests before those of your father."

"You're so harsh, Ellen, and so hard with me, and when you talk of principles, you don't leave me any chance to hope. It's all so utterly oppressive. It's all about my duty and my ailing father when, just once, I would have liked you to see Mr. Nicholls in a more encouraging light."

"You're being selfish, and that's quite unlike you."

Charlotte hesitated for a long while. When she spoke, there was an underlying tension in her voice: "Yes, I suppose it's to everyone's benefit that I remain single. Yours as well as Papa's."

"Charlotte! What are you implying?"

"Unless I were to marry someone like George Smith with good social connections. I'm sure no one would object to *that* match. I should go to London and make all the right kinds of friends, and poor Papa would be shuffled off to lodgings and no one would bat an eye."

"If you marry Mr. Nicholls, my dear, I daresay you will have no friends left at all. You always talk about what a bigot he is . . . well, what would he think of your Mrs. Gaskell? With her Unitarian minister husband?"

"I would manage it, in time."

"And what about Mary Taylor? Outspoken as Mary is! Why, he wouldn't allow her to set foot in your home!"

"Mary's in New Zealand."

"And do you think he'll allow you to correspond with her? Once he takes a look at one of her letters—"

"I would make sure he doesn't read them."

"May I remind you that he is not old and blind like your father, and he will be much more curious about your life than your father ever was."

"Let's not discuss this anymore, Ellen," she said bitterly.

"No," Ellen answered sharply. "Let's not."

My dear Miss Brontë,

I have heard from Joseph Grant that you and your father have recovered, and so my prayers—on that score—have been answered.

I leave Ireland tomorrow and will go to Kirk Smeaton in Yorkshire where I am to take up a small curacy there. I daresay there will be scarcely enough work to distract me. It is a quiet place and sparsely populated.

I am troubled by a sense of embarrassment as I sit down to write to you again—my letters to my friends and family are generally of the most dry matter. Now I find it is absolutely necessary that I look inside myself and try to give you a portrait of my heart. I feel myself almost childlike before the task—I don't know the language of love and I am entirely dependent upon you to understand what it is I wish to say.

I can say this much: knowing I can never see you again, I have tried to forget you, but I cannot. It is a terrifying thing to have the heart tyrannized by one constant idea, which is my love for you.

I have turned to your novels for comfort. On the pages, I hear your voice and I see you move before my eyes. But then, once the book is put aside, I am faced with a stark, empty reality, and you are not there.

Forgive me, my dear Miss Brontë, for my outpourings. Only by writing to you am I able to alleviate just a fraction of my suffering. I beg you for just one word, a word of kindness. I saw as much in your eyes on the day we parted. I cling to the hope of having a letter from you. Even a few words, written in your hand, would bring such boundless joy.

Your devoted
Arthur Bell Nicholls

When this letter arrived, Charlotte showed it to Ellen, hoping to engage her sympathy for Mr. Nicholls.

"I'd like you to read it, Nell. Here," she said, holding out the letter.

Ellen was installed in a chair beside the window, working a piece of worsted with long colored threads. Without dropping a stitch, she said airily, "You would make me an accomplice?"

"I beg you to read it."

Ellen put down her tapestry and looked Charlotte straight in the face. "I daresay, I always fancied that *Jane Eyre* was just a bit of naughty imaginings on your part. I was sure Jane Eyre was not you. Never would you be tempted to such wickedness. Now I'm not so sure. Your mind can be a dangerous thing. I remember when we were schoolgirls and you were so in thrall to your imagination. You recognized the power it had over you and you knew it was not always pure, that your thoughts were sometimes sensational and unhealthy. You used to tell me I was your model of purity and self-denial. Well, I sit here now, as your best friend, urging you to cease this deception."

Charlotte's eyes flashed darkly. Without a word, she folded the letter and slipped it into her pocket.

The visit bore the strains of their dispute, and Ellen departed from Haworth under a cloud of hurt feelings. Charlotte wrote once, and Ellen replied. It was a wounding reply, full of harsh judgment and stern Calvinistic warnings that Charlotte was losing her soul.

Their correspondence ceased after that, and Charlotte found herself more adrift than ever before in her life. All those to whom she would have turned were gone. She still looked forward eagerly to the books George and Mr. Williams continued to send, and to letters from admirers and literary acquaintances, but London grew increasingly irrelevant to her daily life and the concerns that now filled her thoughts.

On the September day when Elizabeth Gaskell was due to arrive, Charlotte was up before dawn. The visit, originally planned for June, had been postponed because of Charlotte's illness, but Charlotte had taken advantage of the delay to make small improvements to the parsonage.

The small Oriental rugs purchased that spring in Leeds had been aired, the new crockery and glassware removed from the paper wrappings and arranged in the china cabinet in the dining room. The mahogany table— bought after the publication of *Shirley*—had been polished to a deep glow, and the warm wood picked up the crimson from the sofa and armchair, which had recently been reupholstered with revenue from her railway dividends. There were new lamps and a new runner for the entry hall. Every inch of the walls and woodwork had been washed, the kitchen stove blackened, the waterspouts and tubs freshly painted white, the counterpanes laundered and ironed. The entire house was scrupulously clean and obsessively tidy. Charlotte had done her best to drive out the bleak austerity and bring a feeling of warmth and snugness to her home.

Elizabeth Gaskell had never experienced such a wild wind; she had to incline her head and clutch her bonnet as she hurried up the gravel path.

"My goodness gracious," she exclaimed, laughing, as she stood in the hallway smoothing down her skirt and brushing her hair out of her face. "I thought I was going to be blown right back to the gate!"

"My dear Miss Gaskell, come . . . come inside. I see you've been welcomed by our local banshees."

"Is the wind always so fierce? And you must call me Lily."

"And you must call me Charlotte. I'm afraid it is, at this time of year. Quite terrifying at night, the way it sobs and moans down the chimney, but wonderful if you're in the mood for ghost stories."

"Then we shall have ghost stories," Lily said with delight.

"Oh, no," Charlotte said with a nervous little laugh. "No ghost stories. I'm afraid I'm all too susceptible to those thoughts. While you are here, we shall talk of real-life things."

Patrick was his typical quaint self, reminiscing about his Cambridge days and exaggerating his friendship with Lord Palmerston in order to impress their celebrated guest. What did impress Lily Gaskell was the loaded musket on the wall in his study.

"He's always fancied firearms," Charlotte explained later. "When he's out of spirits he wants me to describe to him all the weapons in Prince Albert's armory at Windsor—he begged me to visit the place when I was in London last year. I've got it all down in my head, all the displays, the names of the arms, the battles . . ."

"And does it do the trick?"

"Inevitably," Charlotte tittered. "Cheers him immensely."

From their first meeting, Charlotte had been captivated by Lily Gaskell. Lily had a queenly presence about her, softened by a good dose of playfulness, but she was brilliant, too. She brought out the best in people. During her visit, their talk wandered off in all directions, like their rambles over the sweeping moors, and there never seemed to be an end to them. Charlotte confided in her without reservation; she spoke freely of her sisters, her brother, her father, and Arthur. Finally, she had found a sympathetic ear.

"I've known him for so many years, but it's quite a different thing to see him in this light."

"Of course it is."

"I would just like to have a chance to speak to him."

"And you should. I do believe your father is being dreadfully unfair. Is his objection really just a matter of Mr. Nicholls's income?"

"That's really at the heart of it, I believe."

"And your own objections?"

Charlotte hesitated. "Oh, Lily, I would be going against everything in my nature to marry without love. It's certainly not a brilliant marriage— but I would not be alone anymore, and there would be someone to take care of Papa in his old age." She added quietly. "I think perhaps it's time to let go of my dreams."

"I've been meddling again."

It was the first thing Lily said as soon as Katie Winkworth had settled herself on the sofa.

"Oh my, what have you been up to?"

"Well, first of all, I did a little spy work. I'm quite proud of myself. I was able to obtain Mr. Nicholls's address. For Lord Houghton. He's a great admirer of Charlotte's. He met her in London once. He's going to pull a few strings."

"What could he possibly do?"

"Find Mr. Nicholls a good position. Not far from Haworth, if possible. Anything that might improve his standing in her father's eyes."

"Does Miss Brontë know about this?"

"Absolutely not! And you mustn't ever breathe a word of it to her or anyone. My head would go rolling, Katie. I know her scruples, and I'm sure it would mean an end to our friendship." She paused, her eyes swelling with sympathy. "I don't think I've ever met a being so deserving of success and human affection. What she has endured, and yet overcome—her courage and perseverance through the most dreadful personal difficulties—and weathering all of this in utter loneliness, with her few friends always at a distance—and no man on whose steady chest she might rest her head. Can you imagine living like that? Well, I felt compelled to take action. I just cannot sit by and let her be browbeaten into submission by that father of hers."

"You weren't too fond of him, were you?"

"He was very charming—paid me rather old-fashioned, high-blown compliments—but to tell you the truth, I was afraid of him. I caught him glaring at her over his spectacles a few times, very sternly. Made me know my man. And he talked *at* her and me, rather than to us. You know how men can be when they really don't see women but see right through them to the other side."

"I know precisely what you mean."

Toward the end of November, Charlotte received a letter from George Smith. She had not heard from him in more than a month, and she found the tone of his writing disturbing. It was very much unlike him—vague, with an undercurrent of uneasiness, worded in obscure language with reference to some important step in life. Charlotte was too full of dread to answer him directly, and so she wrote to his mother that very day, discreetly asking about his hints at some impending decision.

"If he is going to take an important step, would it likely be conducive to his happiness and welfare?" she wrote, unable to put her fears into more direct language.

Within a few days she had a reply from Mrs. Smith, stating that George was very well and very happy, that he was indeed thinking of taking a very important step in life, one with every prospect of happiness.

"I am very thankful and pleased about it," Mrs. Smith wrote, "and I am sure he will—as soon as it is quite settled—enter into all the particulars with you. I have no doubt in my own mind that all will be as his best friends could wish, and you will soon hear from him."

Charlotte had never allowed herself to think about this possibility, although she had spent many a day and evening with George, watching him eye pretty women. But the reality struck her with devastating violence, ripping every shred of confidence from her heart. She was consumed with jealousy for this unknown woman, undoubtedly some pretty little Polly-like creature from a socially connected family. She thought again of Arthur's mediocrity, and how her expectations had been brought so low.

The following day Charlotte boxed up the latest books that Cornhill had lent her and sent them back to Mr. Williams. Along with her thanks, she added, "Do not trouble yourself to select or send any more books. These courtesies must cease someday—and I would rather give them up than wear them out."

Within a few days, she received a letter from George; he was formally engaged to a Miss Elizabeth Blakeway. In his own delirium of love, he could perhaps be forgiven for his enthusiasm, pronouncing himself the most fortunate man in the world.

Charlotte replied:

My dear Sir,

*In great happiness, as in great grief, words of sympathy should be
few. Accept my meed of congratulation—and believe me*

*Sincerely yours
C. Brontë*

She read through her note. It was cold, stern, and unworthy of the
man who had treated her so graciously, but she did not have the heart to
write him the congratulations he truly deserved. This was the best she
could muster.

Chapter Twenty-six

In January, Arthur made an unannounced visit to the district, stopping at Oxenhope with the Grants and dispatching a note to Charlotte. Charlotte took the note to her father and asked permission to see him. She confessed that she had been corresponding with Arthur since September and that it was tearing her apart to conceal this from him. They had a terrible row, so loud that even deaf old Tabby could hear them; the servants hadn't heard that kind of shouting in the house since before Branwell's death. They had certainly never heard the old parson speak like that to his daughter.

But this time Charlotte stood up to him. She insisted that she would see him, whether he approved or not.

"Father, look at me," Charlotte said with heated determination. "I'm not a girl, not even a young woman anymore. I never was pretty and now I'm ugly. What is there to attract a man? It certainly isn't money. At your death I shall have three hundred pounds along with the little I've earned myself—do you honestly think there are other men who would want me? Men who would serve eight long years in a place like this for a stunted little spinsterish clergyman's daughter?"

When Charlotte came storming out of the parlor, Martha waited a few minutes, then tiptoed upstairs and pressed her ear to the bedroom door.

"Why, she's pacin' the floor an' mumblin' to 'erself like a madwoman. I think I've never seen the mistress so angry!" Martha told Tabby when she came back down.

Tabby was busy mopping the floor in the back kitchen. Her head wobbled back and forth on her shoulders but Martha couldn't tell if she meant anything by it.

Charlotte's reply was hand-delivered to Arthur over breakfast. He had a forkful of ham poised in midair when the servant entered, and he lowered it back to his plate and took the envelope like a man awaiting a death sentence. Life seemed to visibly drain from him, every nerve in his face, the broad muscular shoulders, all of it emptied of vitality. He hesitated, dabbed at his mouth and whiskers with the napkin, then snapped open the seal. As he unfolded the page, his hand trembled.

Sarah Grant sat across from him stirring sugar into her tea, and her heart went out to him. She shot an anxious glance at her husband, but Joseph Grant was knuckle-deep in his toast and scrambled eggs and serenely oblivious to pounding hearts and the drama at hand.

Sarah leaned forward and whispered to Arthur, "I do hope it's good news."

She couldn't tell at first—his face froze momentarily while his eyes scanned and rescanned the words.

"She will see me," he murmured in disbelief. "She will see me. Today. I must go immediately."

"Oh, but you must finish your breakfast," Sarah declared.

Arthur rose so quickly that he caught the tablecloth with his knees and dragged it with him, jerking Mr. Grant's plate right out from under him.

"What the deuce!" he sarted. "Must you be so clumsy, Nicholls?"

"She's consented to see me, at last . . . after a year! A full year I've waited! Do you realize? . . . Why, there might be a chance after all."

"Settle down, Nicholls. Get a grip on yourself. Say, you're not leaving that ham, are you?"

The servant was sent to fetch Arthur's coat and hat, and Sarah saw him to the door.

"Do be careful out there; it's quite cold, you know. And the wind is so sharp. Ah, here's Mary with your coat. Do bundle up. Where's your neck scarf?"

As he was leaving, she stopped him with a gentle hand.

"Mr. Nicholls," she said in that twinkling way of hers, "if you would allow me?" She reached up and plucked a crumb from his beard.

"There," she said with a pleased smile. "Now you're presentable."

She watched from the dining room window as he bowled down the steps. He slipped on the ice, regained his balance, and then barreled down the lane with the icy wind at his back and a mighty fire in his heart.

Tears stung Sarah's eyes, but she blotted them away so that Joseph wouldn't accuse her of sentimentality.

She straightened the tablecloth, then sat back down. Joseph was still reading the paper.

"He's lost so much weight," Sarah sighed.

Joseph shot a frown at Arthur's plate. "Pass me that ham."

"Here, dear."

"No need to waste it."

"Don't you think he has?"

"What?"

"Lost weight."

Joseph had his mouth full and didn't bother to answer.

"I'd say he's dropped at least a stone. His clothes just hang on him. And his face is much thinner." She set down her teacup and stared dreamily out the window, her chin resting on her hand. "I daresay, I've never seen a man so lovesick. I didn't know men ever felt like that."

Joseph knew better than to follow her into that discussion. He made a lot of noise with his newspaper and kept his head down.

Arthur stood in the hallway, covered from head to toe in a white dusting of snow. The house was deadly silent except for the ticking of the old clock on the landing and the sound of Flossy whining somewhere behind a closed door. Then he caught the faintest rustle of silk, a whisper, and she emerged from the kitchen with Martha just behind.

It was his first glimpse of her in nine months. She seemed even more delicate than ever, her pale face strained and her great brown eyes full of alarm.

"My note said this afternoon, Mr. Nicholls," she said in a low voice.

Arthur was flustered. Unable to speak anything but the truth, he blurted through numb lips, "I apologize. I was afraid you might change your mind, or there would be some hindrance."

"Papa's going out to a meeting after lunch. I thought it would be better to meet when he was away."

His voice dropped to a whisper. "I can go down to the Bull and wait—"

"For five hours? Don't be silly. You must be frozen from your walk. Please, do come in."

In the dining room, Charlotte looked on as he passed his hat to Martha and removed his cloak. He smelled of damp wool and clean wind, and when he drew off his gloves Charlotte noticed his hands, rugged, stiff from the cold.

"Where's Keeper?" he asked, when Martha had closed the door.

"He died last autumn. In his sleep. We buried him in the garden."

The expression on Arthur's face reminded her how much he had cared for the old dog. "Your father must be very sad."

"Yes. He's talking about getting another dog, to keep Flossy company, he says, but it's really for himself."

Arthur stood awkwardly in her presence, his hands clasped stiffly behind his back. With a sweeping glance, he took in the surroundings, the old familiar room.

"You've put up curtains," he exclaimed.

"Yes. Papa was quite resistant at first. Change is quite difficult for him at his age, and the amenities of life never held any attraction for him."

"You've done well here, Miss Brontë. I like the changes. Very warm and snug."

"Most of it was done before you left."

"That may be so, but I see it after a long absence." He was battling with his restraint, feeling the need to say much when it was not in his nature. "I have missed this place."

Her head barely reached his shoulder, and for the first time in his presence, alone like this, her thoughts sped to the possibility of intimacy with him. His strong, whiskered face was explored in a new light, the line of his lips examined now for hints of sexuality. Disturbing thoughts that she could not repress. It was far too soon for that.

"Please, come warm yourself."

She led him to the hearth. The fire had burned down and she reached for the coal scuttle.

"Let me do that," he insisted, taking it from her. He scattered a few coals onto the glowing embers, nudged them around with the poker. It was good to find something physical to occupy his hands, and the heat eased the nervous tension in his chest.

"You said in your last letter that your father has had a good winter."

"Yes, he has," she said. "No bronchitis, I'm pleased to say."

"And his eyesight?"

"It's still very cloudy, but he sees well enough to get around."

He wanted to talk about her—about them—but he didn't know how to get there. Nevertheless, for now, he was in her presence, alone, for the first time. She stood with her head tilted up at him, her hands folded across the front of her dress. Trim and neat, and ever so fragile.

"Oh, Miss Brontë," he blurted in a near whisper, "do you think you could love me and be my wife?"

There they were. The very words she had longed to hear since girlhood when dreams of romance had filled her mind. Spoken with all the intensity and passion she had hoped to inspire in a man. But this was not the man she wanted.

"I don't know, sir."

"Please, don't tell me you brought me this far only to reject me once again."

"It's my father—"

"I am all too aware of the obstacles in my path, but all I need is the one thing you continue to withhold from me, a promise of your affection."

"You have my esteem and my regard. You have shown yourself true and constant, and I know your principles to be beyond reproach. You are a good man. But—"

"I beg of you, say nothing to discourage me—first let me speak." And to silence her, he reached for her hand, raised it to his lips, and kissed it warmly.

"I often find it difficult to believe that a delicate creature like you might ever want any part of a great whiskered fellow like myself. I know you are a brilliant woman, with great intellectual gifts—and I admire you all the more for these talents. But when I think of you—and I think of you every moment—I never see you in the light of genius and fame. I think of you as fragile and vulnerable, and easily wounded. I cannot bear the thought of seeing you harmed, in any way, by any person."

He pressed her hand to his chest. "I might wish that you would love and worship me with all your heart, but I'm not your Rochester. I see that quite clearly. And yet, I can confidently avow that I love you far too well, far more than any other mortal. If you could only be content with mortal love—stripped of all delusion."

Through the thickness of his coat she could feel his pounding heart.

"There would be no surprises between us," he went on. "You know my deep-rooted convictions and my conscience. You've witnessed my devotion to my duties. You know what your role as my wife would be."

"I do."

With a sudden racket, the door flew open, startling them both. Charlotte recoiled, snatching her hand from Arthur's chest. Her father filled the doorway—a crusty, unshaven old man in his shabby slippers and old-fashioned neckcloth, trembling with bile and bitterness.

"My dear Mr. Nicholls, *sir*," he began, drawing out the words with exquisite sarcasm, "the next time you are invited to my home—*if* there is a next time, which I fervently hope there will not be—you would be so courteous as to arrive at the designated hour."

Charlotte glanced anxiously at Arthur. His features had hardened into a scowl.

Arthur held his tongue, and the two men glared at each other in mutual contempt.

"I see you do not have the manners to apologize," Patrick snapped.

"He has apologized to me," Charlotte interrupted.

"Well, it's quite inconvenient to have him here right now, because I'm not feeling well. Not well at all."

Her first inclination was always to coddle him, but she would not—not in Arthur's presence.

"I'm not well, Charlotte," he repeated peevishly. "I'm feverish—"

"If you would go to bed, Papa, I'll send Martha up."

Flossy, who had managed to escape from the parlor, wormed his way around Patrick's legs and trotted up to Arthur. Arthur's face lit up with a smile and he bent down to scratch the dog's ears.

"Flossy, my old friend."

"Come away, Flossy," Patrick commanded roughly, but the dog was licking Arthur's hand.

"Flossy!" he boomed. "Come!"

Puzzled by the harsh tone of his master's voice, the dog trotted back with his tail low and sat obediently.

Patrick scowled down at the cowed dog. "So, you've gone traitor on me as well, have you? A whole house full of traitors!"

Turning stiffly, he closed the door with a bang that startled the poor dog and sent him scrambling beneath the dining room table.

The noise sent a jolt through her head, and Charlotte pressed her hand to her temple.

"You have a headache, don't you?" Arthur said, his voice grave with concern.

"Since this morning. Now it's pounding."

"I thought as much when I first saw you. You looked pale." He reached for her arm to steady her. "Here, come sit down."

He led her to the sofa.

"Would you rather I go?" he asked.

"No, Arthur," she said, lifting her dull eyes to his. "Don't go, not now. We've paid a high price for this time together."

"I'll call Martha. You need a cool compress."

"I imagine she's tending Papa."

"Then I'll fetch it myself."

He returned a few moments later, bearing a basin of cold water and a cloth.

He remained with her in the room that morning, sitting in the armchair quietly reading a paper while Charlotte reclined on the sofa. From time to time he would put down the paper and step softly to her side. He would freshen the cloth and lay it gently over her eyes.

"Arthur," she whispered, "if you would prefer to leave . . ."

"I would prefer to remain by your side forever, in sickness and in health."

She lifted the cloth and, with blurred vision, tried to fix her eyes on his face.

"I can't see you, but I think I heard a bit of levity in your voice."

"Yes, you did," he smiled. "But hush now." He resumed his seat near the fire. "Not a word more until you're better."

And so, Arthur courted Charlotte. He remained in Oxenhope for ten days and visited the parsonage with the same rigorous devotion with which he had tended his parish duties. Punctual as clockwork, defying driving hail and numbing wind, he set off each day on the footpath to Haworth and trudged across fields now blanketed in white, arriving on Charlotte's doorstep with astonishing precision. While Patrick—walled up behind his newspapers and his politics—stewed silently in his parlor, Arthur and Charlotte closed themselves in the crimson-toned dining room, with all its memories, for there was nowhere else they could go.

On occasion Patrick would burst into the room with some grievance or another, but Arthur's happiness trumped every indignation and every cruel word. Now that he had Charlotte all to himself, his attitude softened and he tolerated the old reverend's irascibility with good-humored equanimity. His gloominess gave way to laughter and small gestures of affection. His eyes, when gazing down at her, reminded her of the way she had felt when she had once loved deeply.

Charlotte had always known that Arthur lacked the intellectual power to seduce her mind, and she was acutely aware of the limitations of their conversations. Arthur's thoughts never strayed far from his clerical duties and the provincial activities that filled his days. Listening to his earnest chatter, she sometimes found herself escaping mentally to more stimulating places, to lively literary salons or warm nights in a Brussels garden. Sometimes the memories would rise up so vividly that her hands would falter, the clicking needles would fall silent, and Arthur would pause.

"What are you thinking, my dear?" he would ask. "You seem far away."

"I'm listening to you, Arthur," she would answer with a smile. "Do go on. You were telling how you ran into Mr. Sowden's brother in York. What a pleasant coincidence."

At times she stole looks at him through her spectacles, and try as she might, there was never that glow, that rose-tinted vision, that heat. All she felt was a sort of dull gratitude and a sense that she had run out of dreams to dream.

So she brightened her thoughts with memories in order to stir a little excitement into the moment. Into the room where she sat, with the dog and her knitting and Arthur.

With each passing day Arthur settled more and more comfortably into the framework of her life. He showed himself eager to reassure her that she was not marrying down, as her father would have her believe.

"Cuba House is a fine country manor. I should like to take you there. On our honeymoon."

Charlotte sat knitting by the fire, her feet on a stool, and she tossed a stern look at him over her spectacles. "I don't recall having accepted your proposal."

"But you will."

"I have made no promise."

"But you will." He rose from his chair and stood before the grate, stroking his whiskers. "I've been meaning to tell you, I had a surprise visit from Lord Houghton several months back."

Charlotte looked up, curious. "Lord Houghton?"

"He's a great admirer of yours. Claims to have met you in London."

"Yes. At Thackeray's lecture. He invited me to his home on several occasions, but I declined."

"Well, he came on a most unusual mission. He offered me two positions at his disposal, one in Scotland, the other Lancashire. Both of them very generous. I daresay I was puzzled by his interest in me."

"Scotland? What a wonderful opportunity for you, Arthur."

"Of course I refused them both. I would not have been able to come back to you."

She was silent for a moment, and then asked in a quiet voice, "So you would return? You would come back to serve here in Haworth?"

"In an instant."

"After all Papa's cruelty? You would forgive him?"

"For all the past injustices and all the future ones to come."

Still with her nose buried in her knitting, she said, "Tell me, Arthur, if we were to marry, would you be content to live here, in this house, with my father?"

A long silence, with only the sound of the needles clicking and the wind rattling the panes.

"Put down your work, Charlotte, and look at me. Raise your head."

At this command from Arthur, something thrilled in her, the resonant echoes of another voice she had not heard in years.

Willingly, she obeyed.

"I'm not a man of empty words. What I pledge, I will fulfill. I know your worries all too well, and you know my faults—and fraud is not one of them. We'll live here and care for your father until the end of his days, together, as husband and wife. He need never worry about going into lodgings or being abandoned by his only surviving child. You see, I love you, my dear."

His eyes held hers with firmness.

One evening several days after Arthur had returned to Kirk Smeaton, Charlotte rapped on her father's door. She stood before him with trembling hands folded at her waist and told him she had been heartily encouraged by all she had learned about Arthur. That she was inclined to esteem and affection, if not love.

"A curate," he said with contempt. "After all the fame you've achieved, you'd marry this poor curate without a penny to his name."

"Yes, Papa, I must marry a curate if I marry at all. But I would never marry just any curate. It would have to be your curate. And not merely your curate, but one who lives in the house with you, for I cannot leave you."

Martha, who was listening at the door, heard a commotion: the sound of a chair scraping, then a thud, a metal clang, something breaking.

"Live in my house? My house? Never!" he barked. "Never will I have another man in my house!"

The door flew open and Martha scurried to safety. Patrick stormed out and up to his bedroom, slamming the door. Martha rushed into the parlor, wide-eyed with fright.

"Miss! Are ye all right?"

Charlotte sat slumped in a chair in the corner like a rag doll, her forehead pressed into one hand. She lifted red-rimmed eyes to Martha.

"He kicked over his spittoon. It'll need to be mopped up. And there's a broken pipe on the floor over there."

For two days Patrick would not speak to his daughter. He shut her out of his study and took his tea alone; passing her in the hall, he treated her as if she did not exist. This coldness from him was more effective than all his tired ranting. She had been waging an exhaustive war for something she wasn't sure she wanted, and she could no longer sustain the effort. Emotionally drained, she retreated to bed with a pounding headache and vomited up everything Martha brought her to eat. Not once did her father look in on her.

By then Tabby and Martha had had their stomachs full of the old parson. They had seen how things stood between Mr. Nicholls and their mistress. They saw how kindly he treated her—"like a queen," Tabby said—and how calm she seemed when he was around.

On the fifth day, Tabby put on a clean apron and hobbled into Patrick's study.

"Master, I ben with ye nigh on forty years now, and I tell ye what yer doin' to yer daughter is just wrong."

Patrick raised his white head in astonishment.

"Aye, sir, yer old servant is standin' before ye, tellin' ye what she thinks of all this. Well, it's jes' plain selfishness on yer part. Ye're killin' yer daughter. Aye, ye're killin' her. Is that what ye want? Well, the others are all dead, and if ye don't stop this nonsense over Mr. Nicholls and let the two of 'em marry, she'll be dead, too, and ye'll have yerself t' thank for it."

Before going up to her room that night, Martha let Flossy out in the garden, and when she returned she found Mr. Brontë sitting at the kitchen table in the dark.

"Can I be gettin' ye somethin', master?"

With his long-fingered hand he tapped a note on the table.

"Take this up to her tonight, Martha. Before you go to bed."

"Aye, sir," she said. "I hope it's somethin' that'll make the mistress happy. She's not ben well."

The faint moonlight from the narrow window, illuminating the white of his short bristled hair, lent him a ghostly quality.

"She's not strong enough for it." His voice sounded drained. "I've seen what it does to a woman. Bearing children. Charlotte's too tiny."

He covered his face with his hands and wept silently.

Chapter Twenty-seven

The lead-colored sky had been roiling with the threat of rain ever since Arthur left Oxenhope. As he came up on Higher Halstead's field, the storm finally caught up with him. A few heavy drops and then a cloudburst; thunder shook the hills. Arthur was drenched by the time he reached the churchyard. Only a short distance from the footpath, John Brown squatted on a flat box grave, chipping a name into the tombstone.

"Good day to ye, sir," the stonemason called out.

Arthur stopped, and with a hand on his hat he tried to make himself heard over the moaning wind and driving rain.

"That's the Fosters' vault, isn't it?"

"It is, sir. The old man. Passed away on Tuesday."

"Foster was a good man—God give his family strength. His wife is well, I pray?"

"Aye, well as they come, but fer grievin'."

"Give them my condolences, will you? I shall remember them in my prayers."

"I'll do that, sir. They'll be glad to hear from ye."

"I pray you're well, John?"

"Aye, sir. Just a little stiffness in the 'ands and knees."

A lightning bolt split open the sky, followed by a deafening crack. "You'd better take cover, John. Wait until this passes."

With his head bent into the wind, Arthur had started up the path when he heard John call out, "Is it true ye may be coming back to Haworth, Mr. Nicholls?"

Arthur wheeled around, still clutching his hat.

"I don't know, John."

"Well, if ye do, folks'd be mighty pleased."

Arthur stood silently for a moment, the rain dripping down his nose, wondering what on earth to say to the man who had once wanted to shoot him.

"It would please me even more, John," he said before he sped up the path toward the parsonage.

Martha met him at the door with a towel to dry his face, bobbing and nodding in a comic display of exaggerated deference.

"Oh, Mr. Nicholls, sir, ye're a brave one to come out in this."

"You know I'd brave worse than this to see your mistress."

"Would ye like some tea, sir? Warm ye up a little?"

"Not just yet. Where's Miss Brontë?"

"Waitin' in the reverend's parlor, sir."

Seeing Charlotte for the first time after a long absence, all he wanted was to draw her into his arms and hold her close. But he had not yet been granted that favor, nor any favor.

Her father stood peering out the window at the ominous sky. A sour odor hung over the room—the olfactory stew of a reclusive old man careless of appearances, of clothing that had seen too many years of wear, of stale tobacco and cold ashes. He had been dictating correspondence to Charlotte and now she was tidying up his desk, her nimble fingers moving with admirable efficiency. Habits of tidiness and order. Arthur liked that about her. Then she offered Arthur her hand to shake, and reassured him with her eyes.

For the first time in a year, Patrick greeted Arthur with something like his old familiarity and urged him kindly to take a seat. The sky had darkened and rain pelted the glass, and while Charlotte lit a lantern the three of them exchanged light banter about the storm riding overhead.

Patrick sat down behind his desk, twining his gnarled fingers across his chest. Arthur faced him with calm dignity; his black hair sprang in wet curls around his strong, square face. Charlotte had drawn her chair into the corner and taken up her knitting, but her hands were trembling.

"I do appreciate, Mr. Nicholls, that you were able to travel this far on such short notice," Patrick began. "I am only too aware of how difficult it is for one who serves the Almighty to make arrangements for duties that cannot be abandoned lightly. I know your time is limited, so we shall move directly to the point. If my daughter, Charlotte, should decide to accept your offer of marriage—and she has not yet decided in your favor, Nicholls—but if she should, there are monetary conditions she would like put in place. My daughter has earned a good deal of money from her books—"

"A modest amount," Charlotte corrected gently, with her eyes lowered.

Patrick shot her one of his stern glances and continued: "And she stands to earn a good deal more. I insist upon a marriage settlement that protects her interest. Therefore, I have taken the liberty to consult a solicitor. The terms he advised are these."

Patrick opened up a dossier, withdrew a sheet of parchment, and extended it to Arthur.

"I have no need to see such a document," Arthur said mildly.

The clicking needles fell still as Charlotte glanced up.

Patrick sat back with a frown. "What do you mean by that, Nicholls?"

"What I mean is that I accept any terms you ask of me."

"You would be wise to read the conditions."

"Whatever they are, I accept."

"You won't get anything, Nicholls."

"I never wanted anything."

Charlotte dropped her gaze. A smile crept around the corners of her mouth.

Arthur sat calmly, his powerful hands spread on his knees.

"Well, then—here. With that understood, for form's sake, you might wish to read it."

There was a tally of her investments: £500 from *Shirley,* £480 from *Vil-*

lette, £521 from her railway shares, plus miscellaneous sums from foreign copyrights and the various editions of *Jane Eyre.* The settlement provided that her money be transferred to a trust for the benefit of Charlotte and any children she might have, to be paid out at her disposition during her lifetime; if she died in Arthur's lifetime her money would go to her children, and if there were no children, the estate would revert to her father. Arthur would get nothing.

As he read through it, he lit up. "Yes," he murmured, a smile breaking from ear to ear. "Yes. Very good. Very well managed, I say. Exactly what I would have done myself if I had been her father."

With an air of impatience, he returned the document to Patrick and rose.

"I have very little time today, sir," he said. "If you are satisfied, I should like to have a few minutes with your daughter before I take my leave."

Without waiting for a reply, Arthur extended his hand to Charlotte. She laid aside her knitting, and Arthur took her hand and drew her to her feet.

The sky had darkened even further, and the wind-blown rain clattered against the window with raging force as she led him up the stairs and down the hall to the small, garretlike room.

"You'll need a study," she said as she stepped inside. "I thought you might like to have this room. I'm afraid it's the only one."

There was not a speck of dust anywhere, nor a wrinkle on the counterpane, nor a smudge on the well-oiled dresser.

"When we were children it was Branwell's room," she mused quietly, "but then Emily claimed it and he never got it back again. She loved the views from this room—the sky, and the heath on the other side of the valley. When the weather was too bad to go walking on the moors she would spend endless hours up here. It was all the drama she ever needed or wanted in her life."

Emily's German grammar and a book of Schiller had been neatly arranged on the table beside her ink-stained writing desk. Charlotte opened the drawer.

"She hid herself so completely, Arthur. From all of us. It was only when we began to publish together that I felt I was beginning to see her and understand her. We were closer during those short years than ever before. After she died I found a few small souvenirs she'd kept." Charlotte removed a printed program to show him. "Here. It's from a concert we attended together in Brussels. And I found clippings of reviews of *Wuthering Heights*. It was like seeing a piece of a tender heart that she had hidden behind a wall of stoicism. She never really understood all the attacks on her book. She could not see what she had written—not the way others saw it. But she's gone. There will be no more novels. Nor verse. I still can't quite believe it."

Carefully, reverently, she slipped the program back into the desk and then opened the top drawer of Emily's scarred old chest.

"She never really thought her work meant anything to anyone but herself, and I would often sit and watch her toss old drafts of her poetry into the kitchen fire. But at the same time she had this habit of neglect—she would leave her things all over the house. We would have these constant little quarrels; she'd be looking for something and I would have put it away. When she was gone, I gathered up everything and stored it in here. Here, this is her work." She withdrew a sketchbook and passed it to Arthur. The pages were filled with romantic scenes of ruined castles and graceful allegorical figures. There were exquisitely detailed studies of nature: a tiny whinchat perched on a rock, a solitary Scotch fir twisted by the wind. And portraits of the many animals she had so loved: their dogs and cats, their pet hawk.

Coming across a portrait of Keeper, Arthur paused and grew very still. Charlotte was observing him closely, and she saw how his features softened in sadness.

" 'Until the day break, and the shadows flee away.' " he murmured.

There was a long moment of silent complicity, and then she took the sketchbook from him and shut it away.

"It's a great comfort to me that you knew them," she said. "I won't ever have to explain them to you."

Arthur laid his hand on her shoulder—a reassuring gesture, no more.

She turned to him with sudden earnestness. "If I survived when all the others died, I can only think it was because God had a purpose for me. He gave me a gift of words, and intellect, and imagination—although God knows Emily's gift was so much greater than mine. If I write at all, I must write the truth. I don't write out of vanity." Her brown eyes pleaded with him.

He seemed perplexed by her earnestness. "My darling, I never believed you cultivated a desire for notoriety."

"But there are certain things I've written—about the church and about women—that have drawn a good deal of criticism. If we were to marry . . ."

"I confess I sometimes cringe at your opinions on certain matters, but I have always known that we disagreed on these things. My only concern is that you leave yourself open to such wounding criticism. It is from this that I would hope to protect you."

She nodded. Satisfied, for the moment. Thunder rolled in the distance; the storm was passing.

Arthur could no longer restrain himself. He drew her into his arms. She came willingly, her head nestled just below his heart.

"I should never be at peace in here," he said in a low voice. "It's Emily's room and it should remain as such."

When she made no move to withdraw, he lowered his head and brushed her soft hair with his lips.

"My sweet Charlotte," he murmured. "How I've longed to be close to you like this."

She tightened her arms around his waist, and his heart soared.

"Arthur?" Her voice was barely above a whisper.

"Yes?"

"What made you smile when you read the marriage settlement?"

"I smiled when I came to the part about the children."

The rain fell lightly now and the gloom was slowly lifting.

When Charlotte learned from Miss Wooler that Ellen was seriously ill with influenza, it was enough to spur her to write. Ellen, also eager to make amends, replied. Thus their correspondence resumed—brimming with the old warmth and affection but confined to safe topics such as the health of friends and family; there were long pages dedicated to paralytic strokes and remedies for obstructed bowels. The subject of Arthur was scrupulously avoided on both sides.

Until by accident Charlotte posted a letter to Arthur in an envelope addressed to Ellen. Ellen immediately returned the letter to Charlotte. The mistake prompted a speedy confession, and Charlotte replied:

My dear Ellen,

The enclosure in yours of yesterday puzzled me at first, for I did not immediately recognize my own handwriting; when I did, I was deeply vexed, for the letter to Mr. Nicholls ought to have gone on Friday—it was intended to relieve him from great anxiety as he had not heard from me in several days. I must have inadvertently slipped it into the envelope I had prepared for your letter—and sent yours to him. I can only be thankful that the mistake was no worse and did not throw the letter into the hands of some un-scrupulous person.

Since you were here in July, matters with Mr. Nicholls have pro-gressed thus. Last winter I obtained permission to continue com-munication with him. He came in January and was then received but not pleasantly. I told him the great obstacles that lay in his way. He has persevered. He came again and was here all last week. The result of this last visit is that Papa's consent is gained—that his respect is won—for Mr. Nicholls has in all things proved himself disinterested and forbearing. He has shown too that while his feelings are exquisitely keen, he can freely forgive. Certainly I must respect him—indeed I owe him more than mere cool respect. In fact, dear Ellen, I am engaged.

In a few months Mr. Nicholls—I now call him Arthur—will return to the curacy of Haworth. What seemed at one time impossible is now arranged, and Papa begins really to take a pleasure in the prospect.

For myself, dear Ellen, while thankful to One who seems to have guided me through much difficulty, much and deep distress and perplexity of mind, I am still very calm, very inexpectant. What I taste of happiness is of the soberest order. I trust to love my husband—I am grateful for his tender love to me—I believe him to be an affectionate, a conscientious, a high-principled man—and if with all this, I should yield to regrets that fine talents, congenial tastes, and thoughts are not added, it seems to me I should be most presumptuous and thankless.

Providence offers me this destiny. Doubtless then it is the best for me.

Arthur wishes our marriage to be in July. He spoke of you with great kindness and said he hoped you would be at our wedding. I said I thought of having no other bridesmaid. Did I say right?

Do not mention these things just yet. I mean the marriage to be literally as quiet as possible.

There is a strange half-sad feeling in making this announcement. The whole thing is something other than imagination paints it beforehand: fears come mixed inextricably with hopes. I trust yet to talk the matter over with you.

Yours affectionately
C. Brontë

In all of Charlotte's letters announcing her engagement, there was the echo of sad resignation and a kind of forced cheer, a sense that she had to reassure herself that she was doing right for herself. She was far too honest to portray Arthur as anything other than what he was. She could boast only of his moral virtues, not of wealth or standing or worldly connections. There was nothing interesting about Arthur, nothing that would be grist for the imagination or excite curiosity. Her acquaintances in London would not be in the least surprised; they had seen how she floundered amid their sparkling society, with their women of beauty and men of wit. She had landed where she belonged, in the hands of a most ordinary man.

Most painful of all was the letter to George. She framed it as best she could, in the context of her peculiar existence, but she could not feign an excitement that was not there. She wrote:

> *The step is not a hasty one: on the gentleman's side, at least, it has been meditated for many years, and I hope that in at last acceding to it, I am acting right. My future husband is a clergyman. He was for eight years my father's curate. He left because the idea of this marriage was not entertained as he wished. But various circumstances have led my father to consent to his return. Nor can I deny that my own feelings have been much impressed and changed by the nature and strength of the qualities brought out in the course of his long attachment. I fear I must accuse myself of having formerly done him less than justice. However, he is to come back now. He has forgone many chances of preferment to return to the obscure village of Haworth. I believe I do right in marrying him. I mean to try to make him a good wife.*
>
> *My expectations, however, are very subdued—very different, I daresay, to what yours were before you were married. I hardly know in what form of greeting to include your wife's name—as you have never told me any particulars about her, though I should have liked them much. Say to her whatever may seem to you most appropriate and most expressive of goodwill.*
>
> *I sometimes wonder how Mr. Williams is, and hope he is well. In the course of the year that is gone, Cornhill and London have receded a long way from me—the links of communication have waxed very frail and few. It must be so in this world. All things considered, I don't wish it otherwise.*

By April, Charlotte was immersed in preparations for her wedding. The change in her father was radical. Once the whole matter had been settled, he admitted to Charlotte that he had been far too stern. He grew kind again and declared himself happy. He discussed matters calmly and took an interest in all the arrangements. Yet there was a lingering sense of disappointment that pierced Charlotte's heart more deeply than all his months of hostile ranting. Gentleness was far more potent than wrath, and in his quiet acceptance of her fate, she felt all the more keenly her own regrets. There were nights when she retreated to Emily's room and gazed through the window onto the moonlit moors, struggling with her own pride and mourning the loss of something that would never be found.

When Arthur came to visit in April, he found the parsonage in upheaval—with workmen tramping through the house, the servants scuttling about in a flurried state, and a gaping hole in the entry hall opposite the kitchen.

"It's your new study," Charlotte announced proudly. "Come. Take a look."

He extended his hand to her as she stepped over the rubble, into the room where they had once stored peat and coal.

"It occurred to me that all we needed to do was open up a door into the hallway and plaster up the door to the backyard. You'll have a good deal of light from the south. When you next come it will be all scrubbed clean and painted and papered." She tilted her head to look up at him with eager eyes. "Does it please you?"

He slipped a hand around her waist and drew her close to him. "I wish I might have broken into your heart as easily as you've broken through this wall."

She became suddenly nervous, the way she always did when he drew close to her. Reluctant to cross the threshold—knowing she could never go back.

Resisting him, hands pressed on his chest, she flashed him a warning.

"Arthur," she whispered, "please. There are workmen about."

"And what do you think will happen if you kiss me?"

"Don't tease me, Arthur."

"Tell me, am I that pathetic character St. John Rivers? Are you afraid of my nature?"

"You, St. John?" she answered with a little gasp. "But he was all marble and ice. And vengeance. You are none of that."

"But you once thought as much—tell me it wasn't so."

"Indeed, you are outwardly solemn and grave. When you fix your eyes on a body, the way your brows knit together—see, you're doing it just now—such a stern fellow!"

"So I was right to fancy I glimpsed something of myself in him."

"He had none of your qualities."

"Ah, but even you were ignorant of them."

"I was."

"Even when I stood at your side, through all of your terrible sufferings, through all the loss, you read only austerity and ice, and nothing of my feelings."

"I could see nothing beyond my own grief, Arthur."

"I used to keep one of your books with me, wherever I went. I read parts, here and there, my favorites, and at each reading I discovered more of you. But that was before. Now you are my book. And there is a new chapter approaching."

The moment was shattered by the sound of the workmen returning. Charlotte drew back and patted at her hair, although not a strand was out of place.

"Yes, it will be a fine room," she said audibly as she lifted her skirts and turned away.

The next instant Arthur pulled her into his arms and kissed her. In that brief but bold kiss she was keenly aware of the firm outline of his lips—the flavor and texture of his mouth—and an unmistakable sensual charge. Then he thrust her away from him—only seconds before the workmen peered into the room.

"Good day, gentlemen," he said brightly as he steadied Charlotte with a firm grip on her arm and passed her back over the heap of rubble. "Pray, let the lady pass."

In the days that followed, she found it difficult to deter his advances. Once he had kissed her, he deemed it his right to demand more. Because her father had long established the habit of leaving Charlotte on her own, Arthur's visits were entirely unchaperoned, and it was up to Charlotte to keep him under control. He confessed to how difficult it was to wait, that even though he might walk back and forth to Oxenhope a dozen times a day he would not be sufficiently exhausted to maintain his composure around her.

"It's quite alarming, the effect you have on me," he murmured to her one day in the dining room when he had cornered her next to the window and pressed her to the wall.

Charlotte was tense and ill at ease. "Arthur, that's quite enough kissing."

"But we're engaged now, my dear."

"It's not that—I'm just afraid of making noise," she whispered, glancing anxiously toward the door.

He only laughed and said, "And what kind of noise shall we be making when we're married?"

"Arthur!"

"You know as well as I do that these walls are thick."

"But the doors are not."

"And do you anticipate someone standing on the other side with an ear to the door?"

"You're trying to shock me, and it won't work."

"Come, draw the curtains and sit on my lap," he urged.

"I shall not!"

"Why not?"

"You know perfectly well why not."

"If you don't, I swear I'll be quite undone from the strain by the time we're married."

"Good grief, Arthur, pull yourself together."

There was a quick tap on the door; Charlotte broke free and made a dash for her workbox just as Martha entered. But Martha instantly read the situation, and she only gawked, then spun around and hurried out.

"Martha!" Charlotte cried. "Come back! Oh, confound it, Arthur, that was very naughty of you."

"Do you think Martha's never seen anyone get kissed before?"

"That's not the point."

"All right. I'm going for a walk."

Charlotte gave him a crushed look. "You're leaving?"

"You're coming with me," he said firmly. "Go on. Find your shawl and change your shoes."

And Charlotte—who thrilled to his stern commands—instantly obeyed.

On the first of May she set off on a brief bridal tour, stopping in Manchester to visit Lily before going on to Hunsworth to see Mary Taylor's family, and finally to Brookroyd to stay with Ellen. At Lily's, Charlotte found herself in the company of open-minded women who spoke candidly about those things that were troubling her.

"I know there are places where he cannot follow," she said.

"You mean intellectually?" Katie Winkworth asked.

"Yes."

"Oh," Katie laughed. "Intellectual men are highly overrated. They can be such cold fish. Affection and constancy in a husband are worth much more, I promise you."

Charlotte set down her cup of tea and folded her delicate hands in the lap of her gray silk gown. Katie was struck by her resemblance to a swan settling on a quiet pond, gracefully folding its wings and returning to a state of utter stillness.

"Perhaps, but I know myself. I require a good deal of intellectual stimulation."

"You're afraid he won't be exciting enough?"

"The winters in Haworth are long, and by five o'clock there's no light left in the sky. We shall be stuck with each other on many a long evening."

"So, you invite friends."

"Arthur is rather sticky about that."

"Does he disapprove of your friends?"

"Some of them. He is quite intolerant of certain religious views."

"Oh, you'll manage him. You know, the nice thing about"—Katie started to say "dull" but caught herself just in time—"about *uncomplicated* men is that they appreciate it when their wives bring excitement to the table. So you can be the fickle one and be quite unpredictable if you choose, which is ever so much fun."

This made Charlotte laugh. Katie glanced over her shoulder to make sure there were no servants lurking in the hall and then leaned forward. "I've heard—and this is from someone who is very close to them—I know for a fact that Jane Carlyle is a virgin."

Katie sat back and watched Charlotte's wide brown eyes take on an astonished look. "Thomas Carlyle's wife?"

"Yes. That brilliant historian and critic whom we all revere."

Lily came back in at that moment, and Katie repeated what she had been saying.

"Katie, you are so wicked!" Lily laughed.

"I understand his wife is an invalid," Charlotte said.

"Well, she certainly wasn't an invalid when he married her," Katie continued. "How do you think she got that way? I think I'd be quite ill, too. After twenty years in an unconsummated marriage. Can you imagine? How utterly appalling. It's scandalous, but of course no one really cares. At least the husbands don't. Now, I'm sure Mr. Carlyle would provide many an evening of intellectual conversation, but no thank you. Anyway, I don't think you need worry about Mr. Nicholls on that score, according to what you've told us about him."

Lily cried, "Why, Katie Winkworth!"

Charlotte blushed, but at the same time she felt a quick rush of pleasure.

"No," she answered quietly, "he is an affectionate man."

After Charlotte left, Katie said to Lily, "Poor Mr. Nicholls. She really isn't in love with him."

"Oh dear, I thought she would be a little more sure of herself by now," Lily sighed.

"I think she would like him to be more like those impulsive, fickle men she puts in her novels. I suppose her one truly great love was Paul Emanuel."

"Who?"

"The professor."

"Oh! In *Villette*! Do you think there really was such a man?"

"Oh, absolutely, I do. He is far too unpleasant to be made up."

"If her novel is true, then he must be dead."

"Perhaps. Anyway, she never speaks of such a man, so we'll never know."

Chapter Twenty-eight

There were only five letters.

They were not love letters—not like those Arthur had written to her. But beneath Constantin Heger's affection and esteem for his star pupil there lay an intensely passionate and intimate voice, a style and manner of thinking that had seduced her as surely as if he had made love to her. For years after returning from Brussels she had lived off those letters and the wild, futile hope of seeing him again.

After Emily's death she had been tempted to write to him, but it seemed like such a pointless gesture. Then she had written *Villette* with its true-to-life portrait of him. The book had been translated into French and received wide acclaim. He would have read it.

There was no need for any more words between them.

In her nightgown and slippers, she knelt on the hearthrug before the fire, the letters nestled in her lap. She debated whether to read them one last time. But that would only stir old wounds. Hope had lingered long before dying, and she had already suffered enough.

Carefully, she loosened the limp blue ribbon, then paused to study the envelope addressed in her name. His handwriting. How many hours, days, and months had been spent waiting to be handed a letter with that handwriting?

Charlotte rarely kept correspondence. She had saved a few of Mary's letters. For sentimental reasons she had preserved Southey's letter in which he admonished her to put aside her literary ambitions. She kept letters from her publisher pertaining to payments for her books. But little else. Most letters made their rounds to friends, to be forwarded on to all interested parties and then back; once digested, they were consigned to the fire.

But Heger's letters were treasures to be hidden away, locked in a small lacquered box and stored at the back of a deep chest of drawers.

She had thought of finding a more secure hiding place—the cellar perhaps, or beneath the floorboard where as children they had stashed their stories. But there would always be the risk of discovery. A few days hence her home would no longer be exclusively her own. A husband's eyes would pry into corners—perhaps unintentionally, perhaps not; drawers would be opened, and the contents of locked boxes might be cause for mistrust.

In Brussels she had heard a story from one of the Belgian girls about illicit love letters that had been closed in a bottle, hidden in the hollow of an ancient pear tree in the *pensionnat* garden, and then sealed with cement like a tomb. The girl had shown Charlotte the very spot, where the cement was now overgrown with ivy. Heger had laughingly denied the story, told her that there were no love letters buried there, that the cement had been poured to shore up the rotting tree. But Charlotte preferred the romantic version. She had written the incident into *Villette*, having Lucy Snowe bury Dr. John's letters in a bottle in the hollow of a tree.

But Charlotte wanted no tomb. Nothing that might be unearthed one day.

The coals put off an intense heat that would consume the letters quickly.

With a casual gesture that betrayed the great sense of loss in her heart, she tossed the letters—ribbon and all—onto the fire.

She had strongly resisted white—she was, after all, thirty-eight years old—but Ellen sounded off such a storm of protest, quickly joined by every female in their circle, that Charlotte allowed herself to be taken in hand. In Halifax, going from shop to shop, she had tried on a score of white dresses; Ellen had vowed fervently that nothing had ever suited her so well—and that she had to buy white—and so white was what she bought. She soothed her conscience by sticking to muslin rather than the tulle and silk Ellen dangled under her nose.

"Plain book muslin, with a bit of embroidery—that will do nicely," Charlotte had stated firmly. "It will be ever so practical later."

There it was, laid out on the bed with the bonnet and veil beside it. Charlotte's trunk and a smaller traveling case stood packed and ready.

All day long, Martha had been trotting in and out with trivial questions about this or that, but it was really just to keep an eye on the dress.

"Martha, the dress is not going to get up and walk away," Charlotte scolded affectionately, looking up from her sewing.

"Don't ye think it should be covered with tissue paper, miss?"

"I'm wearing it tomorrow. And the only dust in here is what you keep kicking up. Now go. Eliza needs you in the kitchen."

Ellen came in and collapsed at the dressing table, her face flushed from the heat. "It's a madhouse down there," she cried.

"Which is why we're staying up here."

Charlotte turned to Miss Wooler, who sat near the window fanning her neck.

"I am sorry to make you suffer, my dear Miss Wooler. I know it's warm up here."

"Have you asked her yet?" Ellen asked Charlotte.

"Not yet."

"What is it, my dear?" Miss Wooler replied.

"Oh, nothing important," Charlotte said with her tight little smile. "I just wanted to know if you would do the honor of giving me away at church tomorrow?"

"You wish for *me* to give you away in marriage?"

Miss Wooler, that stout old headmistress who had handled with serenity legions of hormonal schoolgirls, momentarily lost her composure. She dropped her fan, retrieved it with a mild exclamation, then raised startled eyes to Charlotte.

"But is that not your father's duty?"

"Papa's not well. He's been having dizzy spells again, and his deafness has returned. He's barely been out of bed these past few weeks. And his spirits are depressed. I just don't think he's strong enough."

"At his age, these kinds of changes are so difficult to adjust to," Ellen said.

"But you're his daughter . . ."

"I assure you, we're quite settled. Papa asked specifically that you do the honor in his stead."

"Oh, my dear . . . but I'm a woman."

"Arthur has consulted the prayer book—he can be trusted on these things, I assure you. At the moment when the bride and groom pledge their troth to each other, it is written 'her father's or friend's hand'— those are the very words, and it makes no distinction about the sex of the friend. So, will you give me away in matrimony?"

"Oh my dear child. Of course I shall." She began to cry. "Oh my dear Charlotte, I remember your first day at Roe Head as if it were yesterday."

"Pray, don't cry, Miss Wooler," Ellen pleaded, "or we shall all be in tears."

Charlotte waited while Miss Wooler tugged a handkerchief from her sleeve and blew her nose.

"It will be quite intimate," Charlotte said, taking up her sewing again with a contented smile. "The Grants are coming over, but they will only attend the wedding breakfast. Arthur has been wonderfully good about that—he's conceded on every point. Sutcliffe Sowden will do the service. There will be the two of you. That's all."

"Now, are you sure, my dear? Perhaps I should try to persuade your father—"

"Absolutely not. I much prefer it like this. I think there will be sufficient drama with just Arthur. He had me quite worried for a while, thinking he had something seriously wrong with him, but it was only his nerves." She added, with an air of sweet complacency, "He's fretted himself thin, I'm afraid."

Martha scurried in bearing a letter.

"For you, miss," she said excitedly.

As Charlotte took the letter, her composure suddenly melted. She opened the seal with trembling hands. It was brief. She tucked it back into the envelope. She spoke in a hollow voice, as if the air had been sucked from her lungs.

"It's from Arthur. He's arrived in Oxenhope. With Mr. Sowden." She looked up at them with wide eyes. "So. This is it. Tomorrow I am to be married."

Mary Burwin was on her cousin's doorstep when the note arrived that afternoon.

"What's that about?" her cousin asked when, after reading it, Mary stuffed it quickly into her pocket.

"Nothin' to worry yerself about. Just work for me to do," she said gruffly. But there was a smile tickling her face when she turned out the gate and hurried up the lane to her own cottage.

Mary waited until dark had fallen; then she fetched the heavy keys and climbed the hill to the church. She took her time preparing the altar that evening, dusting and polishing the ancient dark wood with beeswax and a cloth until it glowed in the light of her lantern. Then she spread the altar linens, putting on the white frontal, the one Mr. Nicholls had requested—the one Miss Brontë had embroidered with a burning bush. Fresh candles were fixed in the tall brass candlesticks, and to the side she placed a vase with a meager bouquet of flowers she'd cut from her little garden. Then she locked up the church and went home.

The next morning, young Johnny Robinson was on his way to school when John Brown waylaid him on the footpath. He had been a favorite scholar of Arthur's, had gone every Saturday morning to the curate's lodgings for private lessons until Arthur had left Haworth. He remembered a good deal from those lessons that was not in the books. He had learned what lovesickness was.

"Listen carefully, lad," John said, "I have a task for ye this mornin'. Reverend Nicholls asked specifically for ye."

"Mr. Nicholls? Is he here?"

"He will be soon. I want ye t' go t' the top of the hill and keep a watch for him. They'll be comin' over the hill from Oxenhope. Soon as ye see 'em, ye run directly t' the parsonage and tell 'em the gentlemen are on their way."

"Is he comin' for the parson's daughter?"

"Indeed he is, John. They'll be married in the church this mornin'."

"Lord Almighty!" the boy cried. "Mr. Nicholls must be a happy man for sure!"

"Now listen up. After the parsonage, you run straight off an' get Josh Redman and bring him t' the church."

"Aye, sir."

"Tell him we need him t' register a marriage and he's got t' come right away."

"Yes, sir."

"And not a word t' anyone else. Ye hear me, lad?"

"Aye, sir. And if I'm late t' school?"

"Don't ye worry about that, boy. Not on a day like today."

She stood before the looking glass putting on her bonnet. It was a delicate confection, white satin and French lace, with a string of tiny satin roses and green leaves twined just back of the brim, and wide satin ribbons that fell down her shoulders. It did not overwhelm her plain face, as she had feared; rather, it flattered her large, dark eyes and brown hair.

Staring at her solitary reflection, she felt a sharp and poignant yearning for her sisters, an ache such as she had not felt in years. A longing for the past. She struggled momentarily, trying to keep her thoughts in the present, on the prospects of her future.

She went to the window and looked out over the churchyard. It was nearly eight. She wouldn't have long to wait. Arthur was always meticulously punctual. She was thankful for that.

Ellen came in.

"It's time to come down. Oh, you've already put on your bonnet! It's lovely! You look just like a little snowdrop. Turn around. Let me see.

Oh, my dearest Charlotte, why the tears? Oh, dear friend, here, come to me. Here, take my handkerchief."

Charlotte rapped on her father's bedroom door, then entered. He was lying in bed, dressed and shaven, in his house slippers. He swung his legs around to sit on the edge of the bed, then turned a stricken face to her.

"How are you feeling, Papa?"

"I'm just resting," he said in a pitiful voice. "I shall be down shortly."

She stepped up and kissed him on his cheek.

"Arthur will be here any minute. I must go," she said gently.

"I do hope and pray that under Providence this change will be for your good as well as my own, Charlotte, both in time and eternity."

"I trust that it will, Papa."

With Ellen and her old schoolmistress close behind, she slipped out the door and quietly down the gravel path, through the gate and down Church Lane. She walked with her eyes cast downward, her pale face concealed behind the lace veil, and a prayer book clutched in a white-gloved hand. She entered the church by the back, through the vestry door. It was a dim, hazy summer morning and no one was about.

Johnny Robinson watched the service from the vestry. He thought he probably wasn't supposed to be there, but no one had bothered to chase him away.

The cavernous gloom of the ancient church swallowed up the muted morning light, leaving only the flickering candles to illuminate the small wedding party gathered solemnly at the altar. Charlotte's tiny figure had disappeared behind the others—but Arthur could be seen inclining his head toward her as he repeated his vows, his face softened by the glow of the candlelight. They spoke in low voices—his grave and confident; hers but a whisper.

Johnny Robinson waited in the shadows as they went out through the vestry. Word had gotten around by then, and there were villagers in the street; they all watched, hushed, as the tiny woman in white and her strong black-clad husband walked arm in arm the short distance up to the parsonage.

Not long after that a carriage and pair arrived with a racket of hooves and wheels clattering on the cobblestones. Those who had been inclined to wait around witnessed Mr. Nicholls coming out with his dainty little bride on his arm and lifting her gently into the carriage. She wore a simple pale lavender silk dress and bonnet, and he handed her up like something weightless and easily broken. Johnny Robinson was seventeen, and it made an impression on him that a big, stern fellow like that was capable of such tenderness.

Chapter Twenty-nine

They traveled southwest by train, passing quickly through the plains of Cheshire. By the afternoon, as the train wound around the deep inlets of the rivers and turned back toward the sea, the first hills of Wales rose up to the north. The weather was wild and windy, with sunlight intermittently breaking through the clouds and warming the compartment in bursts of intense heat. Arthur had taken first-class seats, and the only other occupant was a beefy-faced gentleman who pulled his hat over his eyes and slept in his corner until he was awakened by the porter somewhere just across the border. After that they were alone. By then they had thoroughly exhausted the topic of the wedding, with all its excitement and well-wishing guests, the toasts and tears. Charlotte had been fighting off a cold for days, and her face—earlier so lively—had now taken on a drawn and pale look.

"You must be worn out," Arthur said to her. "Try to sleep a little."

She removed her bonnet and nestled her head in the crook of his arm, but she could not sleep—could not even close her eyes. Her gaze wandered nervously about the compartment: to the window, back to Arthur's hand wrapped around hers, to his sturdy, muscular legs now stretched out across the aisle. In the silence, a new perception of herself crept into her thoughts: *A married woman—no longer single. A husband. My husband. Husband and wife.* The very words invested her with a sense of privilege, as if she had suddenly found herself on the other side of a great divide, enlightened and forever altered. Only now did she admit how desperately she had longed for this. Whatever her failed illusions, whatever her disappointments with the man destiny had chosen for her, she could not wish herself back on the other side.

She felt a sudden rush of gratitude and relief; she tilted her head up and, in a rare spontaneous show of affection, kissed Arthur on his whiskered cheek. It was one of the few times when she had kissed him of her own volition. He turned to her with a gleam in his eye, and she quickly looked away. She had become fully aware of the effect she could produce on him by so much as a gesture or a touch.

They remained quiet for a moment, and then he tugged off her glove and held up her dainty hand to admire the ring on her finger.

"You've made me a very happy man," he whispered into her ear.

He did not ask if she was happy, and Charlotte offered no reply.

As England receded and they sped toward the northern coast of Wales, there was an unspoken sense of leaving behind all that was familiar and known. Wales was a land steeped in nostalgia for the past, and Charlotte listened intently while Arthur spoke of the great castles he planned for them to tour, of the strikingly dramatic mountains and the coastline of steep cliffs and sandy bays. She was reminded of Scotland's rugged beauty and her brief but heavenly excursion with George. She had been far more excited about that journey than this one. Here there would be no literary shrines to visit, and the man by her side had none of George Smith's charm. But this man had made her his wife, and George had not.

Late in the day the train rumbled across the bridge spanning the River Conwy, toward the bleak and barren fortress towering over the medieval village. At the sight of the castle ruins Charlotte's imagination began to stir, awakening briefly all those great romantic ideals of passion, adventure, and beauty.

She leaned close to the window, squinting through her spectacles.

"Have we arrived?"

"We have. This is Conwy."

They took a cab from the station, passing into the walled town through the lower gate. Light rain had begun to fall when they drew up at the doorstep of the Castle Hotel. The rambling old coaching inn had recently been renovated; the half-timber was now masked with an elaborate Gothic façade of stone and red brick. Bay windows were crowned with mantles of intricately carved designs and fitted with small glazed panes that caught the shadows and light in myriad subtle reflections. Although modest in scale, it projected a stately, manorial air.

"Is this our 'comfortable little inn on the coast'?" she whispered to him as he lifted her down from the carriage.

"Are you not pleased?"

"You led me to expect something quite modest," she whispered back.

"We'll have plenty of that when we get to Ireland," he said with a laugh.

"You've a view of the castle, Mr. Nicholls, as you requested," the innkeeper boasted as he led them down the corridor to their room. "Lady Llanberis departed just yesterday—she had this very same room and was very pleased with it indeed."

As he unlocked the door and gave orders to the porter with their luggage, he added with a sly wink, "You never know who you might meet downstairs. Mr. Wordsworth used to stay here on occasion. Said he liked Wales almost as much as his English lakes. Aye, there's a good number of famous people come through here."

"Is that so? Perhaps we might obtain an autograph—"

"Right now we've not got anybody famous. Not that I know of. But I'll be sure to let you know, sir. You bein' a clergyman, I'm sure they'd oblige you, sir. The maid will be right up with hot water, sir, and to start the fire if you'd like. Coals are extra. Supper is served in the dining room at six." With this he gave a quick little bow and hurried out.

"Arthur!" Charlotte scolded as she dusted the rain off her bonnet and set it on the table. "How wicked of you to tease him so!"

"I wonder what he'd say if he knew Currer Bell was under his roof."

"You mean Mrs. Nicholls," she corrected softly.

"Mrs. Nicholls," he said in a low voice as he reached for her and drew her close. "Come here, little wife." He trapped her hands behind her back and pressed her against him.

"I shan't let you go now," he said. "You cannot flee. There's no one coming to frighten you off."

He said these things with his eyes locked on hers, and she was startled by the urgency in his look.

"The maid's coming back with water."

"And the door is locked," he murmured with his lips so close she could feel his breath on her cheek as he spoke. "Look up at me, Charlotte," he said, and she tilted back her head and closed her eyes. His kisses—once snatched so furtively—were long and forceful. He pressed himself against her; she could feel his arousal, and she gasped and recoiled.

"Arthur . . ." she began in protest, but his clasp around her was like iron.

"I do so want you. I've waited so long for you."

She squirmed, but he was pulling up her skirts with one hand, grappling with her petticoats.

"Arthur!" she cried, and at the sound of alarm in her voice he quit groping for her. He lowered her skirts and took her tenderly into his arms.

"Charlotte," he exclaimed softly into her hair. "I'm a wreck," he said. "Do you see what you've done to me?"

"You frighten me."

"I frighten myself sometimes." He stroked her hair to calm her.

After a moment he whispered, "Is there too much light for you?"

She nodded against his chest.

"Then we'll wait until tonight," he murmured. "God give me the strength."

And me as well, Charlotte thought.

They went down together to the dining room and had tea. He was kind and considerate as always, but a dark cloud of restlessness hung over his mood. When they had finished tea he left her to go off and make arrangements to hire a cab for the next day to take them on a tour of the region.

"I'll meet you back in the room," he said with a meaningful glance as he pulled on his greatcoat.

In the bedroom, Charlotte unpacked her trunk and then sat down to dash off a quick note to Ellen. Already she felt a sense of guilt and divided loyalties, and behind the hastily scribbled words there lurked a feeling of loss and longing. The mere gesture of writing seemed to her a frantic desire to hold on to something that was slipping from her grasp.

How to speak of these things to her dear and faithful friend? She could not. They would remain unsaid. Charlotte—loyal to the truth—would never allude to the dread and anxiety churning in her chest. Her hand trembled as she dipped the pen in ink and set it on the paper. She could barely recognize her own handwriting.

"You mustn't expect much at first," Katie Winkworth had whispered to her in parting. "It gets better, trust me."

Charlotte was not a stranger to sexual gratification. She had discovered it during those days at Roe Head and satisfied herself quietly, shamefully, shuddering silently in her bed, alone, at night. She had found it impossible to confide in anyone, impossible to speak of darkly powerful urges of such a private nature. All her life she had heard passions of the flesh condemned as vile and wicked, and during those days, as she succumbed to her sexual desires and fantasies, she felt herself falling away from God. She had cloaked her fears in terms of a spiritual struggle and written dozens of letters to dear, pious Ellen, who had bade her to pray and seek strength and courage from God.

Yet something in her rebelled against this doctrine. Even as a girl she had let her imagination skirt around the perimeters of desire. She knew her body could respond to the fantasies of touch, of hands and lips.

Now she was married. It was her sacred duty to render this pleasure to her husband, but the reality of a man's flesh was something for which she was absolutely unprepared.

She sealed the letter quickly and began a second one to her father. She was still writing when Arthur returned.

She removed her spectacles and rose swiftly when he came into the room.

"My dear, you're absolutely soaked."

"It's pouring out there, and blowing a gale," he said as he sloughed off his wet greatcoat and gave it to Charlotte to hang on the back of a chair to dry.

"I was just jotting off a note to Papa to tell him we've arrived safely."

"Very good."

"I've given Bangor as our next mailing address. I said we should be there by Monday."

"That's our plan. But we'll see how the weather is."

She returned to her desk and picked up her pen.

Arthur removed his waistcoat and the clerical collar, and when she next looked up he was in his trousers with his white shirt open at the chest. Stripped of the decorous trappings of the church, his physicality became strikingly apparent.

He was pouring a glass of port from the bottle the maid had brought up.

"Here, my darling," he said as he set the glass in front of her, then poured one for himself. There was an air of impatience in his manner. She was finding it difficult to concentrate on her letter.

"I ran into a most obtuse man at the stables. A Manchester clergyman. He asked where my curacy was, and when he learned I was from Haworth he claimed to know your father. Said he's here with his wife and was planning an excursion tomorrow to Caernafon. Proposed that we share a cab and see the sights together."

"Oh dear," Charlotte said with a look of horror.

Arthur pulled up a chair, straddled it, and leaned against the back. "I accepted."

"You didn't!"

He watched her with an intense gaze as he sipped his port. "I thought it might please you."

"Arthur, you wouldn't."

He reached out and touched her cheek, and his blue eyes darkened.

"I will unless you put down your pen," he said sternly.

Her hands trembled as she lay aside her pen and stopped the ink bottle.

"Now drink the port."

She took the glass, her hand still shaking.

"Go on, drink," he said. "It will calm your nerves." When she had obliged him, he said, "Now let down your hair."

"Would you at least allow me the decency of turning your back?"

"Not yet," he said gently. "Just do as I ask."

She had never liked her own body. Even now she could not think of it as an object of desire, and as she removed the combs and the hairpins and shook out her hair, she did not dare to meet his eyes.

"I'm not pretty to look at," she whispered.

There was a brief but solemn silence while he struggled to express something deeply felt.

With a touch of his hand, he lifted her chin so that her eyes met his.

"From the first day we met, you have been for me an object of indescribable fascination. But I know that's not your meaning. You speak of conventional beauty. But has that ever mattered to me? Have you ever seen me shy away from you, or turn my gaze from you? Have you not seen—and felt—the effect you have on me?"

She felt herself blushing hotly.

"Here, give me your hand," he said. Timidly, she offered it to him. Her fingers were chilled, and he slipped them inside his shirt, to the bristling hair on his warm chest just over his pounding heart. "There, feel that. Is that not answer enough for you?"

Then he released her hand.

"Now, take off your things and get into bed. I'll sit here by the fire and drink my port. I'll not come to bed until you're ready for me."

He listened to her undressing, following with his imagination the sound of her fingers fumbling with the hooks, buttons, and ties and then drawing her chemise over her head; the rustling of silk as the voluminous skirts and petticoats fell to the floor; the whisper of muslin against her skin as she drew on her nightshirt; her bare feet padding lightly over the creaking wood floor, the old bed groaning as she turned back the blankets and slipped between the sheets.

He finished his glass of port and rose to add coals to the fire.

"Arthur, that will only make the room brighter."

"Whatever pleases you, my dear."

With the poker he spread out the coals. Then, in the shadows, he removed his clothes.

He crept into bed, sliding between the sheets and reaching for her.

Her entire body was trembling now.

She let out a startled gasp as he crawled on top of her and pressed his erection against her stomach; his size and the intense heat of his body overwhelmed her.

The pain was sharp but short-lived, as was the act itself. When he withdrew himself, and fell beside her, and spread his hand across her stomach, curling his fingers into the hair of her sex, she lay there in awe and disbelief.

It was done.

Cradling her in his arms, he kissed her for a long while, and when his breathing had calmed he said, "One day you will take as much pleasure in this as I do."

When she made no reply, he said, "I promise you."

Hot tears slid down her cheeks, but she made not a sound.

"I promise you," he repeated softly.

The intimacy forged from that wondrous strange act infiltrated her thoughts and colored her perception from the moment she opened her eyes the next morning. She felt as if this new sexual knowledge had so changed her that it must inevitably be visible to others. At breakfast in the dining room, she flushed when the innkeeper stopped by their table to inquire if the room met with their satisfaction.

"My dear, you've gone beet red," Arthur teased when the innkeeper had gone. Then he dove into his ham and beans.

She took a sip of her tea and darted a shy look at him. "It's just a little warm in here, that's all."

He swallowed and leaned forward to whisper, "I'm your husband, my dear. Only I can read your thoughts. No one else."

Charlotte flashed him a fiery look. "And what makes you think you have such wondrous powers?"

Arthur broke out into deep laughter, and Charlotte immediately realized the suggestive nature of her comment.

"Arthur!" she scolded in a quiet voice. Then, noticing how quickly his breakfast was disappearing, she said, "Well, at least you seem to have regained your appetite."

He blotted his mouth and said, "Only because another has been satisfied."

She shot him a look of utter shock.

His countenance softened, and he reached under the table for her knee. "Pray don't be so harsh on me. I'm mad about you, my dear. I've never been so happy in my entire life. To whom can I say these things if not to you? My wife?"

A reluctant smile crept around the corners of her mouth. "It's just difficult to hear you talk like this. For years I knew you as a man of such restraint, Arthur. So stiff and reserved."

Arthur had a mouthful of tea. He struggled to hold a straight face while he swallowed.

"Now what have I said?" she pursued hotly, and upon reflection, she blushed again.

"Oh, Arthur!" she scolded. "You're absolutely impossible. I can't talk to you anymore!"

Gradually they adjusted to each other, and Arthur's unfailing kindness and warmth, his unceasing concern for her comfort and happiness always compensated for the awkwardness of the nights. In bed she endured the sexual act. She thought of it as indulging her husband a strange and powerful need. For her the most crucial element was lacking: the feeling she knew to be love. That emotional glue that held a man and a woman together. Without that glue, the realms of her life seemed disjointed. The rational woman told herself she was satisfied. The emotional one had been left out in the cold.

Chapter Thirty

W ere it not for the fact that they were to meet Arthur's family, Charlotte would have preferred any place other than Ireland for their honeymoon voyage.

It was the only point upon which Arthur had insisted.

"I think you'll discover a different Ireland from the one your father has painted for you. It's not as savage as you imagine." Arthur said this to her their last morning in Wales as he stood near the window, trimming his beard. He angled the hand mirror to catch her reflection; she had her chin tucked to her chest as she fastened the front hooks of her bodice. She was only just getting comfortable dressing in front of him.

Arthur smiled to himself, enjoying this furtive surveillance when she was unguarded.

"I imagine no such thing," she murmured, preoccupied with her hooks and eyes.

"Some of us are quite respectable," he said as he put away the scissors. Impulsively, he went to her and kissed her on the back of the neck.

Charlotte answered with an elbow jab to his ribs.

It was true that Patrick Brontë looked with scorn on certain weaknesses in the Irish character and had planted in his children's minds visions of Ireland as a rural society mired in illiteracy and poverty. From the day he'd set foot in Cambridge, her father had wiped the Irish dust from his shoes and never glanced back. He rarely spoke of his ten brothers and sisters, the Prunty peasants, farmers, and ale makers, nor had he ever returned to visit them. He had left Ireland at the age of twenty-five with a hard-earned classical education and seven pounds in his pocket, and over the next four years at St. John's he became an object of awe and admiration for his singular ability to subsist on practically nothing. By dint of his natural gifts, a sincere and ardent faith, and steely ambition, he had overcome enormous disadvantages to achieve outstanding academic success and ordination into the Church of England—thereby earning the right to claim the most valuable prize in all of Britain: the status of a gentleman.

That his brilliant and famous daughter could do no better than a poor Irish curate for a husband had just about broken his heart.

Arthur was perhaps a little to blame for the misperception of his worth. There was much he might have said to disprove Patrick Brontë's harsh opinions, if he had chosen to do so. But it was not in his nature. Had he been more arrogant and boastful, the truth might have come out a little earlier. As it turned out, Charlotte had to discover these things for herself. She would be forced to take the man on faith, and travel with him to a new and unfamiliar place. Arthur's qualities would slowly become apparent, like the refracted beauties of a gem long ignored. When observed in a new light, it was found to be an object of surprising fascination.

She was certainly not expecting to be greeted by such a strikingly beautiful thing as Mary Anna.

The young woman hurried along the quay as quickly as she could, clutching the flapping ribbons of her bonnet with one hand. The awkward gait was noticed first, but then the face took your breath away.

She had tears in her eyes even before she drew near enough for Charlotte to make out their color—the same delft blue as Arthur's.

There was a flash of unconcealed emotion when she fell into Arthur's embrace and turned her cheek for him to kiss. "Oh, Arthur," she murmured tenderly, "we've missed you ever so much."

"Charlotte . . . my cousin, Mary Anna Bell."

"I'm pleased to meet you," Charlotte smiled, offering the girl her hand

and noting the sober elegance of her dress, the spotless kid gloves and silk parasol. There was about her whole person a grave air of competence that seemed designed to play down the ethereal beauty of her face.

She grasped Charlotte's hand warmly. "Oh, Miss Brontë," she said in a softly assured voice that could barely be heard over the clamor of the train station. "We're so glad you've come."

"It's Mrs. Nicholls now," Arthur corrected with a smile.

"Oh, but of course it is!" The blue eyes widened in embarrassment. "How thoughtless of me!"

Arthur saw how this small slip had flustered her, and he reached for her elbow and gave it a gentle squeeze.

"It's quite understandable, dear cousin, since I've been writing to you about Miss Brontë for so many years. And then I went and changed her name."

"And I'm so glad you did," Mary Anna said, once again composed. She allowed her delicate blue gaze to linger on him for just a moment, and Charlotte felt an unexpected pang of jealousy.

"Where's that big brother of mine?" Arthur asked.

"He ran into a gentleman from the Canals who absolutely insisted on detaining him, but I saw you come off the train and slipped away."

"And Joseph?"

"He'll join us tomorrow." She turned to Charlotte. "My younger brother so regrets not being here to meet you, ma'am. He's a student at Trinity, as I'm sure Arthur has told you, and he has duties as a tutor to a family in town. But he's very much looking forward to touring the city with us."

"And your mama?" Arthur asked. "How is she?"

"Like she always is just before you come home. Counting the days and driving the servants into a tizzy."

Charlotte inquired about the youngest cousin, Lucy.

"She's quite well," Mary Anna smiled. "Rather upset at having to remain at home with Mama."

This drew a chuckle from Arthur. "My poor dear aunt."

"Yes, Mama's paying for it, I'm sure."

At that moment Alan Bell strode into their midst—a stout, red-whiskered man with a loose smile and an animated face and the air of a country gentleman. The two brothers fell into a bearlike embrace, and after much hearty back pounding, the elder turned to Charlotte with a mannerly tip of the hat.

"Madam, my deepest admiration to you for having taken on this troublesome old bachelor. I daresay, a few more years of single life and he would have become quite intolerable." His eyes seemed to twinkle with an urge to do mischief, and Charlotte could sense the strong, real affection behind the sparring words.

"Indeed, sir, I believe I saved him in the nick of time," Charlotte quipped.

Arthur broke into a proud smile, and with a protective air he drew her hand through his arm, tucking it snugly into his elbow and pressing her as close to him as her full skirts would allow. It was a gesture that was becoming familiar to her, his response whenever he was at a loss for words or overwhelmed by emotion.

Outside, Alan gave a signal, and a heavy black coach drawn by two bays came clattering toward them over the cobbled drive.

"Thought it best to come up in the old family thing. So much roomier than mine," Alan said in a quiet aside to Arthur. "And Joseph's coming back with us to Cuba House. The earl didn't want to give him leave, but he explained it was to meet your new bride and showed himself quite firm about the matter. Ah, here's Simon. Here we are." He opened the carriage door and lowered the steps. "In you go, Mrs. Nicholls."

Charlotte felt hands on her waist, and she glanced up to see Arthur's whiskered face over her shoulder.

"Yes, Mrs. Nicholls," he murmured lovingly. "In you go."

Dublin took her by surprise. Her first impression from the carriage was that of an elegant city of classical beauty. Magnificent Georgian public buildings and terraced town houses bore witness to the extravagant lifestyle of the gentry during the previous century's prosperity—although there were signs of growing deterioration and neglect. She caught glimpses of fountains, squares, and greens planted with flower beds, of porticoed doorways crowned with elegant fanlights.

Over dinner at the inn that evening, Charlotte found her new brother-in-law extremely well-read and well-informed about politics. He spoke modestly of his work as manager of the Grand Canal linking Dublin to the River Shannon, although Charlotte suspected it was a position of considerable influence. For the most part their conversation turned around familial topics; they talked of the family estate, how they were managing the little bit of farmland that remained, of a favorite old retainer who had passed away, of trout fishing, of stalking and shooting, of horse trading. These were clearly subjects of intense interest to Arthur—the passions of a country gentleman rather than a clergyman. It was not so much a new man but a whole man that began to emerge.

Mary Anna remained quiet. Only Arthur seemed capable of drawing her out. To him she would chatter away in a soft voice as if she believed that nothing she said held any interest for anyone but him. Her manners gave the impression of maturity beyond her years—and upon closer acquaintance one became conscious of a perplexing sadness that somehow dulled her beauty.

That night in their room at the inn, Charlotte sat perched on the bed wrapped in Arthur's wool sweater while he dug through their trunk for his flask of whiskey.

"Arthur, how old is Mary Anna?"

"Twenty-one."

"She seems much older."

"She's always seemed that way, even as a child."

"But what a beautiful girl. She has the complexion of a Madonna. Is Lucy as pretty?"

"Lucy is every bit as pretty, but she lacks Mary Anna's good sense. She's only a year younger, but they are as different as night and day.

Lucy can be a little spoiled and petulant, and Mary Anna suffers it all with the patience of a saint. And Lucy has suitors, which Mary Anna has never had."

"Never. Not any?"

"Not one. . . . Ah, here it is! Now, where are the glasses?"

"On the mantel. And you keep two carriages and a coachman?"

"It's not my property, dearest. It's my aunt's household. As for Simon, he wears a half dozen hats around the house, and the carriage is an ancient rattletrap, as I'm sure you noticed."

"And what about your cousin Joseph? I overheard something about an earl's household."

"Uh, yes . . . the Earl of Kenmare."

"You never told me he was employed by an earl."

"I told you he was employed by a respectable family in Dublin."

"Honestly, Arthur, you might have been a bit more forthcoming."

"Now, don't be cross with me. You abhor boasting, Charlotte, as do I. You would have accused me of being like Sir James if I had started touting our acquaintances."

"Does Papa know these things about your family?"

"No, and I see no reason why it should make a whit of difference to him. How could my young cousin's employer in Ireland brighten my prospects? I'm as poor as I've ever been. And having pretty girl cousins and a well-educated brother and two carriages doesn't make my star shine any brighter. These things are immaterial to us. What's important is that I have the qualities necessary to take care of you and your father and continue in God's work. That's all that matters. That and the fact that I love you madly."

He poured a little whiskey into a glass and offered it to her.

"Here, drink this. You've overexerted yourself now and your cough is getting worse."

He pressed the back of his hand to her forehead and cheek.

"You have a fever."

"Arthur, dearest, I'm warm because you've got me bundled in wool up to my ears. I assure you I'll be quite well enough to see the sights tomorrow. I should not like to miss a thing."

"Then get underneath the covers. You must rest."

He made no demands on her that night. It was the first night since their marriage that he had not urged himself on her. Each night in the cover of darkness he would slide his bearlike hands beneath her nightgown and grapple in his clumsily innocent way with the unformed breasts, the boyish hips and thighs—and she would feel him swell with lust and love, which were one and the same to him.

All through the act she remained distant and alert, noting the startling changes in his body, the sweat and heat, the sensation of his beard on her nipples, the grunts and spasmodic cries when he had been satisfied. She would wrap her arms around his bullish neck and meekly return his kisses, but just as soon as she began to feel her body respond it would be over.

Arthur was only too aware of the one-sided nature of their pleasure.

"Oh, my dear," he sighed one night in Wales as she lay nestled in his arms, "I'm afraid innocence does have its disadvantages, doesn't it?"

"What do you mean?"

"What I mean is, if I had acquired a little experience in these matters, I might know better how to please you."

Charlotte rose on her elbows and scowled at him. "Arthur Bell Nicholls, you are a man of the church."

"I assure you there are many young bachelor clergymen donning surplices every Sunday with blemishes on their souls."

"And do you think they make better husbands?"

"I speak of lovers, not husbands."

Charlotte was silent. She laid her head on his chest and listened to the steady drumming of his heart. She did not know how to talk about these things. She could certainly not talk about her own desires, or how to satisfy them.

He gave a sort of relieved sigh and kissed the top of her head. "Well, we shan't need to talk about it again."

Charlotte felt an instant liking for Joseph. He was waiting for them the next morning just below the college's massive bell tower—a pale, slim figure with spectacles and an appealing air of distraction. He slouched in the shadow, reading a book, his long hair ruffled by the wind; at the sound of their approaching steps he squinted into the bright sunlight, and then he stuffed the small volume in his pocket and rushed forward to greet them.

With Charlotte he seemed mildly starstruck—which they all noted with tacit amusement—and he was clearly relieved when his sister began asking about his examination.

"I think I performed passably well," he replied modestly. "The texts were poetry. Virgil and Dante."

"Joseph's had three firsts since he's been at Trinity," Mary Anna said with quiet pride.

Arthur took command of their little party, shuttling them from chapel to museum, to dining and examination hall. The entire setting thrilled Charlotte to the core; here she was walking the green lawns and cobbled quads of Trinity College in Dublin, breathing the exalted air of an exclusively masculine and privileged domain. As Arthur recounted anecdotes of his student days, Charlotte was moved by a quiet sense of irony. There flashed through her mind a vivid memory of Emily, Anne, and herself as children gathered in her father's study, listening to Branwell recite Virgil in his flawless Latin, and she recalled how she had once dreamed of her brother walking halls such as these at Cambridge or Oxford. She would have visited him. She would have stood in the ladies' gallery of the halls to hear lectures delivered by great men, and sat in the chapel listening to strains of the organ and the glorious choir.

Branwell and his dreams were buried, but she was here with Arthur. It seemed that her own dream had come true in the way that dreams often do, in their own time and in a manner quite unexpected.

When they came to the old library, the spectacular long gallery with towering walls of ancient manuscripts, it was Joseph who stepped to her side and picked up the narrative. As she listened to him speak in a hushed voice, Charlotte could not refrain from making comparisons to Branwell. There was the same impressive command of English, the flashes of brilliance and erudition, the passion for poetry. But Joseph Bell had been blessed with a sense of discipline and a steady temperament that left no doubt that he would succeed where her brother had failed.

When Arthur attempted to usher her down an aisle to show her a section of philosophical volumes, she pulled him aside and whispered, "I would so like to have liberty to take this in my own way, Arthur."

"What? You would forgo my commentary?" he teased.

"It would mean a good deal to me to have a few moments to myself."

"I understand. I shall wait for you here."

"Thank you."

"You won't get lost, I pray."

"If I do, I'm sure you'll find me."

"Arthur said this would give you pleasure," Charlotte remarked as she withdrew a small package from the corner of the carriage and presented it to Joseph. It was evening, and they had just pulled up in front of his lodgings.

He gave her a wide-eyed smile. "Are these your poems?"

"Yes. I confess I didn't know until today that you wrote verse yourself. This was the first thing we published. My efforts are quite juvenile, I'm afraid, and Anne's—well, we indulged our sister out of affection. But Emily's poems are of considerable merit."

"Ellis Bell's novel was the work of a genius," he said quietly.

"You've read *Wuthering Heights*?"

"Oh, madam, I've read it twice."

Then, with an impetuous kiss on her cheek and a murmured word of gratitude, Joseph Bell bade good-bye to all of them and bounded from the carriage.

Chapter *Thirty-one*

T he road to Banagher took them west along the lush green banks of the Grand Canal, past bogs and morasses, and fields of grazing cattle. Night was just falling as they drove through tall wrought-iron gates and up a rutted avenue lined with leafy linden trees. At the end, faintly outlined against the gloom of the woods, stood Cuba House—a great old Georgian pile of the sort built by the gentry in the previous century.

"There's the old home," Alan said as the drive curved and the house came into sight.

Charlotte turned to Arthur with a look of wide-eyed wonder.

"Why, Arthur, it's splendid," she whispered. She reached for his hand, and she couldn't help but feel a sense of vindication. She wished her father could see this. And Ellen. Her father and Ellen, who had convinced her that she was stepping down in the world.

"Gardens are looking fine, aren't they?" Alan said in an offhand manner.

"Very fine." Arthur replied.

"Narcissus gets slower every year. Don't know how he manages to keep up the grounds, but he does."

Harriette Bell was a formidable-looking matron with marked masculine brows and heavily pomaded hair that shone in the candlelight like the lustrous jet cameo fixed to her snowy-white fichu.

"My dear aunt—you must forgive the inconvenience."

"Inconvenience? Pray what do you mean, Arthur?" she said, holding her cheek up to him for a kiss.

"You weren't expecting us for several more days."

"But we're quite prepared. You did send a message, my dear."

"Which was quite unnecessary," Alan said as he passed his hat and gloves to the servant. "Arthur's such a stickler about those things."

Lucy came gaily tripping down the wide stairs and flew up to them in her summer dress of creamy rose-sprigged cotton, aware that all eyes had turned her way.

"You're such a noodle, Arthur," she said, tugging him away from her mother and giving him a peck on the cheek. "Mama's been on tenterhooks for days and everyone's been holding their breath, so it's really much to our relief that you've arrived early rather than late. Hello! I'm Lucy!"

"Lucy, my wife, Charlotte Brontë Nicholls," he said proudly.

There was more commotion as Arthur broke away to greet the household servants who hovered near the kitchen door, bobbing and curtsying and beaming with joy. One or two of them whispered words of congratulations and threw furtive, deferential glances at the tiny, fragile-looking lady who stood awkwardly at the center of attention.

"What's this about your bride not being well?" Harriette Bell asked her nephew in a commanding voice. "I gather Arthur has quite exhausted you—he's inclined to do things a bit too thoroughly."

"I never complain about my husband's thoroughness," Charlotte said quietly. "He arranged for such marvelous excursions in Wales. We saw absolutely breathtaking sights."

"But, my dear Mrs. Nicholls, you are pale. And you, Arthur, you're thin as a rake. What have you done to yourself? Well, I suppose it's to be expected—what with all the excitement. But you're home now, and you shall be well cared for. You must be bone-tired. We shall have a light supper and all go straight off to bed. No, Lucy, I'll not have a word of dissent."

The rooms were spacious and lofty, and the drawing room and dining room elegantly appointed, but as the maidservant led them down the wide, empty hall Charlotte suspected that they had not the means to furnish it as grandly as it deserved. Charlotte was accustomed to close, snug spaces, and their bedroom on the ground floor seemed vast and cold, with only an ancient four-poster bed, a vanity, and a table and chairs by the fireplace. A turf fire was already blazing in the wide old chimney, and the maidservant lit candles on the mantel while the coachman brought in their trunks.

Here, her meager reserve of energy depleted, Charlotte collapsed. Arthur was full of remorse.

"I should have brought you here directly," he apologized the next morning as he sat beside her on the bed. "It was quite selfish of me."

"I do so dislike being weak, Arthur," she murmured. "Why am I not well and strong like other people?"

"Hush," he said, and he kissed her and brushed her hair back from her face.

For two days, Mrs. Bell nursed Charlotte on vegetable and beef broth and a good dose of firm kindness, sitting quietly by her bedside every afternoon with her cat and her sewing basket. Mary Anna and Lucy gathered flowers from the garden and arranged them in cut-glass vases on the tea table, and Joseph lent her books of verse to read. Arthur would blow in and out during the day—followed by his dogs, which would lope up to her and sniff around her head and then curl up on the hearthrug, waiting on their master. During the day he smelled of horses, hot sun, and wind, and when he came to bed in the evening there was the faint odor of cigars. He abandoned his clerical collar and most days set off wearing only a light summer shirt and a straw hat.

"There could be a little something for Arthur if he chose to take it," his aunt said one afternoon, "but he has always insisted that the modest income should go to his cousins and myself. You mustn't find it odd that I speak so openly to you. You are Arthur's wife now, and you should know these things. I doubt Arthur's told you himself."

"I confess, he has not."

"Because he has always put us first. He's a selfless man when it comes to material things. But he has a wife now—and perhaps soon will have a family of his own. If you should ever find yourselves in distress, you must apply to us. We will do what we can. I would hate to think that he has deprived himself and his family of any comfort on our account."

"Mrs. Bell, I assure you, that will not be necessary. You have merely revealed to me another small proof of my husband's goodness. I can only admire and respect his choice."

"Well, things will be easier when the children are all grown. My boy Joseph shows every promise of doing well for himself—I don't fret about him—and Lucy has a serious suitor. I expect we'll announce an engagement soon. But I doubt my dear Mary Anna will ever attract a husband. Arthur is always anxious about her future."

"But she is so pretty."

"Yes, she is, with a heart as pure as her eyes are blue. And men are always quite drawn to her, until she walks across a room, and then, well . . . I've noticed that they turn away and ignore her after that. But then, we each have our burdens to bear, as God sees fit. He will give us the strength to bear up, of that I'm sure." She snipped off a thread and held her work up to the light. "I say this only to reassure you that you have, dear madam, the most loyal and devoted of husbands. When Mr. Bell passed from this world, Alan was at university in Edinburgh, and Arthur insisted that his elder brother's education should come before his own, so he gave up his studies and came home to take care of us. Lucy was only seven, and Mary Anna not even nine. Arthur is very protective—as I'm sure you've discovered. It's in his nature. Eventually he returned to Trinity and finished his degree. It must have been very difficult for him, having taken all those years off, but he never once uttered a word of regret to any of us. Arthur's a bit of a surprise, isn't he? He always strikes one as so fierce and stiff on the outside, and he's certainly not without his faults, but he's got a heart of gold. He's the favorite around here, you'll see."

It was a refrain Charlotte heard all throughout the week. She took to making inquiries whenever she had the opportunity—the housekeeper or the old man they called Narcissus, who pottered in the flower beds beneath her windowsill every morning.

"Sir, have you seen my husband this morning?"

She stood at the bedroom window in her dressing gown, looking out onto the lawn glistening with dew. The air had a clean, loamy smell.

"Aye, ma'am, he's gone off riding with his young cousin."

Charlotte's stomach sank. "Which cousin is that?"

"Master Joseph," he said as he set down his wheelbarrow, shooting her a wary look from beneath his bushy white brows. "The young mistress don't ride, what with her crippled legs, and Miss Lucy goes out only in the carriage." He took off his cap and wiped the sweat from his bald head.

"When will they return?"

"Can't tell you. He's a great one for the outdoors, Master Arthur is. Outdoors from dawn till dusk. And he's always doin' for others. Not got a lazy bone in his body, that one."

"Have you been with the family long, Narcissus?"

"I was the Reverend Bell's manservant back when he was a bachelor."

"So you've known my husband a long while."

"Since he first came to live here. A rugged lad. Always gettin' in fights, but for good cause. Took it upon himself to defend the weak ones. I've always said the lady who wins his heart is a fortunate lass indeed, for there's not a better gentleman in all the country, if ye don't mind me sayin' so, madam."

"No, Narcissus, I don't mind at all."

She had never imagined that marriage would change her in so many subtle ways. She did not shed her anxieties, but the sting of critical glances and insensitive words was mitigated with Arthur by her side. As a newly married couple, they had social visits to make in the neighborhood, and her aversion to meeting strangers would have to be overcome. It was a duty she could not avoid; to snub her husband's friends would be unthinkable. Nor could she retreat into a corner and speak in monosyllables, as she had done in London when she'd felt overwhelmed by a situation. She had made a solemn pledge to herself before their wedding: *Whatever he exacts, you force yourself to perform.*

But she had not understood the transformative power of complicity, the protection afforded by a true and selfless love. Arthur would no more allow her to flounder in a drawing room than he would abandon her to the depths of the sea.

Every day they drove out to call on neighbors—sometimes alone, other times accompanied by his cousins or his aunt. They went on picnics and excursions to distant lakes; they visited friends in outlying country homes. What had once been intolerable now became a higher order of business to her. Her fame was rarely acknowledged in the homes they visited; instead, they saw her as the fortunate wife of a well-liked and highly respected man, and Charlotte began to prefer it this way. As a wife she took pleasure in people and things that she had once dismissed as foolish, and at some point along the way the firmly held notion that she was insignificant and plain began to fade away.

Arthur was impatient to have her to himself again, and at the end of the week he announced that they were setting off for a watering place on the west coast.

"It's terribly uncivilized out there," Lucy claimed.

"But you must not miss it," Joseph replied. "It is glorious beyond words, Mrs. Nicholls. You'll never see a finer coast."

"I wish you might stay longer, my dears. But I do understand," his aunt said.

Mary Anna regretted their departure the most, although she protested the least.

They followed the Shannon to Limerick and then struck off across wild, uninhabited country to a remote spot on the southwest coast, landing in a resort town nestled in a deeply curving bay girdled with stupendous cliffs. Their accommodations were of the most primitive sort and the food appallingly bad, but they were more inclined to laugh about any shortcomings than complain. The coast here was bold and grand, with sandy shores to the south; to the north rose iron-black cliffs that dropped precipitously into the raging Atlantic. They spent the daylight hours exploring the outdoors and their nights in deep, untroubled sleep.

In the days that followed, as their sexual intimacy increased, this last and most powerful bond slowly began to deepen.

One night Charlotte stood before a looking glass brushing her hair while Arthur sat in a chair behind her, a map and train schedule spread across his knees. Gazing at her reflection, her eyes were drawn to the dark buds of her nipples faintly visible through her light muslin nightdress. She was astonished to feel desire creep into her stomach, low between her legs. With a furtive glance at Arthur, she lay down the brush and raised her hand to her breast, lightly grazing the nipple with the back of her hand. A tentative gesture, experimental.

"Arthur?" she whispered.

He looked up. "Yes?"

"I look at my image in the mirror and wonder that you should find anything that fascinates you."

He put down the map and came to stand behind her, wrapping his arms around her and fixing his eyes on her reflection.

"The matter has always been entirely beyond my control, my dear," he said solemnly. "I have only to look at you and it sparks something in me—I find you irresistible."

"Irresistible?"

He kissed her neck and allowed his hands to roam over her body.

"Entirely," he murmured.

She had steeled herself against ever anticipating any pleasure. But she knew at that moment it was possible.

"Arthur," she whispered, closing her eyes. She took his hand and moved it between her legs, quite forgetting who she was and how she should be.

They traveled through seaport towns with islets packed with dense forests, through villages set against spectacular mountain peaks and deep gorges, and Charlotte gave up trying to keep a record of the places they had been. Some parts were beautiful beyond anything she had imagined, and it all became intertwined with a progression of feeling for her husband, feelings so deeply private and fragile that she would only hint of them in her letters home to friends or family.

"Much pleasure has sprung from all this," she wrote to Ellen, "and more, perhaps, from the kind and ceaseless protection which has ever surrounded me, and made traveling a different matter to me from what it has heretofore been."

As for Arthur, by the end of their honeymoon he had gained twelve pounds and reclaimed his hale and hearty physique. That she should be the cause of this transformation was a subject of quiet wonder to Charlotte.

Chapter Thirty-two

The transformation that had first manifested itself on her honeymoon did not vanish in the familiar setting of Haworth. The timetable of her life—the whole range of activities, the shape of the week and the schedule of each day—had completely altered, and her response to this change was shaded by a growing pride and contentment.

Charlotte's letters—sprinkled with intimations of the demands made on her as the wife of a very active and practical man—testified to this: "My kind husband is just now sitting before me kindly stretching his patience to the utmost, but wishing me very much to have done writing, and put on my bonnet for a walk," she would write, or "My husband calls me—give my love to all who care to have it."

Whenever Arthur had calls to make in the outlying towns, he would hire a cab and take Charlotte with him. He sought her approval on his sermons and lectures; she presided at teas given by the Haworth Mechanics' Institute, of which Arthur was now president, and advised on books to be purchased for its library; she corresponded on his behalf, issuing invitations to sundry clergymen to visit for the night and to preach at one of the Sunday services. Her visits to the poor cottagers in the district took on new and deeper significance; she began to understand how wrong she had been about Arthur, how thoroughly he was appreciated by his parishioners, and how much gladness there was at his return. She spent hours tucked away in his snug study with its green-and-white wallpaper and the curtains she'd sewn herself, and Martha would often find her perched on the armrest of his chair, with her glasses on the tip of her nose and her nose deep in some letter or other, and Mr. Nicholls's arm around her waist.

She found it difficult to keep up with her correspondence; whenever Arthur went out, she would hurry to her writing desk and scribble off a hasty note or two before he returned. The French newspapers she had once devoured so eagerly now piled up in the corner. When he was home, she needed to find occupations and tasks they might share. He was jealous of her attention, and to be wanted and possessed filled her with a sense of awe.

Patrick, who had continued poorly for months, had relinquished all his duties to Arthur since their return, and to see how her husband now shared the burden of her father's deteriorating health was a source of immense relief to Charlotte. Patrick, for his part, found little changed in his life. Wrapped up in his politics and his local reforms, he dithered with his correspondence and muddled through his newspapers with his magnifying glass; he entertained distinguished visitors now and then and was grateful to find his routine undisturbed.

Their squabbles were infrequent and of short duration. Arthur often vented his frustration by slogging off with Flossy onto the moors, and during his absence Charlotte—buoyed by a wave of relief at having him out of her hair—would gaily bustle around the house, tending to all the little neglected chores that always seemed to pile up, but within half an hour she would be eagerly watching for his return. If he disappeared for too long, the relief would turn to anxiety and, on a few occasions, tears.

But their separations were few. Arthur wanted her near him, sharing his life and responsibilities, and it had always been in Charlotte's nature to please those who truly loved her.

Whatever the fault lines of their marriage, their solidarity was obvious to all who met them. He listened to her more radical opinions with a sardonic grimace or a groan, and she bit her tongue when he launched into a searing tirade against the Baptists. Arthur defended her fiercely from criticism and continued to protect her from the obtrusive demands of her celebrity. Charlotte—who had so often aired her doubts about

Arthur in her letters before their marriage—became increasingly tight-lipped about her husband's faults.

Arthur was a busy man, and his large, energetic presence electrified the atmosphere of the parsonage. They had frequent callers, the clergy-man sort as well as old friends, and Charlotte never complained. Joe Tay-lor and his wife, Amelia, brought their baby girl; Sutcliffe Sowden came on a visit with his brother; and the Grants were often guests at tea. When Sir James drove over from Manchester to meet the bridegroom and stayed over on Sunday to hear him preach, he took such a fancy to Charlotte's high-principled husband that he offered him the living of Padiham near his house at Gawthorpe, which was within his gift, and worth a good two hundred pounds per year—twice Arthur's present salary. Without a moment's hesitation, Arthur kindly but firmly turned it down.

"Your offer is extremely generous, Sir James, and I am honored, but I have solemnly pledged my support to Mr. Brontë in his declining age," he replied. "I am therefore bound to Haworth for the duration of his life—May God preserve him to us yet for some years to come."

After Sir James had departed, Charlotte said, "It is a pity, isn't it? Such a good situation. A beautiful new church, and quite grand."

Arthur turned one of his stern frowns on her. "But he annoys you to no end. He puts himself into such an excited fuss, and I know how you dread that sort of thing. You couldn't possibly live within walking dis-tance of him—he'd be on our doorstep every day."

Charlotte laughed and drew herself up on her toes and kissed him firmly on the lips.

It was to be expected that her friends adapt to her new role. Lily, who knew how Charlotte feared her husband's reactions to her nonconformist friends, refrained from writing to Charlotte until she was back in Ha-worth.

"She is married and I ought to write to her, but I've a panic about the husband seeing my letters," Lily said to Katie Winkworth. "Bridegrooms are always curious; husbands are not. Oh, I should so hate to be cause for turmoil on their honeymoon. I shall wait until she's home. He'll have less of a chance of intercepting my letter."

"Do you think he'll change her?"

"Certainly not. Miss Brontë could never be a bigot if her life depended on it."

"We shall see much less of her now, I suppose."

"Yes, it is sad, but she has a good and kind husband, it seems—his little foibles apart—and she has had so little affection shown to her— by men, I mean—so we must not regret losing her if it is to such a good cause."

Ellen was the first to visit upon their return to Haworth. She descended from the train on a steamy summer day, nursing a tender heart and a muted resentment of Arthur. Life had not been so yielding of its prizes, despite her pretty blond looks, and she had already fallen into the habits of spinsterhood—the preoccupation with health and heightened anxieties about her future. The life she had once imagined as the surrogate sister of the celebrated author Currer Bell, the dream of living out her days in a house by the sea sharing the limelight with her old friend, all this had been shattered; she held Arthur solely accountable.

Their walks on the moors were always arranged around Arthur's schedule so that he might accompany them. In the evenings as the women sat chatting in the dining room, with the windows open to scented breezes from the garden, Arthur would wander in and out, looking so lovesick and lost without his wife that Charlotte would break down and laughingly invite him to join them, which he always did. Charlotte never seemed to mind his intrusion. She became more spirited in his presence; she would scold him in her affectionate, bossy manner, and he would play the beleaguered husband—parrying with his own sardonic quips. Beneath the sparring ran a current of affection, and on occasion Ellen would intercept a meaningful glance between the two—the sort of sexually charged look between men and women sharing a secret. Through all this, Ellen concealed her jealousy and bore up with frozen smiles, resenting the loss of late hours full of the loose, gossipy talk they had always enjoyed. Now Charlotte retired with her husband—willingly, at his bidding. Ellen would find herself climbing the stairs alone to the back bedroom, feeling neglected and deprived of her closest friend.

Only in the mornings, when Arthur was giving religious instruction at the school, were they able to speak without constraint. After several days, Ellen gave in to her frustrations.

"To be truthful, I find it rather disturbing, Charlotte. The way he's tamed you. You're far too compliant."

Charlotte smiled good-naturedly. "You yourself have often wished for me to be more compliant and less selfish. And now that I am, you regret it."

"It's so unlike you, to be at the beck and call of another, and to enjoy it."

"I do enjoy it. To be wanted continually—to be constantly called for and occupied seems so strange, but it's a marvelously good thing. My life has always been turned inward, and that has been a source of great pleasure but also much anguish."

"But how will you find the time to write? He will certainly not allow it."

"Of course he will. But at the moment I have no desire to write, and I don't think that is a bad thing. I believe it's good for me that he should be concerned so entirely with matters of real life and so little inclined to the literary and contemplative. Look at me, Nell. I've never been so free of sickness. My headaches and nausea and stomach ailments have all but disappeared."

"You should take care. He tires you out. I've seen how he is with you on your walks. He always wants you to go the extra mile."

Charlotte laughed. "My walks with Arthur are one of my greatest pleasures."

"But in the winter!"

"Even in the winter. Just last week when we were out on the moors Arthur suggested the idea of the waterfall. He said it would be fine after the melted snow. It's so powerful in the winter, Ellen. Such a magnificent sight. So we walked on. Oh, it was fine indeed. A perfect torrent racing over the rocks, white and beautiful."

"Yes, and as I recall, it rained on you on the way back. You came home soaked to the skin. How rash of him."

"Oh, but I enjoyed it inexpressibly. I would not have missed it on any account."

Ellen was subdued into a long, sullen silence.

"I don't think he likes me much," she said at last, turning wounded eyes to Charlotte. Charlotte quickly set down the shirt she was sewing for Arthur and reached across the sofa to take Ellen's hand.

"Oh, my dear Nell, that is not true."

"But he seems so hard."

"But he's not at all, not underneath. And he is fond of you."

"I've yet to see proof of that."

"Because he's not an effusive man—but he always speaks warmly of you, and one friendly word from him means as much as twenty from most people."

Ellen sat staring at the toes of her shoes, reluctant to believe in Arthur's good will.

"It was his idea to invite Mr. Sowden while you were here. Did you know that?"

A glimmer came into Ellen's eyes. "Was it truly?"

"It was. And nothing could be more proof of his kind regard for you. Mr. Sowden is his dearest friend and a very worthy gentleman."

"Does Mr. Sowden remember me?"

"From the wedding party? Of course he does. You are far too pretty to forget, Nell."

"When does he come?"

"Next week. And Arthur loves his walks, as you know, so there will be many opportunities for the four of us to go rambling on the moors— and with the weather so warm and fine, we'll have a very merry time, the four of us."

Charlotte sat back and took up her husband's shirt again. "Just imagine, Ellen—now, wouldn't that be something? You and Mr. Sowden?"

She twinkled over the rims of her glasses. "We've talked about it, you know—about getting you settled. Arthur has quite a few bachelor friends."

Sutcliffe Sowden's arrival did lighten the mood. He seemed quietly amused by his friends' attempt at matchmaking and responded with just enough interest so that Ellen went home at the end of two weeks with hopes that everything might come right again.

But Charlotte's allegiances had shifted—fully, irrevocably. She had once written of her desire for a master, "one in whose presence I shall feel obliged and disposed to be good. One whose control my impatient temper must acknowledge. A man whose approbation can reward—whose displeasure punish me. A man I shall feel it impossible not to love, and very possibly to fear."

She had written those words thinking of Constantin Heger. But it was Arthur who was revealed to be the conquering David, the man chosen by God to defeat all the Goliaths in her life.

As the passion and intimacy between them grew, so did he gain ascendancy in her life.

Lily had correctly predicted that he would be curious about her correspondence, and on occasion he exercised a husband's right to read her letters. Martha and Tabby, habituated to years of conspiring for the mistress, once intercepted a letter from Mary Taylor and hid it in the kitchen behind the salt cellar so that Charlotte might read it away from his prying eyes. But Charlotte had no desire to lead a double life; she had found a man who bore her faults tenderly, who accepted her strengths and insecurities in all their complexity, who was undaunted by the task of loving her. His religious prejudices aside, his motives were undeniably honest and pure; he loved her unconditionally and sought to protect her from injury and from the clamoring, grasping, curious world beyond their doors.

Which was why he expressed a growing concern about her letters to Ellen with their wickedly humorous observations of their friends. More than once he had declared them as hazardous as lucifer matches, which Charlotte found terribly funny. It all came to a head one morning when she was dashing off a biting account of a recent visit by Joe and Amelia Taylor; Arthur, leaning over her shoulder, sounded an alarm.

"Good heavens, Charlotte, have you no sense of caution?"

"Caution?"

"Look at what you've written there."

"I've said nothing rash."

"You've called Amelia a simpleton."

"You've said as much yourself."

"But you've put it down in writing. There's a vast difference."

"My dear, letters are a vehicle of communication—that is their purpose; we women write as if we were in the room talking to one another."

He had taken up the letter and was reading it through. "What's all this business about my threatening to bolt the next time Amelia comes to visit?"

"Those were your words, my dear."

"But I should not like to see this kind of thing reported in a letter for anyone to read. You write too freely of other people and that is most reckless. What if it should get into Amelia's hands?"

"That won't happen."

"But you and Ellen share all your letters with your friends."

"Well, she certainly won't share this one with Amelia."

"I do not wish to speak unkindly of Ellen, but she did turn on you once—when I was courting you and she had such strong objections. Have you forgotten?"

"Oh, Arthur, you are being really silly. But if you insist."

"I do. She must burn your letters."

His voice had that stern quality that thrilled her.

"Yes, dear. I'll say as much to Ellen. Now give me back the letter."

She looked up at him, now solemn and obedient, holding out her hand for the letter. "Honestly, I never really attach any importance to these notes, you know. I don't give a penny for their fate."

"Then tell her to fire them. She must give you a pledge."

"And if she does, then we may write whatever we wish?"

"You may write any dangerous stuff you please."

She dipped her pen in the ink and read to him as she scribbled, " 'Arthur thinks I have written too freely about Amelia—he says letters such as mine never ought to be kept—so be sure to "fire them!" as he says, or else he will elect himself censor of our correspondence and you will get such dull uninteresting notes as he writes to Mr. Sowden.' "

She looked up at him with a bemused smile. "There, dear. Is that satisfactory?"

"Quite," he murmured as he kissed her on the back of the neck.

As the year drew to a close, Charlotte kept delaying her much-anticipated bride visit to Brookroyd—her first as a married woman. Ellen's sister fell ill with a fever, and Arthur refused to allow her to go. Several days later, through Miss Wooler, Charlotte learned that the fever had been diagnosed as typhoid.

"It's good that I stood firm with you," Arthur told her. "To think if I had allowed you to go, and you had been exposed! It was most unwise of her to conceal the nature of the fever."

"I don't think Ellen knew."

"Did the physician not tell them it was typhoid?"

"I don't believe he did."

"These medical men ought to be more candid."

"I shall say nothing to her on the subject—but Ellen shall be very disappointed. I must find an excuse."

"Just tell her the truth. Tell her I put my foot down. You need not be more specific than that."

"My dear Ellen," she wrote,

> I shall not get leave to go to Brookroyd before Christmas now—so do not expect me. For my own part, I really should have no fear—and if it just depended on me, I should come—but these matters are not quite in my power now—another must be consulted—and where his wish and judgment have a decided bias to a particular course, I make no stir, but just adopt it. Arthur is sorry to disap-

point both you and me—but it is his fixed wish that a few weeks
should be allowed yet to elapse before we meet.

She showed him the letter.

He groaned. "Well, she'll be very unhappy with me. But if it preserves your friendship . . ."

"It is all so disappointing. I should so like to see her sisters, and all my old friends in the neighborhood."

"Are you already bored with me?"

"Bored? Arthur, I never have a moment's peace. I have to run away from home to be bored."

In December, Charlotte learned that Charles Dickens would be in Bradford to give a reading of *A Christmas Carol.* The thought of attending brought her a twinge of nostalgia as she remembered her halcyon days in London, but it was just the sort of gathering where Arthur would feel at a disadvantage. He would be the husband of Currer Bell, insignificant and ill at ease. Lily would be there, since she and Dickens were great friends, and Lily and Arthur had still not met. Lily's new novel—the story of a clergyman who leaves the church in a crisis of faith—had been coming out in serial form, and the work had stuck in Arthur's craw. It was just the sort of thing to set him off.

"It's a vile book. An insidious attack on the church," he said with one of his dark scowls.

"I don't think it's an attack so much as a defense of those who conscientiously differ from the church and feel it a duty to leave the fold."

"Her husband is a Unitarian minister. They are heretics," he glowered.

"But she is such a good woman. I assure you, when you do know her you will feel as others feel. I love and respect her deeply, and would so like for the two of you to get along. I think she may be a little afraid of you—she knows your opinion of her. I believe that's why she has not yet visited us, despite my invitation."

He gave a deep sigh of resignation. "I should never wish to be a barrier between you and your friends, my dear. I have said that to you before. But I feel these matters very deeply." He sulked quietly for a moment, then drew his book back to his nose. "I suppose I can make myself scarce when she's around."

She rose and went to him; she took the book out of his hands and sat down on his lap, twining her arms around his neck.

"Darling, you know I could never force a person on you against your will."

"Perhaps she might visit in the spring—when you would not be confined indoors." He paused and added grimly, "Without her husband."

"Yes, that could be easily arranged."

So Charlotte did not attend the Bradford reading. They were busy with their own preparations for Christmas, and the day flashed by unnoticed.

The season of Advent had always been celebrated reverently and humbly in the parsonage, but this year Charlotte was inspired to add cheerful new touches. With Martha and Hannah's help, they strung garlands of evergreen over the doors and mantel; they decked the portraits and the old grandfather clock with red holly and green ivy and scented the rooms with oil of cinnamon and cloves.

The kitchen was a hive of activity from morning to night. In addition to the joints and puddings and pies, Charlotte supervised the baking of dozens of spice cakes, which were wrapped in paper and stored in the cellar until Christmas Day, when they would be delivered personally by Mr. and Mrs. Nicholls to the poor. Parishioners walked miles in the cold raw wind to attend concerts in the Haworth church, and there were festive receptions in the parsonage for the bell ringers and singers. The Haworth brass band—all fifteen of them—made their rounds in the village as they did every year, playing their songs and glees, and the musicians were struck by the change that had come over the parsonage. It seemed more brightly lit, and the occupants lighthearted. When the band had finished blasting out the last note of a jubilant "Joy to the World" and

Jeremiah, the trumpet player, stepped forward with his open purse, Mrs. Nicholls—flashing a shy, radiant smile—came down the steps and gave him an extra coin.

No ghosts haunted the parsonage that year.

One night several days after Christmas, Charlotte and Arthur sat together in the parlor. The winter wind howled around the house, but they were warm indoors before a blazing fire; a sense of contentment subtle as perfume hung in the room.

Charlotte looked up from her sewing and said, "Do you know that tomorrow we shall have been married all of six months?"

Arthur turned a page of his book and acknowledged the statement with a grunt. He did not smile, but a rosy tint spread through his hardfixed features.

"You know, if you were not with me, I should be writing just now."

"Would you?"

"After *Jane Eyre,* when I owed more books to Cornhill, I was under a good deal of pressure. Now I'm free to write when I have a tale to tell and feel inspired to tell it."

"Are you so inclined this evening?"

She tilted her head and with a saucy smile said, "Perhaps."

"Then what's stopping you?"

She reflected for a moment, then put down her sewing and disappeared upstairs. She returned clutching a handful of pages.

"This is something I started last year. Would you like to hear it?"

Closing his book, Arthur propped his stocking-clad feet on the fender. "Read away, my dear."

Settling down in her chair opposite his, she read him the first few chapters of *Emma,* the story of a motherless young girl who is abused by the mistress of her boarding school when it is learned that her father is not the wealthy man he had portrayed himself to be and has disappeared without paying her school fees.

When she had finished, she put down the pages and asked him what he thought.

Arthur reflected for a moment. "It's about a school again. I fear the critics will accuse you of repetition."

"Oh, I shall alter that. I always begin two or three times before I can please myself."

After a long hesitation, Arthur said, "My dear, you should not rely solely on my judgment. You know I'm not good at this sort of thing."

She leaned forward and placed her tiny hand on his leg. "I don't care. I want to read my work to you. I want to share it with you. Besides, I rarely agree with the opinions of others. Even my publisher."

"Good. You are the genius. You should do as Genius dictates."

"That I shall."

"I suppose writers write what they know."

"Yes, and I only know schools. And governesses."

"And clergymen," he laughed.

She grew serious. "I told you once that writing is an act of conscience for me. I must speak truthfully about human nature. I cannot force or fake a character, and I take them seriously, as I do all of life. My stories are a product of my experience, and if I have not accumulated enough experience to enable me to speak again, may God give me the grace to be dumb."

A moment passed before he asked her quietly, "Do you think you are finished writing about Brussels?"

After a long, startled silence—waiting until she was sure to have firm control of her voice—she answered, "I believe so. Yes, I'm quite sure of it. I have told the story I wished to tell."

He nodded and shifted his feet on the fender.

She said, "I imagine that I shall write something quite different the next time." There was a pause. "Yes. Something quite different."

The following day Flossy drooped; he would not eat but lay quietly before the fire all day and died silently in the night. It was the only blight on the Christmas season.

Chapter Thirty-three

"I do believe you enjoyed yourself, Mr. Nicholls."

"I did indeed. Much more so than I had anticipated."

"You were quite taken with Sir James's microscope. I thought you'd never come up for air."

"Fascinating contraption. Should like to have one of those myself."

"Then I shall buy one for you with the proceeds from my next novel."

Arthur let loose with one of his great exuberant laughs and stamped on the carriage floor with his boot, waking the dozing driver.

"What's that, sir?" he called through the window.

"Nothing. Mind your driving."

"Yes, sir," the old man muttered. *A miserable day to travel,* he thought as he hunkered back down in his seat, winding his tobacco-stained scarf around his mouth. The cold drizzle had been picked up by a fierce wind, and now the rain stabbed his eyes like needles. The horses didn't like it either; they plodded on with their ears battened down and their flanks twitching.

They were jolted as the carriage hit a rut in the frozen road, and Arthur reached out a protective arm to steady Charlotte.

"Are you all right? You're looking pale."

"I am feeling a little queasy."

"You should have eaten before we left."

"I did, my dear."

"You nibbled a crust of toast. And you ate nothing the night before."

"I had no appetite. Which was quite regrettable. Sir James laid on such a fine dinner. He is kind."

"You were absolutely correct in suspecting there was a motive behind his invitation."

"Sir James never does anything without a hidden motive. I suppose he thought if he fawned over you like he does over me that you might change your mind and take the living at Padiham. He just does not understand that anyone could thwart his wishes."

"Little does he know us."

"I'm very proud of you, Arthur. How you stand firm."

He gave another, more subdued laugh, then abruptly fell still, alarmed by the expression on her face.

"My dear, shall we stop the carriage?"

"No, no. It's too cold," she said, drawing the carriage rug tighter around her legs. "I'll be better once we're on the train."

Arthur and Patrick were waiting in Patrick's study when Dr. Ingham came back downstairs. He was new to Haworth, a young surgeon recently licensed, and they were not wholly convinced of his competence. They shot to their feet and greeted him with intense, anxious stares.

"There's no need for alarm. Her nausea and lack of appetite are both symptomatic."

There was a brief silence. Patrick faced the doctor in a curiously frozen stance, his hands clasped tightly behind his back and his eyes unblinking.

Arthur appeared dazed. It took him a moment to find his voice, and then he stammered nervously, "Do you mean to confirm . . ."

"Yes, she is with child," Dr. Ingham assured him solemnly. "Her illness may be of some duration, perhaps several months, but there is no immediate danger."

He gave Arthur a firm pat on the back, which loosened a smile from the curate's face.

"Congratulations, Mr. Nicholls."

"Thank you. Thank you." Momentarily, Arthur succumbed to the joy, and he clasped the doctor's hand and pumped it. "Yes, thank you. This is good news, indeed." But Patrick stood silent as a sentinel.

Arthur asked, "What can we do for her?"

"There's little to be done except to wait for time to take its course."

"Are there any problems we should anticipate?"

Patrick spoke up sharply. "My daughter is nearly thirty-nine, Dr. Ingham. And frail."

"Yes, indeed, but her age does not necessarily impede a healthy birth. I've delivered many a woman older than she of a healthy baby."

"Her mother died at this very age," Patrick said morosely, and then he turned away toward the window.

Arthur found her sitting erect on the edge of the bed in her petticoat and chemise, her head down. Strands of her hair had come loose, and her fingers moved quickly, expertly, putting all in order again. She looked up at him with dark, probing eyes. She had been waiting for him.

"How are you feeling?" he asked.

"Odd. It's nothing I can quite describe. I just feel very queer. Quite unlike myself."

"The doctor says it will pass," he said as he cautiously lowered himself onto the bed beside her. He was a little flustered and didn't quite know how to treat her. He reached for her hand and found it cold.

"We mustn't speculate, Arthur. It's very early. We must not get our hopes up."

"My only hope is for your health."

"But would it make you happy?"

"If it be God's will."

Beneath his cautionary words she sensed a restrained joy.

"It would make you happy, wouldn't it?"

"Oh, my dear, it would make me very happy indeed," he said. Momentarily she felt herself swept up in his joy, despite the queasiness and the chills.

"Well, again, we must wait," she warned. "Things can go wrong."

"You mustn't talk like that. You're sounding like your father."

"Goodness, I hope I don't sound like him. He's all gloom and doom. He'll have me dead in the grave before long." She said this with her wry, taut grin, but she seemed to half-believe it herself, and her attempts at cheerfulness gave way to a swell of anxiety. "But I *am* afraid, Arthur. I can't say as much to Papa. I've always sheltered him from anything that might worry him. But I must tell you."

"Of course you must."

"I *am* afraid."

"Come here."

He reached for her. She laid her head against his chest and rested quietly in his arms.

After a while she said, "I must get dressed."

"Why? Why don't you rest?"

"I've been lying in bed all morning. I have far too much to do."

She slipped from his embrace and went to take her dress from the back of the chair. Within a few steps she was seized by another wave of nausea.

"Oh no . . ."

She turned toward the washbasin, but Arthur was already on his feet; he snatched it from the stand, thrusting it into her hands just as she heaved. He held her up while she emptied the meager contents of her stomach into the basin. She strained until her face was damp with sweat, and when the sickness had passed, she crawled onto the bed and lay limp, spent.

He poured a glass of water for her and waited while she washed her teeth.

"It will pass. The doctor promised it will pass."

He summoned Martha, who came upstairs to clean away the basin and bring a ewer of fresh water.

"Sir, ye needn't bother yerself with this," she whispered to him on the way out. "This is woman's work."

"I shall tend to her, Martha," he said with quiet assurance. "We must do everything to make her comfortable. Bring some fresh linens. And tend to the fire. It's far too cold in here."

"Aye, sir."

He stepped to the window and pulled back the curtain. Earlier in the morning the winter sun had risen against a canopy of blue, but now the church tower stood lonely and desolate against a blanket of gray. Snow had begun to fall, stirred by the eddies of wind as it swept through the garden and the tombstones below.

He glanced back at Charlotte. She was resting; the fine fairylike hands lay curled, relaxed, on top of the counterpane. Arthur drew the curtains and went about tidying the room. The dress went back in the armoire; the tiny leather boots fell in line with the other shoes against the wall (both of them would have fit easily into one of Arthur's boots); the shawls were folded and draped over the footboard. When everything was ordered as Charlotte would have liked it, he moved the chair beside the bed and sat down. When Martha returned she found him deep in prayer.

Once again, her visits to the Nusseys and the Taylors had to be postponed. She wrote, "Don't conjecture—dear Nell—for it is too soon yet. Keep the matter wholly to yourself. I am rather mortified to lose my good looks and grow thin as I am doing—just when I thought of going to Brookroyd. Papa continues much better—and Arthur is well and flourishing. It is an hourly happiness to me to see how well the two get on together now. There has never been a misunderstanding or wrong word."

Ellen besieged her friend with frantic pleas to be permitted to visit. Charlotte replied, "I am well tended by my kind husband. The presence of another, even yours, my dear Nell, would only add to my worries. I am too conscious of my duties to be careless of your own comfort, and I am in no condition to be weighted down with concerns. Wait a little. Be patient. All will come well and you can visit in the spring."

As the weeks advanced, they hoped for an improvement, but the nausea and sickness continued. Mistrusting the inexperienced Ingham, Arthur sent for Dr. Macturk from Bradford, who reassured them once again that her illness was symptomatic of her pregnancy.

Arthur, in his usual manner, tacked toward the practical.

"Is there a particular diet that would help?"

"Make sure she gets as much nourishment as possible. Anything light that she can keep down. Beef tea is good. She is merely suffering what many women suffer in the early stages. It will pass."

He prescribed draughts, and Ellen and Amelia Taylor sent advice culled from their acquaintances who had suffered the same symptoms in pregnancy, but nothing worked. By February, Arthur and her father had taken up the task of answering her correspondence, for she had become too weak to hold a pen. Tabby, who had been ill since January with severe diarrhea (yet another contagion from Haworth's foul water supply! Patrick lamented), had been moved to her great-niece's cottage in the village, since Charlotte could not care for her. With the news of her death several weeks later, Charlotte sank into despair.

A biting cold settled over the entire region, blown in by a steady north wind, and the snowfall exceeded anything they had seen in many years. There were record deaths, and Charlotte lay in her bed listening to the death bells toll just outside her window.

Day after day she battled her fears; she was shocked to examine her feelings and discover ambivalence toward the child that was draining the life from her. *Do I resent this child already? Before he's made his entrance into the world? Dear God, help me. What kind of mother am I?*

She confided to Martha, "I'm not good with children. Children have never been fond of me."

"That's fool's talk, ma'am. Why, Mr. Joe Taylor's little girl takes to ye like family."

"She finds me odd. I amuse her."

"It's different with yer own wee one. That's what my mother says. Ye'll see. Just ye wait—when ye're holdin' the little bundle in yer arms, ye'll see. An' Mr. Nicholls will be a good father."

"Yes, I think he will be."

"As good a father as they come, ma'am."

Charlotte missed Tabby dreadfully. She missed the old servant's comforting wisdom and nonsense. Her Yorkshire superstitions and love of fairies, her grim, harrowing tales told over the kitchen table on winter nights when the fire burned low, with all the children gathered round, hungering for visions to come alive in their heads.

So many things taken away. The young and the old. The memory keepers. All gone.

In the midst of these bleak thoughts, Arthur came striding into her head, that great whiskered man in black, so solid, so dauntless. Anxieties fled at his approach. She lay in bed with her eyes closed, imagining squat little demons scampering away at the sight of him. Like the washer-women. In her imagination she smiled.

Arthur moved through the days like an iron-clad locomotive: on track, punctual, dependable, his energies thrown into the service of others. When villagers stopped to ask after his wife, his stiffness was so off-putting that no one dared pry. They judged the seriousness of her illness by the increasingly rigid manner of his speech and bearing.

One day late in February the Keighley solicitor who had managed the matter of her will arrived at the parsonage. In the hush of the sickroom, with the wind rattling the windows, he sat at a table and drew up a new will wherein Charlotte Brontë bequeathed to her husband all her property, to be his absolutely and entirely. It was a brief piece of business; she signed it with her shaky hand, and her father and Martha Brown signed their own names as witnesses. Arthur remained stony-faced and silent throughout the proceedings.

She said she had been thinking about revising her will for some time, and that the changes testified to her love for him. She had not given up on life. There was too much to live for. But Arthur took it as a sign. It was a turning point in his resolve. His defenses collapsed.

Only strenuous physical exertion distracted him. He could be seen early in the morning shoveling snow from the wide steps rising to the church, and spreading salt on the steep lanes so the children could make it to school. When a coal carrier's wagon went off the road in a blizzard, dragging the horses into the icy waters of Bridgehouse Beck, Arthur led a rescue team to the site. One of the horses was green, and he'd gotten himself in a hopeless tangle of line and rope. It was treacherous work, unhitching the wagon and freeing the animals in the rushing, numbing water, and the carrier crushed a couple of fingers between a wheel and a rock. They lost the wagon but saved the horses, and for about three hours that day Arthur didn't think about his wife.

It was a daily struggle dealing with Patrick's laments; he bemoaned the weakness of his own frail body, the loss of his strength, his eyesight, his children. All the miseries of his fate had come to reside in the frail body of his last living daughter, whose books were so famous, and who was dying in the bed upstairs. One day when Patrick came into Arthur's study to leave some correspondence related to church business, Arthur looked up at the old man and said, "I can understand if you resent me, sir. That you blame me for this. It's a guilt that has haunted me from the beginning of her illness."

Patrick interrupted: "You are mistaken, sir. I bear you no grudge."

Arthur said, "You should know that if I could have foreseen the future, I would have given her up if it meant saving her life."

"But you forget, Mr. Nicholls, that Charlotte herself had a say in these matters. She knew the risks. If I had a choice, I daresay, I would have chosen otherwise. But God determines these matters. You have made my daughter happier in these past eight months than she has ever been. We must accept God's will and have faith in His mysterious Love and Mercy."

Their talk turned to church business, and for those few minutes at the back of his mind Arthur marveled that this man could lose so much and keep his faith. Arthur admired him but did not for a second wish to be like him. It wasn't that Arthur's faith in God had weakened, but if he believed in the power of everlasting love it had been taught to him not by doctrine, but by a prickly-tempered, insecure, melancholy little woman with fiery opinions. How could this odd little bundle inspire in him, at once, in the same moment, the fiercest desire to ravish and protect? Agape and Eros. Not separate but one.

If there was a Mystery, it was this: that his old self had dissolved into a muddle and the new man made seamlessly whole.

He wondered if Patrick Brontë had ever experienced this all-consuming passion for his wife. Perhaps. But he thought not. Patrick Brontë loved God first and then himself. Arthur felt as if he had quite lost himself altogether in another. If Charlotte should pass from this earth, he could not imagine how he would find himself again.

Arthur abandoned his study and brought his work into their bedroom. He wrote his sermons there and replied to Charlotte's correspondence. When she felt she could eat a little something, he fed her spoonfuls of water mixed with wine, and a little applesauce or light pudding. But most days the very sight of food made her sick, and Arthur took his meals hurriedly in the dining room by himself before returning to her bedside. Twice a day he knelt by her bed for the ritual of morning and evening prayer. Daily he read to her from Psalms, choosing only those that sang of consolation, hope, and love.

Her father checked in on her every day but stayed for only a moment. He could not bear the stifling closeness of sickrooms, with the cloying smell of medicines and draughts.

Their nights were sleepless and utterly miserable. She was constantly ill and would strain until she vomited blood. Arthur nursed her through it all with unfailing patience. Charlotte urged him to take the bedroom next door.

"I would not think of leaving you," he answered sternly. She didn't press him again.

Arthur never spoke of the baby.

She knew that her thoughts should be turned to her Maker in these difficult hours, that she should be preparing her mind for submission to His will. But all she could think about was this man at her side, this mortal who loved her and whom she loved in return. Her thoughts drifted in and out of dreams and memories. Often she was too exhausted to care for life, but then she would hear him shuffling about the room in his slippers, opening a drawer, closing the shutters, drawing the curtains, fanning the fire. The scratching of his pen, the soft lisping of shuffled papers soothed her like a lullaby. She welcomed the smallest utterances, a sigh or muffled cough. The weight of his body as he lowered himself onto their bed, his strong hands so tender in their touch, all these faint impressions sensed through the fog of her suffering formed a cocoon that sheltered her from her fears. She escaped into Arthur and prayed that he would intercede for her, in life and with God. It was the ultimate act of submission. It was not God's will but Arthur's to which she relinquished herself. His prayers. His judgment. She submerged herself in his presence, and in her total exhaustion she believed that his strength would be sufficient to all their needs.

The doctors were baffled. She was wasting away, could not keep down even the smallest morsel of food, and even with her stomach empty she strained to vomit.

What am I doing? Charlotte thought in her dark moments. There was too much time to think. Whenever Arthur left her side, he took his reassurance with him. In his absence she took one of his old sweaters and curled up with it like a lover. The scratchy wool testified to his hardiness and strength.

What am I doing? Am I so afraid of this infant that I reject it from my body?

When she heaved and strained and her muscles contracted like a vise around her abdomen, she felt that her body was struggling to defy human physiology and expel this child through her mouth. Nothing came but bile and blood.

Then one day, a horrid thought: *Could it be that the child wants nothing to do with me? It knows what kind of mother it has and does not want to be born.*

The thought made her weep.

One Sunday late in March, as Arthur came up the lane from church he found Martha shivering in the cold on the doorstep.

"Oh, sir, thank the Lord ye're home—her mind's wanderin', sir.... She don't recognize us anymore ... ben seein' all sorts o' things ... crea-

tures like ghost dogs with moon-yellow eyes, and talkin' like her sisters
was in the room—"

"Did you send for Ingham?" Arthur said as he tore off his coat.

"Aye, sir, we sent for him . . . but he's sick himself. There's that young
Mr. Dugsdale—"

"Yes! Send for him! And send to Bradford for Macturk! Send for all
of them! Quickly!" Arthur cried as he took the stairs in giant strides,
three steps at a time.

From that morning on, Arthur never left her bedside. From Oxenhope,
Oakworth, Hebden Bridge, and all the surrounding hamlets, his
brethren quietly descended on Haworth to take up his duties; they
preached the Sunday services and evening prayers, they took the burials
and baptisms and taught his class at school.

Over the next few days as she drifted in and out of consciousness, her
body seemed to be willing itself to live. Finally she begged for food and
wine, and for the first time in two months she was able to keep down the
little that she ate.

"It's a good sign," Arthur whispered to Patrick outside the bedroom
door. "I think the worst has passed."

The clock on the landing struck the half hour—Arthur had lost track
of the hours—and he looked up from his book to check on his wife. The
fire was banked high in the grate, and the room was still warm. He sat in
his sweater and house slippers in the armchair they had brought up from
his study. He had dozed a little but then awakened, and finding himself
unable to sleep, he had lit a candle and begun to read.

As he watched her, she began to stir. He could tell by her breathing
that she was awake.

"Arthur?" she whispered faintly.

The book fell to the floor as he rose; in two strides he was kneeling at
her bed.

"My beloved . . ."

"...thought you'd gone..." She murmured through a parched mouth.

"Never. I shall never leave your side."

"Thirsty..."

He raised her and moistened her cracked lips with a spoonful of water. Her body had all but wasted away. She lay in his arms, light as air.

"What are you doing?" she said.

"Why, I've been reading a book. A novel."

He fed her another spoonful, and it seemed to revive her. She turned her great compelling eyes up to him.

"...novel? You never read novels."

"This one has quite taken my fancy. Although I've read it before."

Her dark eyes searched his for a long while, and he thought perhaps she was wandering again, but then she murmured, "What novel?"

"Something by an author by the name of Currer Bell."

"Why should you . . . read that naughty . . . Currer Bell?"

"I'm searching for a passage."

He felt her tiny hand—skeletal now—on his chest, tapping lightly, teasing, like a bird.

"Perhaps," she whispered, "I can help you?"

"I think I know the passage by heart—but I should like to find it. It's something about love."

"Love?" A smile glimmered in her eyes. "Currer Bell writes of love?"

"She writes of a 'faithful love that refused to abandon its object, love that disaster could not shake, love that in calamity, waxed fonder, in poverty clung closer' . . ."

He had lost control of his voice. He paused to take a deep breath. "Or some words to that effect."

He couldn't hold her gaze any longer. He fell to his knees beside the bed and began to sob. Weakly she reached out to reassure him. Her hand resting on the top of his head, the fingers sunk into his thick black hair, she tried to calm his fears.

"Arthur . . ."

"Dear God, I beseech you, spare her," he whispered. "Oh God, spare my beloved wife."

She murmured, "I'm not going to die. God won't separate us. We've been too happy."

Charlotte died in the hush of that steel-gray morning, with the earth all stern and still beneath the winter frost.

Epilogue

Arthur lived on in the parsonage, tending Charlotte's aging father and taking the parish duties, sterling true to his word.

They were an odd pair—bound by grief and love, by a fate too painful to share with anyone but each other—the eccentric old father who had lost most of his sight and his hearing and the bereaved husband who had buried his heart.

With the death of the last of the Brontës, the sisters' fame only grew. Requests for Charlotte's handwriting came in from all over the world, and Patrick cut some of her precious letters into tiny strips and sent them off to satisfy the demand. He was careful not to let Arthur know when he did this sort of thing. Arthur abhorred curiosity seekers and he understood—better than Patrick—that these mementos might be collected for material gain. Arthur was incensed at the idea that strangers might enrich themselves from the effects of his self-denying wife who had lived most of her life in poverty, and he guarded Charlotte's few material possessions, as well as all her siblings' writings, as carefully as if they were the relics of a saint.

When George Smith sent a letter proposing that Elizabeth Gaskell write Charlotte's biography, Arthur reluctantly conceded, only because Patrick wished it so. Upon her visit to the parsonage, Lily found the interview with the two bereaved men so painful that she spent but a few hours with them and then hurried away, never to return. Charlotte's friends would have to provide the bulk of the material she needed. Mary Taylor wrote from New Zealand that, as per Charlotte's request, she had conscientiously destroyed her letters. Ellen had not been so faithful; she had hoarded nearly every piece of paper to which Charlotte had set her name and now eagerly supplied the treasure trove of correspondence that enabled Lily to write her book.

Ellen's betrayal left Arthur reeling, for some letters of a very private nature made it into Lily's book—most notably, those in which Arthur was portrayed as a morose and lovesick sniveler, and the local press picked up those parts and reprinted them, to Arthur's keen humiliation. Patrick—of whom Lily had formed some very harsh opinions, based on her own notions of Charlotte's odd upbringing—fared no better. The men dealt with these injustices in their own way. Patrick took his ogre-like portrayal with good humor; Arthur, who felt he had been dragged into sanctioning something that was utterly repugnant, read the Gaskell biography with inexpressible pain but remained silent about it all.

It was to Lily's credit that he never learned about Charlotte's letters to Constantin Heger. Suspecting there was a good deal of Charlotte's story to be discovered in Brussels, she traveled all the way to the Continent to meet the professor. His wife refused to see her, but Monsieur Heger received her warmly. He still had in his possession several of Charlotte's letters, which he showed her—passionate, heart-wrenching letters of un-requited love couched in the language of an adoring pupil writing to her master. Here was confirmation of a suspicion none of them had ever dared to voice: that Charlotte, much like Jane Eyre, had fled the temp-tation of an adulterous love. In her biography, Lily treated the Brussels episode of Charlotte's life shrewdly, with great caution, and Charlotte's letters to Constantin Heger would not surface until well into the follow-ing century.

Neither husband nor father took a penny from the publication of the biography. Monetary gain was never a question for them; they only wished to rectify some of the cruel misrepresentations about the woman they had both loved. Lily was paid handsomely—twice what Charlotte had received for her last novel—and Charlotte Brontë's biography would prove to be her most enduring work.

When George expressed an interest in publishing *The Professor*—

which he had resolutely refused to publish in Charlotte's lifetime—Arthur and Patrick rejected the idea on the grounds that the same story had been successfully told in *Villette*. But forces conspired against them, and Sir James swept down on the parsonage one day and in his determined, insensitive manner managed to wrest the manuscript from Arthur's hands.

Arthur was shrewder when it came to *Emma*, which he felt had merits, even as a fragment. The manuscript was particularly precious to him because it was the last thing his wife had written, and he spent hours laboriously transcribing the heavily revised pages rather than lend out the original. *Emma* first appeared in George Smith's new publication, the *Cornhill Magazine*, along with a glowing personal tribute to Charlotte written by William Makepeace Thackeray.

Conscientious to the end, ever mindful of his wife's personal integrity, when George clamored for more poetry, Arthur read through Emily and Charlotte's verse, and with Patrick's assistance selected only the ones he deemed Charlotte would value. Then he sat down and carefully copied them. It was an excruciatingly painful task, and when the Bells' poetry was republished several years later, no reader would have thought to imagine that the volumes had been produced through the fog of tears.

George would forever benefit from his association with the Brontës; he would live into the next century and die an exceedingly wealthy man.

Patrick and Arthur lived on together quietly, tended by the ever-faithful Martha. Not long after Charlotte's death, the two men acquired a new dog from the Haworth schoolmaster—a young Newfoundland that Charlotte had doted on as a pup—and named him Plato. Patrick, a man of deep, unshakable faith, never questioned God's great wisdom, but it was a bitter cup to drink, to outlive his wife and all six children and then linger on for six long years. In his Sunday sermons he was known for quoting Job, and sometimes from the pulpit he would speak softly of longing for wings like a dove to fly away from the wearisome world and be at rest.

There were some in the village who were of the opinion that his wife's death had worked a little good in Arthur. He showed more tolerance for the failings of his flock, and what he once perceived as insults to the church of God he now saw simply as human weakness or ignorance. When he noticed that Mrs. Barraclough's knees were getting so bad that it took her half the Lord's Prayer to kneel, he pulled her aside after the service and told her that the Lord wouldn't find her any less pious if she remained in her seat from now on. Farmer Butterfield said he'd come across Arthur in a field one day with Plato in tow and a little lad balanced on the dog's back. Arthur had found the boy asleep beside the footpath, exhausted from a day of work in the mill, and had scooped him up and set him on the dog's back; the boy rode the young dog all the way home.

When Patrick died, it was presumed that Arthur would be offered the position that he had single-handedly administered all these years. But there was agitation for change. The church trustees wanted a new man, one with an independent income and the means to restore the crumbling parsonage. One free of bothersome ties to the infamous Brontës and with a little more tolerance for the dissenting sects that were now so numerous in the village. It was by a margin of one vote that Arthur found himself, just months after burying Patrick, without a curacy.

This was a crushing blow to Arthur, and many in the village thought it shabby and heartless to abandon the man after he'd labored so long and lost so much, leaving him with no employment and nowhere to go. They were ashamed of themselves, and no one could pass Arthur in the street and dare to look him in the eye.

Martha thought it was just as well. Arthur was such a lonely and disconsolate man, with his beloved wife and all her family now sealed in a cold vault beneath the stone church floor. With Martha's help he packed Charlotte's dresses, her writing desk, sewing box and paint box, the manuscripts and the little books she had written as a child, her portrait by Richmond as well as all the other family portraits, and the grandfather clock that had stood on the stair landing. Of what remained of the family's personal belongings, Martha took her pick, and the rest went up for auction.

He left Haworth before dawn one September day, taking with him his treasured possessions and Patrick's dog. He never sought another curacy but returned to Ireland and took up farming, slipping into a life of quiet obscurity. After a while, Martha—who had once professed such a violent dislike for the curate—came to live with him in Banagher, bringing her colorful Yorkshire manners and recipes for her tea cakes and, above all, her memories. She was as devoted to Arthur as she had been to his wife and until her death served him loyally.

For years after the publication of Lily Gaskell's biography a good deal of controversy flew around involving libel suits and rights; there were page after page of letters rebutting claims made in the book, quarrels about what was true and what was not; Ellen, who had expected praise and recognition for her contribution, found herself under attack for recklessly divulging Charlotte's personal correspondence. Bitter and bristling with indignation, she attempted to deflect the blame onto Arthur, against whom she would nurse a grudge for life. But Arthur remained distanced from the scandals and the Brontë fanatics. Conscientious to the end, always mindful of his wife's integrity, he did what was asked of him and ignored much of what was written about his famous wife and her family.

Ten years later he married his cousin Mary Anna, but it was widely accepted that Arthur acted out of gratitude to Mary Anna, who had kept his house and been such a caring companion all those years; they retained their separate bedrooms, and there were never any children. Charlotte still lived on in his heart; the portraits that had once hung in the parsonage and many of the Brontës' watercolors now crowded the walls of his modest house; the grandfather clock that Patrick Brontë had punctually wound every night at nine stood on the stairs, and Charlotte's white wedding dress and bonnet were carefully preserved in a clothespress. The dress was in Martha's keeping, and every few months she'd take it out and give it a good airing.

Arthur lived long, nearly to ninety, largely forgotten by the outside world. The few people who made the effort to locate him found him to be a dignified, contented man, idolized by his wife and held in great esteem by his friends and neighbors.

He bequeathed Charlotte's wedding dress to his brother Joseph's daughter, Miss Charlotte Brontë Nicholls, with instructions that the dress should be burned before she died so that it would not be sold.

Miss Charlotte Brontë Nicholls kept her word.

Author's Note

Thousands of readers, writers, and scholars have fallen under the Brontës' spell, as I first did during a graduate seminar over fifteen years ago. Countless plays, novels, and films have been spun from their lives and their work. But what I found so gripping was the true story of Charlotte's personal struggle: her determination to overcome circumstance, even her own temperament and nature, in order to taste just a few of life's splendors, its thrills and its beauty.

From the beginning I was committed to as much historical accuracy as the narrative could bear; it was tempting to omit some of the characters who impacted her life, or tighten the progression of her relationship with George Smith, but it would have meant sacrificing a deeper and more complex portrayal. Likewise, the political and social problems of their time needed to be addressed. Arthur's religious intolerance presented an enormous hurdle to Charlotte personally, and the historical context of their differences needed to be woven into the story.

Nearly all of Charlotte's letters are her own, with minor editing and only occasional invention. Her letters also provided the substance, if not the language, for some of the dialogue. I also turned to her novels for character development, particularly *Shirley,* where I felt she was speaking through her characters of her sisters and their relationship with their father. After countless readings of all the sisters's works and letters concurrently with biographies and historical documents of the region and the period, I felt confident making those choices.

As a novelist I drew on what may have been minor incidents or anecdotes to develop the story, some of which were alluded to in biographers' footnotes, or could be inferred by reading between the lines of correspondence. Necessarily, there was a certain compression of events at the beginning, but even the time frame of their lives during these years is, for the most part, accurate.

A few of the minor characters, such as Miss Dixon, are pure invention.

Arthur Nicholls is an obscure figure about who very little is known, although Charlotte certainly wrote a good deal about him during the difficult months after his proposal. Even then, the portrait she painted of him was skewed by her own prejudices, and later, when that attitude had been transformed by love, she said little about their intimate lives. Thus it was this part of the story that allowed my imagination the most freedom—although I do not hesitate to add that the progression of their romance accurately follows Charlotte's account, and nearly all the scenes toward the end are rooted in authentic incidents, particularly the events that led her to view him in a new light and fall in love with him. Arthur's letters to Charlotte are my own creation, and I suspect, given his deep feelings, I have not fallen far from the mark. Intentionally, his outpourings draw from the same language she used in her letters to Heger. I took enormous pleasure in bringing Arthur to life and giving him his due in the story.

This novel would not have been possible twenty-five years ago; it stands on the shoulders—I should say in the shadows—of remarkable scholarly achievements. I am particularly indebted to Juliet Barker's extensive work, *The Brontës,* which brought to light difficult-to-access sources such as George Richmond's papers and George Smith's autobiography, and to Margaret Smith's monumental three-volume edition of all Charlotte's surviving letters. I would also enthusiastically recommend *The Brontës: Charlotte Brontë and Her Family* by Rebecca Fraser, recently reissued as *Charlotte Brontë: A Writer's Life; Charlotte Brontë: The Self Conceived* by Helene Moglen; and *The Life of Charlotte Brontë* by Elizabeth Gaskell. It is my sincere hope that my novel will inspire the reader to pick up one of these fascinating studies. And, of course, the Brontës' novels as well.

Acknowledgments

I would like to recognize the following for their contributions:

The many Brontë scholars and biographers who, through their decades of research, made possible this intimate portrait of Charlotte.

Barbara Daniel at Little, Brown in London, who urged me to follow my heart and write this novel.

The Brontë Parsonage Museum, and Ann Dinsdale, for their prompt, courteous attention to all our inquiries.

Father Stan Runnels, for reading the manuscript and assuring me that my Anglican curates were sufficiently priestly, but most of all for his warmth, encouragement, and guidance.

Rhoderic Bannatyne, who read the early manuscript, for his meticulous attention to detail and helpful editing suggestions.

My many friends who revived my drooping spirits during the long winters of work, specifically Jan and Les Ryon, who always made sure I was well fed.

My splendid agent, Loretta Barrett, for her patience, support, and enthusiasm.

Linda Marrow, Senior Vice President and Editorial Director at Ballantine, for her lively humor and passionate commitment to this book.

About the Author

JULIET GAEL was raised in the Midwest and obtained her M.A. in French literature before pursuing graduate film studies at USC and English literature at UCLA in Los Angeles, California. She has lived abroad for more than fifteen years, primarily in Paris, where she worked as a screenwriter. She now makes her home in Florence, Italy.

About the Type

This book is set in Cloister Old Style, designed by Morris Fuller Benton (1872–1948) for American Type Founders as a revival of the Venetian types of Nicolas Jenson. Jenson originated a roman typeface, first used in his famous 1470 edition of *Eusebius's De Praeparatione Evangelica,* that soon became the model for all Venetian type designs. In his distinguished career, Benton revived and revised many earlier typefaces, including Jenson's. In *Printing Types: Their History, Forms, and Use,* Daniel Berkeley Updike describes Cloister Old Style as "not very inspired, perhaps, yet quiet and satisfactory because not attempting too much."